Bay
of
Secrets

Rosanna Ley has worked as a creative tutor for over twelve years, leading workshops in the UK and abroad, and has completed an MA in creative writing. Her writing holidays and retreats take place in stunning locations in Italy and Spain. Rosanna has written numerous articles and stories for national magazines. When she is not travelling, Rosanna lives in west Dorset by the sea.

ROSANNA LEY

Bay of Secrets

Quercus

First published in Great Britain in 2013 by

Quercus
55 Baker Street
7th Floor, South Block
London W1U 8EW

Copyright © 2013 Rosanna Ley

The moral right of Rosanna Ley to be
identified as the author of this work has been
asserted in accordance with the Copyright,
Designs and Patents Act, 1988.

All rights reserved. No part of this publication
may be reproduced or transmitted in any form
or by any means, electronic or mechanical,
including photocoping, recording, or any
information storage and retrieval system,
without permission in writing from the publisher.

A CIP catalogue record for this book is available
from the British Library

PB ISBN 978 1 78087 506 4
ISBN 978 1 78087 507 1 (EBOOK)

This book is a work of fiction. Names, characters,
businesses, organizations, places and events are either
the product of the author's imagination or are used fictitiously.
Any resemblance to actual persons, living or dead,
events or locales is entirely coincidental.

10 9 8 7 6 5 4 3 2

Typeset by Ellipsis Digital Limited, Glasgow
Printed and bound in Great Britain by Clays Ltd, St Ives plc

For Ana – with love.

PROLOGUE

The doorbell rang – loud, insistent.

Ruby sat up, still half-dreaming. She was in a nightclub, the lights were low and she was playing her saxophone. *Someone to Watch Over Me.* She rubbed her eyes.

The doorbell rang again. More insistent still.

Ruby groaned as the dream slipped away from her. 'OK, OK. I'm coming.' She blinked. Registered the early morning light. Glanced at the illuminated dial of the clock on James's side, taking in the sight of him as she did so; fair, unshaven, arms flung out as if even in sleep he was saying, *What the hell do I have to do to make you happy?* (*I don't know. I don't know.* She'd always hoped it would just happen).

They'd had another row last night. She wasn't even sure what the rows were about any more. Only that he seemed to be travelling in one direction and that she was careering off in another. They'd been living together for two years. The question was – when would their paths coincide?

And why would the doorbell be ringing at six in the morning? Not even the postman came this early.

She stumbled out of bed. 'James,' she said. 'Wake up. There's someone at the door.'

'Who?' he muttered, voice slurred with sleep.

Oh, hilarious. Ruby grabbed her bathrobe, pulled it on, shivered, padded down the hall, running her fingers through her mussed-up hair. She really shouldn't have had that extra glass of wine last night. She'd met Jude for a drink after work and they'd ended up putting the world to rights over a whole bottle. And then when she'd got home . . .

There were two people outside. She could make out their shapes through the glass; one male, one shorter female. A blurred check pattern; a darkness. Who came round visiting at this time in the morning? A sliver of foreboding slunk into her. Throat to knees.

She pulled open the door.

CHAPTER I

The house looked just the same. Red brick, white front door, sash windows, worse for wear. Ruby exchanged a glance with Mel. 'Thanks for picking me up,' she said. Could she have done it alone? She thought of James back in London and those different directions they seemed to be taking. Well, yes, she could have. But it would have been so much harder.

'I'm not just dumping you here,' Mel said. 'I'm coming in to help.'

'Help?' But Mel was already getting out of the car, so Ruby followed suit. 'You don't have to—' she began.

'Don't be daft.' Mel opened the front gate and took Ruby's arm as they walked up the path. The grass was overgrown, the plants were wild and untended and the garden was full of weeds. It didn't take long.

But Ruby felt the relief wash over her. Mel was her oldest friend and exactly what she needed right now. She was thirty-five years old and yet she felt like a child. She squeezed Mel's arm. It had been two months. It was time. Time to tackle the past and take the first steps towards moving on.

At the front door, Ruby closed her eyes, smelling the jasmine her mother had planted here years ago. The heady scent of the tiny white flowers seemed to wrap itself around her, shunt her forward. *You can do this.*

She put her key in the door, almost heard her mother's voice. *You have to pull it out a bit and wiggle.* The door eased open – reluctantly.

Mel held back, understanding that Ruby had to go first. Ruby straightened her shoulders, stepped over the letters and circulars lying beached on the doormat. And took her first breath of parents and home since it had happened.

Of course Ruby had been back to Dorset since the accident. She and James had driven from London for her parents' funeral. She sighed now as she remembered the journey, the expression on James's face – his mouth thin and unsmiling, his eyes fixed on the road ahead with hardly a glance at the woman by his side. Ruby had barely noticed as the car swallowed up the miles, as the familiar green Dorset hills came into sight. Because the pleasure of coming home had turned into a terrible sort of emptiness. And she hadn't felt able to face the house, not even with James by her side. James. How long had it been since they'd just walked hand in hand down by the river or since they'd talked – really talked, as if they wanted to hear what the other had to say? And now this. Poor James. He hadn't known how to deal with it, how to deal with her. He'd started looking at her as if he no longer knew her. Which in a way he didn't. It sounded a bit crazy. But she'd become someone else since she'd lost them.

After the funeral they'd returned to London. Ruby had

dealt with the awful aftermath. The sympathy cards from friends and from acquaintances of her parents' she hardly knew, and some she did know, like Frances, her mother's oldest friend, who had been so kind at the funeral, giving Ruby a note of her address and phone number and offering her help should she need it. There was the will and the probate; the winding up of their affairs that she'd accomplished somehow, finding a temporary and cold objectivity from some desperate corner of her grief.

Somehow too, she finished the feature she was in the middle of writing – an exposé of a certain hotel chain and the recycling of house wine – and then she'd thrown herself into the next project and then the next. She'd hardly seen any of her friends. She hadn't gone to the gym or had one of those occasional girlie evenings with Jude, Annie and the rest of them that always somehow made her feel better about everything. She simply worked. It was as if all the time she was writing, all the time she was interviewing people and investigating their stories, Ruby didn't need to think about her own life, about what had happened to them, to her. She was functioning on autopilot. And in there somewhere was James and their foundering relationship.

But Ruby wasn't sure she could let it go – not yet. She knew she had to go back to the house in Dorset, had to sort through her parents' things, had to decide what to do with the place now that they were gone. But how could she? If she did that it would be like admitting . . . That it was true. That they had really left her.

Last night the situation had reached a head. Ruby had finished the story she was working on. She had a long bath. She felt as if her head was bursting. Afterwards, she sat on the sofa with her notebook, her sax and her guitar and waited for inspiration, but nothing came. She hardly played her saxophone, she hadn't written a song for months. It wasn't just her parents' death. Something else was wrong in her life. Very wrong.

James came back late from drinks after work, tired and irritable and not even wanting the supper she'd cooked for him. He ran his fingers through his fair hair and let out a long sigh. 'May as well get off to bed,' he said. He didn't touch her.

A final thread snapped. She couldn't hold back. 'What's the point of us staying together, James?' Ruby asked him. 'We seem to want such different things. We hardly even spend any time together any more.' She half wanted him to disagree, to fling her doubts aside, to take her in his arms. She didn't want to keep having these arguments with him. But how could they go on living separate lives? Something had to change.

But he didn't disagree. 'I don't know what you want, Ruby,' he said instead. 'I just don't know any more.' His hands were in his pockets now. Ruby wondered what he was trying to stop them from doing. Reaching out to her, maybe?

What did she want? What did he want, come to that? James loved living in London. He liked going out to crowded bars and restaurants and taking city breaks in Prague or

Amsterdam – preferably with a few mates in tow. Apart from her occasional nights out with the girls, Ruby wanted a bit more peace and solitude these days. She'd rather tramp along the cliffs at Chesil Beach than shop in Oxford Street. He liked Chinese food, she preferred Italian. He was into hip hop, she loved jazz. He watched telly, she read books. He played football, she liked to dance. The list in her head went on. She couldn't even remember how or why she had fallen in love with James in the first place. They used to do things with one another. They used to have fun. What was the matter with her?

She realised that she was crying.

He had his back to her though and he didn't even see.

And that's when Ruby knew what she had to do. She had to take some time off – she had worked as a freelance journalist for over five years, her parents had left her a small inheritance as well as the house, so at least she had some breathing space – and she had to come back here to Dorset. She had to face up to what had happened. She was strong enough now to deal with it. She had to be.

The house, though, wasn't easy.

Ruby went into the living room first. Stopped in her tracks as she surveyed the scene. It was awful. It was as if they had just popped out for an hour or two. She went over to the table. Ran a fingertip over the stiff sheet of pale green water-colour paper. Her mother had been in the middle of a painting; her brushes still stood in a jar of murky water, her watercolour paints thrown into the old tin, her mixing palette on the table, the wilted flowers in a jug. Ruby touched them and they crumbled like dust in her fingers. There were two mugs on the table crusted with long-ago dried-up dregs of tea. And her father's green sweater – slung on the back of the armchair. Ruby picked it up, buried her face in it – just for a moment – smelt the Dad-smell of the citrus aftershave she'd bought him last Christmas, mixed in with waxy wood polish and pine. *They were so young. It wasn't fair* . . .

What had he said to her? 'Fancy a quick spin on the bike? Fancy a ride down to the waterfront? Go on. What d'you reckon? Shall we give it a whirl?'

And her mother would have been busy painting but she would have smiled and sighed at the same time in that way she had, and pushed her work to one side. 'Go on then, love,' she'd have said. 'Just for an hour. It'll probably do me good to take a break.'

For a moment Ruby pictured her, dark greying hair falling over her face as she painted, eyes narrowing to better capture her subject, silver earrings catching the light . . . No. It wasn't fair.

Mel put a comforting arm around her. 'I've got some milk in the car,' she said. 'I'll fetch it and make us a nice cup of tea. And then we'll make a start, OK?'

'OK,' Ruby sniffed and nodded. That was what they were here for. But there was so much stuff and it all meant so much to her. A lifetime of memories.

★

'What I reckon,' Mel said, over tea, 'is that you need to clear away some of the personal things so that you can see more clearly.'

Ruby nodded. She knew exactly what she meant.

'Because you're going to sell the house, aren't you?'

'Yes, of course.' Even if . . . Well, she hadn't come to a decision either way. But on the train to Axminster she'd been thinking. What held her to London – really? There was her job – but being freelance meant she could work just about anywhere she had her laptop. It had been a huge jump after working for the local rag in Pridehaven and then the glossy *Women in Health* in London. But she'd made it after a year of juggling nine to five on the magazine with the freelance articles she really wanted to write – articles that gave her the freedom to research and choose her own remit. And she made a living – though admittedly things were tight sometimes.

It was handy living in the city for editorial meetings and what have you, but it wasn't a deal breaker. She had to be ready to drop everything and go wherever the next story or article might be, but provided she was within reach of a decent airport or railway station, what difference did it make so long as she could email through her copy? There were her friends – she'd miss Jude in particular and their grumpy-women rants over a bottle of wine. And there was James, of course. She thought of him as she'd seen him last, as the taxi took her to the station; framed in the doorway, tall and fair, his blue eyes still sleepy and confused. But was there still James? She really didn't know.

'So we'll do one room at a time. Three piles, darling.' Mel tucked a strand of bright auburn hair behind one ear. 'One for you to keep, one for anything you want to sell and one to give away to charity shops.'

Fair enough.

And by the time they stopped for a beer and a cheese and pickle sandwich at lunchtime, Ruby really felt they were getting somewhere. She'd shed plenty of tears, but she was doing what she'd spent two months plucking up the courage to do. She was at last sweeping the decks. It was hard – but therapeutic.

She looked around. It was warm enough to sit outside at the garden table and good to get some fresh air. The old-fashioned sweet peas her mother had loved were blooming in wild abandon on the worn trellis by the back wall and their scent drifted in the breeze. Her mother used to cut bundles of them for the house. 'To make sure everyone knows it's summer,' she used to say. Ruby decided that this afternoon she'd do the same.

'I suppose you'll want to get back to London as soon as you can?' Mel was munching her sandwich. She pulled a sad face. Mel had missed her vocation in life; she should have been an actress. But she'd met Stuart when she was eighteen and fallen dramatically and irrevocably in love. Stuart was an accountant and Mel had her own business she'd started ten years ago; the hat shop in Pridehaven High Street, which had become a thriving concern. It had branched out to include fancy accessories – quirky ties, screen-painted silk scarves, hand-crafted leather purses and belts. But its speciality hadn't altered. The town even had its own hat festival now, she'd informed Ruby earlier. *Forget about London, darling, this is where it's all happening these days.*

And perhaps she was right. 'I'm not sure about going back.' Ruby lifted her face up to the sun. She'd missed this garden, missed having outside space. And she'd missed not living near the sea.

Ruby had left Dorset ten years ago when she was twenty-five. She'd wanted to be independent, to see somewhere new, to experience a different kind of life. She was bored with following up local stories for the *Gazette*, with interviewing local minor celebrities and with her weekly health file problem page. She applied for the job at *Women in Health* because it sounded glamorous and exciting, and because it was an escape from what had come to seem parochial. When she met James she'd thought for a while that everything had slotted neatly into place. He was attractive, intelligent and good company. They both had jobs they enjoyed and the city was their oyster. It was all happening in London – theatre, music, film, galleries, everything you could want. But . . . It had turned out that *Women in Health* had its limitations and that Ruby wasn't really a city girl after all. She'd lived the life and she'd enjoyed it. But home was where it was real. And although her parents were no longer here, somewhere in her heart this was still home and this was where she wanted to be – at least for now.

Mel's eyes widened. 'What about James?'

Ruby traced a pattern on the tabletop with her fingertip.

'Ah,' said Mel.

'Exactly.' Ruby sighed.

'You haven't split up?'

'No.' At least not yet, she thought. *I'll call you*, was the last thing he'd said to her when she left for the station this morning. But when he did – what would she say? He hadn't made any objection to her coming here. But he'd assumed it was just for a week or two – not for ever.

'What then?' Mel asked.

Good question. 'I suppose you could say we're taking a break.'

Mel knew her so well – she didn't have to say more. But whether she stayed for a week or two or whether she stayed for ever, Ruby wouldn't be staying in this house. It was far too big for her and it held way too many memories. Her parents' ghosts would be haunting her every move.

After lunch, Ruby tackled her parents' bedroom. She'd already pulled out all the clothes, put them in their designated piles. And at the bottom of the wardrobe, tucked behind assorted handbags, she'd found a shoebox. It had some writing – maybe Spanish – on the lid and a thick rubber band around it, but otherwise it appeared ordinary enough.

Ruby sat back on her haunches. Downstairs, she could hear Mel vacuuming. The woman was an angel. Because this was so difficult; harder than she'd ever imagined it would be.

When it happened to you – when the doorbell rang early

in the morning and you opened the door to see two police officers standing there, about to tell you that your parents were dead – it didn't feel like you could ever have imagined. She'd noticed silly and insignificant things. Like the fact that the female PC was wearing a padded body-warmer and had dark circles under her eyes. And that it was 21 March, the first day of spring.

'There's always a blind spot,' the male PC had said to Ruby. 'That's why motorbikes are so dangerous.' He'd glanced at her apologetically. 'It's not that they're badly ridden. It's the car drivers usually.'

There's always a blind spot . . .

'They wouldn't have suffered,' the female PC added.

Ruby had looked at her. Did she know that? For sure?

The woman's words sent an image spinning through her brain – of tyres squealing and smoking, the stench of molten rubber. Her hands gripping his waist. The clashing impact of metal on metal. Bodies somersaulting through the air. Not just bodies. Her parents' bodies. And then the silence. God. Not suffered?

Ruby shook the memory away. Everyone said that time healed. But how much time did it take? Was she healing? Some days she wasn't even sure. She held her hands out in front of her. But at least her hands weren't shaking and she'd even stopped bumping into doors.

She eased the rubber band from around the box. It wasn't heavy enough to be boots or even shoes. She shook it gently. Something rustled.

If only he hadn't bought that motorbike. How many times had she thought that since it had happened? She'd warned him, hadn't she? Hadn't she told him off for trying to relive his lost youth? He was supposed to be close to retirement age. He should have been thinking about playing bowls or cribbage, not riding motorbikes around the countryside.

Ruby let out a breath she hadn't even known she was holding. She had come here for the weekend – a chilly weekend in early March; James had gone off on one of his weekends with the lads. It was the last time she'd seen them. It would probably stay in her mind for ever.

'You'll never guess the latest, love.' Her mother had put a mug of fresh coffee down on the table in front of Ruby and flicked the hair out of her eyes like a girl.

'What?' Ruby returned her mother's grin.

'He's only bought a bike, hasn't he? Can you imagine? At his age?' She put her hands on her hips, tried to look cross.

'A bike?' Ruby had visualised high handlebars, a narrow saddle, a cross bar.

'A motorbike.' Her mother took Ruby's hand and gave it a squeeze. 'A pushbike wouldn't be fast enough for him. Old Speedy Gonzales.'

'You're joking.' But Ruby knew she wasn't. She twisted round in her chair. 'Dad? Are you crazy? How old do you think you are?'

'Never too old to enjoy yourself, love,' he said. His face was buried in the paper but he looked up and treated her to one of his eyebrow waggles. 'I had a Triumph Bonneville 650 for a while before you came along. Always fancied getting another. Blame *Easy Rider* – that's how it started.' He gave her mother a look. 'I always fancied the leathers too.'

'Get on with you.' But she'd blushed – furiously – and Ruby had thought: *they look ten years younger.*

'Maybe it's the male menopause,' Ruby teased. She loved coming back to see them at weekends and she knew they loved having her, but they'd never raised any objections to her moving to London. Why should they? They'd always made it clear that they respected what she did for a living and that they would never try to tie her down. They'd brought her up to be independent; they'd always expected her to fly.

'Maybe it's time he grew up.' Ruby's mother tousled his hair as she passed the sofa and he reached up suddenly, making a grab for her wrist. She tried to pull away, he wouldn't let her and they ended up giggling like a couple of kids.

'You two,' Ruby said. She'd got up, put her arms around them both and felt herself wrapped in one of their special hugs. But she had wished she could be like that, like them. She and James maybe. Or someone . . .

He'd shown her the bike the following day. It was big, red and black and she'd watched, arms folded, while her father roared up and down the street for her benefit. 'I'll give you a ride if you want, love,' he said. 'I passed my test years ago.'

Ruby had put a hand on his arm. 'You will be careful, won't you, Dad?' She didn't like the idea of him racing round the lanes of west Dorset on a motorbike. Nor the idea of her mother on the back of it.

'Course I will.' He winked at her. 'You can't get rid of me that easily, my girl.'

But she had. Ruby blinked back the tears. She had.

She took a deep breath. And opened the shoebox.

Some tissue paper and some photographs. She flipped through them. No one she knew. Who were they then and why were they here? They looked – well, interesting. She picked one up and scrutinised it more closely.

A young couple on some Mediterranean beach were leaning against the orange wall of a beach-house. In the background she could see pale gold sand, turquoise sea, some black rocks and a red and white striped lighthouse. The girl, who was wearing a flowing, maxi-dress with an Aztec design and loose sleeves, had long blonde hair and was laughing. The boy was olive-skinned with curly black hair and a beard, one arm slung casually around her shoulders.

Ruby picked up another snapshot. It was the same girl – she looked no more than mid-twenties, but she could be younger – sitting in the driver's seat of a psychedelic VW camper van. Ruby smiled. It was like an instant flashback to the days of flower power – way before her time, of course, but she could see the appeal. And another; a group of hippies on the beach, sitting on the black rocks, someone – maybe the same girl again, though she was too far away to tell –

playing a guitar. And the same girl again on the beach holding a small baby. A baby.

Something – grief perhaps? – caught in Ruby's throat. Her
mother would never see Ruby holding a baby. She would
never be a grandmother and her father would never be a
grandfather. They would never see Ruby be married, have
children. They wouldn't be proud of her when one of her
articles made the pages of a Sunday supplement. They
wouldn't come to any more of her jazz gigs where she played
the sax in local pubs, mixing her own songs in with all the
famous jazz covers her parents loved – though, truth to tell
she hadn't done much of that since moving to London; she'd
let her music slide. They wouldn't be here for any of that
stuff, for her future.

Ruby blinked back the tears. She put the photos on the
floor beside her and investigated the rest of the contents of
the box. Some pale pink tissue paper was nestling in the bottom corner. She unwrapped it. Out dropped a string of
multicoloured love beads. Ruby let them drift between her
fingers. They were the kind people wore in the sixties and
seventies. The kind . . . She picked up one of the photos
once more. The kind this girl was wearing. They were old,
delicate and fragile. Maybe then they were one and the same.

Gently, she unwrapped some more tissue at the bottom of
the box to reveal a little white crocheted bonnet – so small it
would only fit . . . She frowned. A baby. She picked it up – it
was so soft – and put it with the beads. And unwrapped the
final tiny parcel. A piece of grey plastic. A plectrum. Just like

the one she used when she was playing her guitar. But why would there be a guitar plectrum in the shoebox? She looked at the small heap of apparently random objects. Why was any of this stuff in a shoebox in her parents' wardrobe?

'I've put a pile of papers on the table in the living room.' Mel was talking as she came up the stairs. 'You might want to take a look at them. You probably should have gone through them weeks ago, to be honest.'

Ruby looked up at her. She was standing in the doorway. 'OK,' she said.

'Found anything interesting?'

'Oh . . . Just a shoebox with some things in.'

'Things that aren't shoes?' Mel sat down on the bed and Ruby showed her the photos, the love beads, the plectrum, and the white crocheted baby's bonnet.

'What do you reckon to all this?' she asked.

Mel picked up the photo of the girl with the baby. 'It looks like this lot must belong to her.'

'Yes.' But who was she?

'You don't recognise her then?'

'I don't recognise any of them. I don't remember Mum or Dad mentioning anyone like this either.'

Mel shrugged. 'Maybe your mum was looking after the stuff for someone else?'

'Maybe.' But who?

'That's nothing. You should see all the things I've got at the bottom of my wardrobe.' Mel glanced at her watch. 'I've got to go, darling. Stuart's mum's coming round for supper – and I haven't even gone to the supermarket yet.'

Ruby laughed. It would be good, she thought, to be around Mel and Stuart again and some of the old friends she'd had before she moved away. It was exactly what she needed.

And maybe it was nothing, but she replaced all the items and put the shoebox in the 'things to keep' pile. Just in case it was important. Just in case – for some reason – her parents had wanted her to find it.

That evening, Ruby went into the bedroom that had continued to be hers even after she'd moved away. One of her old guitars still leant against the chest of drawers – she'd left it here, partly because she had a new one she'd taken to London with her, and also so that she could use it when she was staying with her parents. You never knew when a song would stroll into your head and you'd need to strum a few chords.

She picked it up now, sat on the bed as she had done so often when she was a girl, head slightly to one side to listen more acutely, automatically starting to retune. That was better. She put the guitar to one side and lifted her saxophone from its case. It had been a mission bringing it with her on the train, but she couldn't leave it behind. It was the first thing she'd rescue from a fire, something she'd always assumed necessary to her existence – like a third arm. Could it be that way again? She'd let her practice lapse since James, since living in London, since not having a regular band to play with. But maybe she could get together again with the guys from the band here in Pridehaven? Play again at the Jazz Café. Why not?

Ruby touched the shiny keys and the sax seemed to shimmer a lazy response. When she'd first started playing, she could barely hold it. The only sound that emerged when she blew was a kind of desperate squeak. 'Is there a mouse in the house?' her father would enquire, raising an eyebrow. Now though . . . It was her blue fire.

A random line came into her head and she scribbled it in the notebook on the bedside table. Her mother had been a happy person, hadn't she? But she too had loved jazz and the blues. She'd listen to her old albums and CDs while she was cooking, cleaning, painting, whatever. And the sad songs were always her favourites. 'The Nearness of You' . . . Ruby sighed. She missed her mother. She missed them both. She ached for them. For a hug. To hear her father's laughter. Her mother's voice.

Tenderly, she replaced the sax in its case. 'Wish you touched me like that,' James had said once. *Yes, but the saxophone never asked for too much in return.* It was responsive too. It echoed every breath, every feeling, every mood that Ruby poured into it. Faithfully.

'Are you jealous?' she had teased. That was in the early days of their relationship. Before they stopped teasing and before she stopped playing.

'Of course I am,' he'd laughed. 'It gets so close to you. When you play that thing, you go off somewhere without me. You're transported.'

It was true. The saxophone had a way of hitting a spot deep inside. It made her think of a dark nightclub in the early hours. Did she want to go there? There was something inside her that wanted it, yes. Even while it hurt. To escape to another world, she thought. She closed her eyes and started seeing a new song climbing inside her head. Its pattern was rising and falling, she could hear the beat, feel its rhythm. It was coming alive. The lyric she'd written fell into place. Yes, she thought. To escape to another world . . . Sometimes it was all she wanted.

An hour or so later, Ruby went downstairs to make herself some hot chocolate. But she wasn't tired enough for bed so she started going through the pile of papers that Mel had unearthed in her parents' bureau. Letters from banks and utility companies. Letters about mortgages and interest rates and council tax. They were ancient; surely they could all be thrown away? She opened a wrinkled cardboard folder. Medical certificates. And her own vaccination record – very much out of date. She spotted a letter from her old family doctor and quickly began to scan its contents. There could be something important tucked away in this lot. Neither of her parents were the most organised people in the world.

But hang on . . . She refocused on the print. What was that? She sat up straighter, blinked, read it again. *Following our consultations and tests. This is to confirm our diagnosis of unexplained infertility* . . . Infertility? *Should you wish to pursue the option of the fertility treatment discussed, please telephone the surgery to arrange for your first appointment.* What on earth? Ruby checked the date on the letter. It was dated seven months before her birth.

She read the letter again and then again. But it still said the same thing. Seven months before Ruby was born her parents had been told one or the other of them was infertile and unable to have children. *Unexplained infertility.* It didn't make sense whichever way you looked at it. Because seven months later her mother had given birth to Ruby.

Ruby stared at the sweet peas in a vase on the table. Well, hadn't she?

CHAPTER 2

20 March 2012
Should she – shouldn't she? Vivien had found herself thinking this more and more often lately – more often than she was happy with. It disturbed her equilibrium, poked its head into her peace of mind. It had been a long time. So. *Should she or shouldn't she tell the truth?*

To distract herself, she frowned at the flowers she'd picked from her wild patch out back. A cutting of spiky acid-yellow forsythia, a few stems of soft-leafed sage still in bud, a single cream early rose. She rearranged them so that the sage drooped its fragrant herbiness over the lip of the terracotta jug. From yellow to green to cream, back to yellow; colours merging, that was how Vivien liked it. Paint what you see – not what you think you see.

Some famous artist had said that – Monet or maybe Van Gogh. She supposed that was what Impressionism had been about. You resisted *how* your brain was telling you to paint; flat sea, for example, with white waves. And you painted it as your senses perceived it – moving, curling, rippling lines punctuated with pinpricks of light and patches of shade; all colours – grey, green, white, blue, dark violet – separated and merging, shifting with the breeze and the current, paddling into ringlets on to sandy beaches or grey rocks. And Vivien liked to take it one step further in her flower paintings. She liked to merge colour so that it blurred and bled. Wet on wet. So that it was fluid and became one.

Should she – shouldn't she? Similarly, this decision – which had nothing to do with art – was not clear cut and the boundaries were fuzzy. Some truths were like that. For starters, she would have to be very brave.

Vivien shuffled through her paints. She preferred watercolour, which had the transparency, the opaque finish, the fluidity that she wanted. Was she brave? Not really. She was thankful though; goodness, she was thankful.

It wasn't a question of should she or shouldn't she have done it in the first place. *That* decision at least had been clear cut. She had felt she had no choice – *they* had no choice. Someone else might have taken a different pathway after that. But not Vivien. She was done for. It wasn't in her make-up to resist. She'd always been heart over head. So . . .

No. It was a question of whether or not she should tell her secret to the one person who might deserve to know. That was the tricky thing. Whether or not she should tell the truth. Because the truth could be difficult to tell, and even more difficult to hear.

She decided on a pale mint background wash, so frail it was almost not there at all; just the feel of it, like a gossamer stole on her shoulders. She began mixing, humming softly a Joni Mitchell song. 'Little Green', just as this was.

And it reminded her, would always remind her, of that day.

It was, she supposed, a moral dilemma. The dilemma being – did everyone have the right to the truth?

Vivien generally did tell the truth. She liked to think of herself as honest, open, straightforward. And she had never wanted to keep this secret to herself – at least not at the start. But one had to think of the consequences. There were such things as white lies, after all – untruths that protected people's feelings perhaps, that prevented people from being hurt.

Was she protecting anyone's feelings? Was she stopping anyone from being hurt? Maybe. What would happen if she were to tell? Vivien almost gasped at the thought. That was the thing about secrets; they took on a furtive life of their own. She selected her broad brush, swept and smoothed the paper with the bridge of her hand in order to begin. What was the worst thing that could happen?

Vivien heard the front door open and Tom's familiar whistle.

'Where are you, my lovely?' he called.

Vivien smiled. Yes, she was lucky. 'Working,' she called back. She was in their living room. It was large, it was messy and it was home. Vivien had flung open the French windows at the back and the sun flamed the scruffy orange tendrils of the carpet and the faded red of their big, old and comfy sofa, spotlighting the dust motes settled on the wooden furniture – mostly crafted by Tom, like the elegant mahogany bookcase he'd made just after they were married. The table at which she worked was covered – in tubes of paints, a mixing palette, Vivien's jar of brushes and water, paper and the vase of flowers – so that you'd hardly know it was a beautifully mottled walnut beneath. But Vivien knew and it felt good. She loved Tom's furniture; the weeks of painstaking work, love and care that could go into one of his pieces.

'Working? On a sunny day like this?' Tom filled their doorway. He pulled off his sweater as if to demonstrate how warm it was and chucked it on to the back of the armchair. And it was true that it was warm for March.

Sometimes Tom didn't seem much older than when they'd first met more than thirty years ago. Though his hair was greying and he was more world-weary. 'People don't want hand-crafted furniture any more,' he sometimes said wistfully. 'They want cheap and factory-made. Who can blame them?' And Vivien would hug his sad-looking back and she would blame them – fiercely. She would never stop loving what he did even though these days he spent more time fixing kitchen cupboards and skirting boards for people than he did making tables and chests of drawers. Despite this, Tom still had the brown twinkly eyes and sense of fun she'd first fallen in love with.

Vivien had never wanted to be with anyone but Tom.

She remembered the first time she'd seen him, the tinny fairground music and whoosh of the rides, the laughter of the boys and screaming of the girls. The sweet sticky scent of candyfloss and toffee apples heavy in the air, the neon bulbs of light dazzling in the dusk of the summer evening. Charmouth Fair.

Vivien was sixteen. She and her friend Lucy were camping in a field behind a pub in the village – on holiday in Dorset on their own for the first time. They'd told their parents they were hiking and staying at youth hostels; in fact they were hitch-hiking and staying wherever the fancy took them.

The fancy had taken them on this occasion to Charmouth. They had heard the fair was in town. They sat on their sleeping bags with their mirrors and mascara and got themselves ready for a night out that wouldn't include any curfew from their parents. Because they were here on their own. And they were free . . .

The adrenalin hit Vivien as they walked to the green and heard the music. It was past eight o'clock but still light; most of the families had left to go home and the fairground was just beginning to buzz. There were groups of girls and groups of boys, young couples hand in hand, and boys operating the rides, strutting along the walkways, giving the girls the eye.

Vivien and Lucy made for the waltzer. They jumped into the silver car. The ride gathered speed and as the boy spun the car around, they gripped on to the metal handrail with white knuckles, threw back their heads and shrieked with laughter and fear. It was over all too soon, a whirlwind ride.

'Another?' said Vivien.

'You bet,' said Lucy. They giggled.

Vivien saw the two boys making a beeline for them. She nudged Lucy. 'Don't look now . . . ' But she did.

'Room for two more?' the taller one enquired with the raise of a dark eyebrow.

Vivien felt reckless. 'Why not?' She shifted to make room. He sat down next to her.

'My name's Tom,' he said. 'Tom Rae.' He smiled.

Vivien just had time to register that his eyes were light brown with a streak of amber. And then the car spun, the girls shrieked, and the ride began.

'What's yours?' he shouted over the screaming and the music – Amen Corner: 'If Paradise is Half as Nice . . .'

She couldn't agree more. 'Vivien!' she shouted back.

After the waltzer they paired off. Tom's mate Brian already had his arm round Lucy. What would she do, Vivien wondered, when Tom put his arm round her? Would he try to kiss her?

Next up was the dodgems. The two boys took the wheel, the cars sparked on the metal grille above, bumping and grinding and even dodging occasionally. Tom's proximity was making Vivien feel hot. She could smell the hint of sandalwood and sweat on his skin. She closed her eyes.

After that came the big dipper where they hung motionless in the darkening sky for what seemed like minutes and Tom looked into her face as if he were taking note of every feature. Vivien looked back, unblinking, and wondered what he had seen. By the time they got to the rifle range she felt like she was in a trance. The others were chatting and laughing; Tom concentrated and focused, took aim, shot; three minutes later he proudly presented her with a yellow teddy bear. And then they munched toffee apples which got stuck in Vivien's teeth, and drank Fanta from the can.

By the time Tom walked Vivien back to their tent (Lucy was lagging behind with Brian) he had put his arm around her and they had exchanged life stories. Vivien knew that Tom lived in Sherborne in Dorset – a long way from West Sussex – that his favourite subject was woodwork and that he wanted to be a carpenter. A furniture maker. A master crafts-man, if you like. She liked the way he talked – low and quiet with a gentle Dorset burr. And she sensed from the start that Tom Rae would do what he said he would. She knew that he was an only child like her, that he had lost his parents when he was young and was living with his aunt and uncle, and that he was saving up to buy a motorbike.

When they got back to the tent he suddenly fell silent.

Vivien wasn't sure what to say either. She'd had casual boyfriends before but no one that really meant much to her. Was it just because she was on holiday that she'd taken such a shine to this dark-haired, lanky boy with the brown eyes and warm smile? Was it his accent and the unfamiliar male scent of him in the night-time? Or was it the heady excitement of the fairground rides that had churned up her insides?

'I'd better be saying goodnight then,' Tom said at last. He took a step closer.

And then she was in his arms and it felt a better place than anywhere she'd been before. He was a good kisser and he tasted of apple. She only hoped she no longer had any bits of toffee stuck in her teeth.

After they'd gone, she and Lucy analysed the evening to death.

'I really like him, Luce,' Vivien breathed. 'What do you think about staying here for the rest of our holiday?'

'Suits me.' Lucy was lying on her back, arms folded under her head. 'I'd like to get to know Brian a bit better too.' They giggled.

After they returned to West Sussex, everyone told Vivien it was just a holiday romance. She was only sixteen, they said. She had her whole life in front of her. Which was true. The difference was that now Vivien wanted it to include Tom.

'Viv? It's lovely out. Too nice to be stuck in here,' Tom said now.

In reply, Vivien arched an eyebrow and drew her brush wetly across the top of the paper.

Tom pulled a disappointed face.

She felt it. 'If you've finished work, go and play,' she said, smiling to soften the words.

He studied her. 'How long will you be?'

Vivien gave a little sigh and a small smile. She'd had it all planned. Do the background wash. Prepare supper. Sort out some mounting. Do some more to the painting – the first real colours, the exciting bit. Cook supper. Phone Ruby. Have a relaxing evening with Tom and the telly.

She lifted the paper, to allow the wash to curtain down, creating the desired effect with a rhythmic sweep of her brush. She paused, frowning at it. 'What were you thinking of?'

'A trip on the bike to Pride Bay? I need to take her out for a test run. I've been tinkering around with the carburettor.'

'Oh, yes?' He really knew how to tempt a woman . . .

'A 99 ice cream?' he added. 'A walk round the harbour. Maybe a beer?'

'In that order?' Vivien jiggled the paper around a bit.

'We could swap around the ninety-nine and the walk. "Born to be wild", my lovely. What do you reckon?'

She chuckled. 'All right then. I suppose I could do with a break. Give me ten minutes or so?' Vivien mentally readjusted her evening. Spontaneity was, after all, one of the qualities she loved about her husband.

'Good girl. Nice colour.' He nodded approvingly. 'I'll make us a quick cup of tea.' And he was gone.

Head to one side, Vivien surveyed the wash. The hint of colour was about right – only just there.

The worst thing that could happen, she thought, putting her brush in the clean water, was not being forgiven. That was why she hadn't told. There had been many valid reasons for not telling at first. There still were. But now . . . To be not forgiven was too awful to contemplate. The secret and

29

the keeping of it had become a wall between them; the kind of wall that was hard to climb.

And the best thing that could happen? Vivien wasn't sure that there was one. She selected a few tubes of paint from the pile in front of her and clattered the rest back into the large cake tin they lived in. Was honesty its own reward? She squirted a few experimental blobs of colour and shifted them around a bit with her mixing brush. No. The best thing – for her – would be not to have to worry about this any longer. To be open about it all. To explain the whys and the wherefores and how it had all come to be.

Ah. She breathed out. Screwed the caps back on the paints. Later.

That was what she needed to do – explain how it had all come to be.

CHAPTER 3

Fuerteventura, June 2012

Slowly, painfully, Sister Julia got to her feet. It was growing dusk. She brushed the fine dust from the white habit she wore – the visible sign of her departure from the world outside; the symbol of her inclusion in the monastic community of her spiritual family. Dust. *Dust to dust. Ashes to ashes* . . . A reminder – as if she needed another reminder – of all the deaths she had witnessed. Of the decision that she must make.

She fingered the rosary beads she carried. Here there was always dust, even in the chapel, which was decorated with scrolled stonework in pinks and blues, and faded frescos above the altar depicting the Crucifixion. She had been praying for two hours, but these days she hardly noticed time. It simply passed by. There was still so much to ask Him. What should she do? Could He give her some sort of sign?

She must now get on, however. There were only a dozen of them living here at Nuestra Señora del Carmen – the patron saint of fishermen – and this week Sister Julia's duties included picking vegetables and herbs from the garden plot outside. They grew wormwood, aloe and echinacea as well as the more common mint, camomile, and rosemary. Every plant had its uses. *Si*. That was the way God had planned it. And He had given them the strength of mankind to make use of His gifts. But mankind was weak. Hadn't she seen that? Mankind could fall into temptation. Mankind had free will but so often made the wrong decisions. And those decisions could have consequences so far reaching that it was almost unimaginable. Sister Julia did not want to make the wrong decision – not after all that had gone on. There had been so much sorrow, a sorrow that seemed still buried in her very soul.

Sister Julia walked through the cloistered arches of pale crumbling stone and stepped outside the back door. This place was not so different from the Santa Ana convent in Barcelona where she had lived when she was little more than a girl. It was not a closed order – the sisters were free to come and go and they could sell their sweetmeats in the foyer just as the sisters had done in Santa Ana. She smiled, remembering their *suspiros de monja* – nun's sighs – made with a thick batter and candied fruit; golden and crispy on the outside, rich and creamy on the inside. *Ah*. But at Santa Ana things had changed. Something else had been asked of her . . . Sister Julia looked up at their small bell tower which was attached to the chapel on a buttress of stone. Steadied herself.

Outside, the light had changed from gold to a pinkish hue. Towards the south the mountains rested as if in slumber; as if wounded, with their deep scars and furrowed wrinkles;

above them the darkening sky held daggers of red, orange, white. Another day gone. Another day nearer death . . .

Sister Julia had experienced a long life, a life that had held challenges very different from the ones she had been expecting when she was a girl; different too from what she had foreseen when she had been forced to take her first simple vows. It had not been easy – perhaps God's work was never easy – and many times she had questioned what had occurred. She still did. She had lived through such uneasy and turbulent times. But now. *Please God* . . . All she wished for now, was for the burden she held to be eased from her shoulders. For the gentle blanket of peace to put her mind and her heart at rest.

She fetched the roughly woven basket and sharp knife from the outside storeroom and began to collect the salad leaves for tonight's meal from the allotment surrounded by low dry-stone walls. They had fig and almond trees; hens for eggs; three goats for milk and cheese. They ate simply but well. As at Santa Ana, they grew most of their own vegetables and fruit, including potatoes, onions and the small Canarian bananas, although the land here on the Island of Fuerteventura was arid and dry. They still ate *gofio* too – once eaten by workers in the fields, mixed with water and sugar into a dough in a goatskin bag. These days they added it to milk to make their breakfast cereal or used it to thicken their soups and stews. Like many things, it had lived on, adapted to new times. And yet it symbolised, for Sister Julia, the simplicity of the life here.

Sister Julia did not fear death. She never had. Over the years, she had seen many die – sisters in the convent, people in the hospital where she worked as a young novice, her own family too. They were all gone now. And then there was the Civil War. No one could live through the Civil War and its aftermath and not see death, not stare it in the face, not smell it – bloody and rancid in your nostrils – around every street corner. Politics. War. Sister Julia shivered. There had been so much destruction.

And she feared that she was not blameless. They were difficult times, painful times for many. How could you know – unless you had lived through it? She had tried to beg God's forgiveness for the things that she had done. Things no person should be asked to do. Things that could not be right. That could not have been God's will. Not if He was the kind and just and loving God she had always believed Him to be. But did He hear her? Did He understand that she had felt she had no choice?

She paused for a moment to look out over the *campo*, the brown desert earth, so restful to the eye. To Sister Julia it seemed a biblical landscape; a land where you might expect to see camels and donkeys, three wise men travelling by the light of a star . . . But she was old and she was rambling. She must take these vegetables into the kitchen. They would be waiting. She picked up her basket.

It was very quiet here. These days only a few people came to the convent to seek guidance or to pray in their chapel. The road outside was little more than a sandy track leading only to the mountains and the Atlantic Ocean. And the sisters were quiet – although not a silent order. Quiet was regarded as the natural condition for religious women; careless talk had been avoided at Santa Ana and it was also avoided here. Mostly, the only sounds Sister Julia could hear were the faint howl of the wind echoing around their white pockmarked stone buildings, the hiss of the sand being lifted and blown, the distant heave and rush of the ocean waves and the occasional sharp cry of a gull. In the mornings the cockerel crowed and the hens scratched at the dusty earth. The simple sounds of Nature. And that was how Sister Julia wished it to be. After all she had lived through, she craved tranquillity and calm for her soul.

Sister Julia took the leaves through to where they were preparing the food, washed them carefully under the tap in the white enamel sink – the water here was salty but clean. There used to be a well and there was still a lime kiln outside the gate where the barilla plant had been burnt for sodium carbonate to make glass and soap, but some years ago the villagers had joined together to connect the convent to the water supply and to electricity and this had radically changed their lives.

She laid the produce on the kitchen counter beside the stove. They were making a hot soup – *caldo caliente* – with potato and eggs in a thin broth with sweet red pepper. Sister Josefina was stirring it with a wooden spoon. She smiled and nodded her thanks.

Sister Julia retreated to her own room on the first floor. She would have a short time of rest and quiet reflection before dinner. She needed to think. She did not want to get anyone into trouble – not if they had truly acted from the best of motives. But had they? When money was involved, there was temptation and there was corruption. And this had made her doubt everything that she had once believed to be true. It was a long time ago. But she still had the evidence, did she not? Sister Julia's eyes filled with tears as she remembered. Yes, it was a long time ago, but there were still many people who might desperately need to know the truth. Was it not their human right? And she – Sister Julia, humble as she was – could help them.

Her room was small and whitewashed. It had a wooden cupboard for her few clothes and a narrow bed; she needed only one thin blanket, for it did not get cold here on the island. There was no mirror. Why would she need a mirror? God could see inside her to her deepest thoughts – that was all that mattered. She had a writing table, though, on which she kept her Bible and psalm book, and the arched window behind it looked out on to the courtyard. In the writing desk was a drawer, which she always kept locked. In this, Sister Julia had secreted a few precious artefacts, mostly from her previous life before she had taken vows, but also from her time here on the island. There was her mother's wedding ring, some photographs of her family, an embroidered sampler she had made as a girl and a few items given to her by those she had helped over the years.

Here – as at Santa Ana – the sisters sometimes gave advice to those who came seeking guidance. Sister Julia had never sought the role of spiritual counsellor; it had come to her. She listened as people talked of family quarrels, of love that was lost, of sons and daughters who had disappeared. There were men who gambled or drank (always there were men who gambled or drank) and women who had lost sight of their virtue. And other things. Darker things.

She fingered the delicate white tablecloth of lace – like gossamer to the touch – given to her by a woman in the village. Sister Julia could still remember the look in the woman's dark eyes as she had told her story, could still feel her despair. Sister Julia had often prayed for her. She was another one who had been hurt, who did not know where to turn. It had been a story of disillusion and disappointment. But Sister Julia sensed there was more that the woman was not saying. She felt it. It rested there behind the sad eyes. And Sister Julia wondered. Was there another reason why her husband had behaved as he had? Was there more to the woman's story that she could not tell?

'Be still, my daughter,' she had told the woman, placing her palm gently on her head. 'Trust in God. He will show you the way.'

God had helped her give advice to others. He still did. Sister Julia prayed and He sent her answers so that when people came to her for guidance, the words – the right words – would emerge from her lips. Sister Julia was merely a vessel. God's vessel. What greater gift could she ask for? She knew, though, the answer to this question. What she longed for, more even than this, was the gift of peace.

Nestling deep in the drawer of her writing desk was the book. The book of names. Sister Julia touched the cover, which was plain and gave no clue as to what was inside. And let out a deep sigh which seemed to hold all the pain, all the emotion she had witnessed over so many long years. It didn't release it though. Even reading what was inside the book would give no clue of what had been. Unless . . . Names and dates. It was all here. Sister Julia had the evidence. She had written it down.

Every day she asked God for guidance. Every day she yearned to tell her story. Every day she ached for the ability to seek atonement; to do something that – while it might not make it right; nothing could make it right – could, in some measure, help one of these people. Because they needed help. Sister Julia knew this. Such things could not be covered up for ever. Secrets . . . Like a boil under the skin they would grow and fester until they must be lanced. It was the way of the world.

Sister Julia opened the book, read the first few names. 'May God forgive us,' she murmured. So many names. So many tears. So many secrets. Slowly, she closed the book again and put it back in the drawer. *One day . . .*

She thought back to the end of the Civil War – for that was when it had begun. They had all believed it was a new start, a time of hope and the end to poverty and violence. Not so. For Sister Julia it was just the beginning.

CHAPTER 4

The following day, Ruby spent all morning sorting out the contents of the house. Like a woman possessed, she thought. But at least it would stop her thinking.

In the afternoon, Mel called round. 'Just passing, darling,' she said. 'Thought you might fancy a walk?'

Just checking up on her, more likely. Mel sounded casual enough but Ruby kept catching her scrutinising her with narrowed eyes when she thought Ruby wasn't looking. 'I'm fine, Mel,' she said. 'Shouldn't you be working?'

Mel shrugged. 'I'm the boss. I can give myself a half day.'

Fair enough. And a walk sounded good.

Ruby grabbed a jacket, glanced in the mirror and ran her fingers through her short hair. She would do. They walked down the lane arm in arm. At last it was truly summer. The breeze was milder and there was a real warmth in the sun when it poked out from behind the clouds. Ruby and Mel headed for the sea.

'How's it going?' Mel asked as they walked towards Pride Bay. 'You look exhausted.'

'Thanks, Mel.' But she was. Last night she'd hardly slept. And when she eventually did get off she'd woken at dawn, sat bolt upright in a cold sweat. She'd been reliving the accident. Heard the clash of metal on metal, the screech of tyres, the scream . . . It had been pointless trying to sleep afterwards. She'd got up, made tea, watched the day begin and wondered. Was there something going on here that she should know about? Or was she being hopelessly paranoid?

She had tried to remember everything her parents had ever told her about her family. There had been the usual stories. Both Mum and Dad had been only children so there were no uncles and aunts and cousins. Mum had an aunt – who had died when Ruby was small – and three cousins living in Wales who she never saw. Dad had almost no one. There were her mother's parents, living on some island off the west coast of Scotland. But Ruby hardly knew them. They'd come down for the funeral, of course. Ruby had thought they might be a comfort, but they had both seemed so old and confused.

'She's our daughter,' her grandmother kept saying. 'How can she go before we do?'

Ruby hadn't known what to say to her. Her mother had hardly seen them in the last thirty-five years, she knew that much. It happened in families, she supposed. People lost touch, families became fragmented, before you knew what had happened you were practically estranged from your nearest and dearest. 'I'm sorry, I'm sorry.' She murmured this to her grandmother several times, as if it might make a difference.

'Bolt from the blue.' Her grandmother looked straight at her. 'Bolt from the blue.'

It had given Ruby a bit of a strange feeling, to tell the truth. As if her grandmother wasn't acknowledging her somehow. But they'd hugged, and she'd kissed her grandmother's papery cheek. Still, the old lady hardly seemed aware of her. She just looked at her sightlessly and murmured, 'Vivien, Vivien,' until at last Ruby's gentle and white-haired grandfather led her away, stroking her hand. 'There, my love. There, there, my love.'

It was hard to imagine her parents having dark secrets. But perhaps everyone had secrets. And some chose never to tell.

'Have you been in touch with James?' Mel asked.

Ah, James. Ruby looked towards the cliffs. The house martins were back. She watched them swooping and gliding and flapping, all directions; their special dance. 'He's phoned a couple of times.' Though Ruby didn't really know what to say to him. It was beginning to feel as if he belonged to a different life, one that had nothing to do with her any more. 'It's difficult. We haven't really talked.' At least not about the things that mattered. They'd talked about the weather (it was warmer in London) about the flat (he'd got someone in to clean) and about what he had done at work that day (two new clients and an appraisal coming up). But that was about it. Both times he'd ended the conversation by asking her when she was coming back and both times she'd said she didn't know. Was he relieved? Did he miss her? She had no idea.

They walked past the harbour and the old chapel. 'And are you going back?' Mel asked.

The million-dollar question. They scrunched their way

over the stones. The cliffs on the far side of the bay were high and steep, the foam of the incoming waves stretching like a ribbon along Chesil Beach towards the Fleet and Portland Bill, the waves stamping their imprints for just a few moments into the tiny pebbles before they were absorbed and gone. 'Not yet,' Ruby said.

They were approaching the row of fishermen's cottages right on the beach. The end one was the coastguard's cottage, and there was a sign outside. *To be Sold by Auction.* Ruby stopped walking. She looked at Mel and Mel looked back at her. 'Not yet?' said Mel.

'Well . . . ' Ruby had always liked this cottage. It was small and simple, built of yellow local stone with shy square windows at the front – all overlooking the sea. It must bear the brunt of the wind; the stone was pockmarked with years of salt and sea air. So it was strong in the face of adversity. 'It's a really sweet cottage – don't you think?'

'Why don't you give the agent a call?' Mel suggested.

Ruby hesitated, listened. The drag and pull of the waves on to the shore was so powerful, it seemed to thrum into the very centre of her. In front of the cottage and to the side, Chesil Beach rose – a ginger hill of small pebbles. Beyond, the path to Clearwater Beach wound up the tufted green cliff, sandy and ragged, like the promise of a fairy tale, the cliff bricked like the proverbial blocks of gold. It was her fairy tale, she realised; her childhood. Was that what she was trying to recapture?

'I found a letter, Mel,' she said.

'A letter?' Mel blinked at her. 'What sort of a letter?'

'I'll show you.' Ruby dug the letter from the doctor about her parents' infertility out of her bag and handed it over.

Mel frowned. When she'd finished reading she looked up. 'So, what are you thinking, Ruby?'

'I don't know what to think.'

Mel handed the letter back to her. 'I can't see what you're worrying about, to be honest,' she said.

It seemed pretty obvious to Ruby. 'Remember all those things in the shoebox?' she said. 'Those photos? The baby's bonnet?'

'Of course I do.'

'Well . . . ' Did she have to spell it out? Could there be a connection between the letter and the contents of the shoebox in the wardrobe? She didn't want to think so. It seemed impossible. But . . . She kept thinking of that photograph of the young woman with long blonde hair. And the baby in her arms.

'Oh, Ruby, you're tired and you're letting everything get to you.' Mel put an arm around her. 'Come on now. That letter doesn't mean a thing. How can it?'

'I don't know.' *Unexplained infertility.* It didn't sound very technical. But those would have been the days before many technological advances in IVF treatment, she supposed. So her parents had found it difficult to conceive – very difficult to conceive. What was she then? Some kind of miracle baby? How come they hadn't told her?

'Look.' Mel's voice was firm. 'It's perfectly possible that

since visiting the doctor, since doing those tests – whatever they were . . . ' Dismissively, she waved long, manicured nails towards the letter Ruby still held. 'You were conceived. By the time the surgery sent this letter out, your mother was already pregnant. Simple.'

'Yes, of course. You're right.' Ruby felt the tension ease out of her. She smiled. Of course it was possible, probable even. 'Thanks, Mel.'

Mel shrugged. 'Your mum never went back for that fertility treatment because she didn't need it.'

'And the photos?' Ruby murmured almost to herself.

'Are nothing to do with you.' Mel held her by the shoulders. 'Trust me. They belong to someone else. They must do.'

'OK.'

'And are you going to call the agent? It's a nice place – as long as it's not about to fall into the sea.'

Ruby moved closer to the low stone wall that surrounded the cottage. So far it had survived against all odds. The hill of pebbles provided a protective sea wall, but who could tell for how long? She placed her hands on the top of the wooden gate. But although it was a nice place, it wasn't so much the cottage that drew her. It was the view. The view of her childhood that she wanted to snatch back again so desperately. Ruby felt heady just looking at it.

'Why not?' She had to live somewhere. She pulled her mobile out of her pocket. Tapped in the numbers. 'I'd like to look round Coastguard's Cottage in Pride Bay,' she told the girl who answered the call. 'Now, if possible. I'm standing right outside.'

The cottage turned out to be an upside-down affair. The sitting room was on the first floor.

'For the views,' said the agent unnecessarily. She looked young and bored in her high heels, black tailored jacket and pencil skirt, and sounded as if she might have said the same thing many times these past few weeks.

Ruby moved to the window. 'Of course.' From here she could see beyond the pebbles, to the calm shimmering English Channel and the wavy line of a pale and distant mauve horizon. The grass on the cliff top was freckled with yellow buttercups and purple thrift. Pride Bay and her parents . . . Was she trying to get them back somehow? Was that it? She had always loved the mixed-up kid that was Pride Bay – it didn't know whether it was seedy or upmarket, elegant or scruffy, arty or bohemian. It was her past – but could it also be her future?

The kitchen was exhausted. The oven was probably circa 1940, dark with grime and grease; the lino was torn, the sink chipped enamel. Mel looked at Ruby and pulled an expressive face. Ruby ignored her.

'Obviously it needs updating,' the agent said.

'Obviously,' echoed Mel.

And OK, it didn't seem too much like a fairy tale. But doing it up wouldn't be too much of a problem; it couldn't be hard to find a good builder. And financially . . . She could

45

put her parents' house up for sale, if necessary move into rented accommodation until it was ready. It would work. 'When's the auction?' she asked.

The agent consulted her file. 'A week on Wednesday. Three p.m.'

'Right.' Dorset should have seemed impossible without her parents here. Impossible. And yet here she was. Without her parents there was no pathway. Ruby was wobbling along without stabilisers. She had to focus on something or she'd fall.

'Are you sure it wouldn't be easier to live in a modern place that's done up already?' Mel asked. 'Do you really want the hassle of all this?'

Ruby considered. Maybe this was exactly what she needed – a project; something to think about. She couldn't stay in the house. She had to go somewhere. Apart from the fact that it was too big and she needed to release some capital . . . Her parents' house would always be theirs. She didn't need ghosts to help her remember. And those cliffs summed up her childhood for Ruby. That was what she wanted.

Outside, they explored the steep terraced garden. Predictably, it was overgrown, but equally predictably the best view was at the top. All Ruby could hear was the wind, the waves, the shrieking gulls.

'It needs a lot doing to it, darling,' Mel said to Ruby after the estate agent had driven away. 'But I do like it.'

And so did Ruby. 'I'll have to get on to the bank,' she said. There wasn't much capital left, but there was the house to trade on. Yes, it needed a lot doing to it. But she could see herself here. It wouldn't bring her parents back. But it was the kind of place where she needed to be.

Mel raised an eyebrow. 'Does this mean you're definitely going to stay in Dorset?'

Ruby took a deep breath. She'd have to talk to James. Tell him what she'd decided to do. 'I think it does,' she said.

They went back to Ruby's for tea. Mel stretched out on the sofa and Ruby curled up in the armchair.

'It'll be so good having you around,' Mel said. She looked at Ruby thoughtfully. 'But I can't see you staying here for ever.'

'Because of James?'

Mel sat up. 'Not really. More because you seem to be kind of . . . ' She hesitated. 'In limbo.'

Ruby thought about this. James hadn't understood why she had to go back, but she'd felt she had to – in order to go forwards. 'Or in process,' she said to Mel.

She nodded. 'Exactly.' They exchanged a conspiratorial smile.

'Maybe I should get a car?' She hadn't needed one in London. James had owned a Saab convertible which they'd used at weekends, but mostly it had been easier to use the Tube and buses. Now though . . .

'Something cool and sporty?' Mel grinned.

'Absolutely.' Maybe an MX5. 'And a Dutch bike for cruising the country lanes.'

Mel laughed. 'Definitely a Dutch bike.'

If she moved back to Dorset, her life was going to change.

Ruby went to the kitchen to make more tea and when she got back Mel was standing by the walnut table flipping through the old family photo album Ruby had left there.

'Your mum was so pretty,' she said.

'I know.' Ruby peered over her shoulder. There were her parents – in Cornwall the summer before Ruby was born, arms wrapped around each other like a couple of newly-weds.

Mel turned the pages and Ruby watched her parents' lives unfold. Her mother running into the sea and laughing; her father caught off guard as he chatted to a grizzled fisherman beside his brightly painted fishing boat; the two of them posed by some railings, the view of St Ives harbour behind. Ruby sighed. The neat précis produced at the funeral had left her dry-eyed and aching. It was nothing like the real, tangled parent days she'd known when she was a girl. More images came into her mind's eye. Her mother, brushing her teeth with one hand, pinning back her long brown hair with the other; running down the street breathless, getting Ruby to school late. Her father frowning as he smoothed and planed the surface of a table, his grin as he swept little girl Ruby from her feet and turned her upside down to see a topsy-turvy world where everything was standing on its head.

'And I look nothing like her.' Both her parents were dark while she . . . 'Oh, my God,' she said.

'What?'

Ruby grabbed Mel's arm. 'Look at me, Mel. What do you see?'

'You do look a bit tired,' Mel admitted. 'I'm not sure whether you're eating properly. And your hair's a terrible mess, to be honest. But we have just been out to the beach. And—'

'What colour's my hair?' Ruby ran her fingers through it. She'd never had to colour it or even have highlights.

Mel looked confused. 'Blonde?'

'Exactly.' Ruby prodded a finger at the photos in the album. 'Look at them. They've both got dark hair. And brown eyes.' She could hear her voice rising. Why couldn't she see?

'Oh, Ruby.' Mel hugged her. 'Lots of kids don't look anything like their parents.'

'Come on, Mel.' Ruby could picture the shade of her mother's hair as if she was sitting right opposite them. Hazelnut brown. And . . . 'Look at my eyes, Mel.'

'Blue,' she said.

'Exactly.'

Mel frowned. 'But you must have noticed that ages ago. Maybe you're the dead spit of some ancient uncle or someone. Didn't you ever talk to your parents about it?'

'Yes, I did.' Her mother had told her she was their beautiful throwback. When Ruby was a bit older and she'd pressed her for further information, Vivien had enlarged on this and said that her grandmother had been a blue-eyed blonde and that must be where Ruby's genes had come from. But she had never really wanted to talk about it. And after all, what did it matter? But now . . .

'Ruby.' Mel took her hand. 'Please don't let this spoil your memories of them.'

She didn't want to. On its own the fact that she looked nothing like her parents wasn't necessarily significant. But taken with the things she'd found in the shoebox and the letter about her parents' infertility . . . How could it not spoil her memories? How could it not creep into her mind and make her doubt everything she'd always believed?

'I think you're getting this way out of proportion,' Mel said. 'Can you seriously imagine your parents—'

'No.' She couldn't. Didn't want to. She was beginning to feel not quite real, as if her identity had been snatched away, as if her very existence was now in doubt. 'But . . . ' A thought occurred to her. 'Baby pictures,' she said. She pulled the photo album back towards her.

'Baby pictures?' echoed Mel.

Ruby's childhood had been captured on film and processed in the old-fashioned way, and she was glad. It was wonderful to have such a complete record of those years, of her family. But was it complete?

She flipped the pages. There was Ruby playing in her cot; Ruby crawling around the living-room floor; Ruby's first tottering steps in the garden, amongst the grass and the daisies.

'How old do I look to you?' she asked Mel. In the first

photo her eyes were alert and she was smiling at the camera. Blue eyes. A fair down of hair. Fiercely holding Ginger, her teddy bear. When she was seven Ginger had gone on holiday somewhere and she'd never got him back.

Mel frowned. 'Six months?'

'And how do you explain that?' Ruby felt as if her head was exploding. 'Why aren't there any photos of me when I was first born?' She flipped the pages back again. Two months old? Three? Four? Nothing. So this wasn't such a complete record of her childhood after all.

'Maybe they were too busy looking after you to take pictures.' Mel poked Ruby affectionately in the shoulder. 'Babies can be hard work, you know, darling. Though Stuart keeps reminding me that my time is running out and we should start a family before it's too late.' Just for a second she looked wistful. And Ruby knew what she was thinking. If she had a baby it wouldn't be so easy to run the hat shop. And right at this minute, the hat shop *was* her baby.

But who was too busy to take baby photographs? Wasn't it something you did automatically? Kind of top priority when you'd just had a baby? And hang on a minute . . . She turned back to the pictures of her parents in Cornwall. After that there was nothing but the odd landscape until Ruby was six months old. 'There aren't any photos of Mum when she was pregnant either,' she whispered.

'Honestly, Ruby.' Mel sighed. 'What is it with you? Who wants pictures of themselves when they're fat?'

'Maybe.' Although pregnant wasn't the same as fat, was it?

Pregnancy was a time of hope, expectation and excitement. And she was doing the maths. 'That's no photos for about a year,' she said. A year. Even before the digital age that was a long time.

'Unless the photographs they took weren't good enough to make the album,' Mel said. 'Or the camera broke and they couldn't afford to get a new one.'

'Yes. Or I'm not really their daughter.' There. She'd said it.

How many times had she looked through this album? The truth was staring her in the face and she hadn't been able to see it. No pregnancy. No newborn baby.

'What about your birth certificate?' Mel asked.

Ruby stared at her. Birth certificate?

'You must have one.'

Yes, of course she had one. 'It's in London.' With the rest of her stuff – at James's flat. She hadn't looked at it for ages though, she'd just tucked it away in a drawer. But she'd used it to get her first passport. The relief flooded through her.

Mel stood, hands on hips. 'And who does it say your parents are?'

'Oh, Mel . . . ' Vivien and Tom Rae were her parents – they had to be; their names were on her birth certificate.

'If I can't convince you you're imagining things then your birth certificate will,' Mel said. 'You're getting into a state about nothing. Trust me. Ruby Rae is Ruby Rae in every sense of her. OK?'

'OK.' She took a deep breath. 'Thanks, Mel.' She would

phone James, she decided. She would go to London and she would collect all her stuff. She would find her birth certificate and she would stop worrying. Mel was right. She could be getting all stressed out for no reason at all.

But after Mel had left, Ruby took the photograph out of her bag where she'd tucked it for safe keeping. The blonde girl with the little baby on a Mediterranean beach somewhere. She stared at the baby. Tiny face, a fair down of hair. A baby was just a baby – didn't they all look much the same?

She stared at the girl too. At her mouth which was half-smiling and at the love beads she wore around her neck. 'Who are you?' she whispered. Secrets . . . If only photographs could tell.

CHAPTER 5

Dorset, 1977

'I don't understand,' Tom said, 'why it matters so much to you?'

Vivien's fists were tightly balled. She felt that if she let her fingers relax, even for a second, she would lose the will to make him see.

'Neither do I,' she said. 'But it does.' She eyed him helplessly. They never quarrelled – but they were close to it now. She shifted her dinner plate to one side of the table; she couldn't eat any more. She'd thought this would be a good time to broach the subject – in the after-dinner relaxation following Tom's favourite sausage and mash. Not so.

Tom looked sad. 'Aren't I enough for you?' he asked.

'Of course you are,' she said. 'It's just that . . . '

She'd known, hadn't she, when she wrote to him in the months after they'd met at the fair, when she sent him little drawings of stick-Viviens and stick-Toms swimming, cycling and kissing, that he was what she wanted?

And he seemed to want it too, because he'd stopped saving for a motorbike and instead saved up for train fares to visit Worthing as often as he could. But it was never often enough.

★

On Vivien's eighteenth birthday he had phoned her. 'If you were here, my lovely girl,' he said. 'I'd take you out for a slap-up dinner.'

Vivien had held the telephone receiver even closer. 'And would you buy me some flowers?' she said. Some of the girls at college envied her the boyfriend from Dorset who wrote to her and came to stay at weekends. They thought it was dead romantic. But Vivien wanted more.

'Course I would,' he said.

'It's almost the end of term,' she said. 'Maybe I could come and see you in the holidays.' In September she was going on to teachers' training college in Kingston upon Thames. It was all planned. It was what she'd wanted to do – before Tom.

'I was thinking . . . ' Noisily, he cleared his throat. 'Have you never thought about coming to college nearer here?'

Vivien almost stopped breathing. 'Now, why would I want to do that?' she teased.

'To be closer to me,' he said. 'We could move in together if you want.'

If you want . . . It was all she wanted. She'd just been waiting for him to ask. 'All right,' said Vivien, uprooting two years' plans in one casual word.

And that was it.

'You're doing what?' Her mother was horrified. 'It's ridiculous,' she said. 'How can you throw everything away because of some boy? You're far too young to know what you want.'

But Tom wasn't some boy, and Vivien did know what she wanted. Tom was on his own. He needed her. And she was quite keen to live in sin – it sounded both risky and thrilling.

Vivien never went to teachers' training college although she did study art at evening classes. Tom was only just qualified and money was tight so she found a job as a shop assistant. Six months later Tom proposed and Vivien accepted and they got married in the register office in Bridport.

Now, Vivien looked at him with fond exasperation. Tom was her husband, lover, best friend, soulmate. She loved everything about him. Most especially she loved watching his hands as he worked with wood – chiselling and sculpting, planing and polishing. He had started off working for a local company, but he wanted to run his own business eventually, he said. He was ambitious. He knew where he was going. She liked the way he teased her and made her laugh. She liked it when he was grumpy and she could rub his shoulders and kiss the corners of his mouth to make the bad mood evaporate. She liked the way he lost himself when they made love and came to afterwards with a sort of vacant wonder as he held her very, very tight. She liked the life in him, the love in him, his strengths and his vulnerabilities. And yes, he'd always been enough for her. But now she wanted more.

'Why now?' Tom asked. He pushed his plate aside. 'What's the hurry?'

My biological calendar, Vivien thought. 'It's been five years of trying, Tom,' she reminded him gently. She'd thought it would just happen. She watched the candle flicker on the table, stared at the food sitting in congealed gravy on her plate.

'That's not so long,' he said. 'We're still young. There's plenty of time.'

So why did Vivien feel that time was running out? He didn't want a baby as much as she did – that was obvious. How could she show him? A baby wasn't a threat. A baby would be an extension of herself and Tom; part of their love. They would be, not just a couple, but a family. 'Tom, I'm only saying let's both of us do some tests—' she began.

'I don't want to do any bloody tests. Don't you get it?' Then he was up and out of the room, slamming the door behind him.

No, she didn't get it. What was Tom so afraid of?

She began to clear up. No one has it all, she thought as she stacked the plates. Why should they? She had Tom. He was right – that should be enough. It was just that over the years a little gap had opened up inside her and she knew there was only one thing that would fill it. She took the plates and dishes on a tray into the kitchen, put them down by the sink. It seemed like not much to ask. Because that little gap had grown into a well of emptiness. She leaned for a moment on the sink, staring out of the window into the darkness of the side passage. Some days Vivien had an ache so bad she didn't know what to do with herself.

The following afternoon, Vivien called round to visit her

neighbour Pearl Woods.

'You're not looking quite yourself,' Pearl said, as they sat at her kitchen table with their cups of tea and a plate of digestive biscuits between them. 'Is everything all right?'

'Yes, of course.' Though she and Tom hadn't made up – not yet. And this was the longest – and worst – falling out they'd ever had.

'You're not . . . ?'

'No, I'm not.' Though Vivien had confided in Pearl that they'd been trying.

Pearl pushed the plate of biscuits towards her. 'Have another.'

Vivien smiled. She noticed Pearl wasn't eating any though. And come to think of it, she looked a bit peaky herself. 'I went to the doctor,' she said.

'Oh yes?'

The house always smelt of lavender, Vivien realised. It was calming somehow. 'He wants to do some tests to find out what the problem is.'

'It may be just a question of time,' Pearl said.

'That's what Tom says.' And that wasn't all Tom had said . . .

'Tom doesn't want to do the tests, I take it?'

'No.' And where did that leave her, with this ache inside and nowhere to put it? Where did that leave her?

Again, Pearl pushed the plate of biscuits towards Vivien, who took another one absent-mindedly. 'How important is it to you, love? Having a baby?'

Vivien looked back at her wordlessly.

'Ah, I see.' Pearl nodded. 'That important.' She sighed. 'It was like that for me too – more's the pity. Then you should do those tests and find out the truth of the matter. Otherwise it'll always come between you.'

Suddenly, Pearl's face tightened as if she was in pain.

Vivien got to her feet. 'Pearl?' Her neighbour's face was drained of colour and she had bent almost double in her chair. 'What is it? What's wrong?'

'It's all right, love.' She held out a hand and Vivien took it. 'It'll pass. It always does.' She took a couple of deep breaths as if to steady herself.

It always does? 'Let me get you some water.' Vivien went to the sink and ran the tap. Pearl was clearly far from well. And there was Vivien blathering on about her problems . . .

'What's wrong?' she asked again. 'Have you been to the doctor?'

And Pearl told her. About the cancer. About how long she had to live. A year if she was lucky. Maybe less.

Vivien was shocked. It struck her now that she hadn't seen Pearl working in the garden lately, cleaning windows, dashing to the shops. She had always been so full of energy. She'd lived on her own since her divorce. But, 'What about Laura?' she asked. Pearl's teenage daughter had gone off travelling over a year ago and Vivien knew for a fact that Pearl hardly ever heard from her. In fact she'd given up asking. 'Does she know?'

'I don't want her to know.' Pearl's face had regained its colour now and she seemed almost back to normal. 'There's nothing she can do.'

But didn't she deserve to be told? Surely it wasn't fair to the girl not to tell her that her own mother was dying? Vivien thought of her own parents in Scotland. She still saw them, but not often, and they had never been close. They were so different from Vivien – so ordinary and conservative, prim and predictable. When they'd upped sticks and moved lock, stock and barrel to an isolated Hebridean island, Vivien could hardly believe it, hardly believe them. Perhaps, she'd admitted to Tom, she hadn't known them quite as well as she thought.

'If I tell her, she'll feel she's got to come rushing back.' Pearl sighed. 'I don't want that. I don't want her to come until she's ready.' She sighed. 'You do understand, don't you, Vivien?'

Did she understand? With no children of her own, it was hard to imagine how she might feel in Pearl's situation. If she had a daughter, would she have ever let it get to this point? Vivien didn't think so. She might not have been close to her own mother but Vivien was determined that it would be different for her. Her daughter would confide in her, rely on her, would turn to her in times of trouble. Not go off round the world with hardly a word of goodbye, and not even have the simple courtesy to let her mother know where she was and how she was doing.

'I understand,' she said. 'But I think you're wrong. Laura needs to know.'

Pearl sipped her water. Her face was so pale. She'd lost

weight too – Vivien could see that now; her upper arms were thin and the skin hung from them in folds. 'She was angry when she left,' she said at last in a low voice.

'I know.' Vivien bowed her head. Her parents had split up and so of course Laura was angry. But it wasn't Pearl's fault. Her husband Derek had always played around but there was inevitably going to come a time when Pearl had had enough. Marriages broke up. It was hard for everyone concerned. But was it right to stay with someone for the sake of the children when you no longer loved one another? Vivien didn't think so. It was dishonest. And sooner or later those children would find out the lie that their parents had told. She understood, though, that it wasn't always that simple. It was hard and it was complicated.

'I was the one who wanted a baby so desperately.' Pearl smiled sadly, as if remembering that time. 'It's different for you, love, with your Tom. He's a good man.' She shook her head. 'But I knew what Derek was like. And I could have just put up with things as they were. Maybe I should have.'

Vivien took her hand. 'You have to lead your own life,' she said. 'You have to do what's right for you.'

'And if it wasn't right for Laura?' Pearl's gaze slipped past Vivien. There was a vacancy about it, she thought, as if she was imagining her daughter – wherever she was.

'Laura will understand,' Vivien said. 'In time.' Children got over it. They had to.

Pearl glanced at her. *What do you know?* she might have said. After all, Vivien didn't have a child, couldn't have a child

– maybe. But she didn't say it. And would there even be enough time for a new understanding between mother and daughter? Vivien didn't know how long Pearl had or when Laura might be coming home.

But Pearl didn't look convinced. 'I don't want you telling everyone round here either, Vivien. I don't need anyone's pity. I can manage on my own.'

Vivien sank bank into her seat. Her heart went out to her. 'I won't.' But she would have to do something.

She told Tom about it later, when they were cuddling in bed. Everything seemed to be all right again between them, but she'd caught a glimpse of a different side to the man she'd married, and it had shown her how fragile some things could be – things that you thought were built in stone, immovable, unbreakable.

'Poor woman.' He stroked Vivien's hair. 'I'll go round and offer to do her lawn for her. See if there's anything that needs to be done in the house.'

'Thanks, love.' She squeezed his shoulder. 'But don't—'

'I won't.' He tipped her chin so that she was looking into his eyes. 'I'll be the soul of discretion. I can be sensitive, you know.'

'I know.' She held his gaze.

'And about those tests . . .'

'It doesn't matter.' She turned her face away. She didn't want to talk, didn't want to argue. If they weren't meant to have children, then that was all there was to it. It wasn't worth breaking up a marriage for.

'Oh, it does though, love.' He held her face cupped in his palm so that she had to look back at him. 'It matters to you, doesn't it, having a baby?'

She shrugged. 'Yes,' she murmured, under her breath. Oh, yes.

'Then we'll have those tests. I want a baby too, you know.'

'You do?' Thank God, she thought.

'I do.'

She cuddled in closer. 'I'm scared too,' she whispered. Scared of what she might find out. But Pearl was right – they needed to know.

He held her more tightly. 'We won't be scared, love. We need to know the facts. And if there's anything they can give us to help . . . Well, we'll try everything.'

Everything. Vivien let out a deep sigh of relief. It was what she'd longed to hear. 'Thanks, Tom,' she said. She could cope with anything if Tom was with her. And once they knew . . . Well, then they could decide what to do about it – together.

'And in the meantime . . . ' He rolled over so that he was sideways on to her. 'We could always keep practising.'

'Practising?' Vivien closed her eyes.

To have a child. She felt the brush of his lips on hers, his hand on the soft flesh of her upper thigh. And she thought of Pearl – poor Pearl who had only tried to fight for what was hers, who had cancer and who was alone, and who didn't even know where her daughter Laura might be.

CHAPTER 6

Andrés was sitting at a table outside a café on the beach, a café he had begun to frequent more and more. Soon it would be invaded by summer tourists; this was the lull before the storm – particularly at this time of day when most people were packing up to go home to their families. It gave him what he needed – especially out of season. Space to think, a sense of quiet and a view of the ocean. *Si. Bueno.* Even the coffee was good.

But today his coffee had grown cold. Yet again, he'd been staring out to sea. Daydreaming. This sea was very different from the sea he'd grown up with on the island. Vast and a gentle blue-grey, it was another creature entirely. And yet, strangely, there were similarities in the landscape and perhaps that was why he had come here to West Dorset, escaping from the city of London where he had first found himself when he came to England. Another similarity about this landscape was that he loved painting it.

Someone he'd once met on the island, an Englishman, someone who had admired his work when he was painting down at the Old Harbour one afternoon, had mentioned West Dorset; it was as simple as that. 'You should go there one day,' he'd said. 'Amazing cliffs – the Jurassic coast, millions of years old, a bit like this place y'know.' And so – finding himself in England, the land, so they said, of opportunity – Andrés had come here to see. He had wanted, he supposed, despite everything that had happened, to find a small piece of home.

He had put a postcard in the local post office advertising his services. He had done painting and decorating in Ricoroque too – just on a casual basis until he'd decided what he wanted to do, until he made his name as an artist perhaps. And he'd worked on some of the building sites springing up all over the island in order to meet the demands of tourism.

Rather to his surprise, the advert had only been in the window for two days when the postmistress employed him to paint the outside of her house. And that was how it had started. When you were painting the outside of a house, people stopped and talked to you. When you were employed by the village postmistress, people found out about you. Word spread. Andrés Marin was of the old school. He was old-fashioned and reliable and his rates were fair; he did a good job and he could be trusted to be left in an empty house. Andrés had got more work. He could make a living here. And so he'd stayed.

He earned more than enough to live on and began to put money by. He bought a pick-up truck, found a better place to live. In the years since he had left the island, he had built up a small business of his own. He had been right to come here. Here he could make enough money to live as he wished to live and he could paint too – without his father breathing down his neck. He had lived here now for seventeen years. He had studied the English language at his island school and now after so long in England, he was fluent. Andrés watched the waves wash on to the shore, frothing around the tiny pebbles that made up Chesil Beach. Mile upon mile of it, stretching from Weymouth to Lyme Regis. Now, England held fewer surprises. It was a kind of home.

His childhood had been nothing but painting. It was practically all he remembered. Canvases filled not only his father's studio, but overflowed into the rest of the blue and white stone house on the island. That was all there was. And now . . . Andrés had finished work early today and he had a purpose in mind. He wanted to do some preliminary sketches for a big seascape he was planning. The art group he belonged to – all linked to the Barn Studios in Pride Bay where Andrés had a small unit to work in – were planning an exhibition for later this summer and he wanted to get as many pieces finished as possible.

Unlike his father, Andrés had to fit his art in with his other work – in the evenings, if he wasn't too tired, and at weekends. His father . . . Andrés pulled out his sketch pad and a pencil. He hated to think of him and yet the man was never far from his mind.

When Andrés was a boy, his father used to go out to play dominos in the Bar Acorralado – that was his distraction; what took him away from his work. And when he did . . . Andrés used to creep up the stone steps to his father's sanctuary, inhale the rich, dry scent of turpentine and unused paper, touch the stiff newness of canvas and card standing upright in the open cupboard, peer beneath dusty sheets and cloths draped over wooden easels. And dream.

It was the colours. Andrés took in the colours surrounding him now. Not dissimilar, no. English colours were normally subtle and grey. But here on Hide Beach they were also bright – the high cliffs stacked like bricks of honey; Chesil Beach itself rising up and flowing out along the coastline like the mane of a golden lion. And the fields were bright and green as peas – it must be all that English rain. The colours of the island were bright too – especially the sea. The sea could be sweet turquoise and it could be cruel navy. It could be blue as a sapphire or black as ink. He'd never known colour quite like it since.

In his father's studio, paint would always be splattered everywhere – on paper and card and canvas; big dollops on the once-white tiles of the studio floor; rainbow freckles smattering pale walls. Tears of colour streaming and running and mixing – out of control, and yet under *his* control, as they all were. Enrique Marin was a man who could never be crossed.

Almost subconsciously, Andrés began to focus on the shapes he wanted to include in the picture. At this preliminary stage he was just doodling really – unsure as to what would go in. He started on the cliffs though; they were his framework. He loved the way the path wound to the top, the grassy cap which was covered in wild flowers, and he loved the scrolled shape of the sandy cliff edge – which over the years had eroded and crumbled on to the beach and into the sea.

His family had more than most on the island. His father and his father's family before him had reared sheep and goats in the smallholding that surrounded the blue and white stone *casa* with its *postigos*, its little wooden shutters, and they grew the prickly pear cactus for the cochineal beetles, but his father's heart was never in growing crops or keeping animals. He always had other things on his mind.

As soon as Enrique Marin started selling his work, he sold off the land to his neighbour, keeping only two goats and an area for growing vegetables, which Andrés's mother tended. Sometimes – when his father's work did not sell – it was all that kept them going.

The Canary Islands were known to the Romans as the Fortunate Isles; Andrés had learned that at school. But they were not perhaps so fortunate for everyone. They were not so fortunate for those who chose to speak up, for those who would not keep a secret, for those who refused to pretend.

On the paper, Andrés made a rough marker for where the sea would come, and the line of the horizon. And saw himself – four years old or five, ducking his head round his father's studio door.

'Andrés! Out! *Hacia fuera!*' His father, wearing his loose pale blue cotton shirt and paint-spat shorts, would yell at him. Stabbing in the air with his brush. In his other hand was the usual thin cheroot; he couldn't paint without smoking; couldn't walk or think. He drew on it, coughed, flicked ash vaguely towards the ashtray and missed, as usual. He stooped slightly forwards, his shoulders hunched, his unruly dark hair held back from his face with a magenta fabric band that made him look like a Red Indian. He was livid. 'I cannot work if I am to be constantly disturbed!' Flick, point, ash. 'Reyna!'

Andrés could hear him still.

Then his mother Reyna would come running and Andrés would scuttle away like a long-limbed cockroach, head down.

'Never mind, my son,' his mother would say, smoothing back her raven-dark hair and retying her apron. 'You can work here in the kitchen with me.'

One day, back up to the studio she went, wiping her hands on a tea towel.

Andrés heard their voices rising and falling, rising and falling into silence. Those were the days when she was still allowed to enter the studio. His mother came back, shaking her head and clicking her tongue. She was carrying an old paint palette, some discarded sugar paper and a frayed brush. Andrés brightened. Work, she'd said. Work. Andrés liked that. It seemed to elevate him to the position of his father, to give him purpose. And he was to paint.

So, while his baby sister slept in her basket near the open door, where the breeze from the sea softly stirred the bamboo tassels hanging from the doorframe, and his mother did the household chores, Andrés worked.

He painted. He painted the fruit his mother placed in the roughly hewn pottery bowl; pockmarked oranges and Canarian bananas – small, sweet and yellow. He painted his mother, dark and industrious, sleeves rolled, apron wrapped around her waist, brisk and efficient as she prepared *ropa vieja*, meat and potato stew, parrotfish or squid. 'Never mind your father. He is what he is. You get on.'

On another sheet, now, Andrés drew the red fishing boat coming in to shore at Hide Beach. He drew the fishermen too and their tents, which would be a good spot of colour in his painting. Red, he decided, to match the fishing boat and contrast with the blues of the sea, and the yellow/gold of the pebbles. Red was a good balance, a good draw.

His father was still painting too, of course, still living in the village of his childhood which Andrés had not been back to for years. They loved Enrique Marin on the island of Fuerteventura, for his creativity and his flair. He had transformed the place, they said, with his sculptures, his art work, his vision. Because of him, other artists came and created more objects of beauty. Because of him, more tourists came too, spending money and making the island richer. Because of him, there were galleries, exhibitions and grants. He was adored, deified almost.

His father was well off now. His first most notable successes had been at the beginning of the new millennium – Andrés had read about them, thought, *Now will you be satisfied?* Since then Enrique Marin had even become known internationally – an artist and sculptor famous in his own

70

right, able to command small crowds at exhibitions and galleries; sought after, in the enviable position of choosing only select commissions. His parents now owned other houses – one in the south of the island and one in the capital city of Puerto del Rosario – but they had kept the house in Ricoroque, and Andrés suspected that they still spent most of their time there. It was their community, Enrique's landscape – the landscape that he loved and which had given him the success he craved.

He is what he is. Andrés never questioned his mother's words. Not then. But did she know what her husband was? *Chofalmeja.* Did she really?

When Andrés ran out of images in the kitchen of his childhood, he turned to his mind's eye and he painted the sea for the very first time; turbulent waves crashing on the grey-seal rocks by the Old Harbour, great rollers spinning out the surf on Playa del Castillo, turquoise luminescent water looping gently round the sandy lagoon of the bay. Every tide was a contradiction. Every tide brought something new. He painted the sea green, blue, white and every shade in between. He painted it still and he painted it moving. He painted it quiet and he painted it on fire. With people and boats, and alone. And gradually, over weeks, over months, over years, he learnt how to capture its colours and its moods and its energies. He could catch the movement of the surf and the waves, the lilts and the lifts, the curls and the glitter.

Until even his father noticed.

He began to watch what Andrés was working on when he

ran home from school to paint. Enrique Marin pointed with the cheroot he held between nicotine-stained fingers, uttered terse comments: 'More white there.' Or, 'Out of perspective. Use your eye. That's why God gave you two.' Sometimes his father only nodded. Other times he walked over to the window and looked out, and Andrés's mother went to him then and put a hand on his shoulder, murmuring, 'Enrique . . .'

One Saturday, Andrés was working on a particularly challenging subject. His friends were out playing football but he was far too absorbed to join them. *Mañana.* Time meant little to him in those days; there was always enough. There was a fishing boat in the New Harbour painted red, green and blue, emblazoned with a black emblem and the name *Halcon.* The emblem was a depiction of a hawk swooping on its prey; single-focused – from its outstretched talons to its curved cruel beak and flinty eye. Beside the boat, Andrés drew a netful of glittering silver fish and standing by this a leathery-skinned old fisherman who might or might not be Guillermo, wearing his blue fishing overalls and canvas boat shoes. In the distance the sea was boisterous. The waves were shattering on to El Toston, the spray a thousand droplets in the wind.

His father trudged past, collecting the cup of coffee Mama had prepared for him. He lit another cheroot, muttered something that Andrés could not hear.

Andrés hesitated, his hand holding the brush poised above the fish. He waited for the criticism. *Too many fish, the sea is too still, error in the skin tone.*

But his father was quiet.

Andrés looked up. His father was stroking the stubble of his chin. His dark eyes had glazed over. He looked angry. 'What?' Andrés whispered. What was so bad?

His father turned to his mother. 'The boy can paint,' he said. And then he stomped back to his studio.

Just that. *The boy can paint*. But Andrés was dazzled by it. The words crept into his soul and exploded like a firework into sparks of delight. He felt as if he had been acknowledged. Recognised. For the first time, Andrés knew what he was, who he was. The son of his father. An artist. Painting would be his life.

But he had been wrong. He had been a fool. An idiot. *Zurriago*.

Annoyed with himself now, Andrés bundled his things back into the canvas bag at his feet. That was enough for now. He was too unfocused. He had let Enrique Marin get to him, the way he had always let him get to him. And when Andrés couldn't get them out of his mind – his mother, his sister, his father, for whom he would never be good enough – he couldn't work. He had to shake himself out of it before he could go on.

Because Enrique Marin had not taken his son into his studio and encouraged him to paint. He had not passed down any words of wisdom or tips from the great master. Oh, no. On the contrary. Enrique Marin had become more and more enraged with Andrés for following in his footsteps – for daring to think that he could compete with him, that he could even live in the same house as the great man. His own son . . .

'Have you got nothing better to do, boy?' he would shout, when he came across him hard at work on a drawing. 'Who do you think you are? Do you think the world will ever want what you do? Look at it!' And he would stomp over, stab at Andrés's work with his finger or with the cheroot, criticising, jeering, pulling his work to pieces – literally sometimes. Until Andrés would run away, tears in his eyes, unable – as they all were – to speak, to stand up to him. Why did his father hate him so much? What had he done? Why would nothing ever be good enough for the man Andrés so admired?

Or used to admire, he thought now. Now, he knew better. He had known for seventeen years that there was nothing to admire in a man like him.

But back then . . . It didn't matter that his mother and his sister had encouraged him in his painting. What did they know? It didn't matter that his art teacher at school said, 'We can all tell whose son you are, Andrés.' None of this mattered. Because the one voice that did matter was always raised against him.

Andrés first noticed the woman when she was up on the cliff path walking towards Hide Beach. She walked with a sense of purpose, short blonde hair swept back in the wind, shoulders hunched, hands thrust into the pockets of her jacket. He noticed her because she was a solitary figure – which was unusual; most people at least had a dog. And because he had the feeling he'd seen her somewhere before.

Since he'd left his home on the island, since that day when he did what he'd never thought he'd do, Andrés had kept in touch with his mother and sister, even though he knew they didn't tell Enrique Marin.

'Do not darken this door again,' he had said to his son, black eyes glowering. 'Do not dare to come back.' Not much room for negotiation there. And anyway, Andrés had too much pride. Every time he thought of the island and his family, he reminded himself of those words. He would never go back to a place where he was so hated. And yet he'd had to do it, hadn't he? How could he not?

Andrés spoke to his mother regularly though. When Enrique was out of the way, she would phone him — two rings and then four — and he would call her back. They didn't want to risk Andrés's father seeing the phone bills and guessing that they were still in touch. Andrés told her details of his life, snippets about his clients — Mrs Emily Jones (bedroom and living-room ceilings apricot-white) who curled the coat of her black poodle, dressed it up and took it for afternoon walks along the promenade. Old Ian Hangleton (outside of the house in magnolia and a few broken slates) who peered out into the street through net curtains to catch up with the latest gossip and kept his money under the floorboards in his bedroom with a loaded gun by his bedside. *Just in case* . . . Anything that he thought might make his mother smile. He imagined them — Mama and Izabella — sitting with a pot of coffee between them when the old man was out of the way. His mother bringing Izabella up to date on his news, though he called his sister too from time to time and she wrote him occasional long letters in return. She was always careful though, he could always sense her holding back. As if she couldn't risk their father's anger. As if she couldn't allow herself to communicate with Andrés more fully. Until he'd been accepted once more into the family fold.

He also told his mother about the last house he'd done up and how he had transformed it out of all recognition before he sold it on. *It made me feel good* . . . At least something did. Andrés had benefited from rising house prices in the late nineties. He had bought a rundown two-up two-down for next to nothing – been given the tip-off by one of his clients, actually. He was far from being a property dealer, but he hadn't done too badly.

And he'd even told her about this new place he had spotted by the sea at Pride Bay. He touched his jacket pocket to check that the auction brochure was still tucked in there. It had reached out to him, this place, and he'd decided to bid for it. Why not? It had glorious views.

'It sounds magnificent, my son,' she had said. Pride in her voice.

He'd smiled, thinking of the rundown cottage. Hardly magnificent. But maybe one day . . . He had been looking for a new project. And the cottage reminded him somehow of home.

'How is everything, Mama?' he had asked her. '*Qué tal?*'

He heard her pause and understood it. 'Ah,' he said.

'I am well enough, my son,' she said. 'But nothing has changed.'

He knew she would never cross him. She was one of the old school. It was different for Andrés. He was the younger generation and maybe he had been born a rebel; he would question – he had to question – the way things were.

'And Izabella?' he asked, thinking of his sweet-faced sister. She would never cross him either. Out of love or out of fear, he wasn't sure.

'Well,' said his mother. 'Though she still waits for a child.'

Poor Izabella. She had been married now for ten years. It must be hard for her. It was the *Majorero* way – family, children. Not so for Andrés. But Andrés had always felt different from his family; never felt that he truly belonged. Perhaps because his father had never allowed him to belong.

Now, the sun poked out its early evening face and Andrés shielded his eyes, watching the cliffs change colour from treacly gingerbread to pale sugar-gold. He took a final sip of his coffee, even though it was cold. He had it strong and black – a double shot of espresso – and the girl behind the counter knew that and no longer asked him what he wanted.

Andrés stared out to sea, conscious that the woman on the cliff was now in the bay and walking towards the café. She was wearing large white-framed sunglasses, pushed up on to her blond head and he saw that her eyes were red, as if she'd been crying. She was not beautiful, but she was striking. She was small, slim and self-assured. There was a kind of dignity in the way she walked and held herself, and something quirky about the way she was dressed (the red jacket, black jeans, white sunglasses and pink laced walking boots were quite a combination) that piqued his interest.

She negotiated a pathway through the tables and he felt her glance graze over him. Why was she sad? He could see it in her eyes and it hurt him, deep in his chest, as if it had stirred the memory of his own hurt. Had he seen her before? If so, it was a long time ago. He certainly hadn't seen her lately – he would have remembered.

She went into the café. Ah well. Andrés would probably never see her again. He pushed his coffee cup to one side and got up to go. He must start work – the work that really mattered to him. A few of the others would be there at the studio, and they'd work till about eight or nine and then go out for a beer and maybe something to eat.

He thought of his last conversation with Mama. He'd almost said more. He'd always wondered if, now that he was far away, it might be possible to say things that perhaps should be said within a family. But in the end he'd said nothing. That was the problem. Wasn't it always easier to say nothing? Wasn't it always easier to pretend?

CHAPTER 7

Ruby drove from London back to West Dorset, all her belongings stuffed into the back of the small van she'd hired for the day; coats, scarves and other debris over-spilling from the passenger seat beside her. Van hire had turned out to be very popular on this particular day; must be something going on that someone wasn't telling her.

'We've got one left,' a man from the third company she'd tried informed her. 'As long as you're not fussy about the colour.'

'Course not,' said Ruby.

It was pink. Hot pink, to be precise. The kind of hot, fluorescent pink that was getting her noticed – she'd been waved at, hooted at, ogled at since she'd left at eight o'clock this morning. But it was a sunny day and she was quite enjoying herself. Should colour matter? Ruby had taken one look at the van, tied a flowery vintage scarf around her hair and climbed in.

There was a lot of traffic – wasn't there always? – but she didn't mind that either. It gave her the chance to collect her thoughts. And there was a lot to think about. Mel had told her that she must be practical, so Ruby had gone to see the bank manager in Pridehaven and worked out her finances. Alan Shaw was an old friend of her parents; he was both understanding and helpful. Her parents' house was paid for and Alan approved of Ruby putting it up for sale. He wasn't so sure about the auction or Coastguard's Cottage, but he did reassure her that if she kept to her planned budget there would be plenty of money left over for her new project.

'And what else will you do, Ruby?' He smiled in an avuncular kind of way.

Ruby wondered what it must feel like to know so much about other people's financial affairs. He certainly didn't seem uncomfortable with it.

'You'll carry on working, I imagine?'

'Oh, yes, of course.' There wasn't that much spare money. Her parents had never been well off, but her father had inherited some and they weren't the type to have squandered what they had. Still. It would be more than enough. Yesterday, she had walked past the cottage again, along the cliff and down to Hide Café. She'd gone there so many times with her parents that it was quite an emotional journey. But one that she wanted to make. Another part of the process, she told herself.

She'd started putting out feelers for work again too and there were several article ideas in the pipeline. One glossy monthly had suggested she pitch for an article on equal pay in the workplace. It used to be a gender issue; once upon a time it depended on qualifications; now, it was often down to personal negotiating skills. The person sitting at the desk next to you could be doing what you were doing and yet be on an entirely different pay scale. It was hardly fair. There were the usual article opportunities on travel, health, interior design. She'd like to do something else, though, and so she was meeting up with one of her editors later, staying in the loop. She knew what she was looking for. Something big. An article that meant something; that had more global repercussions, not just human interest. But stories like that didn't come along every day of the week, and when they did there was usually a posse of journalists champing at the bit and waiting to write them.

'And your music? Are you still playing?'

'Yes, I am.' She had started practising again and had surprised herself. She wasn't quite as rusty as she'd thought. Over the last few days she'd got in touch with a couple of members of the original band and last night they'd met up to rehearse. It had been a bit scary, but . . .

'We're planning to do a gig.' It was a big step forward but Ruby thought she was ready. Last night's rehearsal had gone well and they'd already told her at the Jazz Café that they were welcome any time. Her parents had always supported her music; her mother especially had always loved jazz and they had both been so proud when she performed. It would be as if they were in the audience once again. This would be for them as well as for Ruby.

'Excellent,' Alan said. 'I'm delighted to hear that.'

Life was too short not to do what you dreamed of doing –

these past few months had taught her that, if nothing else. You could never be sure it wouldn't suddenly be snatched away from you.

And then of course she had spoken to James – and it hadn't been as bad as she feared.

'I've been thinking,' she'd told him.

'You're not coming back.' It was a statement, not a question.

'How did you know?' she hedged. It couldn't – or shouldn't – be that easy, should it?

She heard him sigh. 'I think I always knew,' he said. 'I just hadn't acknowledged it.'

And Ruby realised. It had been like that for her too. So it was over.

Now, Ruby focused on the stream of traffic in front of her. It hadn't been the greatest love affair of all time – but they had cared enough to move in together; they had thought that it would work. But . . . Everybody changes, Ruby thought. It was just good luck if you did it the same way and at the same time. And then there was the other truth. She hadn't loved him enough.

'I want to collect my stuff from the flat, if that's OK?' she had said to him.

'When?' And something about the way he'd said it, a muffled noise in the background which could have been the radio (it was early, before he would be leaving for work) made her think there was someone else there. That James had made it easy for her because he'd already moved on. Well, she couldn't blame him. James wasn't the type to hang around and it was his flat after all.

'Saturday morning?' she'd suggested. 'About eleven?' The thought of someone else there – so soon – washing in their bathroom, sleeping in their bed, was shocking at first. But in a way it made things easier, more clear-cut. And it wasn't her bathroom or her bed any longer – it never had been; it was James's.

'Saturday's fine,' he said. 'I'll be here.'

It felt strange ringing the doorbell of the London flat instead of using her key.

James let her in. He kissed her on the cheek and said, 'You're looking good, Rubes,' without a trace of bitterness. So yes, he had definitely moved on.

'You too,' Ruby told him. He was. His fair hair was slightly longer and it suited him. He looked . . . More relaxed, she realised. That was it. Happy. Ah, well. She should be glad about that too.

Ruby didn't waste much time looking around, but the flat did have a different feel. Kind of antiseptic – as if James (or someone?) had scoured the very life out of it. Someone with a touch of OCD? Or someone desperate to eradicate essence of Ruby?

But it didn't matter. He had piled her stuff in boxes in the hall and Ruby was glad she didn't have to hang about. The place still held echoes of that early-morning call from the police, of the news that had shattered her world. *There's always a blind spot . . .*

James offered her coffee, but she shook her head. 'Thanks, but I said I'd hook up with Leah.' Leah was the editor she did the most freelance work for and over the years they had developed a close and trusting relationship. Ruby knew that Leah would give her any interesting leads she could and Leah knew that Ruby would always deliver good-quality copy on time. And anyway, she didn't want to have to make small talk with James, she certainly didn't want to tell him what had been happening in her life and she didn't want to have to use the bathroom and see someone else's stuff parked on the shelf.

Together they carted the boxes down the stairs and piled them into the back of the van.

'It's a bit gaudy, isn't it?' James had recovered from his initial double-take when he first spotted the flamingo-van. It did kind of stand out from the crowd, but Ruby had got quite fond of it during the journey.

Ruby shrugged. 'It goes.'

When they were done, he waited on the pavement while she slid into the driver's seat. She wound down the window.

'Sorry it didn't work out between us, Rubes,' James said. He held out his hand.

'Me too.' Ruby put her hand in his. It closed around it like a reminder of what they'd shared. Nice, she thought, but never earth shattering. Would they keep in touch? Probably not. Which was a bit sad. But . . . 'Hope you get a new flat-mate soon.'

For a second his eyes flickered and she knew she'd hit the mark. She grinned and squeezed his hand to show there were no hard feelings. 'Take care, James.'

'You too. Bye, Ruby.'

So. The brief lunch meeting with Leah had gone well. They had reconnected and Ruby had run a few ideas past her. They didn't really do personal, but Leah knew about the death of her parents and seemed relieved to see that Ruby was coping – just.

'Don't push yourself too hard, Ruby,' she'd said to her when they said goodbye. 'Take the time you need.'

'Don't worry,' Ruby said. 'But in the meantime . . .'

Leah laughed. 'I know. If anything meaty comes my way I'll run it past you.'

'Thanks, Leah.'

After lunch Ruby had met up with Jude and filled her in on what was happening.

'I'll miss you,' Jude said. 'We all will.'

'Me too,' said Ruby. But the truth was that already her London life seemed to be slipping into the distance of her mind. She would miss Jude and the others, and she would miss James. But it was already her past.

So now she and her possessions were out of the flat and heading west. Ruby was tired. But she'd made the right decision – she knew she had.

Somewhere in this lot was her birth certificate. Something

to prove that a shoebox of photographs and random objects couldn't take away from her who she was and where she'd come from. Never mind that her mother and father had taken a long time to conceive her. Never mind that she looked nothing like them. She was their daughter and this would prove it. She was Ruby Rae.

At last she hit the A31 and sailed over the hills, past her favourite view of the West Dorset valleys and the sea beyond, and down towards Pridehaven. Flamingo-van was doing a grand job. She might look blowsy on the outside, but her engine was all heart. And despite everything else going on in her life, Ruby still felt a sense of liberation, of hope, even. She was doing what she could and she was staying strong. She was . . . well, managing.

Back at the house, Ruby unloaded the boxes and at last sat down with a cup of tea. On the sofa beside her was a box of paperwork from the top drawer of her desk. She hoped it would be there. She could hardly keep her eyes open now but she had to look. She wanted to put the doubt to rest. To put this faint feeling of unbelonging behind her just as soon as she could.

It was there. Phew. Tucked in behind her passport and her full paper driving licence. She unfolded it, trying not to hold her breath. After all, she'd seen it before. She knew what it would say.

It was just an ordinary birth certificate. Of course. It showed the registration district – Pridehaven, County of Dorset. It showed her parents' names and occupations.

Vivien Rae, Tom Rae; no problem there. It showed her name, Ruby Ella, the registrar's signature, the address of the place where she was born. This address. It had been a home birth, then. Ruby hadn't noticed that before. But there was nothing strange about that. Lots of people had home births – even for their first child. And sometimes it wasn't even a choice. Perhaps Vivien had gone into labour suddenly and hadn't even had time to get to the hospital. Ruby smiled. Her mother had never actually told her what had happened. Just that it had been a normal and a healthy birth.

And then she noticed something else. Something that made her stomach dip with alarm. It was in the top right-hand margin of the certificate, printed in red ink. *Delayed Registration*. What did that mean?

Ruby shook off her exhaustion, got out her laptop and Googled. She found a pretty comprehensive article straight off. Births should be registered within forty-two days, apparently – that was the law. But in fact the authorities encouraged registration at any time – otherwise there could be all sorts of problems, like not being able to get a passport, not being on the system, not being able to vote and so on. So even if a birth hadn't been registered within forty-two days, it still could be. It could still be registered years later, in fact. But the birth certificate would be marked *Delayed Registration*. Like hers. She read on. Documentary evidence had to be provided. What would that be? Notification from a midwife perhaps? There'd have to be a midwife, wouldn't there? And witnesses. A midwife again? The husband maybe? The civil registrar would examine all the evidence . . . Ruby scrolled down. Date and place of birth would be verified. Finally, the notice of late registration would be put on public display – a bit like the banns before you got married. If no one opposed the registration you were home free. You existed.

She closed the site and shut down her computer. Why wouldn't her parents have registered her birth immediately? It wasn't the sort of thing that would just slip your mind. She thought of the photos in the family album. No baby photos for the first six months of her life, no birth registration either. What did that mean? Two and two generally made four, didn't it? *Delayed Registration?* Did that mean that someone – other than the birth parents – could register a birth? Did that mean . . . ? Could it mean . . . ?

Ruby was struggling. She was tired. It had been such a long and emotional day.

On its own this might mean nothing – she could almost hear Mel telling her that it was nothing. But added to the other things that she'd found . . . It had to mean something, didn't it? And if there was a reason why her birth hadn't been registered straight away, then why hadn't her parents told her? Was the truth so unpalatable that Ruby couldn't be trusted with it?

She went over to the bookcase and ran her fingers lightly over the recipe books, the volumes of poetry, the photo albums. It was time to get personal. Who would know whether or not Ruby was Vivien and Tom Rae's daughter? Who would know what had happened when she was born –

the true story? Who would know why her birth had been a late registration and why her parents had left a shoebox of photographs – not to mention the love beads, the baby's bonnet and the guitar plectrum – in the bottom of their wardrobe? Who would know about the infertility? Where Ruby had come from and why her parents had never told her the truth?

The only person she could think of was Frances.

CHAPTER 8

Barcelona, May 1939.

Julia was just seventeen. The Civil War had come to an end and her family clustered around the radio listening to the recording of Franco's grand victory parade – taking place in Madrid along the Castellana, now called Avenida del Generalissimo.

'They waste no time in changing the name,' her father said darkly.

'They waste plenty of money though, from the sound of all this pomp and ceremony,' her mother added.

Julia saw her parents exchange a conspiratorial look. The parade sounded lavish, it was true. But Mama and Papa were careful what they said – even in front of their own family, they were careful. They had to be, for there were spies everywhere, desiring to curry favour, wanting to betray their own.

The three girls leaned closer to listen. Julia caught the excitement in Paloma's dark eyes. She grinned. It was infectious. Surely now, things would change, Paloma's eyes seemed to say. Surely this was a new beginning – for them, for the young, the new blood of Spain.

Julia wasn't so sure. What did her sister know of politics

and economics? Those subjects did not interest Paloma – they never had. Julia was young, but already she knew more. She listened, she observed. She stayed in the shadows but she heard everything.

The commentator described General Franco and what he was wearing.

Julia's mother clicked her tongue in disgust. 'Who cares?' she muttered.

'Ssh,' their father told her. '*You* should take care, my love.'

But the girls hung on to every detail. Under the uniform of the Captain General, they learnt, Franco wore the dark blue shirt of the Falangists. And a red beret.

'All colour,' said Julia's father. 'All show.'

There were 120,000 soldiers in the parade. 'A hundred and twenty thousand,' breathed Matilde. 'Imagine.'

Julia could not. Paloma looked as though she could though. She looked as though she longed to be there among them. Being admired, thought Julia.

And in the sky above, they were told, aircraft formed the words VIVA FRANCO.

'Glory,' said Paloma. Her skin was faintly flushed. Julia guessed what she was thinking; she knew her so well. Hadn't she listened to her sister's inconsequential chatter all her life? *Now things will change. Now I will get my chance. I will find a man to love me.*

'Would you like one of those soldiers to come looking for you?' Julia teased. Life had been hard for the family these past years. Paloma wanted a man to look after her; she – more than any of them – deeply resented not having the money to spend on clothes and other fripperies.

She tossed her dark head. 'And what if I would?' she said.

Julia shrugged. 'There are other things in life.' She caught her father's gaze on her, thoughtful.

Paloma let out a snort of indignation. 'It is different for you, Julia,' she said.

'And why is that?'

'You are so serious.'

'Perhaps.' Julia turned away from the radio to look out through the window at the world outside. A world in which everything had changed. She was more serious, it was true. And what was wrong with that? She was not looking for a man; not yet. She thought of the Vamos boys who lived next door; of Mario who she often caught watching her with narrowed eyes and a considered expression. He was unruly, she did not trust him, and besides, she had more important things to think about. She wanted to know about the world, about what was happening to them, and so she eavesdropped on Papa and Mama's whispered conversations and stood in the shadows of the city cafés where people discussed such matters.

She turned now to her father. 'What do you think about the new regime, Papa?' she asked. 'Will things change now that the general has won the war? Will we get more food? Will you get more work? Will everything settle down?'

'You are so young, Julia,' Mama said. 'Too young to worry about such things.'

'Hope to God she never has to worry about such things,' her father said. 'Hope to God she never goes hungry again.'

Julia heard the desolation in his voice. But Paloma and even Matilde could not get enough of what they were listening to on the radio. 'If only we could be there,' Paloma said with a deep sigh. 'To witness such a spectacle.'

'God is their witness,' their father muttered. '*Cielos santos.*' He cursed softly and shook his dark head. 'I never thought they could do it. I never imagined.'

Yes. Julia understood what he meant. He had believed, had he not, that the Republicans would win through? They all had.

They had indeed seemed to be winning. By 1937 most of the street fighting had been over and the Republicans controlled their city. Julia was only fifteen and she had quickly got used to the changes, though some had felt strange at first.

'We must not say "*Señor*" and "*Don*" any more,' her father had told them. 'It is considered servile.'

Julia was confused – she had thought it good manners. 'But what should we say, Papa?' she asked.

'Comrade,' he told them. 'This is the correct greeting.'

Julia and her sisters started using this at every opportunity – it became almost a game. 'Good morning, Comrade,' they would say to each other first thing, and, 'Goodnight, Comrade,' when they went to bed.

Her parents didn't seem to mind. But what did they really think? Even then, Julia had sometimes sat at the top of the stairs, when she was supposed to have gone to bed, listening to their late-night conversations, and she found out. They admired the sense of fair play. They felt this new way was necessary in order to escape the control of dictatorship. They had high hopes of a new and prosperous Republican Spain. Would it happen? Maybe it would – because there were other changes too. Businesses became collectives, private motor cars were commandeered; the Workers were in control.

Julia, and most of the other young people she knew, felt that this was no bad thing. Why shouldn't there be equality? Why shouldn't the old ways change? It felt rebellious, daring and exciting. Julia watched the transformation of their city in wonder. Buildings were draped with red and black flags and painted with the symbol of the hammer and sickle; even the trams and taxis were painted black and red. Revolutionary posters were pasted on street corners, and down the Ramblas the songs of the Revolution were played through loudspeakers day and night.

Paloma had responded to the excitement too. She clapped her hands. 'It makes me want to dance,' she had laughed.

Julia had laughed with her. But would dancing be frowned on by the Republicans? It seemed likely. They did not appear to smile very often.

'The important thing,' Papa had told them, 'is that there is enough food for everyone. No one will go hungry.' And this was true. Both Julia's parents had work; her father in the construction industry and her mother as a primary school teacher. And Julia only had to look into the faces of the people on the streets to see something even better. Belief in the future. Hope.

But it had not lasted. In the winter of 1938 the city of Barcelona was heavily bombed.

'Why have they attacked us?' Paloma whimpered as the sisters clung together in Matilde's bed late at night. 'What have we done?'

'Nothing,' Matilde soothed. 'We have done nothing.'

But they all knew that three houses down the street had been hit. The families of two of Julia's closest friends had died; many others were killed and wounded. Buildings were destroyed. The city was in turmoil. And Julia knew why, because she had heard her own father say it. *Barcelona is being bombed for what they call its Republican sins.* The Nationalists had hit back.

The whole family was in shock. But this was only the beginning.

At the start of the following year Franco's troops closed in and they all had to hide in their homes in terror as Fascist troops paraded down the city streets.

'Save us, save us,' Paloma cried in terror. Even she was too scared to go out and look at them.

Julia watched her mother cry and she saw her father hold her hand and comfort her. 'Do not be scared, my love,' he said to her. 'At least we have been spared.'

'But for what?' Julia's mother cried. 'What will become of us? Will we ever be safe again?'

Julia's father could not answer that – because he did not know.

But like everyone else, after the city had been taken, he took care to sever his connections with the people who had become the wrong people to know, the dangerous people to be affiliated with. Julia understood why it had to be done. Everyone did the same. People scurried around, heads down, eyes averted. And anyone with the wrong political connections had to leave Barcelona – fast.

In March, Madrid fell, and then Valencia.

'It is all over,' Julia's father said. '*Dulce Jesús!*' He swore, but in capitulation rather than anger.

He was right. On 1 April, the last of the Republican forces surrendered and Nationalist victory was proclaimed.

One night, a few weeks after they'd listened to the victory ceremony on the radio, after Julia had gone to bed, as the cathedral bells tolled midnight, she heard the rise and fall of her parents' voices once again. She pulled her robe around her and sat huddled on the stair to listen. It scared her. The words poured from her father in a stream – like lava from a volcano; it was as if he had to talk or he would go mad. He spoke of political militants and 'Bolshevik infection'. Of the madmen, the tramps and the beggars who kept all their worldly goods in a bundle underneath the arches of Calle Fernando. And of the prison camps such as Montjuïc Castle and the continuing executions there; of those who had been tortured and yet still lived with the scars. His voice rose in panic; it grew louder and then faded. Her mother was trying to soothe him; Julia could hear her voice, could imagine her stroking his hair from his face, drawing him to her for comfort.

She sighed as she returned to her bed. Since the war nothing was the same. How could it be? Spain's economy was in tatters. Bridges, railways, roads, all was in chaos. But it was more than that. After what she had heard last night, Julia was worrying for her father's sanity.

That night they had eaten their fill but it had not been a happy family meal.

'Where did you get the food?' her mother had asked Papa.

'I earnt it,' he replied. His eyes were wild.

He did not have to say more. Chaos had brought corruption and since the end of the war the black market had flourished. Beans, meat, olive oil, flour . . . They were all hard to procure and cost so much more than the official levy.

Had Papa earnt it? What exactly had he done? Julia had seen how hard he had to look for work – despite the destruction that lay around them, despite the desperate need for rebuilding. His shoulders seemed to hunch lower with every day. And she knew from what she had overheard that he had to be careful who he worked for and that people had to be cautious about who they employed. Please God he would not be thought a former left-wing sympathiser.

'We all know,' she had heard him say, 'what happens to them.'

The following night there was almost nothing to eat. Mama cooked a little rice and a few beans – though Julia knew she had to be thrifty; she did not know where the next meal would be coming from. There were days when their family went to bed hungry – too many days.

And Papa returned home in a terrible temper.

'Tomás? What is wrong?' Julia's mother asked.

He looked around him, twisting his head from side to side. Once again his dark eyes had a look, almost of madness, that made Julia shiver. 'Almost half the tram workers have lost their jobs.' He clicked his fingers. 'Just like that.'

Julia's mother laid a restraining hand on his arm.

Instantly he quietened, staring morosely into the distance as if he was trying to make sense of it all.

'I can scarcely believe it,' Julia's mother said. But she too had lost her job some time before. She had no choice. Like all women, she must now stay home, must obey her husband in all things because his word was law. And if he was afraid – or turned half mad from what was happening? If he could not get work and they had no money? What then?

'But who will teach the children?' Julia had asked. She had been hoping – once, in a different lifetime – to be a teacher herself. Clearly that would never happen now.

'Someone who holds the correct beliefs and has the accepted record of behaviour,' Mama had said without a hint of irony in her voice.

'The church is now the power behind education,' Papa muttered. 'But at what price?'

Julia still fought to understand. She knew that churches had been closed down – even gutted – during the Civil War. And she knew that many people had not wanted this to be.

But what people thought now . . . Who could tell? People – truly – were not allowed to think. Their thoughts were dictated to them, it seemed.

'Almost half the workers!' Now Papa was shouting once more. 'It is madness!'

'Hush, Tomás.' Again, she calmed him. Julia's mother could always calm him.

But Julia knew that both her parents were afraid. She was afraid too. Everyone was.

'We cannot go on like this.' He looked at their mother, hard, until she looked away. And then he peered out into the hazy glow of the streetlights glistening on the cobbles of Puerta del Angel. His anger, the wildness in his eyes had dissipated now. But what Julia saw there seemed worse.

'I tell you,' he said. 'Something must change.'

What could change? Julia shivered with a sense of foreboding as she lay in her bed and listened to their voices as they talked that night. They were arguing about something – but what? She did not get up to listen. She wanted to know, but she could not bear to know. It sounded bad. But could things get any worse?

The following evening, her parents took her to one side.

'Julia,' said her father. 'You understand how things are with us?'

'Yes, Papa.'

But Julia wanted to slink away and never be seen again. She wanted to disappear in a puff of smoke, or fly out of the window to somewhere safe and calm, where everyone was allowed to be who they wanted to be. She did not want to hear this.

'We have to think of your welfare,' he said.

Julia blinked up at him. What about the welfare of the rest of the family? She might not be her father's favourite – Paloma was the one who took his arm and made him smile – but she had always known she was loved.

'And so we have been talking – your mother and I.'

Julia looked at her mother. Her eyes were red. She guessed that this – whatever it was – was what they had been arguing about at the dead of night. Perhaps she should have listened at the top of the stairs. Perhaps she could have changed their minds.

'And I have been making enquiries.' He cleared his throat.

'About what, Papa?' Julia dared to ask.

'About your futures,' he said.

It was, then, as Julia had feared. 'Mama?' She reached for her mother's hand.

'Hush,' she said. But Julia knew her heart was not in it. She was beaten, defeated by her own life and what it had become.

'You will enter the sisterhood,' her father said.

The sisterhood? She was to become a nun? Julia looked wildly from one to the other of them. 'The sisterhood?' she echoed.

Her mother squeezed her hand. 'You will be safe there, Julia,' she said. 'You will not want for food—'

'But . . . ' Whatever she had been expecting, it was not

this. Their family was not remotely religious in their beliefs. The sisterhood? It had never even been mentioned as a possibility.

'It has been decided,' her father said. 'The Church will provide. It will have to.'

'Papa?' Julia searched for compassion in his eyes. But she saw only despair. She had always tried to understand him, she had always respected and obeyed him. But this . . . ?

'It is the right place for you.'

'And Matilde?' Julia was angry now. She felt it rising up inside her like fire. 'And Paloma?'

Her mother put her arms around her. 'They must make sacrifices too,' she whispered. 'We have done our best, my daughter. We can do no more.'

Sacrifices? Julia broke away from her embrace and ran. She ran out into the street blindly, not knowing where she was going, just needing to get away, to escape. Tears streamed down her face, her hair was in disarray – blowing madly like the leaves in the autumn wind. What sacrifices would her sisters have to make? They were pretty girls. How hard would it be to marry off a pretty girl in the aftermath of the Civil War if you didn't much care who you married her off to? Not so Julia. She was the plain one, the quiet one, the passive one who could always be told what to do, where to go.

She thought for one fleeting moment of Mario Vamos, of the look in his black eyes. She had made it easy for her parents to decide. They had all received a good education but Julia had studied the hardest. Her English language was of a high standard; her main interest was history. Her sisters would be married off – she knew it. Would that be better or worse than being married off to God?

At last Julia found herself outside the Ateneo Library. She didn't feel calm or passive any longer. She felt desperate, wind-blown, hardly able to breathe. She steadied herself and looked up at the grand building. Inside was a web of passage-ways and reading rooms which had somehow survived the Civil War bombings and where Julia still loved to wander and read. Now, she would no longer be able to do such things. She would be a prisoner. She would be estranged from the family she loved. From the world.

Julia wandered the streets for an hour before she returned home. She walked past the beggars and the tramps and she wept for what had been taken away from them all. It was their individual liberty – but it was their identity too. Their heritage – which was part of their very soul. Even in the Ateneo forbidden works in Catalan had been destroyed. Their press had been banned, and other newspapers were no doubt censored and controlled. To all intents and purposes there was no Catalan. There was no rousing music now being played along the Ramblas. Instead, posters pro-claimed, 'Speak the Language of the Empire'. Now they were Spanish and Spanish alone. He had taken away even their voice.

Was the convent in Barcelona the right place for Julia? She bowed her head and felt a final solitary tear weave down her face. Her father had said that the Church would provide.

And what choice did she have? Their family had no money. Otherwise they would starve.

She walked back into their house with her head held high. She would be strong. She would not let them see what this had done to her. She would accept her parents' decision. She was an obedient daughter and she would obey.

CHAPTER 9

On Friday night Andrés made his way to the Jazz Café. Gone were the days of people sitting at the bar with a beer and a cigarette and yet somehow the place retained its smoky atmosphere. Low lighting. A guy on the piano. Wooden tables scattered cabaret-style with red cloths and tea-lights in stained glass holders. The walls – like the music – were deep blue.

The Jazz Café was part of Pridehaven Arts Centre – an art deco building that housed exhibitions and had a small theatre; the café at the back echoed the centre's sinuous curves – the room was oval and the mahogany bar followed the line of the top wall's curve like a comforting arm around a shoulder.

'Andrés.' Tina was behind the bar. She looked pleased to see him. She leant forward to kiss him on the cheek, once, twice. He tried to inhale her perfume but he was too slow. 'Beer?'

'Please.'

Tina was a brunette with generous curves and a shapely head which Andrés had drawn on several occasions. In fact he'd done a painting of her behind the bar, hand on the beer pump, showing the reflection of her back in the mirror behind, which he liked to think was reminiscent of the café images favoured by Manet – an impressionist painter he admired. Not that he aspired to those dizzy heights. But he rather liked the idea of painter as *flaneur* – strolling and observing life rather than loitering, of course. He'd definitely put that one in the exhibition. He enjoyed the sweep of Tina's eyelashes as she surveyed her clientele, the angle of her cheekbones, the faintest aura of superiority she assumed. Tina had worked here for a long time – she was most definitely in charge of the Friday night Jazz Café.

A well-cut bob swung back and forth as she walked, as she bent to fetch a San Miguel from the fridge behind her. Nice.

'You OK?' She flipped off the bottle top. Tina always asked him if he was OK. He knew she worried.

'Fine, thank you.' He was looking forward to the auction next week. He needed something more in his life – wasn't Tina always telling him he needed something more in his life? – and he hoped the project of doing up Coastguard's Cottage would be that something.

'Yeah. Right.' Tina raised an eyebrow. She was wearing a close-fitting black T-shirt and jeans that were surely too tight to be comfortable. It had to be said though, she looked good.

It was a spider's web, thought Andrés. Which was beautiful. Which could be supportive – and flexible too. It could catch you in its sticky threads, stop you from falling. On the other hand – it could trap you, and eat you right up. Once you were in, you were in. There was no moving on. There was no escape.

'You are busy tonight.' Andrés nodded towards the rest of the room. The place was maybe half full, which was healthy for just after eight p.m. By nine it would be buzzing. And it was good sometimes to be in a place which was buzzing. It stopped you from brooding. Though Andrés had got used to his own company, his own self ticking away the evening like a railway station clock waiting for the next train. But other nights his head was screaming with images of the island, of his father, of his mother and his sister, and he needed something to drown it out. When a place was buzzing, you could let it slip over you, you could melt into it, even feel you were part of it for a while.

'There's a band in. Last minute, but we put up a poster.' Tina shrugged. 'People get to hear.' She took his money and turned towards the till.

This time he caught the faint waft of her perfume. Geraniums. In Ricoroque they always grew geraniums in the tubs outside the front door. Geraniums grew well in *picon*, the dew-collecting gravel of the Canaries, and they didn't mind being thirsty. 'Any good?' he enquired.

'Yeah. They're good.' She gave him his change. 'They used to play here every week. Then they broke up. Because—'

But Andrés didn't get to hear why they broke up because another customer wanted a drink and Tina was already sashaying to the other end of the bar to serve him.

So he waved a hand to her and grabbed a stool.

He liked to sit here at the end of the bar. He could have his back to the wall – so there'd be no surprises – he could talk to Tina when she was free, and he had a decent view of the stage and the rest of the room. Sometimes the music absorbed him, sometimes he liked to people-watch, sometimes he forgot where he was and it was a shock when it came to closing time and he realised he'd spent the entire evening in Ricoroque.

I'm a voyeur, he thought, as he settled himself more comfortably on the bar stool and took a pull of his beer. A *flaneur*. For ever on the sidelines of life. Watching everyone else have a good time.

Andrés had first met Tina several years ago. She and Gez were his first friends in West Dorset; real friends, that was, as in people who cared. He'd wandered into the Jazz Café one night when it was quiet, and got talking to Tina. She was easy – light to talk to, quick to smile, direct; no games. He liked that. He even toyed with the idea of asking her out for a drink. She wasn't really his type. But then again, what was his type? He wasn't sure that he knew.

But Tina had made it clear early on that she wasn't available. 'You'll have to come in another night and meet Gez,' she said. 'You'll get on. I can tell.'

'Your husband?' Andrés asked, though he hadn't seen a ring.

'Boyfriend,' she said. 'Lover.' And she fixed him with her direct gaze. Hazel eyes, he guessed, though in the dim light of the café it was hard to tell. 'You?'

'Me?' For an awful moment, Andrés had thought she was proposing a threesome.

'Do you have someone? A girlfriend? A lover? A wife?'
She laughed. Even then she could read him like a book.

He laughed back – pure relief. 'No,' he said. 'No one.'
Idiot. There had been women – of course. He wasn't a monk,
for God's sake. But as soon as things began to get serious, as
soon as they tried to get too involved in his life or wanted to
move in with him, he cut himself free. Maybe he wasn't
meant to have a woman in his life. Maybe what he'd seen of
his own parents' marriage had put him off. Maybe he wasn't
the type to make a commitment. Tina had her theories –
well, she would, she was a woman, wasn't she? Her theory
was that he hadn't yet met the Right One.

At the time, she'd just shrugged and said, 'Come in on
Sunday. Meet Gez.'

But she'd been trying to fix him up ever since.

As Tina had predicted, Andrés and Gez did get on well and
suddenly Andrés realised he had acquired a social life. Easy,
really, like finding a key. He could wander into the Jazz Café
and talk to Tina whenever he chose, he was invited for supper at Tina and Gez's at least once a fortnight and he played
tennis with Gez most Sunday mornings – followed by a pint
at the Black Lamb near the tennis courts. And – thanks to
Tina – he had a succession of blind dates.

These were not so easy.

Andrés put the bottle of beer to his lips. Not that he
blamed Tina for trying. She thought it would make him
happy because Gez made her happy. Man needed woman;
woman needed man. We were never meant to live alone. But

Andrés knew his life wasn't quite so simple. He suspected it wasn't just a case of him not having met the right girl.

The first date was shy and self-conscious and made Andrés feel so nervous that he knocked over his glass and spilt beer all over her dress; the second date spent most of the evening surreptitiously texting her ex; the third tried to get him into bed after two gin and tonics and scared him half to death.

'What's wrong with all my friends?' Tina complained one evening at supper. She counted them off on the fingers of one hand. 'You are so damned fussy, Andrés.'

'Nothing,' said Andrés. 'They're all really nice ladies.' For someone else, just not for him.

'Women,' corrected Tina, spooning out generous portions of lasagne.

Andrés exchanged a conspiratorial glance with Gez, but Tina being Tina neatly intercepted it. 'Fuck you,' she said genially.

'OK.' Every time Andrés considered himself fluent, some cultural nuance of the English language raised its confusing head. 'Women.'

'Which one did you fancy the most?' Tina was in analytical mode. She threw some salad into a glass bowl in the centre of the table and passed around kitchen towel for napkins. 'To help me for next time.' Her suppers were always simple and always delicious. Tina had a warmth, a way about her that made Andrés feel comfortable and welcomed.

He frowned. But what was the correct answer? He glanced

again at Gez, but Gez was looking innocent in a kind of *You're on your own this time* sort of a way. 'Er, number three?'

'You mean Jane,' snapped Tina. She tossed balsamic vinegar on to the salad leaves and added a deft swirl of olive oil.

'Yes, Jane.'

'You like women to be small and slim then. And blonde.' Tina narrowed her eyes. 'Do you have protective issues, Andrés?'

'Protective issues?' He blinked at her. 'Not that I'm aware of.'

Gez helped himself to a heap of salad. Andrés followed suit.

'Small, blonde, fluffy, needs looking after,' Tina pressed.

'I never said anything about fluffy.' And she was quite wrong. He liked independent women, those who had opinions and something to say for themselves. He wasn't interested in a doormat he could walk all over – you could get those from the Pound Store in town.

Tina frowned. 'You need to loosen up a bit,' she said. 'You're a bit stiff, a bit too formal.'

Andrés shrugged. He was what he was. It was how he had been brought up.

Tina put a hand on his arm. 'And you would tell me, wouldn't you, Andrés?'

'What?'

'If you were gay?'

He laughed. Though it would be easier, perhaps, if he were. Knowing that the next weekend some vaguely Jane lookalike would no doubt be dangled before him like a bone in front of a dog.

From the other end of the bar, Tina gestured to him. *Another?* He nodded, realising he'd drunk the first already. He was thirsty, but now he'd slow down.

After a few months of non-starters in the blind-dating department, most women would have given up. Not Tina. Even now, she still made regular offerings and Andrés had to admit he'd met a lot of interesting people, been on quite a few dates and made several more friends. Where did she get them all from? Had she advertised? He didn't have a girl-friend, but he had a social life. It had wrapped itself around him with strong, silken strands.

Tina brought over another beer. 'What's up?'

'Nothing.' He dipped into his pocket for change. Though lately he'd been thinking about them more and more often. His family. The island. Part of him ached to go back there. But how could he go back where he wasn't wanted? *Nothing has changed*, his mother had said. And she was right.

The music changed now, though. The pianist shifted rhythm and the notes seemed to vibrate through Andrés's body. He closed his eyes. If he were deaf, he thought, he would still hear this music. He would feel it in every fibre of his being. He knew it.

The vibrations took him back to the drumming in his old island home. The villagers were always practising the drumming for *festa* time. They would gather after dark in the square outside the cultural centre for singing, drumming and dancing. The islanders had their own traditions; the *Malagueña*, the *folias* and *seguidillas*; their own folk dancing in national costume for *festa*. And on holidays – Sundays and *festa* days – there would be a barbecue down in the village square; pungent fragrances and smoke billowing from huge baths on wheels filled with charcoal with meshing over them, roasting sausages, ribs of pork and slabs of goat meat; boiling vats of small wrinkled Canarian potatoes. Dozens of trestle tables set up in the square, the local wine flowing, the drums pounding, their heavy vibrations spinning through the night air.

Later, their family would sit in the *casa*, their mother working at her embroidery or making a dress for Izabella from a piece of bright scarlet cloth, perhaps. Ricoroque had once been a port for cochineal – the red dye from the beetle had made the village prosper; a stone jetty had even been built down in the bay. Cochineal had coloured the Spanish conquistadors' *bayetas* and the Navajo women used to unpick these vibrant blankets and reweave the threads to create their own colourful garments.

Andrés vividly recalled one time when he was still a boy. Mama had pinned the cloth around Izabella, fastened a red flower in her dark hair and as they opened the windows and the doors to the thudding rhythms of the primeval drumming, so Izabella had begun to dance. His quiet and shy sister seemed to be under a spell that night. She swayed and swirled, arched and twisted, her raven hair opening behind her like a fan. On and on drove the drums into the night. Faster and faster Izabella danced. Until Andrés joined in too, his limbs responding instinctively to a rhythm he didn't even understand. Laughing, he had pulled his mother up to join them.

Enrique Marin though, would never dance. He watched his family and his eyes were as black and unreadable as the volcanic rock of their island.

Andrés wiped a tear from his cheek. He didn't look at Tina just in case she was watching him. *A spider's web* . . .

The music stopped and some different people emerged on to the stage of the Jazz Café. Some of the audience clapped and someone cheered. This must be the band Tina had mentioned, Andrés thought.

There was a drummer, a keyboards man, someone on double bass and . . . A girl came on to the stage. No, a woman. Andrés blinked. She was wearing a red dress and, rather spookily, she too had a red flower pinned in her spiky blond hair. He knew who this was. The woman from the cliff top, the woman who he had thought he might have seen before. And he had. It was coming back to him now. This was where he had seen her. Years earlier – back in the days when he had first come here to the Jazz Café. He had seen her before onstage with this band. And then she had disappeared.

They did a bit of a warm-up. The keyboards guy said

something into the mic and then the woman in red picked up an instrument from its case, a gleaming saxophone. She held it lovingly, almost caressing it with her fingers.

And the band began to play. 'Summertime'. Unbearably slow, achingly sad.

When they'd finished their set, people began to drift away and Tina slowed down. She was collecting glasses from tables, stacking them on to the bar.

'Who is she?' She had played with such melancholy and Andrés wondered how anybody could be so sad. He was mesmerised. Her sadness had wrapped itself around him. He wasn't sure whether it was her playing or his own state of mind. Maybe both.

'She . . . ?' Tina stood next to him hands on hips. 'You mean Ruby?'

'Ruby.' The name was perfect.

'Well, don't get your hopes up.' Tina went back behind the bar. 'Tonight's a one-off. Ruby doesn't live here any more. She's been based in London for a while.'

London. Was he interested? Andrés slid off his stool. He wasn't interested in long-distance relationships, that was for sure. Not even in relationships. Still . . . 'I just liked her playing,' he told Tina, ignoring her smirk. 'I've seen her around lately. I just happened to notice—'

'About time,' she muttered.

He ignored this too.

But maybe Tina was right about what was missing from

his life. Maybe the cottage would not be enough. Maybe he should try harder. And on the way back to his place, Andrés actually found himself whistling.

CHAPTER 10

Ruby headed for the auction on her new bike. She'd bought it from the Dutch bike shop in town when she was walking back from lunch with Mel yesterday. Couldn't resist really. It was shiny black, had a basket in front and made her feel windborne, almost carefree. She wouldn't allow herself to be beaten down by circumstances, loss and discovery, she decided. And today she had every intention of buying herself a cottage.

Even Mel had been forced to admit that the words 'delayed registration' on her birth certificate suggested that all was not quite as it seemed. 'Stop protecting me,' Ruby had told her in the end as they left the café. 'Say what you really think.' And so Mel had. 'I think you should talk to someone who was around at the time you were born,' she said. 'What about your grandparents?'

Her grandparents . . . The memory slammed into her.

Bolt from the blue, her grandmother had said at the funeral. Ruby had assumed she'd been referring to the accident, the motorbike crash which had killed her daughter – certainly a bolt from the blue, a terrible shock, a tragedy. But her grandmother had been looking straight at Ruby when she said it. And she'd been so confused.

Ruby stared at Mel in horror.

'What?'

She shook her head. 'Nothing.' But supposing Ruby's birth had been the bolt from the blue? Combined with the shoebox, the letter and the lack of early photographs . . . It all made a horrible kind of sense.

'Or one of your mother's friends?' Mel said gently when they got to the hat shop.

They kissed goodbye. Yeah, thought Ruby. Like Frances.

The bike was faster than she'd expected and Ruby loved the feeling of the wind in her hair as she gathered speed. Had her mother – Vivien – felt this way just before the accident, she wondered? Had she closed her eyes just for a second, before . . . *There's always a blind spot.* Ruby pushed the thought away.

She remembered how supportive Frances had been at the funeral. She was upset herself – Vivien was her closest friend, although they hadn't seen quite so much of each other since Frances had moved to North Cornwall to be nearer her daughter and grandchildren. 'If there's anything I can do, my dear,' she had said as she scribbled her contact details on to a scrap of paper which she pressed into Ruby's hand, 'just ask.'

And Ruby was going to do just that. Thank goodness she hadn't thrown it away. The scrap of paper was still tucked inside the zip pocket of her handbag. She was just plucking up some courage and waiting for the right time. Was she Vivien and Tom's daughter? Was she Ruby Rae? She desperately needed to know. But afterwards – there would be no going back.

She freewheeled down the hill past the museum and the library where the Wednesday market was in full swing. The auction was being held in a town hall four miles away. She had enough time – hopefully, although the bike was taking a bit of getting used to; the back brake was operated by back-pedalling and the saddle was almost too high for her to put her foot down. But she loved it anyway. It was fabulous to sit upright and survey the cropped fields and green Dorset hills. It was like going back in time; back to that childhood she dreaded was about to be snatched away from her.

Saturday night's gig at the Jazz Café had been dedicated to her parents and it had felt like a much more potent and personal goodbye. And although the sadness had almost overwhelmed her . . . It had been good for her. And it had gone well. When she saw the audience out there, when she heard the applause, when she felt that pure rush of adrenalin at performing and playing . . . She had been on such a high. She'd almost forgotten about shoeboxes, photographs and birth certificates.

And if they weren't her parents? She couldn't stop the thought edging once more into her mind. She had lost them both and now she was in danger of discovering that they might not have been hers to lose in the first place.

She pushed down on the pedals, drove the bike faster. But they were still her parents in the real sense of the word. They had cared for her. They had loved her. No one could take that away. *Even if* . . . This thought seemed to float in the air and stream away, like gulls' wings in a thermal.

Auctions were weird. The auctioneer weaved his way through the proceedings, arms raised, eyes in the back of his head and his ears, pushing the price up every time it seemed to be stagnating, firing out the standard phrases: 'It's with you'; 'It's against you'; 'Who'll give me . . . ?'; 'Now two'; 'Am I seeing three?' It was like a chant, a poem; it was almost hypnotic. Ruby was a bit nervous – she'd never been to an auction before and this was a huge purchase. She knew her budget though. She could only go up to £200,000. That was her absolute limit. She wasn't allowed to go a whisker more, no matter how tempted she might be.

There was a picture of Coastguard's Cottage in the auction brochure, looking suitably desolate and in need of adoption, and she allowed herself a brief daydream. In the fantasy, she was up a ladder wearing paint-stained overalls, daubing the sitting room white. White walls, wooden beams, polished floorboards, good antique furniture. A leather sofa? A chaise longue?

She recalled the view of Chesil Beach – the rolling tide, the cresting waves, the sea that stretched into infinity. The promise of a twisting pathway up the green and golden cliff. The fairy tale. Yes, but could it really exist for her again?

At last the bidding began on Coastguard's Cottage; quiet at first, raising her hopes – *no one was interested, no one but Ruby*; then gaining momentum, blast it. Her first bid – at

£115,000 – took some courage, but her waving arm was spotted immediately by the auctioneer. Not waving but drowning. She was in the game.

At £120,000 they lost a few of the players and at £135,000 Ruby realised there were only two of them left in the race. Damn. She had a rival. She couldn't see him properly from her position – he was right over the other side of the hall – but she could hear him. His voice was low and soft, slightly foreign-sounding.

She agreed £139,000 with a decisive nod. Just her luck. She was competing with foreign money. Someone who didn't know what a risk he was taking with Coastguard's Cottage, someone who didn't know what he was doing, who had just wandered in. Some idiot who—

£140,000. The bids went on. Back and forth. At £155,000 Ruby craned round the pillar to get a better look. He shifted in his seat and she got a good view of her rival. He was tall and dark and seemed vaguely familiar. Perhaps he lived in the area after all. £160,000, she agreed.

Neither of them wavered. The hall was prickly with tension; everyone was quiet, waiting, looking from Ruby's position near the back by the door, to his – near the front on the other side. It was like ping-pong, she thought. With danger. The adrenalin streaked through her, she was charged up and determined. £190,000. She mustn't let him hear it in her voice – the fact that she could not, must not go much further, the fact that she was reaching her limit.

'One hundred and ninety-five,' he said.

Ruby couldn't believe she might lose this. £200,000, she agreed. Without a tremor.

He raised it by a grand.

It was too much, she knew that. She raised it five. It was like a game of poker. You had to bluff and scare your opponent out of it. It was a risk, but the cottage was a risk.

He raised it another ten grand.

Ruby knew she was done for. She shook her head.

'Going once at two hundred and sixteen thousand,' intoned the auctioneer.

There was a collective sigh. Everyone knew she'd been beaten. The people sitting near her adopted sympathetic expressions. Ruby put her sunglasses back on to protect herself.

'Twice,' said the auctioneer.

'Two hundred and thirty,' said a voice from the back.

Everyone turned to see. A man in his fifties in a well-cut pinstriped suit. There was another rustle of excitement. Everyone looked towards the other guy to see what he would do. He caught Ruby's eye, shrugged.

There were no further bids.

'Sold,' said the auctioneer, bringing down his gavel with a crack of finality.

Ruby made her way out of the hall. Shit. It was only a house, she told herself. But it was the fairy tale she'd lost. The dream that now she knew she would never get back.

'Hey!' Someone was running after her.

Ruby didn't want to talk to anyone. She walked faster, but knew he'd catch up with her by the bike.

'Hey, Ruby!'

She spun round. It was the half-familiar man with dark hair who had been bidding against her. What the hell did he want? And more to the point – how did he know her name?

CHAPTER 11

Barcelona, 1940

Julia's mother took her to the Santa Ana Convent on that
first day. It was late autumn and a chilly breeze blustered
down Las Ramblas as if it might push Julia and her mother
there with still more speed. Julia's mother held her hand fast
and sure; it seemed she would allow no doubt or second
thoughts to creep in there.

She only paused as the convent came into view.

Would they turn back? Julia gazed ahead at the gatehouse,
beyond which the convent buildings stood, bleak and austere.
Was there still time? But her mother squeezed her hand. 'It is
for the best, my daughter,' she whispered. 'It is all we can do.'

So. They entered the gatehouse and rang the bell in the
foyer. Julia glanced at her mother but her head was bent.
Were there tears in her eyes? She could not tell.

A nun dressed in a simple white habit came to the foyer.
She did not speak.

Julia's mother raised her head. 'We are here to see the
mother superior,' she said in the clear voice Julia recognised
as her teacher's voice. A voice that would brook no nonsense.

The nun simply bowed her head and drifted away.

Again they waited. It was, Julia thought, the worst part. She almost wished that she had come here alone, that she had said goodbye to her mother back at home with the rest of her family. Instead of this. This . . . deliverance.

The mother superior appeared in the foyer, distinguishable by the blue in her habit and a look of authority in her eyes. She was old, her face as wrinkled as a prune, but she held herself erect and with dignity.

'Reverend Mother.' Again, Julia's mother dipped her head. 'This is my daughter Julia.'

Julia followed her lead and as the mother superior scrutinised her with a piercing gaze, she too looked down. But she wondered.

What deal had been done so that she could come here? What had been promised? Had money changed hands or were her parents calling in some old favour? Julia had no way of finding out.

Her father had gripped her by the shoulders this morning before they left. 'I am sorry, my dear,' he said. 'God knows I never meant this to happen to our family.'

Julia could hardly look at him. But she understood. With three daughters who were not allowed to work and food in such short supply, they had to marry them off or all starve. Simple economics. And when two of your daughters are pretty and one is plain . . . The Church at least offered another option. *No muerdas la mano que te da de comer.* Do not bite the hand that feeds you. Yes, she understood. But still. She blinked back a tear.

The reverend mother showed them around. The convent buildings surrounded a square, half-ruined stone cloister, whose air of tranquillity touched Julia almost at once. Beyond this, the reverend mother indicated the living quarters for the nuns. There was a kitchen and a storehouse, an infirmary and a refectory.

'It seems very well organised,' said Julia's mother, looking to Julia for something – reassurance, maybe.

And peaceful, thought Julia, struck by this despite everything; at least compared to the world outside. This was a small comfort.

The reverend mother showed them the chapel. Julia stood at the ornate altar and gazed at the frescos whose vivid colour had faded with time. Could she live in this place? Could she make it her home?

The reverend mother nodded to Julia's mother and Julia shuddered. She knew it was time to say goodbye. But with the old nun standing there over them hands patiently folded . . . It seemed impossible.

Julia's mother embraced her and kissed her cheek. 'Be content, Julia,' she whispered. 'Please be content.'

'Mama . . . ' But Julia saw her mother's broken expression. How could she make it any harder for her – after all she and Papa had been through? So she swallowed hard and was silent.

'Goodbye, my daughter.'

Julia watched her mother walk away. This was it then. The end of her childhood. The day she was abandoned by her

x

x

own family. Given up so that she might have a better life. So that she might not be hungry. So that she could live without fear. She wanted to cry out to her, she took a step forwards as if she might run after her, as if she might fling herself into the warm arms of the mother she loved.

But the reverend mother laid a restraining hand on her arm. 'Be still, my child,' she said. 'For it is done.'

And then Julia's mother was gone.

'We are mostly self-sufficient here, you will find,' the mother superior told her, leading Julia away. 'This is the herb garden.'

Julia gazed at the lavender, comfrey and soapwort, but the plants became a mere blur from her tears.

'And the vegetable allotment.' She pointed to the onions, root vegetables and tomatoes.

Julia brushed the tears from her eyes and saw beyond this a small orchard and a fountain. 'Thank you, Reverend Mother,' she said, since saying something seemed to be required of her. What else could she say? What else could be done? Now, there was no going back.

One of the other nuns showed Julia to her room. She did not speak; just smiled and nodded, but at least her eyes were kind.

Julia stood in the doorway. The room was small and plain and nothing at all like home. Where was her pale blue counterpane? The treasured photograph of her family standing together outside the front door of their house? Where were her clothes and her books? Her sisters' combs for their hair?

Their dresses, their shoes? Julia swallowed back the tears. She must be strong.

Because this was not an uncomfortable building to live in. The feeling of peace – which she'd recognised immediately like a long-lost and unfamiliar friend – would surely be restful after life on the streets of the city these past few years. There was no young man in her life – she'd hardly had the chance and anyway, so many young men were gone. Indeed, they had all suffered so much hardship and fear that she was almost content to retreat from the world she lived in. And that was what she must cling to.

And so Julia took her first simple vows. She forced from her mind the family and friends who had filled her life for so long. She forced away the soft comfort of being held in her mother's arms, of cuddling up to her sisters in bed, of hearing the familiar deep tones of her father's voice. In their place she must welcome God. He was just and He was true. He would help her survive this parting.

The daily life of a nun, however, was not as she expected. Prayers began at five fifteen a.m. when the chapel was cold, dark and windy. And there were three services even before breakfast. Sometimes – in the early days, until her body became accustomed – Sister Julia felt faint from kneeling on the cold stone and from the pangs of hunger. It would take all her energy to make the effort to stand, to walk to the refectory to break her fast. And all her willpower not to bolt down her food as if it was her last supper.

The morning services began with a quiet chanting and although Sister Julia was given a service book she found that she was soon able to say parts of the service by heart. *Gloria al Padre al Hijo y al Espíritu Santo. . . Amen.* She found some comfort in it. The monotony, the ritual – it was soothing to the senses; soon she was softly chanting as if she had been doing it all her life.

The rest of the morning was devoted to work duties. According to the reverend mother, work encouraged the sisters to avoid vain thoughts, idleness and gossip. Certainly there was no gossip. Most of the time no one spoke at all, and this was hard at first for Sister Julia, who was used to the chatter of Matilde and Paloma and their friends at home.

In the evenings they assembled for Vespers – evening prayers – and then proceeded to the chapel. In the quiet, Sister Julia found plenty of room for her own thoughts and her own prayer. But she missed her home and her family with a physical ache that stayed in her heart from morning to night. Could reflection ever replace it? Surely this was impossible – no matter how dedicated she tried to be?

She tried so hard to find peace through prayer. She tried to find the simple rituals of monastic life calming. Nothing was demanded of her – apart from the simple tasks she was allotted and to pray. Nobody expected her to laugh or talk or to comb their pretty hair. There were no reminders that she was the plain one, the serious one. Here, they were all plain and serious and it did not matter a jot. She did not have to worry about herself or her family – God would provide. *What would be, would be . . .* If only she could bring herself to believe that this was so.

Meals were taken in the refectory – a high-ceilinged and vaulted grand hall – and silence was maintained whilst one of their number read aloud from a history of the order in Catalonia. Sister Julia thought of her mother's cooking – when she could procure the ingredients. Her sisters' laughter and complaints as they helped and simultaneously got in the way at mealtimes. Oh, this was so different from home. The food was basic and simple, but good. For breakfast there was coffee, bread, jam and ham; for dinner there was soup – perhaps a broth of leftovers – and salad. They never went hungry and for Sister Julia it had been a long time since she'd felt so replete. Even so . . . She would much rather have been hungry and at home. How were they all? And when would they come to visit? These were the questions that filled her mind.

The convent at Santa Ana subsisted through the same means as most others. They accepted donations from the better-off members of society, they sold needlecraft, they made sweets and cakes like *rosquillas de almendra* and *yemas* which they sold from the foyer of the convent. One day, Sister Julia took a turn at selling. Inside the main front door was a revolving tray. The customer would enter the foyer, press a buzzer and place their order – after the requisite words had been spoken. *Ave Maria purisima* (most pure, Ave Maria), *sin pecado concebida* (conceived without sin). They would then place the money on the tray, Sister Julia would spin it, take the money and place the sweetmeats there in exchange. And then. *Eh aquí.* There you go. She would spin the tray back, the customer would take the sweets and the transaction was complete. *God would provide*, said the reverend mother. And it seemed to Sister Julia that He provided rather well.

But she was lonely. She missed her family, she missed her home, and she missed her own belongings. She might not have had much, but she did have things she valued – her books and her few dresses and shoes, the photograph of her family, the special linen handkerchiefs embroidered by her grandmother. Such luxury items were not allowed at Santa Ana. How, she wondered, could she ever fit in?

In her second week, one of the other sisters took her aside. 'It is characteristic of the modern world to think first of what is excluded and what is forbidden, rather than what is embraced and intensified through living the simple life,' she said. And then she bowed her head and left the room.

Sister Julia thought about this. Since she had been living here, she had wept and she had felt anger. Why her? Why had she been banished from her home in this way? Why was she now destined for a life that meant she would never have a family of her own, no husband to love her, no child to care for? She would never know what it felt like to lie in a man's arms, nor to give birth to a son or daughter.

But what was the use of raging against it? It was, she realised, a matter of perspective. And if she was going to serve God, she must learn to see the positives. She must learn to live without her family and the things that would remind her of home. She must embrace the discipline in order to be fulfilled by it. Somehow. Perhaps this was why her family did not come.

After only three weeks in the convent, Sister Julia was summoned to the mother superior's rooms.

The reverend mother wasted no words. 'You wish to do God's work, my child?'

Perhaps it did not matter to her why Sister Julia had entered the sisterhood; that her family were not staunch believers. It was a commitment, and whatever the reason, the reverend mother assumed it to be a wholehearted one.

Chastity, poverty and obedience . . . Sister Julia bowed her head. Anything that took her out into the world, that allowed her to do something useful, something that would stop her brooding and her loneliness. Anything would be better than this. 'I do, Reverend Mother.'

The reverend mother nodded. Although the order was enclosed, and enclosure was considered the most appropriate condition for contemplative retreat, there was still public work to be done, she explained. And Sister Julia had as yet only taken simple vows. 'There is much work remaining,' she said. 'It is good work. It is a rebuilding of our land and of our people. We will send you to the hospital, my child. It is God's will.'

At the hospital Sister Julia volunteered for long hours; many people no longer worked there and so there was much to do.

The reverend mother had warned her that she must keep her own counsel. But people talked, and one of the nurses – who talked more than most – told her more about what had happened to the Church during the Civil War. Sister Julia knew already that fifty churches had been gutted in Barcelona alone, though the cathedral had been spared, but now she learned that General Franco had restored all the Church's wealth, power and privileges. Perhaps she should not listen. Perhaps it was a sin to be curious. But old habits, Sister Julia found, died hard.

'Very kind of the general, do you not think, Sister?' the young nurse asked. 'Very worthy?'

'Indeed.' Sister Julia would have liked to say more – to ask more. But those times had gone. Her position in the world had changed.

The nurse laughed – but without humour. 'And what – I wonder – does he want in return?' She put her hands on her hips and raised a questioning eyebrow.

Sister Julia knew what she was implying – that there had been an unspoken condition attached to Franco's generosity. And perhaps she was right.

'Obedience from your church perhaps?'

That the Church was to serve the State in all things? Sister Julia kept calm on the outside, but on the inside she felt a tremor of fear.

'But you'll know about that,' the nurse said. 'Being a nun.'

Sister Julia said nothing, just turned away to her duties.

Perhaps someone had seen them talking; she did not

know. But she did not see that nurse again. It was as if she had vanished into thin air.

Back at the convent the reverend mother surprised her further by telling her of some of the Republican atrocities that had occurred during the war. Nuns who had been raped and made to swallow their own rosary beads, priests who were castrated or forced to dig their own graves. 'It was unspeakable, my child,' the reverend mother said, even while she clearly thought it necessary to speak of it to Sister Julia. But why?

The following week, Sister Julia was moved to obstetrics, to the maternity ward. The beds were narrow and quite close together on both sides of the long room, and were made up with white sheets and hairy brown blankets, although there was a movable screen that could give the women some privacy. As in the other part of the hospital, the overwhelming smell was of disinfectant. Sister Julia wrinkled her nose. But it was tolerable; certainly more bearable than the smell of blood or disease. At one end of the ward was the kitchen area and nurses' station; at the other, the sluice.

A middle-aged nurse in a crisp white uniform showed her around.

'This is Dr Lopez, our specialist obstetrician,' she said as they approached a short but important-looking man with a shock of dark hair. He was wearing a white coat and had a stethoscope slung around his neck. 'Doctor, this is Sister Julia.'

The doctor gave a little bow of his head. But when he looked up at her she felt a small shudder inside. He was perhaps only five years or so older than Sister Julia herself. And yet he seemed so much older. His eyes were so cold, and yet his gaze so hypnotic. She felt immediately pulled in. And trapped by it – as if she was a small animal or a bird.

'We have been expecting you, Sister,' he said. 'We have an important task for you.'

Glory . . . Sister Julia tried not to look as terrified as she felt. Was she ready for an important task? She did not think so.

'You are to help look after the fallen women,' he said. 'As a daughter of Christ, it is your duty.'

'Yes, doctor,' Sister Julia murmured. Fallen women. How was she – a mere novice with no experience of such things – to look after the fallen women?

'They have taken the wrong path,' Dr Lopez said sadly, shaking his head. 'It is up to us to help them make amends.'

And as he continued to instruct her on her duties, Sister Julia realised what her role was to be. She was to provide moral support, comfort, and – more importantly – show the women the right path, the path of God, the path which Dr Lopez wished them to follow.

After the doctor had gone, the nurse went off to supervise the rosters and the cleaning of the sluice room and Sister Julia was left alone with one of the women.

She was dark and slight of figure and in the first stage of labour, having regular contractions which made her gasp and grip Sister Julia's hand – hard. Her brow was filmed with sweat and Sister Julia instinctively laid a cool dampened flannel on to it and smoothed the young woman's hair from her face.

'*Madre mia*. Thank goodness you are here,' she muttered. 'Otherwise I should be alone.'

Sister Julia's heart went out to her. Nobody in her situation should be alone. Dr Lopez had advised her to discourage the women from talking to her. 'You must be firm with them,' he had said. 'The lesson they must learn is a lesson from God.' But this was a fellow human being, a woman who was suffering and who needed her. She had to help her through the traumatic experience of childbirth, not just talk to her of God.

'Be still, my sister,' she said. 'The pain will pass. And then you will have a beautiful child.' And she held her hand and rubbed the woman's back when the contractions came.

'If only my husband were here . . . ' the woman gasped.

Sister Julia stopped in the action of dampening the flannel from the bowl of water on the trolley beside her. 'Your husband?' she said. Hadn't she been told that this woman had fallen from virtue? If she had a husband, how could that be? Unless ..?

'He is imprisoned,' the woman muttered. And then she gripped Sister Julia's wrist so tightly that she feared it might snap. 'He is lost, perhaps tortured, perhaps dead. How can I know?'

Sister Julia thought of what had happened before with the

young nurse and how careful her parents had taught her to be. She looked quickly down the ward of narrow beds to check that no one was listening. No one seemed to be paying them any attention and none of the nurses or doctors were around. It was something, Sister Julia thought, when a novice and untrained nun was left to tend to a woman in labour while the nurses and doctors were doing who knew what elsewhere.

Swiftly, she pulled away from the woman and drew the screen around the bed.

'What do you mean?' she whispered. She remembered her father's faltering voice back home in the dead of night when he had spoken of Fort Montjuïc and the prisoners there. His words, his voice – they were branded into her mind.

The woman looked straight at her. 'He was a Republican, Sister,' she said. 'Too proud to run away. They came for him in the dead of night.' She moaned, as another contraction gripped her body.

'Shallow breathing now,' Sister Julia urged. She might not know much but she knew enough. Hadn't she helped boil the water when their neighbour had been in labour during the Civil War, while her mother had stayed with the mother doing more or less what she was doing now? 'Deep breathing as the pain recedes.' Which would at least ensure a good supply of oxygen to the foetus, she hoped. The woman was undernourished; there was practically nothing of her. What was wrong with a country that could not even look after its own?

Later, the woman was taken away to the delivery room.

Sister Julia searched for Dr Lopez. She found him at the nurses' station at the end of the ward, joking with one of the nurses.

'Please may I speak with you, doctor?' she asked.

His face clouded. 'Yes, Sister Julia,' he said. 'What is it?'

She explained to him what the woman had told her. 'Can we not help her find out what has happened to her husband?' she asked him. 'He may even be still alive.'

Dr Lopez shook his head sadly. He drew her aside. 'You have much to learn, Sister Julia,' he said.

She was aware of that. But even so . . .

'Her husband has been punished for his sins,' he added gravely. 'It is not for us to reason why.'

'But at least we could help—'

'There is only one way to help these women,' the doctor said. 'They must repent.' He looked deep into her eyes. 'And you, Sister Julia, must understand why you are here. You are here to further God's purpose, you know.'

Sister Julia could see from his stern expression that this was the end of the matter. But . . . God's purpose? Wouldn't God want the poor woman to know if her husband was dead or alive?

One of the other women – unmarried, Sister Julia was told – gave birth an hour later. Sister Julia was by her side in the delivery room attending her while the doctor and a mid-wife delivered the child and then the placenta. The woman's legs were still in stirrups and she writhed from side to side.

'She is *primipara*,' Dr Lopez told Sister Julia as he made his sutures. 'It is her first baby. Sometimes it is not easy.'

And she saw that he had made a long incision, so that she would not tear.

But the woman seemed to be in considerable pain. 'My God, my God,' she whimpered.

Sister Julia tried to soothe her. 'It is all over now,' she said. 'Your child has been safely born.'

The doctor shot her a warning glance. 'She has repented,' he said. 'Quite rightly, she has decided not to keep her baby. He must be taken from her.'

But the woman was holding her child to her breast.

Although he was not a tall man, Dr Lopez seemed suddenly to tower over the woman. He grasped the child and firmly removed him. 'He must now be examined. There will be no delay.' He strode out of the room, ignoring her cries, carrying the child with him.

The woman grasped now at empty air as she wept. Sister Julia comforted her as best she could. But it was heartbreaking.

Dr Lopez waylaid her as she was about to return to Santa Ana. 'I see that you do not truly understand our work, Sister,' he said.

Sister Julia bowed her head. She was trying. Indeed she was trying.

'To give up a child . . . ' he said. 'This is sometimes a necessary part of their repentance. Otherwise what future will these women have? And what future will there be for the children?' He was passionate; his dark eyes shone.

Unmarried mothers were stigmatised, it was true. They had fallen from the right path, the virtuous path, and society would know it. Sister Julia knew it too. And as for the children . . . It would be hard for them, she could see that.

'How can a woman like that adequately care for a child?' he demanded. 'How is it possible?'

Sister Julia did not know. She supposed she had not thought it through.

'They have no money and no way of making a living – no virtuous way.'

He gave her a certain look and Sister Julia shivered. He was almost saying – was he not? – that if a mother kept her child she might be forced into prostitution simply to have the wherewithal to feed it. And that could not be right.

'How will the child live, Sister Julia? How will it survive? Can we be responsible for the life of that child?'

Somehow, the doctor was making her feel guilty for the thoughts she had had. He seemed to possess a power – though what sort of power, she could not say.

She bowed her head. The truth was that she could not answer these questions; it was too complex a matter for a girl of barely eighteen. Clearly, the doctor knew best; the reverend mother had told her that he was a good and wise man and should be obeyed in all things. And when Sister Julia looked into his eyes – she could not avoid this although she tried to keep her head bowed at all times – she felt his strength, the force of him. It would indeed be hard not to obey.

So she did as he asked. She cared for the women during their confinement and helped give them moral support and comfort as they gave birth. The pain of this procedure – which Sister Julia would have expected to be a natural event – shocked her, but she grew used to it. She found that a calm and quiet presence by their side helped these women in their hours of need. After the birth she would look after the babies too and after that . . . It was out of her hands.

After some months, Dr Lopez took her aside. 'Can I now trust you, Sister Julia, to do God's work?' he asked her earnestly.

'Yes, doctor,' she replied. At least, she was willing to try her best. She had become involved with these women and their precarious situations. She wanted to help them all she could.

'Then I should like you to come and work for me in my private clinic,' he said.

When Sister Julia returned to Santa Ana it transpired that the reverend mother already knew of the doctor's request.

'You must not feel flattered, my child,' she said. 'Although you have done well and you have done your duty. Your life is here with us at Santa Ana but your work must be with the doctor – for now. You will be our representative. We trust that you will not let us down.'

Sister Julia bowed her head in acquiescence. 'I will try not to, Reverend Mother,' she said. It was clear that the reverend mother thought as highly of the doctor as if he were a monastery leader, as if his power was indeed come from God. It was true that he was a most religious man; he quoted passages from the Bible frequently. But . . . whether or not Dr Lopez's power came from God, she knew that she could indeed be of some use.

Slowly, she was growing accustomed to her new life – at the convent and caring for the women. What she could not get used to, however, was the pain of a woman who had made the decision to give up her child. She heard their mournful, desperate cries and their empty weeping and she thought of her own mother. How could she not think of her own mother? She would never – she thought – grow used to that.

CHAPTER 12

Ruby chose a quiet corner in The Gull restaurant in Pride Bay. She'd arrived early, tried not to think about the fact that it was Friday the thirteenth – something that had escaped her attention when she and Frances had fixed up the meeting.

'There's something I need to talk to you about,' Ruby had said when she finally phoned her. 'Are you planning to come down this way soon? I wondered if we could meet up?'

She heard Frances's hesitation. 'What's this about, Ruby?' she'd asked gently.

Ruby hadn't really wanted to say too much; it was something that she'd rather do face to face. But . . . 'It's about my parents,' she said. 'About me, really. About the circumstances surrounding my birth.' It all sounded a bit formal. But how else could she say it? And if there was anything – she was pretty sure Frances would be in the know.

'I see.' There was another pause. 'To tell you the truth, Ruby, I've been expecting something like this.'

'Oh.' That didn't sound good. That sounded as if there was something to know. That she hadn't been mistaken. That there was some big secret surrounding her birth.

'I'll come down to Dorset.' Frances sounded brisk now.

'The sooner the better, I think, don't you? Next weekend perhaps?'

'Fine.' *The sooner the better . . .* Ruby gulped. 'Thanks, Frances.' But she needed to know. And with her parents no longer alive, Frances was the only person who could tell her.

Ruby looked around her at the cream and red old-fashioned decor, the white tablecloths, the folded napkins. What was she about to hear? She'd better order a drink – she'd probably need one . . .

'Ruby, my dear.'

Ruby got up to greet her and felt herself immediately enveloped in a hug. 'It's good to see you,' she said, and meant it. Frances's calm eyes, warm smile and loose curls now flecked with grey, white and pepper-brown, were like a tug at the blind of her memory bank. Not from the funeral, but from before. She felt such a pull of emotion that she had to blink back the tears as Frances kissed her cheek. Frances was so associated with her mother; she could see them sitting together at the kitchen table of her childhood, nursing mugs of instant coffee when she came in from school; Frances with her feet up on their couch while Vivien caught up with her ironing pile. Serious chat, a bit of gossip, lots of laughter.

'How are you?' Frances settled into her seat. 'How on earth are you managing with everything? I had been wondering, you know.'

Where to begin? 'I've got the house up for sale now,' Ruby told her. 'I've been looking for somewhere else to live, but no luck yet.' She thought of the auction. And the cheek of that man . . . Not only bidding against her but having the nerve to try and chat her up afterwards – if that was what he'd been doing. God. Ruby had been so angry she could have whacked him one with her handbag as she rode away – if she hadn't been wobbling so precariously at the time.

'Who are you?' she'd asked him. 'And how do you know my name?' What was he – some sort of stalker?

'I saw you playing at the Jazz Café,' he said. And, 'I didn't know I was bidding against someone I knew in there.'

What was that supposed to mean? He didn't know her and she certainly didn't know him. She frowned.

'Or knew of,' he added. 'Know of?' He seemed a bit desperate now. 'Seen around?'

'You don't.' Her tone was crisp. 'You haven't.' She was not amused. 'You don't know me, and I don't know you.' She pushed herself off with some difficulty and prayed she wouldn't fall. 'End of.' That would tell him.

'So you're staying here in Dorset?' Frances asked her.

'Yes.' Ruby shrugged. 'At least for a while.' For the moment they were on safe ground. She glanced across at Frances. How long before they stopped skirting round the difficult stuff and got down to the nitty-gritty?

Frances seemed to know what she was thinking. 'Shall we order before we talk?' she suggested.

Ruby nodded. In some ways, Frances was the closest she now had to family. She didn't really count the grandparents in Scotland who she hardly knew and who had barely acknowledged her at the funeral. At least Frances had been a constant presence during her childhood. But Ruby had yet to become accustomed to the new, true meaning of 'only child'. There was no one left. She repressed a sigh. Even her memories were at risk of irreparable damage – after tonight.

She chose fresh whole local plaice with salad and new potatoes; Frances opted for sea bass, vegetables and chips. They decided to share a bottle of Soave.

'You'd better tell me everything that's happened, my dear,' Frances said. 'And then I'll do what I can to fill in the gaps.'

Ruby took a deep breath and out it came. The photographs in the shoebox, the baby's bonnet and love beads, the guitar plectrum. The doctor's letter about her parents' infertility, the lack of early baby photos in the album, the fact that she looked nothing like either of them. And her confused grandmother's 'bolt from the blue'.

Frances nodded. 'I see.'

By now their food had arrived, but neither of them was eating much. Ruby was pushing her fish around her plate – at least it gave her something to do. Frances was looking grave. Her gaze kept drifting beyond Ruby as if she was seeing her friend Vivien throwing back her head and laughing in that way she had or frowning as she stood a distance away to look at one of her watercolours.

'And then I took a proper look at my birth certificate,' Ruby said.

'Ah.' Frances nodded. And was it Ruby's imagination or did she see a faint blush on her cheeks?

'The registration of my birth appears to have been delayed,' Ruby said. 'For some reason.'

'Yes, it was.' Frances looked thoughtful.

For a few moments they were both silent.

Ruby smoothed some white fish from the bone and took a mouthful. She'd kept her part of the bargain and now it was time for Frances to come clean. Why was she hesitating? Had she promised to keep her mother's secret?

Ruby swallowed. 'Mum would want you to tell me the whole story,' she said. Family secrets were all very well, but didn't everyone have the right to the truth surrounding their own birth?

'Oh, I know she would,' Frances agreed. 'She wouldn't want you to be floundering around in the dark. She told me so herself.'

'Then . . . ' Ruby took another deep breath. 'Is she my mother?' she asked. 'My birth mother, I mean.'

Frances took a sip of her wine. 'Your mother – and your father for that matter – did what they did for your own good, my dear,' she said. 'They may have done wrong. But they only ever had your best interests at heart.'

She'd have to see about that, Ruby thought. But what did they do exactly? 'You'd better just tell me,' she said.

'Vivien was a good woman.' Once again, Frances's gaze became distant.

But that was the past. This was the present and Ruby wanted some answers.

'She loved you more than the world,' said Frances. 'Whatever I tell you, you have to understand that. No one could have loved you more.'

Ruby could feel her eyes filling yet again. Damn tears — they were round every corner. And that was all very well. 'But she's not my mother? Is that it?' Ruby took a gulp of wine. 'Come on, Frances. Spit it out.'

Frances sighed. 'No, you're not Tom and Vivien's daughter,' she said. 'Not biologically, at least.'

CHAPTER 13

Dorset, April 1978

The knock on the door was a quiet one. But Vivien heard it.

With the faintest of sighs, she put down her paintbrush and got to her feet. There was never enough time to work on her painting and when Tom went out it didn't take her long to grab her materials and the opportunity. She adored him. But. Time alone . . . Sometimes it seemed an almost forbidden luxury. She opened the door.

For a moment she didn't recognise the girl standing there. It was beginning to rain – big, fat drops splattering on to the dry stone path. Tom had been planting some marigolds (to keep away the slugs, he said) and they were squatting in the border like trainee soldiers determined not to step out of line. Then she realised. 'Laura?'

Well, she hadn't seen her for quite a while. But her mother . . . *Oh, my heavens*. 'Laura.' Her voice was softer now. She had known this would happen. But still, it had taken her by surprise. Vivien put out a hand and drew the girl gently inside.

Laura Woods blinked. 'Hello, Vivien,' she said.

She was wearing a long cheesecloth skirt decorated with

red roses and an embroidered smock top. She'd lost a lot of weight since Vivien had seen her last and her blonde hair was long and straggly. In her hands she dangled a tatty wicker basket and over her shoulder hung a brightly coloured fabric bag.

'Come in,' Vivien said, though she already was. It was more something to say, Vivien knew that. Instead of what she must say. 'I'm so sorry, Laura.'

The girl nodded, didn't look up. She seemed kind of vague and not quite with it. Which was hardly surprising. How must it feel to lose your mother at – how old was she? – only twenty?

Laura shivered. 'I came back as soon as I heard,' she said at last, as though Vivien had accused her of something.

'Of course.' Vivien nodded. Although she had been angry with her before for not keeping in touch with her mother, she did understand what Laura must have been through when her parents' marriage broke up. Going off like that so soon after the divorce, disappearing from her parents' radar so completely had seemed, even at the time, an act of rebellion. Perhaps she'd found it hard to forgive her parents for splitting up, perhaps she wanted to assert her own independence, perhaps she simply needed to get away from the mess at home. Whatever the reason, Laura had gone – and she'd rarely looked back.

'Why didn't she tell me?' Laura's eyes were wide, blue and accusing.

'Tell you?'

'That she was ill. That she was dying.'

Vivien had guessed this would happen too. 'She was trying to be brave, Laura,' she said. Though privately she agreed with the girl. Of course she should have been told. Poor Laura. Her heart went out to her.

'Brave!' Laura shook her head as if she couldn't believe it.

Vivien could only imagine what she was feeling. Pearl might have had the best of intentions but not to tell your own daughter that you didn't have long to live simply wasn't fair. In her determination not to make Laura obligated to come back and see her, Pearl had denied her daughter the right to say goodbye.

'Where were you?' Vivien led the way into the sitting room. Automatically she put her paintbrush in the jar of water as she passed the table. *When you heard the news*, she meant.

'Spain.'

'Oh.' Not that it made any difference. Vivien gestured towards the sofa and Laura perched on the edge, as if she might want to make a quick getaway. Her wrists were bony, her brown fingers constantly fiddling with a thread from the blanket in the basket she'd placed on the sofa beside her. Her face was brown too. She looked so different. Weather-beaten at twenty, Vivien thought.

'I had to get the money together to come back,' Laura said. 'It wasn't easy.'

'Didn't your father—'

'No.' Laura cut her off. Her face hardened. 'I don't want a penny from him.'

Vivien nodded. She could understand that too. 'Let me make you some tea,' she offered. Although she looked as if she could do with something stronger.

'Thanks.'

In the kitchen, Vivien took stock. Pearl had lost her battle with cancer a few months earlier. She had spent her final two months in a hospice. Vivien had visited her every day and watched her fading away before her very eyes. It had been agonising.

And now Laura had come home . . .

'Do you take sugar?' she called. What could she say to her? How could she help her cope with the loss of her mother?

'One, please.'

From the other room, Vivien heard a snuffling sound. Oh, God, she was crying. She had come back to a country that must seem so alien to her, to a motherless house that was no longer a home. And now . . .

Vivien hurried back in with the tea tray. Perhaps she should suggest that Laura stay with them for a while. She shouldn't be alone. She needed time in which to adjust to life back in England, time in which to come to terms with her mother's death – somehow. Was she very short of money? Did her father even know she was back? She'd need a job. She—

'Laura?' Vivien stopped in her tracks.

'Mmm?'

Laura wasn't crying. Laura was holding a baby and the baby was crying – or beginning to. It – he/she? – was still half wrapped in the blanket and sling that Vivien now realised had been bundled up in the basket Laura was carrying. And the baby was nuzzling into Laura's neck, whimpering.

Vivien put the tray down before she dropped it. 'You've had a baby,' she said, somewhat unnecessarily.

'Yeah.' Laura looked as if she hadn't yet become used to the idea herself.

'When?'

Laura glanced at the baby in her arms. 'A couple of months ago,' she said. 'I can't remember exactly.'

'You can't remember?' Vivien digested this information as she got closer to the sofa. The little one was still waking up. It was one of the prettiest babies Vivien had ever seen.

Laura shrugged as if it was all a bit of a blur.

'A girl?' She was wearing a pink Babygro and a white cardy.

'Uh-huh.'

'Did your mother know?' Vivien realised her breathing had become shallow. She gulped in some air. Pearl had been a grandmother . . .

Laura shook her head.

Dear God. She hadn't known. Of course she hadn't. This baby must have been born only a week or so after her death. 'You poor, poor girl,' she said with feeling.

'She's hungry,' Laura said. 'I need to make up a bottle.'

'Oh, yes. Of course. You're not . . . ?'

Laura shook her head again. 'No. I tried, but it was pretty useless.'

Hardly surprising, Vivien thought. She was such a slim wand of a girl. She probably wasn't healthy enough to be feeding her own baby. There was nothing of her.

Laura rummaged in her shoulder bag and produced a bottle, a teat, some formula powdered milk in a tin.

'Sterilising tablets?' Vivien asked.

'Sorry.'

Well, no. She couldn't imagine Laura worrying about those. 'Shall I do it?' she asked, since Laura had made no move to do so. And anyway, she had the baby to look after, and she was crying more loudly now. How come Laura didn't have a bottle made up and ready? Vivien certainly would have. But then Vivien didn't have a baby, did she? And she wasn't Laura either – a girl who had been travelling around Spain and God knows where else. Who probably lived the kind of lifestyle where you didn't worry about babies crying or bottles of milk being made up in advance. And a girl, she reminded herself sternly, who had just lost her mother.

'It's no trouble.' Vivien got to her feet. 'I'll soon read the instructions on the tin.'

She needed to *do*.

By the time she'd prepared the baby's milk, the little one was howling and Laura's eyes were big and hollow as eggcups. She was clearly exhausted.

'Would you like me to take her?' Vivien had never fed a baby before. There was something so appealing about this little one, even with her gummy screaming. Her fists were as scrunched up as her red pixie face. Vivien couldn't help smiling. She had quite a temper on her.

'Oh, yes please.' Laura seemed relieved. She handed the baby over and sank back against the cushions. 'I'm so tired.'

'Doesn't she sleep very well?' Vivien took the screaming bundle carefully on to her lap, tested the milk on the back of her hand, supported the baby's head and offered the bottle. Immediately the little one latched on to the teat. Silence. Again, Vivien smiled. Such simple needs.

The baby closed her eyes for a few seconds and then stared up at Vivien. Her steady blue gaze was disconcerting. Her brow was hot with the state she had got herself into and with her little finger Vivien smoothed the faintest wisp of fair down away from the baby's eyes. 'There,' she said. 'Isn't that good?'

The baby sucked noisily. Vivien felt strangely calm and she sat back in the chair a bit. The little baby fists had opened now, spread-eagled like starfish, palms up, and Vivien experimentally put her little finger in the centre of one tiny palm. The baby hand closed tight around it. Goodness . . .

'No, she doesn't,' Laura said suddenly, making Vivien jump. 'She wakes up twice in the night usually. Sometimes I can't stop her crying. You've got no idea.' Her shoulders slumped.

It was true, Vivien thought. She had no idea. She thought of the tests they'd had. *Unexplained infertility*, had been the result. She and Tom had just looked at each other helplessly. What did that mean – and more to the point what could they do about it? In the end they hadn't done anything — at least not yet. There was the option of treatment — there were drugs; injections of a fertility hormone — gonadotropin, it was called; try getting your tongue round that. There were clinics too. The next step was to find out more information, discover what was available. Or maybe even to accept that it wasn't meant to be . . .

She eased the bottle to one side of the baby's mouth and let the teat refill for a moment. The baby blinked and she replaced it. Vivien was trying to come to terms with child-lessness. She knew she had a good life, she had work, she had her painting, she had Tom.

'Lots of people choose not to have children,' Tom had said, trying to make her feel better maybe. But that was the problem — Vivien had had the choice taken away from her. It wasn't the end of the world and she'd come to terms with it if it wasn't meant to be. But still, she thought, looking down at the baby in her arms. But still . . .

'What happened when you had her?' Vivien asked. 'Were you in Spain?'

'Yeah.' Laura was slumped even further into the sofa now, half swallowed by it. She'd drunk her tea and eaten at least six biscuits. Life must be hard in Spain, Vivien thought.

'What was the hospital like? Did everything go OK?' She simply couldn't imagine.

'I didn't have her in hospital.' Laura yawned.

Oh. 'Where then?'

'In the camper van.'

'The camper van?' Vivien tried not to look too shocked. But – how could you have a baby in a camper van? It wasn't exactly hygienic was it?

'We put down some sheets and stuff,' Laura said. 'We had hot water.'

Vivien looked down at the baby. 'It must have been difficult,' she said. But she found herself wondering other things. Like who had cut the umbilical cord? And had there been any pain relief available for Laura – or had she just got stoned?

'It's where we sleep.' Laura sounded defensive now.

Vivien gave her a reassuring smile. 'She looks healthy enough,' she said. And she did. She was a small baby, but perfectly formed. Her cheeks were slightly flushed but now that she had her milk she was the picture of contentment. 'And you had someone with you, did you – for the birth?'

'Yeah.' Laura didn't elaborate.

Vivien wanted to ask so many more questions. But something in Laura's expression stopped her. For God's sake, Vivien, she told herself. The girl has just lost her mother. It wasn't important. None of it was really important.

'So when did you say she was born, this little one?' she asked brightly.

'I told you I couldn't remember.' Laura sounded sulky now. 'A few months ago. Does it matter?'

'Well, it matters to her.' Vivien forced a lightness into her voice. 'Otherwise how will she know when her birthday is?' *Birthday cake, candles, children's party games* . . . Her mind spun out the images.

'We'll choose a day,' Laura said. She stared out of the window.

Choose a day? Perhaps she had post-natal depression. It was understandable – more than understandable after everything that had happened. 'You haven't registered her birth then?' Vivien asked carefully. Really, the girl didn't seem to have a clue.

'We don't believe in it,' Laura said.

'Oh?'

'Being labelled, being controlled, being dictated to by society,' Laura said. 'Why should she be "registered"? She's just a baby. A free spirit, you know?'

'Hmm.' Vivien was sure that there were lots of reasons why births had to be registered, but she decided now was not the time to discuss it. And Tom would say – quite rightly – that it was none of her business.

'Will you be staying here in Dorset, Laura?' she asked instead. 'Or will you go off travelling again?' With the baby, she was thinking. Free spirit or not, was that the right way to bring up a child? Without boundaries? Without structure? Without even knowing when she had been born? Laura would have to stay around for a while, of course. Vivien supposed that as next of kin she would have to deal with the sale of Pearl's house and all her effects. It would be hard for her. A nightmare, actually. She would need all the help she could get.

'I'll stick around for a while.' But Laura was still looking out of the window and Vivien suspected that she couldn't wait to be gone.

'I'll do what I can to help,' Vivien promised. 'I'll look after the baby for you whenever I can.' It wasn't just that she felt sorry for Laura. And it wasn't just for Pearl. It was more than that, of course it was more than that.

'Thanks.' Laura stared at her, reminding her uncannily of the baby, her daughter. Once, Laura's straggly hair had been nothing but wispy down like this; once, she too had been innocent and helpless. And now . . .

'Who's her father?' Vivien asked. 'Is he here with you?'

'No.' Laura's eyes moistened.

Gently, Vivien removed the teat from the baby's tiny mouth and wiped a dribble of milk from her chin. She put her on her shoulder. Gently, she patted the baby's back, feeling the soft, dimpled flesh under the little white cardigan. A feeling of contentment washed over her. So this was what it felt like.

'But Julio's a nice guy,' Laura said, straightening up and looking animated for the first time since she'd arrived. 'I'm with him now. We drove the VW back here from Spain.'

'That's good.' Vivien was glad she had someone. She wondered where the VW was parked. It sounded as though Laura was more likely to stay in the camper van than live in her mother's house. And in a way, she couldn't blame her.

'We got stopped loads of times,' Laura complained. 'We were targeted just because of the way we look and because of the van.'

'Really?' Drugs, she supposed.

'It's a great life though.' Laura's expression was dreamy.

'Having the freedom of the road, you know. No rules or regulations. Stopping wherever you want. Waking up and hearing the rain beating down on a tin roof.' She laughed self-consciously. 'All that stuff.'

'Yes, I can imagine.' Though Vivien couldn't, not really. Casual drugs, parties, not following the rules. Her life had been very different. Living with Tom before they got married was about the limit of her rebellion.

'I'd better get off then,' Laura said. 'He'll be waiting for me.'

'OK.' But Vivien didn't want her to leave. Or to be more accurate, she didn't want the baby to leave. 'What's her name?' she whispered, for the baby's head – surprisingly heavy – had nodded into her shoulder. She was asleep. Already. How incredible was that?

Laura looked at the baby girl.

Vivien couldn't quite read the look, but it was a kind of exasperation.

'Ruby,' she said. 'Her name is Ruby.'

CHAPTER 14

Barcelona, 1942

Every morning at the Canales Clinic, Sister Julia began by taking morning prayers. Dr Lopez had asked her to carry out this duty and she was happy to oblige. After this, she would help with the bedmaking, personal washing duties and breakfast, and then after the nurse had checked the temperatures and blood pressures it was time for Dr Lopez to carry out his morning round. The clinic was not large. There were only eight narrow beds in the first-floor medical room, and two small delivery rooms adjoining. As in the hospital, there was a sluice room at the other end of the ward with the lavatories and sterilising equipment and the small kitchen was beyond that.

On this particular morning, the doctor paused at the bedside of Ramira Baez – a woman who had come to them in response to an advertisement placed by Dr Lopez in the local paper offering help to fallen women who had no one to come to their aid in their time of need. When she'd heard about this, Sister Julia had been surprised – but impressed – by the doctor's kindness. He seemed at least to want to make the facilities of the clinic available to everyone who needed them. Even better, he did not insist that his patients must be rich women, nor did they have to be married. Better in fact if they were not. He preferred, he said, to give help to the most vulnerable members of society and he was not interested in material reward.

'My only goal is to help these poor women, Sister Julia,' he said. 'I only wish to do the work that God has preordained for me.'

Dr Lopez did, however, treat these women as if they were lucky to be there – which Sister Julia had to concede that they were. And he expected them to repent.

'Well, Ramira,' he said now, after he had examined her, for he tended to be familiar and on first-name terms with many of his patients. 'You are advancing satisfactorily, I think.' He glanced at the report that the night nurse had given him.

Ramira had indeed progressed well in the first stage of labour. Her face was pale but she seemed healthy enough. And God knows that was rare enough in these times. The doctor had listened to the foetal heartbeat with the trumpet-shaped tube he called the Pinard and he had placed this back on the trolley beside him. Now, he returned to her bedside and regarded her with his strangely intense but dispassionate gaze. 'But have you said your prayers and asked forgiveness for your sins?'

Sister Julia moved forwards and rested her hand on the young woman's brow. Dr Lopez had already spoken to Ramira on this subject at some length in her initial consultation and yesterday when she was first admitted. He was not happy because she was at present refusing to give her unborn child away for adoption. Sister Julia could understand his frustration and his concerns. But surely now was not the time to further harangue her? She was in pain. She was about to give birth.

'I have, doctor,' Ramira whispered.

He nodded. 'And have you thought more about the welfare of your child?'

'I have.' Her face was ashen.

'And?' Dr Lopez came closer to the head of the bed, bent his face closer to hers. 'What is your conclusion?'

She cringed away from him, her body quivering with the pain. 'Perhaps his best welfare is with his mother,' she panted.

Sister Julia held her breath. This was not what the doctor would want to hear. He wanted women such as Ramira to be aware of the bigger picture. There was so much poverty and hardship still in their country. And yet there were those who had the means of providing a good home for an unwanted child. Dr Lopez was, as he so often said, thinking only of the children.

The doctor made a strange noise in his throat. He lifted his hand and for an awful moment Sister Julia imagined he might strike Ramira. But, no. Of course he would not do such a thing. 'What sort of future do you imagine you can offer him?' he growled instead. And as he spoke, the doctor pulled away from the woman in the bed and again seemed to grow in stature as he stood over her. *A woman like you*, he might have added – but did not.

Ramira breathed more easily as the contraction faded. 'I am his mother,' she said.

'And do you think only of yourself?' the doctor demanded. 'A woman in labour with her child and she thinks only of herself.' His voice rose.

Sister Julia suppressed a sigh. She rinsed out the flannel in the bowl of water by her side. Perhaps Ramira was being selfish. But could she blame her for desiring to keep the child she had nurtured in her own belly, the child who was a reminder perhaps of a love she had lost? For Sister Julia still remembered some of the patients at the hospital who were wives – women who had not fallen into sin at all. So many Republicans had either fled from the city in fear for their life or been imprisoned or executed for their political beliefs. She was not sure whether or not Ramira Baez was one of those women. But this unborn child might be all that was left behind.

'It is my right to keep my own child,' Ramira muttered.

Seldom had Sister Julia witnessed a woman strong enough to stand up to Dr Lopez. She almost wanted to applaud her, but of course that would be wrong. Most of these women were vulnerable and soon had their confidence and their wills crushed by the unquestioning authority of Dr Lopez, by his unshakeable belief that what he was doing was the Right Thing. What else could they do, they might ask themselves, in their situation? Even Sister Julia's presence added to the credibility of his argument — she knew that. Many women were grateful to the doctor and the clinic. To many, Dr Lopez performed what was seen as almost an heroic rescue.

'You cannot be helped,' Dr Lopez said to her in a tone of disdain. 'You will not be helped.' He turned away, intoning from the Bible as he so often did. '"For the word of God is alive and active. Sharper than any double-edged sword, it penetrates and judges the thoughts and attitudes of the heart."'

Ramira's eyes were bright with tears. But her mouth was clenched tight as another contraction came. Sister Julia supported her upper back and tried to rearrange her pillows to make her more comfortable. She was hardly in a position to assert herself. But she had.

'I pity you,' Dr Lopez said. 'I pity you for being unable to see.'

The woman gasped with the pain. Sister Julia swept her dark hair from her sweating brow and laid the damp flannel back on to it.

'I will be back.' The doctor strode away and out of the door.

The midwife, who had been attending to another woman, hurried across to take over.

Sister Julia squeezed Ramira's hand and Ramira looked up at her. A moment of understanding seemed to pass between them. And then Sister Julia saw on Ramira's face that the pain had returned. And the moment was gone.

But Sister Julia looked down the length of the medical room, the walls of which were dingy and brown, the chipped tiles, the hard, uncomfortable beds, the trolleys of cold metal instruments, the sharp smell – of bleach and surgical spirit. She pitied these women too. She pitied them all.

Dr Lopez's consulting room was on the ground floor at the far end to the front door – through which women in varying stages of pregnancy would enter and take their places in the waiting room to the immediate left; a dark, rather dismal room with hard wooden chairs and what Sister Julia could only describe as an air of grief about it. Although birth should symbolise hope and new beginnings and happiness, should it not? In an ideal world.

After lunch, Dr Lopez took afternoon appointments with the women before returning to the labour ward or delivery room for his final round of the day. At other times he would be attending births and examining the newborns. There were experienced nurses working in the clinic and two midwives who worked separate shifts, but Dr Lopez was very much in charge – even more in charge than he had been at the hospital. This was his domain.

It was one of Sister Julia's duties to fetch the women when their appointment time came and to accompany each one down the long hallway that led to Dr Lopez's sanctuary. This could be a daunting journey and Sister Julia hoped that her presence might put the women at ease.

The last patient that afternoon was Agnese Jurado – a girl

of about twenty in the early stages of pregnancy. Her eyes were large and dark in her heart-shaped face and her black hair was thick and lustrous and hung loosely down her slender back. She was very pretty. But she had such a look of sadness about her too. She reminded Sister Julia of her sister Paloma. Dear Paloma . . . How she missed her inconsequential chatter. How different it all was from the life she had now.

Dr Lopez sat behind his large wooden desk next to a glass-fronted bookcase full of medical journals and religious tomes.

'Please sit.' He indicated the low seat opposite his own somewhat higher, leather swivel chair.

Agnese sat, shoulders hunched, head bowed.

Dr Lopez nodded. He liked to see that women were remorseful and ashamed. Sister Julia waited. Sometimes the doctor requested her to stay, sometimes to leave. Today he indicated that she should remain.

He filled in Agnese Jurado's personal details, writing laboriously and muttering every now and then to himself.

'And who is the father of your child?' he suddenly demanded.

The girl flinched. The lighting in the room was dim but the lamp on the desk seemed to be directed at poor Agnese as she stammered and stuttered her responses.

'I do not know, doctor,' she said, blushing furiously.

'You do not know?' His voice seemed to vibrate around the room.

Sister Julia watched the doctor pick up his heavy wooden crucifix from the desk. She knew what would come next. And it did. '"For all have sinned and fall short of the Glory of God",' he said sadly. 'Romans. If you repent, my child, you will receive the gift of the Holy Spirit.'

Agnese looked up at him, wide-eyed and terrified.

His voice rose, his colour heightened. '"The wages of sin is death."' He thrust the crucifix towards her.

Sister Julia began to pray too, silently.

'I was raped, doctor.' Agnese spoke so quietly that Sister Julia had to lean forward to hear her words.

Raped. Sister Julia held her breath. The poor girl. She waited for Dr Lopez to question her further. *When did this happen? Who was the man? Had she reported the incident to anyone?* There were many questions, were there not? And so many horrors in the city that even Sister Julia had not seen.

But he asked none of these questions. Instead he eyed the girl gravely. 'You wish the child to be adopted,' he said, in a manner that was not a question, in a manner that brooked no argument.

Sister Julia had to bite her lip to make herself remain silent.

The girl bowed her head. 'I have no choice, doctor,' she said.

'Indeed, that is so.' The doctor became almost brisk.

And Sister Julia could see that this was true; that clearly this was the best pathway for both Agnese and her unborn child. But it seemed so speedy, so unconsidered. The girl had been through so much.

'Take her behind the screen,' Dr Lopez told Sister Julia. 'I will do the initial examination now.'

'Yes, doctor.' Gently, Sister Julia took Agnese over to the narrow bed on the far side of the consulting room where there was also a trolley with the doctor's surgical gloves and instruments, a bin for soiled dressings and a washbasin. 'Please undress,' she said, drawing the curtain, trying to convey her sympathy with her eyes. She could do no more. It was not her place. But her heart went out to the girl.

Dr Lopez's manner became almost jovial as he carried out the examination. Was he simply trying to make Agnese feel more comfortable? She hoped so. He placed her feet in the stirrups and for a moment seemed to loom over the poor girl, who lay there with her frightened eyes wide open and her legs spread apart.

As if she is being raped again . . . Sister Julia thought this before she could stop herself. It was nonsense, of course. The girl had to be examined and Dr Lopez was not rough. Even so. Sister Julia stood to one side in case she should be needed. And once again she said a silent prayer.

'You are approximately five months pregnant,' Dr Lopez told Agnese. 'Which confirms the date you provided.'

The date that she was raped, Sister Julia thought. How did a girl such as this one – so pretty and so innocent – recover from the trauma of becoming pregnant with her rapist's child? And again she thought of Paloma. She too was pretty and innocent. It was a cruel world indeed that her God resided over.

After the girl had dressed, Sister Julia showed her out and arranged the next appointment for her. Her habit was to speak as little as needed, for this was what she had been told to do, but now she rested her hand on Agnese's thin shoulder. 'Please do not worry,' she said. 'You will be well looked after here.' And she vowed to make sure that this was true.

'Thank you, Sister,' said Agnese.

Sister Julia shut the door behind her and returned to the doctor's consulting room.

'Two more visitors will be here shortly, Sister Julia,' he said, rearranging his papers on the desk and looking at her over the half-moon glasses he had recently begun to wear. They did not, however, diminish the power of those eyes. On the contrary. 'Please show them through when they arrive. And then you may go.'

The couple arrived five minutes later and she let them in. They were well-dressed – he in a smart suit and tie and she in a navy skirt and jacket and white blouse and wearing a lot of gold jewellery, her dark hair well cut to just above her shoulders. Sister Julia guessed they were about forty years old. They were the kind of couple that they saw a lot of at the clinic; the kind of couple who had money and a certain position in society. And who desired to adopt a child.

Dr Lopez greeted them effusively and waved Sister Julia away. 'Your duties are done for today,' he said, and closed the consulting room door firmly behind them.

Sister Julia lingered. She shouldn't – but she was curious. There had been quite a few occasions when Dr Lopez had made it clear he did not want her to know what went on behind his consulting-room door.

'Good news and bad news, my friends,' she heard the doctor say. 'Which would you like to hear first, eh?'

'The good news, doctor,' said the woman. She sounded less cool and self-assured now. In fact, she sounded almost desperate. 'Please tell us the good news.'

Sister Julia could imagine the doctor leaning towards them over his desk. He would tap his pen on the desk top and rearrange his papers into a still neater pile.

'I have seen a girl,' he said. 'A good girl. And the father of the child she will have . . . ' His voice dropped. 'There is no replacement for the proper Nationalist values,' he said. 'You will not be disappointed with this child. I guarantee it.'

Sister Julia hurried off. She wanted to hear no more. She had been hoping to check up on Ramira's progress, but now she simply had to get away. She collected her things and left the clinic, the door shutting behind her with a thud of the brass knocker. She looked back at it — a palm with ringed wedding finger holding a ball. It was ironic, she thought, considering the business of the clinic. Even the nameplate of the place was small and indistinct, as if it wanted to keep itself secret.

She followed the familiar streets which wound their way through the Raval quarter of the city, where the clinic was situated, close to the Calle Arco del Teatro. An unseasonal mist seemed to hang in the air. She was so confused about what she had overheard. What did it mean? Certainly the couple had visited the clinic in connection with an adoption – this was not unusual. But had the doctor already arranged the adoption in question? Had he been forced to disappoint the couple in some way? And could he have been talking about Agnese Jurado's baby? Could the father with the proper Nationalist values be the same man who had raped her? It seemed impossibly heartless for a man of the stature of Dr Lopez. Sister Julia hurried back towards Santa Ana. Of course the doctor cared for the welfare of the children – but shouldn't he also show some compassion to the mothers? Especially girls like Agnese who had been treated so abominably during the aftermath of the Civil War.

Sister Julia looked around. It seemed to her that she could still feel the sorrow clinging like moss to the very city walls. The people in the streets had their sadnesses too; she could see it in the way they walked, the way they stood smoking in shop doorways, watching the world go by and maybe wondering what it was all for. She saw the shadowy forms of beggars and smelt the undertow of the city streets – the rotting vegetables, the stale urine, the city's rubbish mingling with exhaust fumes and tobacco. And death, she thought. The sorrow lay in the shadows of the city. It was winter and soon darkness would fall. Still . . . Darkness was a veil, but it could not cover what this city had lived through; what Sister Julia had seen.

Men had been imprisoned and tortured because of what they believed. Women had been left to bring up their children alone – or to give them up in the hope that they would have a better life. And girls like Agnese were raped and impoverished and then made to pay over again for the crime of having a sweet face and a body that men wished to possess.

It could not be right.

Sister Julia walked down the cobblestones towards Las Ramblas, past the milk bar and the empty market stalls. She thought of her family – of Mama and Papa and her two sisters. She saw them so rarely now; they only visited when there was family news to impart – once a year, if that. They all lived in the same city, yes, but now they lived so far apart. And her father never came . . .

The last time it had been her mother and two sisters who sat awkwardly in the foyer of Santa Ana waiting for her.

'Where is Papa?' Sister Julia had asked, as she always did.

Her mother's gaze swivelled away from her. 'You know he is busy, my daughter,' she said.

'He has work? You have food?' Because she could not help but worry. Entering the sisterhood had relieved her family of the strain of providing for her – but there were still four of them remaining. She examined their faces. All three were thin, but not too undernourished.

'We have enough,' her mother reassured her. 'You must not be anxious on our behalf.'

'No indeed, sister,' said Paloma, her eyes smiling at Sister Julia just as they always had.

'And now, Matilde—'

'I am to be married off.' Matilde had looked sullen ever since they had arrived and now Sister Julia understood why.

'To whom?' she enquired.

'To a man almost old enough to be my father,' she replied glumly.

'Matilde . . .'

But Sister Julia caught the looks passing between the three of them and she understood how it was. It was the second sacrifice her family had been forced to make.

'He is a good man. A wealthy man,' said their mother.

'You do not care for him?' Sister Julia whispered to Matilde.

Her sister looked her straight in the eye and what she saw there made Sister Julia almost sink to her knees, to beg her mother not to allow it.

'I cannot care for him,' said Matilde.

'Then—'

'It has been agreed.' Their mother's voice was firm.

Sister Julia bowed her head. 'And did Papa send a message for me?' she asked.

There was a pause.

'He thinks of you often,' said Mama.

But he never comes.

Perhaps he could not bear it, Sister Julia thought. Perhaps he could not bear to see her in her nun's weeds and witness what she had become.

Now, Sister Julia's steps quickened as she passed the newspaper kiosks and shops. She did not allow her glance to linger on the shop windows; not for her were the clothes and bags and finery that were perhaps the world of other women.

Sister Julia thought again of Agnese Jurado. What was her world? What would happen to her and to her unborn child?

The church bell tolled. Sister Julia was glad to get back to the convent; to the safety and serenity of Santa Ana. She rang the bell and a sister came to let her back inside the heavy gates, into the foyer which smelt of wax and of damp.

Immediately, she went to see the mother superior. She must share this with someone. She told her about the adoptions at the clinic and she told her about Agnese Jurado. She wanted to tell her more, explain that it felt so wrong. But . . .

'You are confused, my child,' the reverend mother said kindly. 'Dr Lopez is simply protecting the innocent, which is God's will.'

Sister Julia thought of Agnese and the rape. 'But Agnese—'

The reverend mother raised a hand. 'She has suffered,' she agreed. 'But we cannot now undo that suffering. No one can. The doctor is able, though, to help her unborn child.'

Put like that, Sister Julia could see that it all made sense. But the way Dr Lopez had spoken . . .

'You misunderstood, my daughter,' the reverend mother told her. 'Your imagination is overactive and you must make it still. You are allowing yourself to be anxious about things which are not your concern. You must have faith and trust in the doctor. He knows what must be done for the greater good. He is a highly respected, highly educated pillar of our society. His way is the Right Way. God's Way. He is to be obeyed without question. Do you hear me, child?'

'Yes, Reverend Mother.' Sister Julia bowed her head. Of course, she must have misunderstood. No doubt the doctor had been referring to some other girl, some other father. And even if he had not . . . He did what he did for the best of motives – she must not doubt it. He was trying to help the vulnerable, the innocent, the unborn.

'You must surrender your will to God.'

'Yes, Reverend Mother.'

'You must continue to be a lamp of faith, of hope and of charity,' she added. 'Remain rooted in the heart of Christ.'

Sister Julia went to the chapel to kneel and pray. Of course this was so. She had questioned the doctor and the good work that he was doing. She had been weak but now she would ask for the strength to do better. She closed her eyes and let the quiet of the chapel sink into her soul. She imagined that she could hear a choir of angelic voices singing a psalm from the Bible. Their voices soothed her troubled spirit. Sister Julia heard in those voices the faint music of hope. And so she prayed.

My Father, my Father, help me to do your will. Show me the way . . .

CHAPTER 15

Who am I . . . ? For weeks now, this question had been at the edge of her mind. And at last Ruby was beginning to get some answers. At least she now knew the identity of her birth mother. Laura – the girl in the photos she'd found. Even then, when she'd first seen her face, she'd felt something, hadn't she, though she'd tried to deny it.

And what of the parents who had brought her up and cared for her and let her believe she was theirs, really theirs? Well, they weren't her parents at all. Ruby let this sink in. Felt the loss of them once again. She had lost something elusive. Her roots? Her anchor? She wasn't sure. She just knew that suddenly she felt rudderless, as if everything she'd always believed had shifted away from under her.

She looked helplessly across the table at Frances. *What now?*

'I'm sorry, Ruby.' Frances's eyes were brimming with sympathy. But that didn't help.

She tried to take stock. She sipped her wine, thought back to what Frances had told her so far. 'So now I don't know when I was born either.' The people she'd thought were her parents never knew her date of birth and her birth mother couldn't even remember . . .

'Not the precise date, no.' Frances reached out and patted her hand. 'They did what they could, my dear.'

'Yes.' Ruby thought back to those childhood birthdays; the presents and the party games; her eighteenth coming-of-age party when she'd suddenly felt so different; as if magically metamorphosed into an adult. Older or younger, did it really make that much difference? Well, yes, actually. Everyone had a birthday. It was special. Why should she be any different? But it wasn't her parents' fault. Frances was probably right. They'd done what they could.

Still . . . It had all been a lie.

'Why didn't they ever tell me?' she asked Frances. She heard the anger in her own voice. She didn't want to hate them. But why hadn't they ever trusted her with the truth?

'Your mother wanted to.' Frances ran her fingers along the stem of her wine glass but didn't lift it to her lips to drink. 'We often talked about it.' She sighed. 'She believed you had a right to know. But your father wasn't so sure it would do any good. And he had a point. After everything that happened . . . Well, it just wasn't that simple, my dear.'

Ruby shook her head. She didn't believe that for a moment. How complicated could it be? Right now she was struggling. Trying not to resent them for keeping it from her, for taking control of her knowledge, for assuming a right to choose what she could know and what she couldn't. For pretending. All those years. All that love.

'Ruby . . . ' Once again, Frances put a hand on hers and

this time she left it there. 'Have you considered that perhaps Vivien left those things for you to find?'

Ruby stared at her. 'You mean that was her way of letting me discover the truth?'

Frances nodded.

'And Laura . . . '

'Laura was too young to take responsibility for you,' Frances said. 'She was just a girl.'

Ruby tried to imagine what it would be like having a baby to look after when you were just a girl. How would you cope? How had Laura coped? With no money, no job, just a VW camper van and some romantic ideal of freedom.

'Not only that,' Frances continued. 'But she must have been traumatised by hearing of her mother's death, when she had no idea poor Pearl was even ill.'

'Of course.' Ruby could empathise with that. She still had the nightmares.

'To start off with, Vivien just wanted to help her,' Frances said. 'She felt sorry for her.'

Ruby nodded. She pulled the envelope of photos out of her bag. Picked out the one of Laura and the baby. The baby . . . The photographic history of her childhood was complete now, wasn't it? This was her as a newborn. She handed it across the table to Frances.

Frances smiled. 'That's Laura,' she said. 'And that must be you.'

'Yes.' Ruby remembered the plectrum. 'Did she play the guitar?'

'I believe so.'

So had Ruby inherited her birth mother's love of music? Was that why she had started playing the saxophone? Why she wanted to write songs? It was a weird feeling – discovering that genetically you were from an entirely different background, a different stock.

'What was she like?' Ruby whispered. She knew what Laura looked like, but she wanted to know more.

'I hardly knew her, my dear,' Frances said. 'I can only tell you what Vivien told me.'

'What did she say about her?' Ruby asked. Though she could imagine.

'She liked her. She felt sorry for her. But she also felt she was, well . . . '

'Irresponsible?' Ruby guessed.

'Perhaps.' Frances handed the photo back to her.

Ruby ran a fingertip over the picture. Mother and daughter . . . When this photo was taken, Laura hadn't known, had she? She hadn't known that her mother had died. That she would be returning to England and that when she did – she would lose her baby too. *What had made Laura give her up?* Was it just because she was so young? Other young girls kept their babies, didn't they? Especially when Pearl had died and Ruby was all that Laura had left . . .

Ruby sighed. The love beads were Laura's. And the baby's bonnet must have been her own.

'Where do you think these pictures were taken?' she asked

Frances, passing another photo over to her. Where exactly had she been born?

'I don't know, I'm afraid. I think Vivien said she'd been travelling in Spain somewhere.'

Ruby looked again at the golden beach, the turquoise sea, the wand of the lighthouse, pointing towards a cloudless blue sky. It looked idyllic. And yes, it could be Spain. Did that make her half Spanish? Who was her father? Would she ever be able to find out? She was part of other family units that she hadn't even knew existed. Her father's family – whoever they were – Laura's family . . .

'What happened to Laura?' Ruby asked Frances. 'Where is she now? Do you know?' For one wild moment she imagined that perhaps Frances had kept in touch with her, that she could tell her Laura's whereabouts. She imagined finding her, meeting her, being reunited with the mother she'd never even known she had.

'I don't know where she is now, my dear,' Frances said kindly. 'Vivien and Tom did try and trace her at one time, I believe. But,' she shook her head, 'she simply disappeared.'

'I see.' Ruby forced her shoulders to relax. *Simply disappeared*. 'So what happened exactly, after Laura turned up with me at Vivien's house? Did she just hand me over?' Like a sack of potatoes, she thought. 'Was I adopted? Fostered? Or what?'

'Not exactly adopted, no.' Frances fiddled with her napkin.

Ruby sighed. No, she wasn't adopted, was she, because

Vivien and Tom Rae were the parents named on her birth certificate. She looked across at Frances. 'You'd better tell me the rest of the story,' she said.

CHAPTER 16

Dorset, April 1978

Vivien parked the car by the harbour, got out and retrieved the bucket of spring garden flowers from the floor of the passenger seat of her green Morris 1000. It was breezy, but the sun was just breaking through the clouds, boat masts clinking in the wind, the gulls shouting as they soared overhead, drawn to the harbour, no doubt, by the sweet scent of fish caught earlier that day.

Vivien locked the car and made her way across the rough concrete past the piles of warty crab pots and fishing nets laid out to dry. The water was sleek and rippling and the little harbour was full of boats – cabin cruisers and sailing dinghies, brightly coloured rowing boats and larger fishing vessels – all gently rocking on the water, though some, like *The Dusky Rose* tethered to the rusted mooring ring on the stone wall by the general stores, were somewhat the worse for wear. Not so much dusky as faded to a frazzle, she thought, surveying the peeling paint and rotting wood beneath.

Vivien's favourite time here was winter, when the tourists left and the place snatched back its soul. But now it was spring half-term so there were lots of people milling around – families eating ice cream or fish and chips, toffee apples or candy floss bought from one of the seaside kiosks lining the harbour. Others were going to the amusement arcade and the penny slot machines, or for a stroll along the front, and a few were tackling the windy cliff-side path up to Warren Down and the Beacon. On the quayside kids were collecting spider crabs in buckets, seagulls zooming down to steal the bait.

Vivien headed for the old chapel. A young couple were getting married there on Saturday – they were neighbours of Frances's and didn't have a bean to pay for a florist, so Frances had asked her to take over some spring flowers from the garden. Vivien always had lots of narcissi blooming – she'd cut loads and barely made a dent in the clusters around her garden path and in the front borders. Anyway, Vivien was happy to help out – they were a nice couple and in this village you did what you could to lend each other a hand.

The bucket was quite heavy although she hadn't put too much water in it, and it swung gently in Vivien's hand as she made her way towards the ginger beach and the old Wesleyan chapel, the water slopping from side to side and the small pale yellow heads of the narcissi nodding with the movement. The scent of the flowers – sweet and heady – drifted up to her as she walked, mingling with the seaside smells of the harbour and the sea.

Weddings and families . . . Vivien's mind drifted. She stood for a moment at the pathway which wavered along uncertainly behind the pebbles of Chesil Beach. Beyond the high rise of stones – the natural sea wall – the ocean was green and slinky, crusted with white foam, the waves whipping with the wind. She breathed in the fresh salty air. Vivien loved it here. It made her feel alive.

She thought back to when she'd married Tom. Her father in his unfamiliar dark blue suit and stiffly starched white shirt and navy tie; his firm and dutiful hand on hers, as they linked arms and he led her down the aisle between the rows of seats in Bridport Register Office. Her mother in blue and cream standing at the front, smiling nervously. *Why couldn't you get married in a church?* That's what they'd said. But what had they really been thinking that day?

It was strange, she supposed, that now she saw her parents so rarely. Since they'd moved to their Scottish island, they had become reclusive – Vivien suspected that they'd always had this tendency, had never really wanted to be part of a sociable, interacting world. Perhaps that was why she had often felt lonely as a child. She had yearned for the type of house always full with chatter and laughter; longed for neighbours or friends to just drop in for a cup of tea. But instead, the house was invariably quiet. And so Vivien was quiet too – her world became the world of the books she read and the friends of her imagination.

Her parents had a telephone in their remote island home, but hardly ever contacted her. Vivien phoned them from time to time, but within every stilted conversation was the sense of something missing, something that made her not want to call again for a while. It was as if the geographical distance they'd put between themselves and their only daughter was so much more than that – it was a personal distance, a spiritual distance. It was as if she had lost them.

Vivien thought of Tom. She was lucky to have him. What she had with Tom . . . Well, she couldn't even contemplate the loss of that. With her parents so far away, he was all she had.

A child ran past her – a girl of about ten, in a flowery pink dress and plastic beach shoes. She stuck her arms up in the air as she ran down the mound of pebbles on the other side shouting with delight. Vivien smiled. She could see the girl's parents up by the café. They were laughing, and there was a little boy with them too, tugging at his mother's hand. A perfectly formed family. She sighed.

Goodness, what was up with her this afternoon? What had brought this on? Vivien turned her gaze from the sea and the child and continued walking down the sandy path towards the old chapel. She knew though.

'Vivien!'

She swung around. Put her hand above her eyes to shield them from the sun. And then she saw it. Parked by Chesil Beach, a brightly painted camper van – in psychedelic colours, swirled with fluorescent pink, lime green, dark purple, dotted with silver moons and stars. And standing by the open door was Laura – waving. 'Hey, Vivien!'

'Hello, Laura.' She waved back, left the bucket of flowers on the worn step of the old chapel and made her way over. So this was the famous VW camper van – in which Laura and

Julio lived with little Ruby. In which Laura had given birth, and in which she'd travelled back to England from Spain. Vivien looked at the intrepid and luridly painted machine. She was surprised they'd made it.

Laura seemed more cheerful than the last time she'd seen her. 'This is Julio,' she said, indicating a surly-faced individual with dark curly hair who was stretched out on a bench seat inside the van at the back.

'Hello,' said Vivien. She noted the stickers on the windows – *Love and Peace*, *Ban the Bomb*. A rainbow. And the scent of patchouli joss sticks drifting out and away with the breeze. She could quite see why they'd been stopped by the police more than once on their journey home. But actually, the inside of the van was rather lovely. It had a pop-up roof so there was room to stand upright and an up and over door at the back. Opposite the sliding door was a compact little cooker and a sink with cupboards underneath. There was a gas kettle on the hob and a loaf of bread and a knife on the counter. The windows had gay, jazzily printed curtains and there were cushions on the bench seat where Julio was sitting and a guitar propped by the open door. But where was Ruby? Ah. Vivien spied her asleep in her basket on the front passenger seat.

'We were wondering about what you said, Vivien.' Laura was wearing a long blue dress today, with a string of multi-coloured love beads hanging around her neck. In her long blonde hair she had pinned a daisy chain. She looked as if she had just come from Woodstock, a real sixties flower child. Vivien smiled indulgently.

'Oh, yes?' Vivien looked back towards the passenger seat. It was difficult not to stare at Ruby. She looked so peaceful, so contented.

'About looking after the baby.'

'Oh.' Vivien hadn't mentioned her offer to Tom, hadn't honestly thought Laura would ask her. She'd told him about her visit, but as soon as she'd mentioned the child, he hadn't wanted to know any more. And there had been a warning light in his eyes. Since then she hadn't seen Laura anyway, although she'd told herself that if she did, she would invite them round for dinner. Pearl had been a lovely woman and a good neighbour. It was the least Vivien could do. She'd wondered about them though, how long Laura would stay now the house was up for sale. She seemed the type who wouldn't stay anywhere for very long. A free spirit. A wanderer.

'Could you have her this afternoon?'

'This afternoon?' So soon?

'Well, yeah.' Laura looked across at Julio, who just shrugged. But it wasn't as if Ruby was his child. It couldn't be easy for any of them – living in a camper van.

'I'd love to,' Vivien murmured. How could she refuse? And anyway . . . She would love to.

'Great.' Laura opened the passenger door and picked up the basket. Without further ado, she handed it to Vivien.

'Oh, you mean now?' Vivien had somehow imagined that one had to prepare for leaving one's baby with someone. That Laura would have to get some spare clothes ready, make up some milk formula, locate nappies and creams and what have you. Apparently not. She blinked.

Julio said something in Spanish.

Laura didn't acknowledge him. 'The stuff's all in the basket,' she said.

'Oh. All right.' Vivien held the basket close to her. 'Er, what time will you collect her? Or shall I bring her back here?' She looked down at little Ruby as she stirred in her sleep.

Laura shrugged as if this was immaterial to all of them. 'We'll come and get her,' she said. 'Sometime later. OK?'

'Well, OK.' It all seemed very vague.

And then there she was, walking towards the old chapel carrying a baby in a basket. When five minutes earlier she had been alone. Once again, Vivien looked down at the baby. And Ruby was still sleeping – unaware that responsibility for her welfare had just been passed to a stranger. When was her next feed due? Vivien had forgotten to ask. But then again she suspected that if she had Laura probably would have had no idea. No doubt she simply fed her when the baby was hungry. No matter – Vivien would do the same.

But she'd also have to do the flowers before she took her home.

Inside the chapel, the interior was cool and calming, the musty wax scent of candles intermingling with wood, incense and damp stone. Vivien walked carefully over the old flagstone floor, towards the simple altar decorated with the cross. Silence. She breathed deeply.

Did the baby feel it too? Vivien smiled and placed the basket tenderly down on the front pew. 'Stay here for a minute, little one,' she whispered to the sleeping child. 'I won't be long.'

She returned for the bucket of flowers she'd left on the doorstep, came back in and looked around for the vases Frances had said she'd bring. The chapel was bare, apart from the faded tapestry on the wall, the embroidered cushions on the wooden pews and the cream church candles in brass candelabra. For a moment she paused to imagine the atmosphere on Saturday, when it would be filled with people and smiles and spring bridal flowers. She glanced at the basket as she passed. The baby stirred again. Opened her mouth as if she was rooting for food. Bless her.

Just as she was going into the tiny kitchenette behind the curtain with the bucket of blooms, Vivien heard Ruby begin to cry. *Oh-oh*. You didn't get much warning then.

She put the bucket down on the stone floor and hurried back towards the pew. The baby's eyes were now open wide. 'Hello, Ruby,' Vivien murmured.

Ruby looked at her and yelled. She did have a voice on her. And from the sound of her she needed to be seen to. Straight away.

'Now, now. What's all this noise?' Vivien bent down, gathered the little one up in her arms. Ah, but she felt good, even though she was already writhing around as if she hadn't been fed for days. 'Less of the racket, now. You're in a chapel, you know, lovey.'

Another deep breath and off she went again.

Vivien rocked her. 'Ssh, ssh,' she told the screwed-up red face. Gently, she rubbed a thumb across the puckered brow.

The baby didn't stop screaming. She was getting hot with it; well and truly het up.

'All right then, we'll soon sort you out.' Vivien scrabbled through the contents of the basket with her spare hand. There was a bottle of milk already made up. Thank goodness for that. Though it wasn't warm, of course.

She took bottle and baby through to the kitchenette, still shushing and rocking. It was just a sink really but there was a boiler for hot water.

She ran the tap, putting the little one on her shoulder where she arched and wailed, but at least Vivien could move around more easily, keeping a firm one-handed grip on the contorting little body, which proved surprisingly strong. On the drainer were the vases Frances must have brought over. Vivien found one which would do as a container for the water, filled it, and stood the bottle in it upright, shaking it every so often to warm the milk through evenly. Every action was confident; she knew instinctively what to do. Laura must have known, surely, that Ruby would be wanting something soon though? She should at least have warned her she'd need feeding. It wasn't, well, very responsible, was it?

After a few minutes of murmuring and rocking and warming and shaking, Vivien tested the milk on her hand. It would do. She cradled Ruby in the crook of one arm and offered the bottle. The breathless baby rooted for it desperately, drank, spluttered, coughed and at last began to suck and was silent. Bliss. Vivien exhaled a breath she hadn't even known she was holding. This was what it was like then, she thought. Motherhood. This was what it was like.

Still feeding her, she made her way back into the chapel, sat gingerly down in the front pew, smoothed the wrinkles of the baby's brow with her forefinger, just as she had before. The redness in her face was already fading; she felt relaxed now and soft in Vivien's arms.

'There,' she said.

There was a click as the chapel door opened.

Oh my heavens, thought Vivien. Were you allowed to feed babies in here?

'Vivien?' But it was only Frances. 'Goodness,' she said. She came closer. 'Who's this then?'

'This is Ruby,' she said. She explained about Laura. 'I think she needed a break,' she said, 'so I'm looking after her for a bit.'

'Oh, lovely.' Frances sat down next to them, clucked her tongue at the baby. 'Isn't she a sweetheart?'

'Yes. She is.' Vivien held her slightly closer than before. She would have liked a few precious moments when it was just her and the baby, but that was foolishness, nothing more.

Vivien put the baby on her shoulder and gently patted her back. She should have invited them to stay at the house – Laura, Julio and little Ruby. They probably wouldn't have. But . . . Truth was, when she'd seen the little one she'd been almost frightened to.

'Do you mind if I leave you to it?' she asked Frances. 'It was all a bit last minute. Laura—'

'Of course not.' Frances nodded. But her kind eyes seemed to take it all in – Vivien, the baby, the way she was feeling.

'The flowers are in the kitchen.'

Frances nodded. 'I'll do them.' She got to her feet. And was that a tear in her eye? 'You see to that baby.'

CHAPTER 17

Barcelona, 1945

And so the years went on. Sister Julia continued to work at the clinic. It was a half-in, half-out kind of life. Perhaps she was fortunate. She had the security of Santa Ana – its peace and tranquillity which was restful to her soul – and a position in the outside world. But what a world. It was said that Spain was heading towards even greater economic disaster than they had ever known before. Towards bankruptcy even. But how could this be? Spain had not even been involved in the Second World War. She had remained neutral. So how come her people were still suffering?

One spring day Sister Julia made her way to the clinic as usual. She had much to think about. Yesterday evening her family had visited her again – the first time for more than a year – just her mother and Paloma this time. Indeed, she had not seen her elder sister since her marriage and still her father never came. She knew there must be news to impart.

'How is Matilde?' she asked them as they sat stiffly and uncomfortably in the foyer once again.

'Well,' their mother replied.

'Is there a child?' Sister Julia thought of the women she cared for at the clinic. She hoped to God her sister's experience would be more fulfilling.

'Not yet,' their mother said.

Paloma stifled a giggle.

'What, sister?'

Paloma shot an exaggerated look around the foyer of the convent as if to check that no one was listening. 'They say he cannot,' she whispered. 'They say he is far too old.' And she rolled her eyes.

'Indeed?' Sister Julia tried not to be shocked. She saw so much in her life at the clinic. But she had forgotten the looseness of her sister's tongue.

'Hush, child,' their mother scolded.

'And Papa? How is Papa?' Though Sister Julia would no longer ask if he had given them a message for her. She knew that he had not.

'He is not as well as he could be,' her mother said.

Sister Julia sat up straighter. 'What—'

'Nothing to worry over,' her mother added. 'We all have our aches and pains, you know. We are none of us getting any younger.' She smiled. 'But how are you, my child? How are you finding your life here at the convent? Have you learnt to be content?'

Sister Julia hardly knew what to say to her. How could she even begin to describe the work she did? And indeed, she must not, as she had been sworn to secrecy from the start. And was she content? No. It was not contentment she felt as she walked to the clinic each day, as she held flannels to the brows of women in labour, as she did what she could to ease their pain. It was not even acceptance — since she still felt keenly all that she had lost. What she had, what she had always had, was understanding. That was all. So she did not answer. She merely bowed her head.

'But never mind all that,' said Paloma in her usual direct fashion. 'For we have come to bring you wonderful news!' She clapped her hands.

She was still such a child. Hands folded in her lap, Sister Julia waited. Gone were the days when she too could shout and jump and run and feel the life blood flowing through her veins. Although perhaps she had never been like that, she thought. She had never, she knew, possessed the vitality of Paloma.

'I am to be married!' Paloma shrieked.

'Quietly, child.' But their mother was smiling.

Sister Julia could not help smiling too. As always, Paloma's happiness was infectious. Life might be still hard for them all but there was still Paloma's joy to brighten the world. 'That is wonderful,' Sister Julia agreed. 'I am happy for you, my dear sister.'

Paloma waggled her left hand in front of her and Sister Julia saw the ring. It was small but pretty. 'Don't you want to know who is the lucky man?' she teased.

'Indeed I do.'

Paloma leaned forwards. 'Mario Vamos,' she whispered.

'Our neighbour?' Sister Julia said it without thinking. It

was a long time since she had watched Mario Vamos as he laughed with the other boys, since she had seen that look in his thoughtful eyes. She considered the news. Cocksure and arrogant, even as a youth, he was just the sort of young man she would have imagined Paloma falling for. And she had clearly fallen. The light of love was shining from her dark eyes.

'Paloma is fortunate,' Mama said quickly. 'She is marrying for love.'

'Oh, yes,' breathed Paloma. 'I love him, Julia, I really do. For so long, I have loved him.'

And Sister Julia was glad for her. For that look Mario Vamos had once shot her was a long way in the past. And perhaps the conditions of post-war Barcelona had made him a better man.

There were more cars and motorbikes now in the streets of the city and it was noisy, even in the early morning before many people were up and about, the air already heavy with exhaust fumes. Down Las Ramblas the bootblacks and lottery sellers were already setting up their stalls and street sweepers were clearing the debris of the day before. The milk bars and cafés were busy too with the early morning trade and the fruit and vegetable stalls were open and ready for business. Sister Julia glanced up at an advertisement hoarding, at a picture of what was described as the wondrous machine of the future – the television. Would people want it? Her family had always loved to listen to the radio. It would be like that, she supposed. But with pictures too. Would there be nothing left to the imagination?

Sister Julia knew now more than ever that her family lived in a different world. Her world was Santa Ana and the clinic – nothing more. But she still loved this city of her birth – though it was changing. As she turned the corner she heard the conductor's bell and saw the blue tram pulling away; some things did not change. Barcelona still carried the scent of the sea in the breeze, but if you looked closely, you could make out the bullet holes in church walls from machine-gun fire. The heart of her city had been damaged. And perhaps it had to change to survive?

Sister Julia passed a newspaper vendor and slowed, straining to catch a glimpse of the headline. She caught the name of Hitler. Ah, yes. It seemed that the other war – the world war – was finally coming to an end. And that wasn't all.

Yesterday she had lingered outside a café on the way back to Santa Ana, listening to a conversation between two men sitting at a table outside. She might be a nun, but she still wanted to know what people were saying about Spain – just as she had back home when she used to listen to her parents from the top of the stairs. Spain was still her country, was it not, even though she had given her life to God?

'Bad times,' the man had said to his companion. 'Have you heard about this latest appointment?' He glanced furtively around.

Sister Julia tried to melt into the very stone wall against

which she was standing. But she needn't have worried – to all intents and purposes she was invisible in her nun's habit and the man seemed satisfied that no one was listening.

Still, his companion dropped his voice. 'Every day, more government posts are going to Catholic politicians,' he muttered. '*Si, si*. And we know what that means.'

What did it mean? Sister Julia frowned. She supposed that it would increase the power of the Church. Or make the government more Catholic. Was that the same thing? She wasn't entirely sure. *Una, grande y libre* – one, great and free. This was Spain's new motto. How did it all fit in?

'We do indeed,' said the first man. He leaned in closer and Sister Julia had to strain to hear the words. 'We are living in a world of National Catholicism now, you know.'

Ah. Sister Julia understood his meaning. She had read a newspaper which a woman had left at the clinic in which General Franco was described as 'the man sent from God, who always appears at the critical moment and defeats the enemy'. Those words – strong words – had stayed in her mind. The newspaper was *Arriba*, admittedly the press of the regime. Nevertheless, Sister Julia had thought. Nevertheless. It was a joining, was it not? The Nationalists and the Catholic Church. Who then was in charge?

Una, grande y libre. There was another motto heard on the streets these days. 'From the Empire towards God.' Had her church become a political animal? And if it had – what repercussions would there be?

At the clinic, two women – both *madras soltoras*, single

mothers – were nearing the end of the first stage of labour and due to be wheeled to the delivery room.

Sister Julia said the morning prayers more hurriedly than usual and Dr Lopez arrived early for his round and took charge, the midwife and nurse also in attendance. Sister Julia stood beside the bed of one of the women, Lenora Sanchez, holding her hand, trying to offer prayer and comfort.

'Help me, Mother, help me, Mother,' moaned Lenora.

'Your mother will not help you now,' said Dr Lopez grimly. 'You must ask your forgiveness of God. You must repent your sins and give up your child to God's good grace.'

So. Sister Julia rubbed the woman's back as the contraction came. Now the pains were not far apart. Lenora had not then agreed to give up her child for adoption. Had she wanted to become pregnant in the first place? Presumably not. Did any single mother? But it happened and once it had happened . . . 'It is a terrible thing,' the doctor had once said to Sister Julia. 'But in some countries it is legal to take a child's life – even before that child is born.' Not so in Spain. Abortion was deeply frowned upon. What then were women such as Lenora to do?

Dr Lopez shook his head in despair. 'I must see how dilated you are. Nurse!'

Lenora's legs were stirruped and spread. Dr Lopez craned over her as he made his examination.

'Be still,' Sister Julia murmured. 'Be still.' The position she was in seemed to be making the pain worse. When had women been forced to lie down to be delivered so that they were denied even the help of gravity? When had inventions like the stirrups been introduced so that the doctors might see more clearly and the woman in labour be able to barely move?

Dr Lopez turned to the midwife. 'She needs to go to the delivery room now. The child is coming.'

Lenora screamed as if to confirm this fact. But she gripped Sister Julia's hand and she could sense the excitement there too, the passion of childbirth.

'Hush now,' said Sister Julia. 'God is with you.'

'We shall see,' snapped the doctor.

But the midwife was busy with the other mother-to-be, a girl giving birth for the first time, a girl not much more than a child herself who wanted nothing more than to be free of it, once her child was born.

'Stay with her,' said Dr Lopez, reassessing the situation. 'Sister Julia will take this woman through.' He seemed to dismiss Lenora with a wave of his hand.

She screamed again.

Sister Julia did not like the look of her. Her eyes were bloodshot and her face was white. 'Can we give her some pain relief, doctor?' she asked. She unstrapped the woman's legs and prepared to move the bed. The junior nurse hurried over to help her.

'It is too late.'

Another scream, long and piercing.

'"In sorrow thou shalt bring forth children",' Dr Lopez bellowed at her. 'Genesis.' He came closer to the bedside and looked down at poor Lenora. '"Because you have eaten the forbidden fruit."' Abruptly, he turned from her.

Dear God. Sister Julia was aware of the doctor's belief that women must suffer pain in childbirth because of Eve's alleged sin, but was it truly God's will for women to experience such pain? The doctor — and others — might ask why women like Lenora had allowed their virtue to be taken away so freely. Had they not worried what might happen to them? What position they might find themselves in? Sister Julia thought of Paloma. She was safe now that she was about to be married. But Sister Julia could see how some men might take advantage of a poor foolish girl who was ready and willing to be flattered. Men who were unscrupulous and who showed women little respect; men who used charm and perhaps even force to get what they wanted.

Lenora hung on to the sides of the bed, her eyes wide and dilated. 'I am a woman,' she panted. 'And I am alive.'

'So we see,' said Dr Lopez.

Lenora cried out again. And they still hadn't got her out of the medical room. The other women were becoming distressed now. But Dr Lopez remained as cool as a mountain stream as he moved away to check on the other mother in labour.

Was he leaving Sister Julia in charge? She tried not to panic. 'Gas and air, doctor?' she asked. He often administered this late on in labour — when he chose to do so.

'No need.' He turned and touched his nose. 'Doctor knows best, Sister Julia,' he said, almost flippantly, apparently oblivious to Lenora's screams. 'She is to be a mother. She will manage.'

An unmarried mother. A mother who wished to keep her child. They moved the bed into the delivery room. Sister Julia rearranged pillows and sheets and tried to make Lenora as comfortable as possible. Were they fallen women, as Dr Lopez said? Or were they simply women who had some life in their bones? She fetched some water in a bowl and dipped in a flannel. But it was true that a single woman pregnant with an unwanted child presented a social problem. And if Sister Julia doubted his methods . . . The clinic and the adoptions encouraged and arranged by Dr Lopez at least provided a solution – for both mother and child. No one could deny that.

It was a difficult birth. Sister Julia did not think she had ever heard a woman make so much noise. Lenora was in pain and she had a streak of wildness in her too. However, Sister Julia comforted her as best she could and Dr Lopez delivered the child. There did not seem to be any complications.

Dr Lopez handed the baby to Sister Julia while he delivered the afterbirth and checked that all was well with the mother.

'A healthy boy,' Sister Julia told Lenora as she began to wash him. His cheeks were already flushed with colour, there was a dark fluff of hair on his little head. He was a darling.

'Indeed.' The doctor looked up from his examination. 'But I think I must be the judge of that, thank you, Sister.'

'Of course, doctor.' She bowed her head.

When he had finished, Dr Lopez nodded at Sister Julia. 'As

soon as you like, Sister,' he said. And then he left the delivery room.

There was a fixed procedure. After a baby was born to a mother, Sister Julia must take the infant to the doctor as quickly as possible, so that a proper examination could be carried out.

'Let me hold him,' begged Lenora. She was quieter now and calm. She had that look of peace about her that women wore after childbirth. When Sister Julia saw that, she had to remind herself: this experience was not for her. She would never know what Lenora had known – that passion and pain, that losing of control, that marvellous and momentous feeling of giving birth.

Sister Julia hesitated. Most of the women wanted to hold their newborns to their breast; they wanted to keep them by their bedside and watch over them. But she was not supposed to allow that to happen. 'Just for a moment,' she said. 'Then I must take him through to be examined by the doctor.'

'Phoof,' said Lenora. 'You can see he is as healthy as a young horse. What does he need to be examined for?' She held him close. 'My love,' she murmured. And kissed him softly on his forehead.

Sister Julia was moved by the simple gesture of affection. But, 'It is procedure.' And she took him back. 'However would it be,' Dr Lopez had said, 'if there was a health problem with one of these children? How would it look if a baby died before I had even had a chance to examine it? What sort of a reputation would my clinic have in this case?'

And if he were to lose his reputation – Sister Julia did not need to be reminded of this – then he could no longer help these children. He could no longer do what he always referred to as 'God's work'.

'I will bring him back soon,' Sister Julia promised.

But she did not. She took the baby down to the doctor and then was sent to help in the medical room. It was some hours later when she returned to the delivery room only to see Dr Lopez already standing at the door.

'Alas, Sister,' he said. He was holding his crucifix in his hand.

Alas? Sister Julia felt the dread of foreboding in the pit of her stomach. Alas? She followed him inside.

Lenora's eyes flickered open. She looked at them both and Sister Julia saw the same look of dread on her face that she herself was feeling. She put a hand on the bed rail to steady herself. Surely not?

'Where is my baby?' Lenora looked from left to right, her eyes growing wild with fear. 'What have you done with him?'

'I am very sorry.' The doctor's voice was heavy with grief. 'But your child has been taken by God.'

Taken by God? But the child had seemed so healthy. Sister Julia crossed herself.

'No!' Lenora's wail was heart-rending. It was a cry of pure grief.

Sister Julia hurried to her side.

Dr Lopez nodded. 'There was nothing I could do,' he said.

'But rest assured that your son has passed on from this earth to heaven.'

'It cannot be! It is not true!' Lenora tried to grasp the doctor's arm. 'Give him to me. Give me my boy!'

'Hush, Lenora.' But Sister Julia did not know what to say.

'He has gone to God, I tell you.' The doctor held the crucifix in front of him. 'Be happy for him. For he has been saved.'

Lenora burst into a fit of uncontrolled weeping. Sister Julia put an arm around her and tried to offer some words of comfort. But in truth the words stuck in her throat. Lenora was inconsolable.

Dr Lopez was about to leave the room when she shrieked at him. 'Let me see him. Let me see my baby!'

Of course she must see the child. Sister Julia moved towards the door – about to go and fetch him, for he must surely still be in the examination room downstairs – when she heard the doctor's reply.

'I cannot give permission for you to see your child,' he said. 'You are in no fit state. It is not healthy. It is not good for you.'

Sister Julia dithered. This was true enough. It had not occurred to her, but she had to admit that hysteria would do no one any good. There were other women to think of and besides, this poor woman could lose her sense of reason, being confronted by such a trauma.

'I must see him!' Lenora insisted. But she sounded less forceful now. Grief had overtaken her. She was crumpled, beaten.

And Sister Julia thought for a moment of her mother's expression when she had left her at Santa Ana Convent that first time. She too had been defeated.

'What was wrong with him?' Lenora whispered. 'How did he die?'

'An infection in his heart,' Dr Lopez replied immediately. 'It was very sudden. A malfunction. No one could have known.'

No one could have known. Life and death. These things happened. Sister Julia had seen more than her fair share. Mothers were often poor and undernourished; they were unhealthy and had perhaps passed dangerous germs on to their unborn infants.

But poor Lenora was suddenly beside herself. 'No, no . . . ' she cried. She tried to drag herself out of the bed. She was becoming hysterical.

The doctor's expression changed abruptly from sympathy to irritation. 'Sister Julia,' he snapped, 'a sedative, if you please.'

Sister Julia scurried off for the sedative. She could not believe it. The child had seemed so healthy. And yet . . . She couldn't rid herself of that feeling of dread.

'Children are born without the natural defences of you and I, Sister Julia,' Dr Lopez said sadly as he accompanied her out of the delivery room. 'Sometimes we cannot protect them and we cannot save them. It is God's will to take them at once. We must accept this.'

Sister Julia bowed her head. She knew that he would have done everything he could to save the child. He was upset himself – though he hid his emotions well. 'And she will see her child later when she is calm?' she asked him.

'I think not.' Dr Lopez was brusque. 'What good will it do to brood on the past? She must look to the future now.'

Sister Julia wrung her hands. Lenora needed to see her son – she knew that. She needed some sense of closure – or she could be traumatised for who knew how long. Sister Julia remembered that look of peace on her face after her child had been born. All those long months of the baby growing in her belly, all that pain experienced in order to deliver him into the world. And now this.

'I am sure that if I could talk gently to her for a moment, she would be able to cope with the sight of her baby,' she said. 'It might help her contemplate her future without him.'

'Her dead baby, Sister,' the doctor reminded her.

'But surely, doctor . . . ' Sister Julia knew she was becoming too emotionally involved but how could she help it? Yes, Lenora's child was dead and it would be upsetting for her to see him. But if she did not see him . . . 'I feel that she needs—'

'Oh you do, do you, Sister?' Dr Lopez opened the door of his consulting room and brusquely ushered her inside. 'You think you can vouch for her emotions, eh? You feel that you know exactly what this woman requires?'

Sister Julia summoned all her strength of will – which was hard, because she had been cultivating acceptance and faith for so many years now through prayer at the convent of Santa Ana. 'I think I do, doctor,' she said.

'So you know better than I what is good for this woman, do you, Sister?' His voice was dangerously calm. 'You, a woman who is part cloistered, who knows nothing of the real world outside this clinic and her own convent? You think you know better than I?'

'Oh, no, doctor, forgive me.' Sister Julia bowed her head. She had not been saying that at all. How could she possibly know better than he? She had simply wanted to convey her own thoughts, her feelings . . .

'Be still.' He put a hand on her shoulder. 'And listen to one who knows.'

His hand felt heavy as lead. The weight was one which Sister Julia could hardly bear.

'It would be too sad for her,' he said. 'She is in a dangerously vulnerable state following childbirth. Trust me, Sister Julia, it is better this way.'

Later that day, Sister Julia had occasion to go into the doctor's consulting rooms to collect a report that he had left there. She saw the death certificate for Lenora's child and had to stifle a sob. The poor woman was still sedated but soon she would be discharged into the outside world. And did she have anyone to support her, to comfort her? Probably not. It was a heartbreaking situation.

There was a birth certificate on his desk too – that of a boy who had been born during the night when Sister Julia had

208

not been at the clinic. He was to be adopted. She glanced at it with interest. Frederico Carlo Batista – the surname of the couple who were to adopt him; she herself had shown them into the clinic earlier today when they had joyfully collected their swaddled and wrapped baby boy and without further ado disappeared.

No mention of course of the little one's birth mother's name. Even Sister Julia did not know it, since apparently the mother had been discharged even before Sister Julia had arrived this morning. And it was not on the birth certificate since General Franco had seen to it that the names of the adoptive parents were the only names ever recorded.

'It is a new law. A good law,' Dr Lopez had told her when she questioned it. 'It ensures that our young people will receive the right ideological upbringing. They will be brought up to love God; they will be brought up in the right way, the only way a Spaniard should be brought up, in His name.'

Sister Julia understood the reasons why. But this new law meant that every adopted child would remain ignorant of their roots. That there would be no record of their biological parents, nor even that they had been adopted at all. She could not argue with the doctor's logic. But did this not flout another fundamental right? The right to know your own origins? And wasn't such deceit likely to lay the foundations in their damaged country for more and still more deceit?

Now, Sister Julia memorised the names of the child and of the adopted parents. She checked the discharges book and found the name of the mother who had left this morning. She memorised all the names.

On the way back to Santa Ana late that afternoon, Sister Julia purchased a plain hardback notebook from a stationery shop in Las Ramblas. She took it back to the convent, went to her own simple whitewashed room and she wrote down the date and all the names. And then she added another. Lenora Sanchez. The name of the woman whose son had died.

She could not even say why she had done it. She kept it secret and she locked the book in a drawer. But she would continue to do it, she decided. She would stay at the clinic and try to help these women. And she would write down all the names.

CHAPTER 18

Dorset, April 1978

Vivien drove cautiously back home from Pride Bay, glancing in her mirror regularly to check that the baby, wrapped in her blanket and tucked into the basket, was still secure on the back seat. What else could she do? Laura obviously transported her in much the same way – the poor mite didn't appear to even have a cot to sleep in. Vivien sighed and gripped the steering wheel of her Morris 1000 a little more tightly. And just for a second she allowed herself to think – didn't Laura realise how lucky she was? Probably not.

Tom was home – she spotted his bicycle leaned against the side wall as she parked in the driveway of their two-bed semi. Goodness knows what he'd have to say. But she was only babysitting, wasn't she? People did that all the time to help out. And Laura wasn't to know what they'd been through, how desperately Vivien longed for a child.

Ruby didn't stir as Vivien walked up the garden path. She brushed the soft cheek with her little finger, felt an echoing pulse of warmth inside her own body.

No, Vivien.

The house next door looked mournful as ever. It hadn't

had the windows or doors looked at in years and the cream paint was cracked and flaking, revealing the bare wood underneath. What would Pearl have made of this little one – her granddaughter? Vivien smiled. Wouldn't she have loved her?

Tom was in the kitchen eating a sandwich – cheese and tomato, Vivien could tell by the debris on the kitchen table. She lifted Ruby gently from the basket.

'Hello, love,' he said, glancing up, back to his paper, then back at her as he registered what she was holding. 'What's this?' he said.

'A baby.'

'I can see that.' He stared at her. 'Whose baby? Where did it come from?'

What did he think? That she'd abducted her from somewhere? For heaven's sake . . . Vivien sat down with Ruby snuggled in the crook of her arm. She shouldn't just be kept in a basket – she needed human warmth and affection. 'Laura's baby,' she said. 'She asked me to look after her for a bit.'

Tom rustled the folds of his newspaper in a way she recognised. 'And you thought that was a good idea, did you?' His voice was gruff.

Vivien looked down at the baby. 'It was hard to say no to her,' she said. 'What with Pearl and everything.'

Tom got to his feet. 'You take care, love, that's all,' he said.

'Course I will.' Vivien smiled.

'I'll put the kettle on then.' As he passed, Tom bent down to peer at the little one.

Vivien saw his eyes soften. For a moment she could see how he would be, how they could be. Something tightened in her chest. 'I'll put her down and make the tea when the kettle boils,' she said. But already Tom's eyes had glazed over. He'd closed down. She saw it.

'Do you think she's finding it hard to cope with her?' he asked.

'Probably.' Vivien recalled what Laura had said about the crying. Though Ruby seemed such a good baby. She just wanted feeding and changing regularly, that was all. And she didn't want to be living in a camper van for ever.

The kettle boiled, Tom gave her a look and Vivien settled the baby – not back in the basket, but in the soft and deep old armchair in the corner. She tucked in the blanket, put a bolster in place to keep her safe and watched her for a moment. It hurt a bit to let go of her. She was so warm and now the place where she had nestled in close to Vivien's body felt empty and cold. Vivien brushed at the deserted space with her hand, as if she could whisk that elusive baby presence away. The baby half-smiled in her sleep. Dreaming rainbows.

Laura didn't come to collect her until almost midnight. By that time even Vivien was frantic. She'd used the last bit of milk formula too. What was she supposed to do the next time she woke up? She wasn't equipped for a baby. Laura hadn't left Ruby's night things or any more spare nappies or anything. What was she thinking of – leaving her here for so long?

Tom had already gone to bed with a sigh and a 'I knew no good would come of it'. But Vivien sat up waiting, watching Ruby and worrying. What if something had happened to Laura?

When the knock on the door came it roused Vivien from a half-doze. She was in the rocking chair in the kitchen, Ruby still in the deep lap of the armchair.

She got to her feet and let Laura in. 'I didn't know you'd be this long,' she said.

Laura looked back at her, vague, not quite with it. 'Was she any hassle?' she asked.

'No, she was fine,' Vivien said. She went over to the armchair and lifted Ruby gently out and into the basket. She felt a dip of desolation in her belly. 'Bye, Ruby,' she whispered.

Laura was watching her. 'You like her.'

'Of course I do.' Vivien handed her the basket. 'Who wouldn't?'

'Plenty wouldn't.' Laura looked down at her daughter, a mixture of love and resentment on her face.

Vivien reminded herself of the facts. Of Laura's mother's death, of the lifestyle she was living, of the fact that Ruby's father had left Laura. And that Laura was still just a girl herself.

'She's lovely,' Vivien said. Be grateful, she thought. Be very grateful. Because you have no idea.

'Not when she's crying all night, she isn't.' She sounded so dispassionate. And so casual in the way she turned around and opened the door, swinging the basket as if Ruby were nothing more than the week's groceries. Vivien wanted to snatch her back there and then.

'I'll look after her again,' Vivien said as Laura stepped outside. She tried to sound more casual than she felt. 'Any time you want.'

'Will you?' Laura brightened. She eyed her with more interest. 'That's great. Tomorrow afternoon, maybe?'

'Oh.' Once again, Vivien hadn't expected it to be quite so soon. Did Laura really know what it meant to be a mother? Did she understand about responsibility of care? 'Well, yes. That's fine,' she heard herself saying. 'As long as it's after three.' Which was when she finished work. Vivien still worked part-time at the post office, though she finished early so that she could keep up with her art – some of which she'd already got into a few of the local galleries.

'Great.' Laura gave her a cheery wave. 'Thanks, Vivien.'

The following day, the van was already parked outside Vivien and Tom's when Vivien got back from work. She hadn't told Tom about this afternoon – she knew he wouldn't like it, and she knew the reasons too.

'We won't be so late tonight,' Laura said as she handed over the basket. The love beads she was wearing swung from her neck.

Vivien looked down at Ruby. 'That's all right.' She'd popped to the chemist's earlier. She had formula, a spare bottle, some nappies, a changing mat and even a little pink sleep suit – though she wouldn't tell Tom about that either. She was only helping out, wasn't she? Laura was Pearl's daughter. No harm done.

There was no pushchair or pram so Vivien couldn't take her out for a walk to the park as she'd like to. Instead, she set up a garden chair outside and laid Ruby on that, surrounded by cushions so that she couldn't possibly roll over or fall off. It was good for babies to get some fresh air. And while Ruby was sleeping, Vivien did the gardening, looking over at her every now and then, pausing in her weeding or digging to smile at her, or check she was all right. She thought about doing some painting but decided not. She didn't want too much of her attention to be taken away from the baby.

When she woke up for her next feed, although Vivien had the bottle ready to be warmed up for her, little Ruby didn't start her screaming like she had before. Instead, she cooed and chuckled and waved her tiny fists around. She was enjoying the garden, Vivien realised. She could see the leaves moving in the breeze, hear the rustle and the sounds of the birds. The fact that she loved it made Vivien feel good too.

'What, again?' Tom said when he came back from work to find Vivien talking to Ruby as she did the ironing.

'I don't mind,' Vivien said. 'It's nothing.' Though it wasn't nothing. Of course it wasn't nothing.

Tom shot her a warning glance. 'Don't get too used to it, love,' he said. 'Don't get too fond of her.'

'Stop worrying. Look.' And Vivien made Tom tickle Ruby's palm with his little finger, until she grabbed and squeezed.

He laughed. Couldn't believe how strong she was, he said.

This was how it would be, Vivien thought again. This was how it would be.

Tom looked at her. 'Someone needs to worry though, love,' he said. 'I'm telling you. I know you want to. But don't offer to look after her too often.'

'I won't.' She was such a sweet baby – but quite a character, bless her, with that gummy smile and those lovely blue eyes. And it was so nice to just hold her and even for a moment to pretend . . .

She'd take Ruby to the post office if she had to. She'd help Laura out – whenever she needed it. Because of Pearl, because she felt sorry for her. And because . . .

Tom didn't mind having the baby, Vivien knew that. He liked having her. But she knew why he was worrying. She'd come to terms with their childlessness – or at least he imagined she had. But Ruby was bringing it all back. How would Vivien feel when Laura left – as she would do one day in the not too distant future? How would she feel when Ruby was no longer around? And he was right to worry. She looked down at the sleeping baby. Because already, Vivien could hardly bear to think about it.

A few weeks later, Vivien woke up in the middle of the night to hear a hammering on the back door. 'Oh, my Lord.' She sat up. It was a noise loud enough to wake the dead.

But not Tom. 'Tom.' Gently, she shook his shoulder and tried to rouse him. But he was out for the count. He'd been working so hard.

Vivien checked the clock. It was actually only just past midnight. But the rain was lashing down like nobody's business and the wind was blowing a gale. A summer storm, it must be. Had she imagined the knocking on the door?

No. It came again. Who on earth . . . ? Vivien glanced again at Tom. Still snoring like a wild boar. She got up and grabbed her dressing gown. Peered out of the window into the rain and the darkness to see who it might be. But she couldn't make out a thing. And all she could hear was the pounding of the rain on the lean-to, the dripping from the roof and that wind howling. Was she in the middle of some kind of horror film?

Then a flash of lightning lit the sky and that's when she saw it parked outside. The VW camper van.

Ruby. *Oh, my heavens.* She ran downstairs in her nightie. Ghastly scenarios fast-forwarded through her brain. She pushed them away again, dashed into the kitchen, switched on the light, unbolted the door and pulled it open. The breath was heaving inside her chest. Ruby . . .

Laura stood there like a ghost. She had on a long dress the colour of indigo, which was wet through and clinging to her slender frame. Over this she had flung a black crocheted shawl – which gave her about as much protection as a headscarf on a building site, Vivien reckoned. Her long hair was bedraggled, rain dripped down her face like teardrops. Her blue eyes were wide. 'Vivien,' she said. She just stood there in the rain. She sounded scared.

'What is it, Laura? What's happened?' There was a growl

of thunder. 'Is it Ruby?' But Vivien had seen already that Laura was holding the basket, cradled in her arms this time, not like the way she had held it before. And she was holding something else tucked under one elbow – what looked like a shoebox.

Vivien pulled her inside out of the rain, helping to support the basket as she did so. She felt a jolt of fear and glanced down. 'Is she all right?' Even to her own ears, her voice sounded harsh.

Laura took just a step inside. She thrust the basket at Vivien. 'Take her,' she said. 'Here. Just take her.'

Automatically, Vivien took the basket. She glanced down again, reassured by the sight of the baby's sleeping face. Though how she could sleep through this racket . . . 'What's happened?' she asked again. 'Is it Julio? Is it—'

But already Laura was stumbling back through the door, crying now. 'Look after her for me,' she cried.

'But, how long . . . ?'

She had gone. She was running in the pouring rain – down the path at the side of the house, splashing through the puddles. She pulled open the passenger door and jumped into the van.

'Laura?' Vivien stared after her. 'Laura?'

The second she was inside, the van's engine roared into life. And just as another spear of lightning illuminated the night, the psychedelic VW camper van pulled away and was gone. Just like that.

Well. Vivien glanced at Ruby. She seemed perfectly fine,

fast asleep still, blissfully unaware of the drama. Vivien rebolted the door and tiptoed back up the stairs, holding the basket carefully in front of her. In their room she took the wide drawer from the chest and emptied all their clothes out of it. She took a single sheet from the airing cupboard and methodically made up a little bed in the drawer. And all the time she was thinking. What had happened? What did Laura mean – look after her for me? When, exactly, was she intending to come back?

She lay awake for what seemed like hours listening to the baby's breathing. And just as soon as she fell asleep – or so it seemed – she woke to the sound of Ruby's whimpering. She got up, scooped her out of the drawer and took her downstairs to feed her. She didn't want to wake Tom – not yet. Time enough for that.

It was too late though. Ten minutes later, as she sat in the rocking chair giving Ruby her milk, he was downstairs, standing in the doorway rubbing his eyes. He took in the sight of her and the baby. 'What's going on?' he asked.

Vivien told him what had happened. 'There was nothing I could do, Tom,' she said. 'She just disappeared into the night.'

'And what's this?' Tom had picked up the shoebox from the kitchen table where Laura must have left it. What with everything else happening, Vivien hadn't even noticed.

'I don't know,' she said.

Slowly, Tom lifted the lid. 'Photos,' he said. He held them up to show her. 'A little hat.'

Ruby's bonnet. Vivien nodded. 'Just some of her stuff then,' she said.

'And this.' He held up a small piece of plastic. Vivien had seen them, didn't know what they were called. You used them to play a guitar though, she knew that much. She thought of the guitar she'd seen in the camper van. Did Laura play? She guessed so.

'And . . . ' Tom held up a string of tiny beads. Love beads. Vivien had seen Laura wearing them more than once. 'So why would she have left this stuff, for Christ's sake?' Tom sounded angry now.

'Sssh.' Ruby looked so peaceful; Vivien didn't want her to be disturbed.

'It looks like she's not reckoning on coming back this time,' Tom said. And with a dark look at her – as if it were her fault – he left the room and she heard him stomping back upstairs.

Not reckoning on coming back this time. Vivien let the words sink in. What did that mean for her? What did that mean for her – and Ruby?

CHAPTER 19

'It was fortunate,' Frances said, 'that your mother – Vivien, that is – was around when Laura came back to Pride Bay. If not for her . . . ' She let the words hang.

It certainly sounded that way. 'Do you think Julio put Laura under pressure?' Ruby asked. 'Maybe he gave her an ultimatum. I want you but I'm not prepared to look after some other man's baby – that sort of thing.' Perhaps she was conveniently shifting the blame, but Ruby hated the idea of Laura just dumping her on Vivien whenever she felt she couldn't cope. What sort of a mother did that? Even when she'd been through what Laura had been through.

What sort of a mother . . . What would have happened – if Laura hadn't come back to England? If Ruby had been brought up in Spain as her daughter? She simply couldn't imagine. How different would she be?

'Very probably.' Frances shrugged. 'You know what young men are like. A baby can cramp your style somewhat.'

Ruby thought of James. Would Frances class him as a young man? Probably not – he was in his late thirties. And yet he had never shown the slightest intention of settling down, wanting a wife, a baby, any of that. A baby would cer-

222

tainly have cramped his style. He was far too busy with his London life and with his clients. As for Julio – he was probably only in his mid-twenties at the time. He was young and into freedom and a lifestyle that didn't include responsibility. He probably just couldn't wait to get the VW van back to sunnier climes. To roll his next spliff and have his next swim. And who could blame him?

'At least Vivien wanted me,' Ruby said. It sounded a bit pathetic but it was the most important thing, wasn't it? To be wanted, to be loved.

'Oh, she wanted you.' Frances smiled. 'She wanted you more than you'll ever know. You were a gift to Vivien from some maternal goddess on high.' She laughed. 'You should have seen her. She was like a cat with the cream when she was looking after you.'

'But why didn't they tell me who I was and where I'd come from?' Ruby asked again. That was what she still couldn't get. 'How come it was all such a big secret?'

'They were protecting you,' Frances said. 'At least that's what they thought.'

Because her birth mother hadn't? That seemed to be the subtext. But things were never black and white. She'd learnt that through her work when she was investigating a subject for a feature. There were always shades of grey. You had to ask around – get other points of view. Not just hear one side of the story.

Ruby leaned forwards across the table. 'Doesn't everyone have the right to the truth, Frances?'

'Perhaps.' Frances had finished her meal and now laid her knife and fork on the plate in front of her. 'Although it also depends on how many people get hurt along the way, doesn't it, my dear?'

Did it? Ruby wasn't so sure. Deceit usually led to distrust. Honesty might hurt but at least you could move forward and make your decisions in life with a clear sense of the facts.

After a while, Frances ordered coffee for them both.

'I appreciate you coming here tonight and telling me the story.' Ruby stirred her coffee and tasted it. It was strong and bitter.

'Vivien talked to me a few months before the accident,' Frances said thoughtfully. 'It was on her mind. I'd come down for the weekend and we met up for coffee.'

'What did she say?' Ruby asked.

'We talked about you. She said that if anything happened to her and that if you were ever to ask, I should tell you everything you needed to know.' Frances sighed. '"What makes you think I'll still be around when you're not?" I asked her. "You might be, Fran," she said. "Who knows what's round the corner for any of us?"'

Ruby nodded. That was true enough.

'But to be honest, Ruby,' Frances continued, 'I always believed she'd tell you herself one day. Whether Tom wanted her to or not.'

Perhaps she didn't have the chance. Perhaps she had left it until it was just too late.

Ruby's eyes filled. 'I still have some more questions,' she whispered.

'Ask away. I'll help if I can.'

'What happened next?' Vivien had looked after her friend's daughter's baby and then suddenly found herself wholly responsible for the child's welfare. How had she felt? How had she justified bringing up that child as her own? There was so much more that Ruby still needed to understand.

CHAPTER 20

Dorset, May 1978

After two weeks, Vivien and Ruby had got into a routine. Truth be told, with a complicit look, they slipped into it from the first. But now it felt established and real.

To start with, Vivien didn't take time off work. She took Ruby in with her to the post office and spent her breaks feeding and changing her. Fortunately, Penny had been longing for a grandchild for the past few years and was delighted to have a little one around. Vivien told her Ruby was the daughter of a close friend; that the mother wasn't at all well and that they were looking after her for a bit. 'You're meant to be a mother, love,' Penny had said, giving her a sympathetic glance. 'And she's no trouble at all, bless her.'

Frances was the only one who knew the truth – Vivien had told her one afternoon when she popped by unexpectedly and found Vivien bathing the baby – the same baby she'd been feeding in the old chapel. 'Oh, Viv,' she'd said. 'Take care.' It was almost as if she'd known how it would be.

When Tom didn't have work, he chipped in and did his bit and at weekends they did everything together. Like a real family, something whispered to Vivien – or she whispered it to herself, maybe. Like a real family . . .

At first, she lived in a state of semi-permanent fear, half waiting for Laura's return. Sometimes when she was feeding her, she held Ruby almost too tight, as if anticipating that moment when she'd be gone. How would she cope? She would have to smile as she handed Ruby back to her birth mother and pretend that her heart wasn't breaking.

After a while though, Vivien began to relax. She knew what she had seen. Laura was young, irresponsible, in love with a boy who wasn't interested in the daughter she'd had with another man. Vivien must have been like the answer to a prayer. A woman without children and yet desperate for them. A woman whose very yearning must have shone out of her eyes like a beacon.

And yet. Every so often Vivien would get the shoebox out of the wardrobe where she'd tucked it out of sight, so it wasn't a constant reminder. She looked at the plectrum and the crocheted baby's bonnet. So tiny . . . Even now, it no longer fitted Ruby's blonde head. She looked at the photographs – Laura holding Ruby in her arms, happy and unaware at this point that her mother had died; Laura with Julio, Laura in the VW van. And she looked at the love beads. They told her all she wanted to know. Laura had loved little Ruby – in her own way. She might have given her up, given her the chance of a different kind of life – given herself the chance of a different life too. But Laura had certainly loved her.

Which meant – didn't it? – that one day, Laura might come back.

Vivien closed her eyes and rocked the baby. Ruby was just out of her bath and smelt of talcum powder. Vivien inhaled deeply. The scent of a baby's skin . . . Was it so wrong of her to want Laura to stay with Julio on some foreign beach somewhere? She supposed that it was, because a baby needed her mother, didn't she? The maternal desire that flooded through Vivien's veins when she held Ruby was no excuse. Neither were the years of frustration and longing, nor the overwhelming love she felt for the child. No. There was no excuse. Apparently she wanted Ruby on any terms she could get. She really was as heartless as she feared.

Tom wasn't happy – Vivien could see that. It wasn't Ruby, nor the fact that Vivien had given up her job – which was only temporary; Penny said she'd have her back any time. It was more of a moral issue. 'We should try to find Laura,' he said. 'It isn't right, this, and it isn't fair. The child's not ours.'

Vivien didn't need reminding. But she didn't want anything to change. 'Laura doesn't want her,' she said, praying that if he did try to find Laura, he wouldn't succeed. 'She won't look after her properly – she doesn't want to.' Vivien didn't care if it was emotional blackmail. She'd do what she had to do.

'Even so,' said Tom. But when Ruby woke up, gurgled and looked up at him with blue forget-me-not eyes – well, the poor man didn't have a hope. He was smitten.

★

The days slipped by. A few folk – neighbours mostly – asked where Ruby had suddenly sprung from, and Vivien said she was fostering. No one appeared to have seen Laura since her return to Dorset, so no one knew she'd even had a baby. Only Frances knew the whole story.

Ruby was growing. Vivien stashed money from the housekeeping and bought her a few new clothes. She'd started her on solids too. The baby stayed awake for longer during the day, and had taken to staring up at Vivien in a way that should have been unnerving, but wasn't. Vivien loved it. She began teething and Vivien rubbed extract of oil of cloves on her flaming gums. She tried not to enjoy this new life of hers too much, just in case it was suddenly snatched away. But the truth was that having Ruby had transformed her world.

One evening, Vivien had sung the little one a lullaby before putting her down for the night and she looked up to see Tom standing in the doorway of what had become Ruby's room – at least in her mind. There was a look on his face that Vivien understood only too well.

'What, Tom?'

'We've no official rights, love,' he said. 'It's not just Laura. If the truth ever comes out, Ruby might be taken into care.'

Vivien shuddered. She couldn't face that. Along with Ruby, she had been handed a responsibility. Pearl's grandchild was not going to be given over to some stranger for adoption. It didn't bear thinking about.

'We'll have to move,' she told Tom. 'Out of West Dorset

and away from here. We can't risk losing her – not now.' Fear was making her desperate.

Tom stuck his heels in – as only Tom could. He had his business to think about, he said. He'd spent years building up a client list; he couldn't just chuck it all away. Did Vivien want him to work for some company fixing other people's windows and skirting boards? And this was his childhood home – the place he loved. He wouldn't give it up – not even for Ruby. 'She's not ours, love,' he told Vivien. 'And that's the truth of it.'

That might be the truth of it but Vivien did persuade him to a compromise. They moved to East Devon – only twenty miles away but at least in another county and he could keep all his clients and work-base. The only person Vivien kept in touch with from Pride Bay was Frances.

'Is there anything else we can do?' Vivien asked him. To be safe, she meant.

Tom balled his fists. 'We could make her ours.'

'But how?' They were getting ready for bed, Ruby safe in her cot next door.

Tom took her by shoulders. 'We could adopt her ourselves, Viv,' he said.

Adopt her themselves? It sounded like the perfect solution. But wouldn't they have to ask Laura's permission? And would they be able to find her? Vivien wasn't sure she wanted to risk it.

'And if we can't do that . . . ' His expression changed. 'Then we'll have to hand Ruby over to the authorities eventually. We can't just go on pretending she's ours.'

Vivien stared at him. Like hell, she thought.

'Viv?' Tom was giving her a strange look.

But she couldn't even speak to him. In that second she almost hated the man she loved. It scared her what else was she was thinking. *Over my dead body.*

Vivien never knew how hard Tom had tried to find Laura because she didn't ask him. Something had changed between them that night. For the first time Vivien had been willing to put Tom second in her life and he had seen it. They didn't acknowledge it, but there was no more talk of handing Ruby over to any authorities. It wasn't an option. End of story.

As Ruby grew into a sturdy, blonde-haired toddler, Vivien often thought about Laura. Where was she? What was she doing? And she worried. Had they done the right thing? They had Ruby. But would there – one day, when Vivien was least expecting it – be a price to pay?

Tom – ever practical – was the first one to realise that without a birth certificate for Ruby, there would be problems. She would have no official name or identity, no nationality even. And how could they get a copy when they didn't even know exactly when or where she'd been born?

'We'll have to get one made for her,' Tom said, as if he was talking about one of his commissions – an oak table, perhaps, or a mahogany chest of drawers. 'Otherwise how will she be able to get a passport or a driving licence? She won't exist – not legally.'

They looked at one another in horror. They really hadn't thought this through.

'But how can we? That's not how it works, is it?' Vivien could hear her voice rising in panic. How could people like them find out how to get a birth certificate made? And it would be illegal, of course. She shivered. But what else could they do? Here in Devon, they had passed Ruby off as their own child. She seemed like their own child. Some days Vivien could hardly believe that she wasn't.

'There must be a way. Forgery's an ancient art, isn't it?' But Tom looked as helpless as she felt.

Forgery?

Tom put his arm around her shoulders. 'Don't you worry, my lovely,' he said. 'We'll get it sorted. It'll all work out – you'll see.'

But it was Vivien who grappled with the problem late at night when she couldn't sleep. How could they get a birth certificate? Vivien remembered Laura saying that she'd never even registered her daughter's birth. Which meant, didn't it . . . ? *That no one could prove Laura was her mother?* Vivien didn't want to think it, but it just slipped into her head. It was a way of making everything safe.

And that's when she talked to Frances. She took Ruby back to Pride Bay one afternoon and had tea with Frances in the café on the beach.

'What happens,' she asked her, 'if someone doesn't register a baby's birth straight away?' Frances was a nurse – she'd know about these things. There must be plenty of mothers who didn't get round to it – especially those, like Laura, on the fringes of society.

'You can get a delayed registration.' Frances explained how it worked. 'But if you have a hospital birth it'll be registered automatically.' She caught Vivien's eye and Vivien saw her twig.

'You're thinking of Ruby.'

Vivien pulled the buggy closer. 'Yes, I am thinking of Ruby. We need to get her a birth certificate, Frances. And if we tell the authorities what really happened . . . '

Frances nodded. She didn't have to say it. 'What about trying to trace Laura?' she asked. 'She wouldn't object, surely?'

'We've tried.' Vivien was certain they could have done more. But at what risk?

Frances stared at her. 'You want to apply for a delayed registration and say that you're her birth mother.'

Vivien watched the waves beat on to Chesil Beach. Olive grey and inexorable. Some things never changed. 'It seems the best thing,' she said.

'For you?' Frances asked. 'Or for Ruby?'

Vivien sighed and met her friend's steady gaze. 'For us both,' she said.

She had worried that it wouldn't be possible, but in fact it proved surprisingly easy. The authorities wanted children's births to be registered, they disliked loose ends, and Vivien's story of a home birth and post-natal depression, of not getting round to registering the birth and even of not consulting a doctor when she was pregnant, was apparently not as unusual as she'd thought it would be when concocting it. She even managed to persuade Frances to be a witness.

'I don't like it, Vivien,' Frances said. 'But I'm doing it for you and Ruby. Because you're a good mother and because she needs what you can give her. That's all.'

'Will we tell her, love?' Tom asked Vivien when the application was in and they were just waiting for it to be displayed publicly and then approved. 'Will we ever tell Ruby what we've done?'

'Why not?' When she was older, she would understand. Her birth mother had more or less abandoned her. All they had done was stepped in.

But Tom shook his head. 'I don't reckon I can,' he said.

Vivien couldn't really believe that they were doing it either – although by now she thought that maybe she would do anything to keep this child. She had never – to her knowledge – stepped outside the law before. She and Tom, well, they just weren't like that. But what choice did they have?

'Oh, Tom . . . ' For a second, Vivien allowed her head to rest on his shoulder. Was it really going to happen? Could she let herself believe that now Ruby would be theirs?

She wanted to, but the very last image that danced behind her eyelids that night as she tried to sleep was of Laura. And Laura's voice as she said those final words. 'Look after her for me.'

★

Once it was done – once Vivien held the crisp birth certificate in her hands, seeing their names written in as Ruby's parents – Vivien forced herself to put it out of her mind. They hadn't done anything so very bad. It was illegal, yes, but who would ever be able to prove they had lied? In the end it made little difference. Ruby had belonged to them for a long time. This piece of paper just made it a bit more official. It would protect them and protect Ruby, that was all.

But as Vivien put it away in a drawer, her fingers lingered on the brass handle. 'Forgive me,' she whispered. Whether she was saying it to Ruby, to Laura or to Pearl, she didn't know. 'Forgive me.'

Tom persuaded Vivien to move house again back to a place just outside Pride Bay. He missed the golden cliffs, he told her. They had been away for long enough. He wanted his daughter to grow up close to Pride Bay as he had; it was important to him. And they were out of danger now. Laura would never come back – why should she? Even Penny had given up the post office and general stores and moved away to Norfolk. Nobody – except Frances – would ever know what they had done or that Ruby wasn't truly theirs. Frances had been sworn to secrecy. They were safe.

CHAPTER 21

Barcelona, 1951

Even while Sister Julia was aware of the changes taking place in her mother country, even while Spain slowly recovered from the damage and desecration of the Civil War and its bloody aftermath, she was aware that her monastic community, the community of Santa Ana, functioned much as it had five hundred years ago. They still lived in a medieval building, they still ate simply, they still spent most of their time praying to God. Prayer, psalms, catechism, Holy Communion – this was what made up the everyday life for her sisters. All their pursuits were ordered; routine was the structure of their days. A bell signalled the end of each activity – be it prayer or work or repast. And the day always finished with night prayers. It was a ritual that Sister Julia found comforting.

Since the nuns at the convent did not indulge in idle talk, they did not discuss how they had come to be where they were. Sister Julia sometimes wondered though. Had they joined the order because they wanted to commit to God, because they desired a life of contemplation and prayer? Or had they joined the sisterhood for security – to ensure that there was one person fewer in the family to feed? Perhaps the fact that she still asked such questions – even inwardly of herself – indicated something lacking in her? Did she lack the passivity that was necessary for true faith and surrender to God? Would she never be able to give of herself in the way that the rest of the sisters in her community gave so willingly? Perhaps she had simply been born too curious? Or perhaps her work for Dr Lopez had made her question things that should not be questioned?

In the foyer of Santa Ana was the portrait of a devout nun, her eyes turned to God in ecstasy. In her hands she clutched a crucifix, in the background was a library of edifying books. It had been commissioned by the nun's rich family, some years before Sister Julia had joined the convent. That family was clearly proud of their daughter. But what did Sister Julia's family think of her? She often reflected on this.

Her mother and sisters had visited her at Santa Ana only a few days earlier. It had been a shock, for Sister Julia had not seen them for two years and it was a full six years since she had learnt of Paloma's forthcoming marriage to Mario Vamos. The last visit had been a hurried one and her mother had come alone. But Sister Julia understood. Family visits were not encouraged and besides, she was so often working at the clinic. In some ways it was almost easier not to see them.

'Julia.' Her mother's eyes filled but she did not embrace her.

'Mama. Sisters.' Sister Julia bowed her head so that her

emotions would not spill out and overflow. For they had changed. Mama, once strong and upright, seemed bent and tired, Matilde was dressed smartly enough but her eyes were so cold. And Paloma . . . The sight of Paloma was what affected her the most. Her sister seemed to have lost the light of life that had made her Paloma. How could that have happened in just six years?

They sat as usual in the room adjoining the foyer, upright and apart as they exchanged their items of news. A cousin she had hardly known had died. An old work colleague of her mother's had lost her husband. Sister Julia, though, was quiet. She had grown accustomed to listening to others, she supposed. Even at the clinic she spoke little – and never of herself.

But, 'How is Papa?' she asked at last.

'His health is not what it was,' her mother admitted. 'But some of his burden has eased.'

Paloma snorted. 'Now that he has no daughters to worry over,' she remarked.

Matilde looked straight at Julia. 'You were the lucky one,' she said.

Sister Julia bowed her head. Her sisters were both clearly unhappy. And so perhaps this was true. Though no one had thought it at the time.

'It is not so bad for you, Matilde,' Paloma shot back at their older sister. 'At least your husband adores you.'

Sister Julia glanced at her in surprise. It was Paloma, after all, who had married for love. 'How is Mario?' she asked gently.

Paloma looked away. But there was no light of love this time in her eyes. Indeed, Sister Julia feared that she might weep. Life under the new regime with the handsome and charming Mario Vamos had clearly not turned out to be what her fun-loving, pretty sister had hoped for.

'There are no children,' their mother said, as if that explained everything.

Sister Julia was confused. Paloma had been married less than six years. Was it so urgent that she and her Mario should immediately start a family? They were still young. Was it a reason for the love to fade between husband and wife?

Paloma shrugged her slender shoulders. 'And so already he strays.'

She made it sound as if she did not care. But Sister Julia knew her sister. Her looks and her ability to command slavish devotion were her very identity – without them she was lost. And Sister Julia thought of the way Mario Vamos used to watch her when he was a boy. No doubt he watched other women in that way too. It did not sound as if he had changed so much.

Matilde was examining her fingernails. They were long, painted red and perfectly manicured. 'Perhaps you should be grateful he no longer wants you,' she said to Paloma.

Glory. Sister Julia tried to conceal her shock. Had it been so long since she had listened carelessly to such talk? Clearly it had. She lived in a world so apart from her sisters that it seemed almost as if they spoke another language.

'Matilde . . . ' their mother gently admonished.

'Well, why should I not say it? Miguel is repulsive!' Matilde shuddered. 'You know it. Any fool can see it. My life is just rules. What I must say, how I must behave, when we should have dinner or take a walk. You do not know what it is like. And in the bedroom. You have no idea what I have to do . . . '

Sister Julia blushed. She hoped Matilde would go no further or she would have to ask them to leave. There should not be such talk in God's house.

'Hush,' said her mother. 'We have all made sacrifices. It is the world we live in.'

Indeed, thought Sister Julia. It was indeed the world they lived in.

'But look at you, Julia,' Paloma said.

And all three of them looked at her. How did she appear to them? It was impossible to say. But at least she was not invisible to her own family. They did not seem to expect her to say much, but at least they addressed her. At least over the years they had come occasionally to visit.

'*Si, si* . . . ' Matilde nodded her agreement. 'You have been given a social role so much more important than looking after a man and bringing children into the world.'

Had she? Sister Julia considered. She thought of the women in the clinic and she thought of the life she led. Yes, perhaps her role was more important than she had sometimes perceived it to be.

'All right for you to say it is not important to bear

children,' Paloma retorted. 'When you are not married to a man who thinks it is the only thing that matters.'

Matilde shrugged her shoulders. She got to her feet and wandered over to the arched window which looked out on to the courtyard. 'Who would want to bring children into this world anyway, when it is a world of war and poverty and heartbreak?' she asked. Her voice was almost expressionless, her dark eyes inscrutable. Sister Julia's heart went out to her.

And she thought again of the women in the clinic. It was strange that she and her family should be talking of this, when the subject was so close to her heart. And the answer to the question? The answer was that many women still wanted to bring children into the world, whatever that world was like. It was an urge buried deep within them.

Their mother nodded sadly. 'I fear that you are right, my daughter.'

And the three of them looked again at Sister Julia. Was she the lucky one? It was true that entering the sisterhood had given her security. It had in some ways been a relief to retreat into a world away from the atrocities she had witnessed as a girl during the Spanish Civil War. She had a refuge, she did not want. The sisterhood had also given her an identity outside marriage. When she was not working or praying, Sister Julia was able to continue her English and history studies; her reading. She had found some solace in her growing faith. And as for her work in the clinic . . . This was demanding and difficult – physically and emotionally. But it gave her a purpose.

'Are you content in your life, my child?' her mother asked her as she had asked her some years before.

Sister Julia saw her mother's sadness. She had given her daughter up to another world in much the same way that many of the *madras solatas* gave up their children – in the hope that they would have a better life than the one their own mother could provide.

How could she be the lucky one? How could she be content? She had lost her family and she had lost the chance to live the life of a woman in the outside world. But Sister Julia did not need to say such things. She did not want to hurt the mother who had sacrificed so much. She could not undo the loss, but she could ease the burden of guilt. So. 'I am content, my mother,' she said.

At least, Sister Julia thought, as she made her way to the Canales Clinic, her work gave her the freedom to walk in the city of Barcelona, which might be a greater freedom than that enjoyed by her two married sisters. To walk and to observe and to think – probably much more than she should. Was she a rebel? She smiled to herself. Perhaps in her own small way.

As she walked, she passed by grand houses and she also passed the pensions rented out by landladies – no doubt of varying repute. She had seen them outside talking with their neighbours or cleaning their windows. And wondered. What were these rooms like? Damp and grimy? A naked light bulb swinging in a bare hall? Broken floor tiles, window sills thick with dust? Threadbare sheets and old wormy furniture? She could well imagine . . . So perhaps Matilde and Paloma were right. Perhaps Sister Julia was the fortunate one.

Yesterday, she had left the clinic early, for they were very quiet and something had compelled her to visit Montjuïc cemetery. She still remembered her father's stories of the men who had been imprisoned and even executed there. She took the bus at Pasea de Colon, a bus which went around the Montjuïc mountain and then up the road to the eastern gates of the cemetery. *Dear God in heaven*. Even from here she could see the rows of tombs; the highways and byways of gravestones and mausoleums. The tombstones continued up to the very top; the avenue of the cemetery lined with a regiment of cypress trees silently watching over the dead. Thousands upon thousands of graves, it looked like. It was a cold and empty place which seemed to echo with the horrors of what had gone before.

Sister Julia continued her walk to the clinic with a heavy heart.

Dr Lopez's waiting room was full that day, with women with appointments to see him. Sister Julia often remained to assist during the examination, or simply stayed in case she was needed during the consultation – for so often the women became upset and emotional. The doctor was always professional but it was rare to find sensitivity and empathy in a man, let alone a man as busy as Dr Lopez, and here again Sister Julia felt that her contribution was worthwhile.

Sometimes, however, her presence was not required and

the doctor would indicate this with a wave of his hand or a curt dismissal. Sister Julia had no idea why some women did not need her to be present during their physical examination. But she would watch these women coming for later appointments, observe the changes in their body as their pregnancy advanced. And again, she would wonder.

This afternoon, she took in a woman who was wearing a loose coat but otherwise had no visible signs of pregnancy. This time it was she who asked to see the doctor alone.

Dr Lopez raised one thick dark eyebrow and nodded for Sister Julia to leave them. She did so, waiting a little way down the hall in case she should be called.

Instead, several minutes later, the woman suddenly burst out of the doctor's consulting room and hurried towards her.

'Are you quite well, *señora*?' Sister Julia asked. She was behaving rather strangely, and a woman with child must be cared for.

'*Si, si . . .* ' The woman was heading for the front door.

'Please wait a moment.' Sister Julia could not allow her to race away from the clinic before she had collected herself and become calm. Indeed, the woman's face was quite flushed and angry.

The woman spun around to face her. 'I am well, Sister,' she said.

Had something happened in the consulting room with Dr Lopez? Sister Julia took her arm. 'Please, won't you rest a while?' she asked. 'Can I fetch you some water, perhaps?' She looked back towards the consulting room but the doctor had not yet called her. Perhaps he was making notes or writing up a report?

The woman shook her head. She was definitely overheated, at the very least. 'Such things, Sister,' she said. 'Such things.'

Sister Julia knew she shouldn't, but she wanted to hear more. So she took her into the quiet room opposite the waiting room, reserved for the more emotional women who needed a few moments alone. She fetched her a glass of water and sat with her for a moment until Dr Lopez should call for his next appointment.

'Children should be with their mothers,' the woman said. 'It is an offence against civil liberty.'

Warning bells sounded in Sister Julia's head. She rose to her feet. What should she do? She wanted to hear more but she dare not.

But the woman did not talk of the clinic. 'The children are taken from their own families,' she said. 'They cannot stop them. How can they?'

'Surely not,' Sister Julia soothed, for the woman seemed to be rambling. 'Why should children be taken from their own families? Who do you speak of?'

'Those who they suspect to be Reds. It is how things are. It has happened to my own sister.' The woman took a handkerchief from her bag and wiped her eyes. 'When the parents are suspect – why take a chance on what they might teach their children? And brainwashing can be very effective, you know, Sister.'

Sister Julia crossed herself. 'But how can this be?' She knew that she should not engage the woman in conversation, and she hoped that Dr Lopez would not emerge from his consulting room and find them talking. But again, she remembered her father's words in those first weeks after the end of the Civil War. About what they had lost. About how things were. What was happening to their country? What would become of them all?

'But where do the children go?' she whispered.

'They send them to orphanages. Religious institutions. Run by Falange or Church, what difference?' She named a couple of these places, both in Catalonia. 'Thousands of them are taken,' she said. 'To be indoctrinated with nationalist beliefs. Some are even adopted – against their mothers' will.'

Adopted? Sister Julia was shocked. Children who already had parents living who had always cared for them? Forcibly taken from them and adopted? And yet – was this so different from what they were doing at the clinic? Yes. For at the clinic the mothers wished their babies to be adopted. It was their choice. Many were poor and also unmarried. They did not want to care for them. They had neither the will nor the means. And if Dr Lopez put pressure on them? This was to ensure that the right thing was done. It was an entirely different situation.

Still . . . Why had the woman come here? 'You must go,' she said to her, ushering her out. She could hear Dr Lopez talking to someone in his consulting room. Thank goodness he had been distracted.

Here at the clinic it was not a political matter. Dr Lopez was not a political man. He was only interested in helping people, in carrying out what he saw as the will of God. His methods might be dubious at times, but his motivation was surely sound. Still, Sister Julia reflected on what the woman had told her. Had those child abductions also been carried out in the name of God?

Later that same day, there was a minor emergency in the medical ward and Sister Julia had to run for Dr Lopez. He should have been present anyway. Not that it was for Sister Julia to say, but the woman was clearly in some difficulty and considerable pain. And the baby was breeched. The midwife was doing her best, but there was another woman also in labour and the doctor was required.

Sister Julia was so flustered that she rushed into his consulting room without knocking – the first time she had ever done this.

She stopped in her tracks. What was happening?

A woman was standing by the narrow bed where the doctor carried out his examinations. And yet it was not the time for appointments. And there was no nurse in attendance.

Sister Julia recognised her as a regular patient, however. She was one of the women who had been coming to the clinic regularly for some months, one of the women whom Sister Julia had never herself attended during an examination. And now she could see why – though in truth she could scarcely believe her eyes.

'Sister Julia!' thundered Dr Lopez. 'What in God's name do you think you are doing? You know the rules. You knock before you enter the room. And you wait for my invitation to do so.'

The woman quickly moved behind a screen. But not before Sister Julia had seen what the doctor was doing. He had been attaching some padding to her underclothing – or at least that was what it had looked like. But why? It made no sense.

'I am sorry, doctor,' Sister Julia said. She looked down at the brown tiles on the floor. 'But you are needed in the medical room as a matter of urgency.'

He clicked his tongue. 'Even so . . . ' he muttered. 'Even so.'

He spoke gently to the woman. 'Do not worry,' he said. 'I will be back shortly.' And he marched out of the consulting room, propelling Sister Julia along with him.

She did not know what to think. Was the *señora* not pregnant? And if she was not then why was she trying to appear to be?

'Do you trust me, Sister Julia?' Dr Lopez asked on the way to the medical room. 'Do you trust me in all things?'

Sister Julia looked into his eyes. He reminded her of a bird of prey – he always had. 'Of course, Dr Lopez,' she said. Was it a lie? Indeed, she was not sure. She had tried not to doubt him. Over the years she had tried more than she could say. She knew he only wanted to do what was best. And that was why she stayed at the clinic. That and the fact that she wanted to continue her work of supporting the women. She let out a silent prayer. *May God forgive me.*

He took her hand and patted it. But his touch was not warm as she expected, but cool and smooth as marble. 'You are a good girl,' he said. 'I knew you would understand.'

Sister Julia saw that woman a few times afterwards when she came to the clinic. But she did not attend her and was not asked to be present during her examinations.

'The *señora* is a personal friend,' Dr Lopez told her after one such visit. 'I cannot tell you more. But she is a good woman. Rest assured. She has fostered needy and damaged children for short periods as a favour to the local priest. Many times she has done this for no material reward.' He retreated behind his desk and grasped the crucifix with both hands. 'She will get her reward in heaven,' he muttered. 'If not before.'

'Very good, doctor,' said Sister Julia. She was glad that the *señora* was a good woman. But it was not her business. Her business was to do all she could to help both the women and the children. This – she hoped – was truly God's work.

When the time came for what was referred to as the *señora*'s confinement, she came to the clinic but she did not enter the medical ward, only a private room. Sister Julia was not asked to attend to her. The only person who saw her was Dr Lopez.

The following morning, Sister Julia arrived at the clinic, only to hear that there had been another death. *Glory*. There were too many infant deaths. What did it mean? She did not want to imagine. She could only suppose that conditions were getting worse in her beloved country, that there was more malnutrition, more disease, a higher fatality in newborns.

Dr Lopez was worried by it too. He had recently decreed that some women should be sedated before they gave birth, particularly those prone to hysteria or who were highly strung. 'It will make the procedure much easier,' he said. But for whom?

When Sister Julia arrived at her bedside, the woman who had given birth was still sobbing. She had just been told that her child had been stillborn.

'We tried to revive him,' the doctor muttered to Sister Julia, 'but it was not to be.'

He turned to the woman, who clung on to his sleeve as if he had the power to bring her baby back from the dead. 'Please, please . . . ' she begged. Her speech was slurred. She hardly seemed to know what was happening.

Sister Julia could not bear to listen. She stroked the woman's hair and tried to comfort her. But she seemed to be performing this duty far too often these days. It scared her.

'God has chosen him.' The doctor's voice shook with emotion. 'He has chosen him and He has taken him to heaven.'

'But what shall I do?' the woman cried. 'What shall I do?'

'Do not be anxious, my dear,' the doctor said. 'We will

take care of everything for you. You will not have to worry about a thing.'

Not worry? Sister Julia supposed that he was trying his best. But surely he could be a little more tactful? The poor woman had just lost her child.

'We will even organise the funeral service,' he said. 'And pay for it too. You must focus on growing strong again.'

Sister Julia sighed. She was aware that the doctor wanted things seen to quickly and without undue fuss and attention. She knew that he thought it best for all concerned. He even advised that mothers did not attend the funeral of their own child. And unsurprisingly, most mothers did not dare to argue with him. He was after all a doctor, and as the reverend mother had once reminded Sister Julia, a pillar of society.

'Thank you, doctor,' the woman said. And she collapsed against the pillows. She had been sedated, Sister Julia could see that. And naturally she was grateful. How could these women afford to bear the cost of a funeral when they had so little?

After the woman had gone to sleep, Sister Julia went to the private room which had been reserved for the *señora*, the friend of Dr Lopez. The door was open and the room was empty. She had gone. Already she had gone.

What could she do? Was there nothing she could do? Was there no one she could tell? Sister Julia thought about this long and hard and when she returned to the serenity of Santa Ana that evening she prayed to God for guidance.

She had tried to speak to the reverend mother and she had

tried to speak to the doctor. Where else could she turn? Who would listen? It seemed that there was only one thing she could do. Sister Julia wrote it down in her book. She wrote down every name. Sister Julia was indeed beginning to understand.

CHAPTER 22

Ruby took the shortcut down a footpath leading to a row of stone houses with long, narrow gardens. Pridehaven was a rope-makers' town and gardens were created for a purpose in those days. She was trying to magic up some enthusiasm for tonight. It was only dinner with friends, but she was feeling a bit fragile – probably still in shock from what Frances had told her.

When she reached the old church, she paused and pulled the photographs out of her bag – she'd started carrying them around with her wherever she went; seemed to need to keep looking at them. *Mother and child* . . . Laura was holding her close. But was she holding her with love? Had Laura loved her? And if she had – then why had she given her away?

'Are you sorry you asked about all this?' Frances had said as she came to the end of her story – or Vivien's story, Ruby supposed. Her eyes over the rim of the coffee cup were concerned. 'Do you wish you could turn the clock back and not know any of it?'

Was she sorry? The early evening sun was combing the church wall with strands of dark gold. Ruby touched the stone. It was like a biscuit; it felt like it could be dipped in a rainstorm and crumbled, and yet it had been here for centuries. Which was somehow comforting.

No, she decided – though there was a conflict of emotions. She could understand why her parents had come to the decision they had. They were protecting her. That's what they'd always done – protected her. Even so, she could hardly believe that her law-abiding parents had actually given false information in order to register her birth. That they had actually claimed to be her natural parents. She sighed. And she still found it hard to accept that they had deceived her over something that was just so important.

Ruby walked on. And yes, she was angry at not being told the truth before. Angry that she had nowhere to direct her emotions, no parent to have it out with. She had been betrayed by the people she most believed in.

'I needed to know,' she'd told Frances.

'And what now?'

'Well . . . ' As Frances had obviously realised, this wasn't the end of the story for Ruby. 'I'll try and find Laura,' she said. Not just out of curiosity or even to hear her side of things. There was a feeling that went deeper. Ruby might be scared of it – but she couldn't run away from it either. It had been building as Frances had told her the story. She wanted to meet her birth mother. She wanted to find out the identity of her natural father too. She wasn't who she'd always thought she was. So who was she? She had to know.

'I thought you'd say that.' Frances looked worried. 'But it won't be easy.'

'I know.' Ruby had no idea where to even start. All she had were a few photographs and the little information she'd gleaned from Frances. Unless Laura had unexpectedly become a fully paid up member of conventional society – which seemed unlikely – it would be a tricky and maybe impossible trail.

'And if you do find her . . . '

'She may not want to even acknowledge me.' Ruby stirred her coffee once more. 'I know that too.' If she didn't have high expectations, she shouldn't be too disappointed. But she had to at least try and find out what had happened to her.

Frances had finished her coffee and signalled for the bill. 'Let me know, Ruby,' she said. 'How you get on.'

'I will.'

'And good luck.'

'Thanks.' Ruby reached for her purse, but Frances wasn't having any.

'My treat,' she said. 'Next time maybe we'll meet under happier circumstances.'

Ruby smiled, though she wasn't even sure if she would be seeing Frances again. Frances didn't live here now, and Ruby . . . well, she hadn't quite made up her mind. She had thought she needed to come back here to Dorset. But now, after this bombshell, she wasn't quite so convinced. Where did she belong? She didn't know any more.

'And I'm so sorry,' Frances added. 'About all this. About the accident. Your father. Your mother. I'm so very sorry about your mother.'

Ruby nodded. 'Thanks, Frances,' she said. But which mother was she sorry about? Which mother?

Ruby headed towards the riverbank cottage of her host and hostess. They weren't old friends; she'd met them not long before she moved to London and the invitation had been a bit unexpected. She'd been undecided about what to wear and had finally chosen an emerald green skirt, a red fitted shirt tunic with tiny buttons, and black shoes. It wasn't exactly casual. Was she too dressed up? Too colourful? Did she look too much like a flag? But Mel had urged her to get out more, and she was right. Dinner with friends was part of leading a normal life – whatever that was. They wouldn't care what she was wearing, as long as she didn't burst into tears over the pudding.

Ruby was conscious of the touch of the breeze on her face as she crossed the old bridge. She held on to the damp and mossy wooden handrail to look down into the river. The water was high and fast-flowing but clear – she could see past the weeds and stones right down to the rocky bottom. From force of habit, she bent to pick up a twig, tossed it into the water and quickly turned to the other side to check its progress. A lot of people were afraid of alone time. When others were around, you didn't have to get too close to yourself, that was the thing. Not so for Ruby. She reckoned she was just learning who she might be.

She'd phoned Mel after her meeting with Frances to tell her what had happened. 'So you were right,' Mel had said.

'I suppose I was.' Though she'd still believed, hadn't she, right up to the last minute, that there would be some reasonable explanation that hadn't occurred to her before. That Frances would make it all clear. *Make everything right again.*

'And how do you feel?'

'Numb. Relieved to know the truth. Angry. Sad. Lost. Incomplete.' Ruby sighed.

'That's an awful lot of feelings,' Mel said.

Yes, it was. And Ruby wasn't sure how to begin coping with them.

She walked up the path of the riverside cottage and rang the bell. Outside the door were tubs of summer blooms – red and white geraniums and big blowsy poppies – while a pale pink wild rose was blossoming in wild and thorny abandon around the porch.

Tina opened the door wide. 'Ruby!' She beckoned her inside. 'Great to see you. How're you doing?'

'Good, thanks. You?' Ruby handed her the wine. She'd first met Tina when the band played regularly at the Jazz Café.

'We invited another friend,' Tina said. 'I hope that's OK.'

Ruby's stomach dipped. Oh, hell. It would be a man, it had to be.

She was in the sitting room before she knew it – Gez giving her a drink and a quick hug. She avoided looking at first. Then she glanced over and did a rapid double take.

'Christ,' she said, without thinking.

'Hello.' He was getting to his feet. Auction man. The

potential stalker. 'It's er . . . good to meet you again, Ruby.'

Gez and Tina exchanged a questioning glance. 'This is Andrés Marin,' said Tina. 'Or do you know that already?'

OK. Ruby would never accept another invitation to dinner again. He must have fixed this. She had been only half serious when she'd called him a stalker. But it seemed as if she was right. Only . . . He looked about as surprised as she. And besides, what choice did she have? It would be much, much too rude to just walk out.

'Hello, Andrés,' she said. *Shit* . . .

'So . . . ' Tina looked from Ruby to Andrés expectantly. 'Where did you two meet? At the Jazz Café?' She frowned as if trying to remember when.

Ruby selected a green olive from the bowl offered by Gez. It tasted sharp and surprising on her tongue – maybe it was stuffed with anchovy. She wasn't thrilled with Tina – she should have told her she was planning some matchmaking. But then she would have guessed that Ruby wouldn't come.

'I saw Ruby playing one night.' Andrés replied to Tina but looked at Ruby. 'And enjoyed it – very much.'

Tina seemed as if she was going to add something to this, but changed her mind.

'Thanks.' Ruby gave a little nod. Flattery would get him precisely nowhere.

'She's great, isn't she?' Gez smiled fondly before offering the olive dish to the others. He bent to refill Ruby's glass, though she'd hardly touched her wine. 'London's loss is our gain.'

Ruby was embarrassed. 'Actually, I hardly played in London.'

'You have moved back here for good?' His eyes were green but his hair was very dark – almost black.

She nodded – still wary. She didn't want to go into what had made her come back – the death of her parents, the need to start again – not now at a dinner party and certainly not with Auction Man. But she could see he was confused – about the cottage and everything.

Tina got to her feet. 'So where *did* you meet?' she persisted.

He looked across at her and Ruby found herself exchanging a small smile with him. Well. She was surprising herself. 'At an auction,' she said. 'He tried to steal my cottage.'

Over the first course of Parma ham, parmesan shavings and sun-dried tomatoes, they told the others the story, each taking it up when the other paused. Tina had placed them opposite one another, so it was easy to see where the other was going. The momentum was growing; they seemed to be on a similar wavelength – though that was ridiculous, wasn't it? She hardly knew him. But by the end of the story – and significantly, after another glass of Sauvignon Blanc – they were all laughing.

'It is a strange way to meet,' Andrés said. 'I probably should not have charged outside to speak to you like that.' He was very formal. Was he Spanish? Italian? Ruby wasn't sure. Though when they had got up to take their places at

Tina and Gez's wooden table, she had noticed that he was quite tall and – she had to admit – rather attractive.

'Why did you then?' Ruby asked.

Tina started clearing the plates. 'Ruby must have thought you were a right weirdo,' she commented. 'She didn't know you from Adam.'

'Adam?' Andrés frowned.

'It's just an expression,' Ruby said, sorry for teasing him. 'Adam as in . . . Well.' She blushed. 'Adam and Eve.'

Tina raised an eyebrow. 'Exactly,' she said.

'I did not want you to leave without speaking to you,' Andrés said. 'I recognised you from the Jazz Café as I said. I felt . . . ' He paused and Ruby waited. 'As if I knew you.'

Ruby fiddled with her wineglass. She didn't quite know what to say to that and Tina and Gez had both disappeared into the kitchen. 'So what will you do now?' she asked.

'Do?' He raised his glass to his lips.

'Find another cottage?'

He shrugged. 'It will wait. There is always another cottage. But what about you, Ruby? Were you planning to live there?'

She thought of the view. 'Oh, yes.'

'And do all the work that needed to be done?' He was teasing her now, she knew.

And perhaps he was right. Perhaps it had been unrealistic. It was just that she had seen that coastal view from the upstairs window and been blinded to all the things that needed doing. 'It was just a dream,' she said. Of her childhood, of something that she was trying to recall, to snatch, before it was lost for ever. And now that she'd talked to Frances . . . Was it lost for ever? She hoped not. Just before Frances had left that night, as they stood outside the restaurant, she had handed Ruby an envelope.

'It's a letter from your mother,' she said. 'From Vivien.'

Ruby had looked at it. Her name was written in huge loopy letters on the outside – her mother's handwriting. She swallowed hard. 'Thank you.' But she hadn't opened the envelope. She still hadn't opened it. She had put it on the mantelpiece and she looked at it every time she walked into the living room. But she hadn't opened it. She was still too angry.

'Ah, a dream . . . ' Andrés nodded.

As if he knew all about dreams, Ruby thought. 'I'll find somewhere else,' she said. It was a lovely cottage and a nostalgic dream. But clearly it wasn't meant to be.

'Maybe I can—'

But he was interrupted as Tina and Gez re-entered the room, armed with another bottle of wine and more plates. From the corner of her eye, Ruby sensed them exchanging glances, no doubt very pleased with themselves that their guests were getting on so well. Careful, Ruby, she thought.

'Maybe I can help you there,' Andrés continued.

Ruby looked across at him in surprise. He was wearing an open-necked blue shirt and jeans. His legs were stretched out under the table on to her side. She could see his boots, brown leather, loosely laced. 'Really?' She needed to find somewhere to live – and the sooner the better. She needed to escape from all those ghosts.

Gez was putting out plates for their main. Tina was holding a casserole dish in giant oven gloves and she placed this in the centre of the table and took off the lid. It exhaled a gust of steam and herby wine fragrances.

'Here we go,' said Tina.

'It smells yummy.' Ruby suddenly realised how ravenous she was.

'Good.' Tina passed Ruby a bowl of steaming rice. 'Just help yourself.'

Andrés dished out the beef casserole. It looked as good as it smelt – tiny shallots, neat glistening mushrooms and large chunks of beef in a rich wine-laden sauce. 'Ruby?'

She held out her plate. 'Thanks.'

'Ruby's a writer,' Gez said. 'A journalist. Did she tell you?'

'No.' The serving spoon hovered. 'What sort of things do you write?'

'Oh . . . ' He had a slightly lopsided eye-tooth and high, almost Slavic cheekbones. And he was looking at her in a kind of intimate way that scared the hell out of her. Quickly, she looked down at the serving dish, at the brown hand holding the spoonful of beef heaven. 'Features for magazines mostly,' she said. 'And songs.'

When she looked at her watch some time later, Ruby was surprised to see it was almost one a.m. Funny, but she'd intended to make her excuses and leave before midnight. The evening had flown by and she'd enjoyed it. She'd talked, laughed, yes, even flirted a little. Why not? She was having fun. She felt like she'd had a wake-up call.

She looked across at Andrés who raised his glass to her. Their eyes met and this time Ruby found it hard to look away. Why on earth? She hadn't woken up *because* of this attractive stranger. Of course not. And yet . . .

'I must go.' She got to her feet. 'It's been lovely.' And she meant it. Hallelujah, she thought. 'Thanks so much.' She hugged Gez and Tina, not sure what to do about Andrés.

He got to his feet. 'I could walk you home,' he offered. 'It's a lovely evening. Or would you prefer to call a cab?'

Something – the prospect of going home? – had made him stiff and polite once more. Ruby smiled. 'I can walk myself. Don't worry.' She picked up her bag.

'But I insist.' His gaze was intent. 'A gentleman should escort a lady home, I think.' He took her jacket from Gez who had retrieved it from the hall and held it out for her.

'Well, OK. Thanks.' She turned and slipped it on.

The night outside was cool on her face as she stepped out of the door. Nice, actually. She zipped up her jacket and waved a final goodbye. Gez and Tina were standing on the step watching them like fond parents. Gez's arms were wrapped around Tina as she stood in front of him; Ruby just knew they'd have a lengthy discussion about this before they went to bed.

'Which way?' Andrés stood waiting on the river path.

She pointed. 'I've got a torch.' She delved into her bag to look for it.

'That's very organised of you. I didn't think of it. I drove. But . . .'

She nodded and produced the torch with a flourish. Yes, they'd probably all drunk far more than they'd intended.

After a moment's hesitation, he took her hand and tucked it under his arm. An Englishman wouldn't make such a gesture, but Ruby liked it. It felt warm and safe. She felt warm and safe. Which was equally ridiculous. *Careful, Ruby . . .* she reminded herself again.

She shone the torch beam in front of them with her free hand. It didn't illuminate much more than the sparse grass and mud that constituted the path, but should stop them falling in the river at least. 'I was a girl guide,' she quipped. 'Be prepared.'

He laughed. His walking style was loping, kind of easy. She fell into his rhythm without having to try.

'There were youth groups on the island too,' he said. 'Kids do all kinds of sports there. Football's big. Tennis. Dancing.' She felt him smile. 'And drumming.'

'The island?'

'Fuerteventura in the Canary Islands.' He said it with a kind of sadness. 'We are *Majoreros.*'

'*Majoreros?*'

He shrugged. 'Natives of the place. "People who originally wore goatskin shoes" is the literal meaning of the word.'

Ruby smiled. She liked that. 'Why did you leave?' she asked.

It was a simple enough question and yet he was silent for

what seemed like ages. And as they walked, Ruby watched the trees which seemed to bend towards the path as though they wanted to listen to the non-conversation. The darkness was so dense that she could only sense the river. The ground flickered in front of and beneath them as if it was no longer solid. Shadows, she thought. It must be one hell of a complicated reason.

'I did not get along well with my father,' he said at last. 'Something happened. We quarrelled. I came to England.'

'To find your fortune?' Ruby lightened her tone. He'd clearly given her the abridged version. She had the impression that Andrés's father was not a judicious topic of conversation right now.

And sure enough, she felt him relax. 'In my dreams.'

Dreams again, she noted. 'You've done well enough at least to have been able to afford to buy a Dorset cottage,' she pointed out.

Once again she felt his smile. He didn't seem offended by her rather personal comment. 'You are right, of course. There were not many opportunities for work on the island. I did some building work there, but here . . . There has always been plenty for me to do. I have done up houses for others – and for myself too.'

They reached the bridge and he looked over the parapet into the water, just as she had done. Ruby shone the torch. The beam seemed to dance on the surface, just for a moment and then was lost. 'You have your own building company?' she asked.

He turned to her in the dark. He had let go of her hand and it was utter foolishness to feel bereft. But she did. 'It is just me,' he said. 'I bring others in only when I need them. An electrician, perhaps. A plumber. Most of the work I do myself.'

She couldn't see his expression, couldn't read him. Did it work in a different way with people of other races? she wondered. Did their varying cultural experience give them a different mindset, a disparate code? No, she thought. On the contrary. There was a familiarity about Andrés. A sameness. They had even wanted to live in the self-same cottage. What she had denied outside the town hall after the auction had actually come true; it seemed to have created some kind of a bond. Did that mean that they were going to become friends? Or . . . 'Have you known Tina and Gez long?' she asked.

He took her arm again. 'A while.' He shook his head. 'Tina has produced a long line of women for me,' he explained sadly. 'Apart from that she is a good friend.'

Ruby smiled. Pictured that long line of women. She probably even knew some of the contenders. 'Some men would be grateful.'

'Perhaps,' he said. And then: 'Of course, I was not referring to you, Ruby.'

She acknowledged the compliment with a wry smile. But he was not 'some men'. There was something different about him. 'She's been good to me too,' she added. Sympathetic, but not over the top. Offering a shoulder, but not insisting Ruby lean on it.

The path was narrowing. There was a hedge on one side, a wall on the other. It should have felt claustrophobic, but it didn't. 'I expect they think I need to be dragged back to the land of the living. Hence the dinner invitation. And you.'

'Dragged back from . . . ?'

A cloud edged over the moon.

The dark side, she thought. 'My parents died a few months ago. Didn't they tell you?' He should have been forewarned about this particular damaged contender.

His pace slowed, but she wouldn't let him stop now; she kept on walking.

'You must miss them very much,' he said.

'It's not so much missing them.' Ruby found that she wanted to explain. 'I only saw them once every couple of months.' Living in London, she'd already made that initial break. 'It's more basic.' What could she compare it to? Like a rug being lifted from beneath your feet? Like a chair being whipped from under you? You might have stopped noticing the pattern of the rug or the cushion on the chair, but you knew they were there; you took their presence for granted. You certainly noticed when you lost your balance and fell over.

But Andrés bowed his head. 'I understand,' he said.

And she had the feeling that he did.

After a short while the path widened out and they emerged on to the pavement. Ruby gestured towards the High Street and they crossed the road. Although there were no lights on, with the houses and parked cars the darkness now seemed less complete, the sky more open. And as they got to the church, the cloud passed and the tower loomed in front of them, silhouetted in the moonlight. Wow . . .

Andrés too had paused. 'If I could just paint this,' he murmured.

'You're an artist too?' Ruby looked at him. His face was still in shadow. She thought of Vivien, her mother. What was in that letter she had left for Ruby? And why hadn't she told her – face to face?

'Yes. I work in one of the units in the studio near the Arts Centre.'

What would his work be like? Ruby tried to imagine. She'd like to see it. They were standing so close together now, she was beginning to wonder if he would kiss her. And if he did . . . If he did, what would she do?

But he moved away and they walked past the dark stone cottages and through the car park. They had slipped into silence once more. He wasn't the most forthcoming of men, Ruby thought. He'd be hard to get to know. But on the other hand, after the last few weeks, she was no stranger to secrets herself.

'This is me,' she said when they reached her house. She wouldn't ask him in. It was late and she was tired. And she hadn't quite made up her mind about Andrés Marin. What had happened with the other women Tina set him up with? Had he walked them home too? Did he tell them about his painting, about his father?

'I know of a cottage coming up for rent in Pride Bay,' he

said. 'If you like I will take you there. It belongs to a client of mine, but I do not think he has advertised it yet.'

'Oh.' That must have been what he was referring to earlier. 'When were you thinking of?'

He frowned. Put his hands on her shoulders.

And if he should kiss me, Ruby wondered again. She looked up at him.

He kissed her on both cheeks; once, twice. Nothing more. What she felt was the scent of him – amber like tree resin, his warm breath on her cheek.

'Would you come for a walk with me? Next weekend perhaps? We could go and see the cottage too.'

'All right.' She agreed quickly, before she had time to find reasons why not. He was a complication, he had to be, and she had no need of a complication in her life. Her coping mechanisms were vulnerable enough already. She didn't want to get involved with anyone. It seemed like the wrong time. But . . .

'Shall we say Saturday morning? Eleven o'clock?'

She nodded. 'OK.'

'I will look forward to it.' At last, he smiled.

Ruby stared at his mouth, at the slightly lopsided eyetooth that somehow made him even more attractive. Was she mad? Was she totally mad?

'Goodnight, Ruby.'

'Goodnight, Andrés.'

And he lifted his hand in a wave and strode off into the darkness.

CHAPTER 23

On Saturday Andrés drove the pick-up truck to Ruby's house. He'd never seen the need for buying another vehicle other than the one he used for work, but now he was a bit embarrassed about the cement dust and the bags of tools – though he had given it a bit of a clear-out at home. He was nervous too.

Ruby opened her front door before he even got out of the truck. Either she couldn't wait to see him – which seemed unlikely – or she didn't want to risk inviting him into the house. Andrés sighed. What was he getting so het up about anyway? He was the one who wasn't supposed to be interested in a relationship – at least not this kind of relationship, he thought; a relationship which could definitely get tricky. Was Ruby part of the spider's web? Would she be his new project now that the cottage he'd wanted to buy at auction had been bought by someone else? Hah – chance would be a fine thing.

Tina had phoned him the morning after her dinner party when he was up a ladder investigating a damp patch the size of a football in old Martha Hutton's ceiling. He was tapping around it carefully – there could be pipes or electricity cables running behind – but he might as well make a hole straight off; he'd have to replace this part of the ceiling in any case. Martha didn't have much money to spare, so for now he'd just make an opening big enough for him to take a look, see if he could spot where the water was coming from.

And then his mobile rang.

He groped for his phone in his back pocket.

'Andrés?'

'Hi, Tina.' He sat down on the step and put down his hammer. He'd been expecting this call, but he wasn't going to make it easy for her.

'You're not mad at me, are you?'

Andrés smiled. 'You did promise – no more matchmaking. Didn't we agree?' He looked up at the black hole in the Artexed ceiling. Martha would have a fit.

'But this was different, wasn't it?'

Yes, he thought, this was different. 'You think so?'

'I know so.' She laughed. 'I remember how interested you were – when Ruby was playing at the Jazz Café. Though I didn't know you'd actually met and spoken to her, you dark horse.'

Dark horse? The English language was forever surprising Andrés. 'So you thought you would give me a nice surprise?' he suggested.

'Exactly.'

'And Ruby?'

'Ruby?'

He'd seen her face when she walked in. Even before she'd

realised that her blind date was none other than the man bidding against her at the auction. She'd been horrified. And when on top of that, she'd seen Andrés . . . Well. She'd looked as if she'd been thrown into her worst nightmare.

'I haven't spoken to Ruby yet,' Tina admitted. 'But I was only trying to cheer her up. She's been through such a hard time.'

'And I am the right person to do that?' Andrés enquired.

'You can be funny,' Tina said. 'When you try.'

'You are so generous.' But Andrés knew Tina had their best interests at heart – him and Ruby. She was kind, even if she did think that no one could be happy without the other half of a couple by their side.

'And you clearly got on like a house on fire,' she said.

'Like a house on fire?' This sounded more negative than positive to Andrés, but it was simply the strange behaviour of the English language – again.

'I've never seen Ruby so animated,' Tina added. 'And as for you . . .'

'As for me what?'

'Well you were clearly smitten. Gez and I could both see that. You were completely and utterly gaga.'

'Gaga?' Andrés frowned. Another new one.

'So . . . ?'

'So what?' But he knew what she was after. Information. And he wasn't going to oblige – not yet at least. 'Thank you for the dinner, Tina,' he said. 'And thank you for introducing me to Ruby. I am grateful.'

'And?'

'And what?'

'And what happens now, Andrés?'

'What happens now, Tina,' he said, 'is that I pick up my hammer and once again try to make a hole in the ceiling.'

'Oh.' She sounded disappointed. 'And what about Ruby?'

'What about her?' Andrés was enjoying the tease. He was usually on the other end of it.

'Well, I just wondered.'

'Wondered what?'

'How the walk home went? Did you kiss her goodnight? Are you going to see her again? That's all.'

'That's all?' He chuckled.

'And anything else you might want to tell me,' she added.

'I will bear it in mind,' Andrés said. 'But for now . . .'

'Yes?'

'I must get back to work.'

He said goodbye, grinning to himself as he tucked his mobile back in his pocket. Ruby, yes, she was an enigma. It was odd, he thought, that he kept running into her everywhere. Hide Beach, the Jazz Café, the auction. And finally at Gez and Tina's. Was it perhaps a sign? He had never believed in signs the way his mother and his sister did. On the island the old stories and legends seemed to be embedded in the female psyche and he knew for a fact that the native Guanches had been a very spiritual people. It was true that Andrés had sometimes felt the pull of something he couldn't quite understand – and it had been a bit like that with Ruby.

His intuition perhaps? Something instinctive that coursed through his veins in his very life-blood? Who could tell? He preferred to let things happen, to run with the wind.

He picked up his hammer and tapped gently at the ceiling. Easy was the way.

It might be the way with Ruby too. He visualised her as she had been the day of the auction. Fierce and angry and trying desperately not to cry as she wobbled off precariously on that silly over-sized bicycle of hers.

He hadn't wanted her to disappear up the lane and out of his life. He'd wanted, even then, to take her in his arms and make it better – though this impulse had surprised him. He'd wanted to put his arm around her as they walked home after Gez and Tina's dinner party too. And when they arrived at her house and she'd lifted her face to say goodnight . . . It was all he could do to simply kiss her on the cheek and walk away.

And now? He wasn't quite sure what to do. He wasn't looking for someone, was he? He thought of his father in his studio throwing wild splashes of colour on to the canvas, painting portraits subtle and soft with an underlying passion that rested just below the surface, barely visible to the naked eye. No, he was not.

The hole in the ceiling was now big enough for Andrés to get his hand in and wiggle it about. There didn't seem to be any cables around, so he knocked out the edges to make the hole a bit larger. This time the hammer hit something solid. Hmm. He worked at it a bit more.

What was under Ruby's surface? He couldn't help wondering. He hadn't wanted to frighten her. She reminded him of a wild animal. Strong but vulnerable. More vulnerable than a man might think. Stronger than a man might think. Easily scared. He had to be calm and go slowly and let her come to him. Tina was right; she had been through so much. He must be patient and let her learn to trust him. That was the way.

But did he want Ruby to come to him? Did he really want to embark on a relationship with a woman – a woman who would mean something to him? Since leaving the island, since coming here to England, he had only ever had short relationships – meaningless flings, as Tina called them. With women who were nice enough but who would never make him love them. Safe women, shallow women, women who could never touch him or hurt him. This was best. Tina called him a commitment-phobe, and perhaps she was right. Perhaps Andrés was too accustomed to the bachelor life.

And yet . . . He thought of the way Ruby looked when she was playing her saxophone, saw again the sadness in her eyes. Did he want her to come to him? Yes, he thought. Yes, he did.

He saw now what had caused the stain on the ceiling. There was a copper pipe above, with what looked like a leaky compression joint. That made sense. It had probably been put in back in the sixties – maybe it was the cold water supply feeding the upstairs bathroom; it was a system now known to be prone to problems.

And then Andrés saw something else. He saw what had felt solid just now. He saw what looked like part of a wooden beam. And as he stuck his head into the hole and felt with his fingers, he could feel the beam. It was about eight inches wide. The whole original ceiling must be beamed and someone had covered them up with a different ceiling that looked like an Arctic Wonderland – in the name of modernisation.

He'd have to talk to Martha Hutton before he went any further. He could take the whole ceiling down and have the beams sandblasted to take them back to the natural wood, or he could just fix the leak and cover them up again. It would, he suspected, be a question of money. But he would explain to Martha that a beamed ceiling would increase both the character of the cottage and its value. Wooden beams were special. England was of course a land whose woods had not been destroyed by man and Nature as had the woodland of the island of Andrés's birth. You would never know now what it had once been; a land of trees, of rivers and streams. Now, the land was dry as a desert. Ah. So many things had changed.

Andrés watched Ruby come round to the passenger side. It just showed though, didn't it, what could be under the surface?

Ruby was wearing a red fleece, blue jeans and the same laced walking boots he'd seen her in before. Simple and uncomplicated. His kind of girl, he found himself thinking. Though of course she wasn't – simple or uncomplicated. Nor was she his girl.

'Hi.' She got in the car and smiled – definitely a good sign. Andrés had been concerned that she might cancel; she was bound to have had second thoughts – he was prone to them himself, so he quite understood. And decisions made after several glasses of wine at a dinner party were not always the wisest ones. But cancelling hadn't been an option for him today – he'd been really looking forward to seeing this girl again. Once more, she was wearing her signature red lipstick and she still had that slightly hunted look he'd noticed at Gez and Tina's. But at least she was here.

'Hello, Ruby.' Andrés was going to apologise for the truck, but decided against it. He was what he was. He checked the mirror, indicated and drove off. He was going to take her to Langdon Woods and Golden Cap. It was the perfect day for it.

In the woods the ground was spongy but not too wet and the bluebells of course were long gone. You could see their leaves thick on the high banks of the Hollow, clothing the ground of the woods beyond with an eiderdown of lush green. The air seemed thick with the fragrance of shady woods and sappy sweetness and the sun filtered through the leaves of the trees, creating jagged patterns on the path ahead of them.

'Tell me about your island,' Ruby said.

And so, as they trudged along the wide path of the Hollow, he told her about his childhood home. About the blue and white stone house in which he'd grown up, his father's studio and the land out back where they had grown vegetables and kept the two goats – at least when he was a child. He told her about the surfing beach backed with the gentle, purple *morros* – hills – and he told her about the Old Harbour and the bay. He described the barrenness of the island, the *calima* – sand-blasting winds – the quiet cultivated valleys and the isolated farmsteads; the palm trees and tamarisks; the valleys called *barrancos*, and the Barbary squirrels. Andrés was surprised. There was, suddenly, so much to say. And as he talked, he could picture the pale sand and the turquoise lagoons, the deep navy and white curls of Playa del Castillo, the gentle mushroom lunar-landscape of the mountains, the black volcanic rock, the bitter-yellow late afternoon light. The palette of the island seemed to shimmer in his mind, until he longed once again to paint it.

'How could you bring yourself to leave?' Ruby asked. 'It sounds wonderful.' She shivered. It was a bright day but the woods were cool and shady.

He smiled. It was true that England could be damp, cold and grey. He still wasn't entirely used to it. *How could he have brought himself to leave?* What could he tell her? 'When you are young,' he said, 'the island – it can feel like a prison.' Which in itself was true enough. He and Izabella had often talked of moving away – to Paris, Barcelona or London. But he had been pushed into leaving, while Izabella was still there, now rooted to the island she had wanted to escape from.

'The other man's grass is always greener?' Ruby asked.

'Good,' he pointed out, 'to even have grass. We do not get a lot in Fuerte.'

She laughed. He liked that feeling – of making her laugh.

'But is it still home?' she asked. She ran her fingers through her short blonde hair. It managed to be both tufty and spiky at the same time, he thought. And would it be soft to the touch? He thought so.

'Well . . .' They paused to take in the view. From here you could see past the fields, hedgerows and drystone walls down to the village of Seatown and the ocean beyond. *Was it still home?* This was not an easy question either. Yes, England had held more opportunities. But . . . It was still a big but, he realised. 'I do not know,' he said. 'I am not sure what it is that I want to find.'

Ruby's thoughtful glance flickered over him. 'I don't know that either,' she admitted.

They smiled at one another. And in that moment he felt something encircling the two of them; separating them from the rest of the world. He knew that his instinct had been correct. The second he saw her, the moment she began to play the saxophone, the first time they spoke.

The path divided and they turned off for Golden Cap.

'You have walked here before, of course?' he asked her.

'Not for a long time.' She hesitated. Her eyes filled and she looked away from him as if she was looking into the distance of the past.

'What is it, Ruby?' But Andrés thought he knew how she felt. She had lost her family just as he had – although in a different way. Was that the bond between them?

'I was about to say that I'm rediscovering some of the places of my childhood. Since my parents died.' She hesitated as if about to say more. 'Since I came back here to Dorset.'

He reached out his hand to help her over the stile. Her hand in his felt small and chilly. 'Does it feel like a good thing to do? To go back? To revisit?' He was asking for himself as much as her. And yet the memories were always there, in his head. The feeling was still there, in his heart. No one could take that away.

'Most of the time it does feel like a good thing, yes.' She jumped down lightly from the stile. 'And I need the connection with them. Especially now.'

He could understand that too. The connection. Though he wasn't sure what she meant by 'especially now'. He wouldn't ask though – let her tell him in her own good time. He felt a shaft of anger. The usual shaft of anger – against him: his father.

They began the climb up to the Cap. 'Do you miss your family?' she asked him.

'Yes,' he said. Especially his mother and his sister. 'We were close once. Very close.' Like the rocks of a *corralito*. Like the waves of the sea.

Ruby touched his arm. 'Perhaps one day you'll go back,' she said. She let out a breath as they reached the summit.

Andrés remembered his mother's words. *Nothing has changed*. So how could he go back? He gazed down at the sea and the village. It was breezy up here on the Cap but all very calm below. He could see the houses on the hill and people down on the beach at Seatown quite clearly now. He looked at Ruby. She wasn't like most people. Sometimes she didn't say much, but she seemed to know how to say the right thing. 'Perhaps,' he said.

They walked across the grassy top of Golden Cap, to the other side. It was the highest point in Dorset and today it was clear, so there was an excellent panoramic view along the coast – past the Fleet and through to Weymouth one way, and almost to Salcombe on the other; way beyond the Cobb of Lyme Regis. They sat down to enjoy the view and chat of other things – Ruby's music, the Jazz Café, of Tina and Gez and about the forthcoming summer exhibition of Andrés's work.

After a while, Andrés pulled the sketchbook out of his bag that he always carried with him. He had a sudden urge . . . He drew fast with strong sure strokes, the woman sitting on the grassy cliff top, hugging her knees, her short hair catching in the breeze, the sea a backdrop behind her. She regarded him, head on one side. Her expression was dreamy. Andrés liked that. He wanted to find out more about what went on inside that head.

When he'd finished, he tore off the sheet and handed it to her.

'For me?' She clapped her hands, like a child.

'If you like it.' It was a decent resemblance. He watched her expression – delighted at first, and then thoughtful, as if the sketched portrait had reminded her of something – or someone.

'It's very good,' she said. 'Thank you.'

He shrugged. 'It is nothing.' He stared out to sea. 'My father is the expert.'

'Your father?'

'Enrique Marin.' He could hardly bring himself to say the name. 'He is the portrait painter,' he said. Did he sound bitter? Probably. But his father had done well, very well. Still. Had he become the *caballero* he had always wanted to be? A gentleman? An image materialised in Andrés's head. His father in his paint-spattered shorts and overalls, skinny cheroot held between his fingers. Hardly. Another image resurfaced – the one that made Andrés shudder. *Some fucking gentleman* . . .

Later, they strolled back down towards Langdon Woods.

'And where is this cottage you wanted me to see?' Ruby asked.

She smiled up at him and suddenly, with that smile, he longed to take her into his arms. She was that kind of woman. You thought you knew exactly how she would feel, how she would smell; the texture of her skin, the softness of her hair, the fragrance of her sinking into your senses. You could be wrong. Oh, there was a sadness about her still. But it attracted him, it drew him.

'Pride Bay,' he said. 'We could go there after lunch, if you like? I have the key.'

'Lunch?'

'I thought the pub by the beach.'

'You're on.'

After lunch they walked along Chesil Beach. Like Andrés, Ruby seemed glad to be down on sea level. And like him, she seemed to love the beach. He watched her pick up a stone and skim it over the waves. Like him, she had grown up on the coast; the sea was in her blood. He took deep breaths of the fresh salty air. The flamboyant golden cliffs always reminded him sharply of the Playa del Castillo back home – his favourite stretch of honeycombed sand, baked by the sun, blown by the wind, backed by the mountains. Andrés had surfed there as a boy – most of the kids had. But he had stopped surfing when painting had taken over his life.

They cut through to the cottage which was half a mile inland. It was a simple two-up two-down, white-rendered place and belonged to one of Andrés's clients who lived in Sherborne. He had asked Andrés to give it a paint job and a top to toe spruce-up so that he could get it rented out.

'So it hasn't been advertised yet?' Ruby asked when they got there. She turned to look at him, her face slightly flushed. In the pub they'd both drunk a pint of beer; lager for Andrés, a dark local ale for Ruby. He'd been surprised. He had visualised her sipping Chardonnay or even knocking back a shot of vodka and ice.

'Not yet.'

'And how much a month does he want for it?' Her expression was deadpan now. Did she like the place? He had no idea. Just because he could imagine her here. What did he know? You had no need to analyse expressions on the island — people tended to shout what they thought. English people were more reserved. You had to guess what they were thinking. Perhaps it was the weather that made them all so damned inhibited.

Andrés told her. It was a fair price and she seemed to agree because she nodded and smiled. 'When would it be available?'

'As soon as I have done the work.' They were in the kitchen now, which was basic, to say the least. 'I could put you up some more cupboards and a better worktop,' Andrés said. 'And some shelves in the living room maybe?'

'With the landlord's approval?' she teased.

He shrugged. 'He will not mind as long as he does not have to pay for it.'

She raised an eyebrow. 'Why would you do that, Andrés? You hardly know me.'

'I just would.'

'But, Andrés . . . ' And the way she said his name made him shudder for a moment inside.

'Ruby.' He put his hands on her shoulders.

She looked up at him, all sadness and dreams and forget-me-not blue eyes.

And he couldn't resist it any longer. He bent towards her and he kissed her, firmly on the mouth to stop her saying more – and because she would probably taste good. She did. 'I think we have a deal,' he said.

She blinked at him. 'Do you kiss everyone you make a deal with, Andrés?'

Andrés wondered what he would say to Tina the next time she asked how he and Ruby were getting along. He took her hand and pulled it into the crook of his arm. It was becoming a habit. 'You are my first,' he said.

CHAPTER 24

Barcelona, 1956

Things were changing – slowly – in the city as the decade progressed. Ration books disappeared and in the press, Sister Julia read that earnings were rising. The economy was still fragile though. In 1956 a severe frost hit Spain's citrus production and olive harvest – this affected the farmers and in turn the people; it seemed to be two steps forwards and one back. But still, Sister Julia thought, at least there was now some sense of hope. This morning she had walked along the street towards the clinic and she had heard a man whistling a bolero. Her spirits had risen. The Spanish were a strong race. They could not easily be trampled on.

Now, it was seven p.m. and Sister Julia was exhausted. Three babies had been born in the Canales Clinic that day and she had hardly stopped to rest.

The first, a healthy baby girl, thank the Lord, had been born at midday. This baby was due to be adopted and the new parents would be arriving very soon to take her away.

Sister Julia had spent some time in the afternoon comforting the mother, a woman called Inez Leon, who had made her decision to give up her baby with what seemed to be a heavy heart.

'I am alone in the world, Sister,' she had said. 'I want my daughter to have a good life. I want her to have everything I cannot give her.'

'*Si, si*, of course you do,' Sister Julia murmured, as she helped Inez express her breast milk. This would be a relief to her and it would give her baby daughter the best possible start in life.

'But do you think my little girl will ever forgive me, Sister?' Inez asked.

Sister Julia stopped what she was doing for a moment. She glanced across the room to see if anyone had heard her – especially Dr Lopez. But the doctor was conferring with one of the nurses at the door to the sluice room and no one else seemed to be listening.

It was not a question that Sister Julia was accustomed to hearing. Mothers either kept their babies or they gave them up because they had been persuaded that it was for the best. *Forgiveness* . . . What could she say? She could hardly tell Inez that her little girl would probably never know that she had once had a different mother.

'Of course she will forgive you,' Sister Julia said. 'Your daughter will be grateful to you, I am sure.' And she offered up a silent prayer. Would God understand that the truth was sometimes too painful to bear? She hoped so.

Inez sighed. 'But I will always wonder about her, Sister,' she said.

And what if the child too ever should wonder about her true birth mother? It was possible, was it not? She might be told that she had been adopted, or indeed, she might find out. And if she did — she too was very likely to wonder. Which was one of the reasons why Sister Julia had continued to keep her book of names. That little girl — like all the others — deserved the right to know.

The second child — another girl — was born mid-afternoon following induction. This mother — Danita Diez — was married and was keeping her child. The midwife had been massaging her in an attempt to improve the presentation of the foetus. She seemed to be a long way off her time still to Sister Julia, but Dr Lopez had instructed for her to be given an enema and castor oil first thing in the morning.

He examined her later. 'The cervix is favourable,' he pronounced. 'And the presentation is now good. I will perform the rupture.'

Sister Julia knew what was coming. Once the amniotic fluid was released the pressure of the baby's head would increase the force and frequency of the uterine contractions. She helped the nurse prepare the surgical trolley and then drew the screen around the bed.

The nurse put Danita's legs up in the stirrups and Dr Lopez worked quickly and professionally as ever.

'She will get better care in the daytime, Sister,' he muttered as he pulled off his white mask, having completed the procedure.

Danita shrieked as the first strong contraction pulled at her. Breaking the amniotic waters in this way might reduce the amount of time she was in labour, but it always made it more painful for the mother. The pains were so sudden, so fierce.

Sister Julia and the midwife took her through to the delivery room. The midwife was shaking her head.

'Should she have been induced?' Sister Julia dared to whisper.

The midwife glanced at her. 'It is simpler this way,' she said.

Sister Julia was aware of that. But simpler for whom?

While Dr Lopez was busy dealing with the third birth of the day, Sister Julia slipped down to his consulting room on the pretext of fetching something a patient had left in the waiting room. She found an excuse to do this two or three times a week – frequently enough to ensure she kept abreast of the birth and death records; frequently enough for her to be able to memorise names so that she could write them in her book, later, in the privacy of her room at Santa Ana. Sister Julia had to do this often, she found – or the files would disappear. Were they destroyed so that there was no evidence of what was going on? She feared so.

Did the end justify the means? Swiftly, Sister Julia flicked through the files in the cabinet. She thought not. She understood that it might help the children and even the mothers – to save them from suffering personal and possibly social deprivation. She even understood that it could – in the long run – be good for Spain. But she had seen the heart of it. She had seen the pain and the anguish. And worst of all, she had seen the deaths.

The third baby died. He was a boy – just as Sister Julia had expected.

She had not been present at the birth and the first she knew of what had happened was when the white-faced midwife ran to fetch her. 'You are needed to offer comfort, Sister,' she said. 'It is another death.'

Sister Julia did not see the child and neither did his mother.

'How did he die?' she asked Dr Lopez before she left that night.

He was writing up a report. 'Low infant weight,' he said. 'Undernourished by the mother. He was distressed – a forceps delivery.' He barely glanced up at her.

And what would he write on the death certificate? Sister Julia wondered. Sometimes he was overconfident. Which meant that sometimes he was careless.

A knock on the door signalled the arrival of the latest couple come to collect their adopted child. Sister Julia sighed as she went to let them in.

'Hello, hello there.' The doctor was effusive as they entered his consulting room.

Sister Julia could not stomach it. She turned to go.

'It has been my aspiration for so many years,' the man said, as he shook hands with Dr Lopez, 'to have a son.' His voice was low and full of emotion. 'And you have helped me. For that I am eternally grateful. It is all I ever wanted. I will give him the best life.'

But at what emotional cost, Sister Julia thought. At what cost?

Later that evening, back at the Santa Ana convent, Sister Julia unlocked the drawer of her writing desk and withdrew her book of names.

Slowly, she turned the pages. It was filling up now. It was becoming as complete a record of the adoptions and deaths at the Canales Clinic as she could make it. Sister Julia took her pen and carefully wrote the entry for that day. She had done this every day since she had started writing in the book. The women who had given birth. The children. The adoptive parents. The deaths. All the names and the dates were here.

So how could she leave?

She closed the book and replaced it in the drawer, locking it and pocketing the small key. And she stared out into the darkness of the courtyard below. How she longed to be free of it all. To be free to live simply here at Santa Ana, to study and to read, to pray and to reflect. To be free of the clinic and the pain. Because the years did not lessen that pain. She still felt every maternal parting as if she was once again reliving her own.

Could she do more? Every day and every night she asked herself this question. She had challenged the doctor so many times and she had tried to make the reverend mother see how it was. But what power did she have – a nun in a convent – against figures of authority such as Dr Lopez? She had seen the people who came to the clinic. She knew how many connections he had in high places.

No. All she could do was what she was doing already – helping the women and children as best she could. Keeping a record of it all. It might not be much, but while she was doing these things, how could she leave?

When Sister Julia's own mother came to visit her this time her eyes were red with weeping. She was dressed in black and immediately Sister Julia knew.

'Papa?' she whispered.

Her mother nodded. 'Pray for him, Julia,' she said. 'For he has gone.'

The following week, Sister Julia stood with her family at his graveside. She watched the simple wooden coffin as it was lowered into the earth and she held her rosary beads gripped between her fingers. It seemed impossible that his body was encased within that box. That she would never see him again. And her loss seemed all the greater when she thought of all those years they had not been together, all those years she had been cloistered away from her family. Lost years. Years which could have been so different if she had stayed in the family home, suffering with them – the hardship, the hunger, the pain.

She looked around at the small group that made up her

family. At her mother, the webs of her black lacy shawl only half hiding her tears; at Matilde, cool and erect, her arm in her husband's, but barely touching. And Paloma, sad Paloma, here without her husband Mario who had found something so pressing to do that he could not attend his own wife's father's funeral.

The priest intoned the words that Sister Julia knew so well. *Our Father . . . Glory to God . . . In his name. Amen.* Sister Julia murmured her responses. Her sisters did not speak. And their mother cried.

When the service was over Sister Julia stepped forwards. 'Why did he never come to see me at Santa Ana, Mama?' she asked. She had to know.

'He could not bear to, my child,' her mother said. She turned from the graveside and took Sister Julia's arm.

'He could not bear to see me?'

Her mother slowly shook her head. 'He could not bear to see what he had forced you to do.'

Sister Julia looked down at the ground. Dear God in heaven, she thought.

'Your father was a proud man, Julia,' her mother went on. 'It shamed him that he could not look after you as a father should.'

And Sister Julia felt the tears come to her own eyes. For her father, for her mother, for her sisters and for herself. For all those who had suffered, and those who were suffering still.

CHAPTER 25

It was Wednesday lunchtime. Mel had left her assistant in the hat shop and she and Ruby stepped out of the shop door and straight into Pridehaven's weekly market.

'Are you OK, darling?' Mel asked. 'What's been happening?'

Where should she start? As they strolled past the stalls – antiques, bric-a-brac, vintage; bedding plants, herbs and home-made curry – Ruby tried to explain to Mel how the bombshell from Frances had left her feeling. As if some sort of tornado had picked her up and spun her into ever accelerating circles before throwing her to the ground – until she wasn't quite sure of where she was or what she was thinking, let alone feeling.

'And what about your mum's letter?' Mel picked up a brass pig doorstop and eyed it suspiciously. 'What did it say?'

Ah. 'I don't know yet,' said Ruby. 'I haven't opened it.'

Mel raised a perfectly plucked eyebrow. 'Why not?'

It was a good question. Ruby might have put it on the mantelpiece but she certainly hadn't forgotten about it. 'I don't know,' she confessed. 'I suppose I still just feel so angry with her, with them.' So many years of deceit, and then her mother does the old cliché – leaves a letter with a friend to be given to her daughter after she dies. Honestly. She turned to Mel. 'Why couldn't she have had the courage to tell me face to face?' she demanded. 'It's just not fair.' She knew she sounded like a child, but she felt like one right now.

They had moved on to a vintage jewellery stall. Ruby picked up an art deco brooch nestling in a dusty blue velvet box. A cocoon. Did jewellery absorb the vibes of its wearer? Absent-mindedly, she fingered the gold locket of Vivien's, which she'd found in her old jewellery box. It was bevelled on the outside and engraved with a rose. Even though Ruby now knew that she wasn't her biological parent, this locket – with the picture of both her parents inside – seemed to embody Essence of Mother in some indefinable, intangible way. It seemed to give her back a bit of what she was missing.

'So you're being a rebel?' Mel asked. 'By not reading the letter you're saying yah boo sucks to them all?'

Ruby had to smile. 'Maybe.' She would read it – but she would read it in her own time; when she was ready to. After all, she knew the whole story now – what more could it possibly say?

'Hmm.' Mel took her arm. 'Just be careful you're not saying yah boo sucks to yourself,' she said.

They wandered past the fruit stall and on to local ceramics. Mishmash market. No wonder it was so popular. No wonder people came from London for the weekend just to experience it. The sun was warm. Ruby had just finished a health and beauty feature commissioned by Leah with two days to spare. So tomorrow she could do some song writing, maybe fix up a rehearsal for the band. She thought of the cottage she'd soon be renting and she thought of Andrés. Smiled. Her emotions felt as if she'd been through a cement mixer. But things weren't so bad.

'You're looking rather cheerful, considering.' Mel narrowed her eyes and flicked back her auburn hair. 'Is there something else you're not telling me?'

Was there? Ruby wasn't completely sure. Not yet. She'd had a lovely day with Andrés. And then of course there was that kiss. It had taken her by surprise. It had been nice – given her a warm glow inside. And she was quite keen to repeat the experience. 'Well . . . '

'Who is he then?' she asked.

'Who?'

'The man who's brought a smile to your face.'

You could never fool Mel. Ruby shrugged. 'Remember that dinner party you persuaded me to go to?'

'Ye-es?'

'Well . . . ' After a bit, she stopped talking. Mel was staring at her. 'What?'

'You really like this man, don't you?'

Did she? They were at a vintage clothes stall. Ruby grabbed a faded print dress and held it up against her. 'What d'you reckon?'

Mel stood, hands on hips. She shook her head. 'You don't do faded.'

No, she didn't do faded. 'He's nice enough,' she admitted. He certainly had something. And he was different too. About as unlike James and some of the other men she'd met in London as he could be.

'And?'

'And nothing.' She met Mel's gimlet stare. 'Honestly. There's nothing to tell.' Not yet anyway. And right now she had plenty of other things on her mind.

She picked up a little honey pot. A tiny yellow and black bee sat on the top of the lid. She checked the price and got out her purse. Like . . .

'Where would you go to look for someone?' she asked Mel.

Pridehaven market was an odd place to be having this conversation but sometimes it was easier to talk when strangers were shifting in and out of your orbit. The market was a transient place. People were only within earshot for seconds.

'As in your birth mother, do you mean?'

'Yes,' she said. 'As in Laura.' Her birth mother. It was a weird thing to say, to think. She still hadn't quite accepted it, she supposed. Laura was the woman who had carried her and given birth to her. What had that experience meant to her? It must have meant something. And what about her father – whoever he was? Did he even know of Ruby's existence?

'You're going to look for her then?'

'I have to, Mel.' Ruby had been given a glimpse into the past – and now she wanted more.

But where should she begin? She had the photographs –

that was a starting point. Where had they been taken? She thought of the turquoise ocean, the orange beach house, the lighthouse. But she could hardly travel around the beaches on the Mediterranean looking for an orange beach house and a lighthouse. And even if she ever found the place – how likely was it that Laura would still be there? Although . . . In the photos they'd seemed like a community; it seemed like the kind of place Laura might go back to.

'Have you checked out her last known address?' Mel suggested. She paused to dip a cracker into some chilli sauce taster on a local produce stall. 'Ouch, hot!' She fanned her face and rolled her eyes at Ruby.

'I've tried that.' She'd gone back to her parents' old house, spoken to the next-door neighbour – where Pearl Woods used to live with Laura – in the hope of getting a forwarding address.

'And?'

'A complete blank.' It was much too long ago; the house had changed hands a couple of times at least since then. *Laura and Pearl* . . . Ruby had thought as she stood on the doorstep. Her mother. Her grandmother. Would she ever be able to get her head around it?

'What about Laura's father?' Mel suggested. She had moved on to another stall and was now examining a cream-coloured platter with red hand-painted poppies.

Ah yes, Ruby's grandfather. Derek Woods. Was he still alive? 'He'd be well into his eighties,' she said. 'But Laura hated him.'

'Maybe they were reconciled,' Mel said. They moved apart to examine the sheen of a blue glass jug (Mel) and the design of a Clarice Cliff plate (Ruby). Then back together again. Like a dance, thought Ruby. They drifted apart to opposite sides of the stall, sent one other a contemplative look and then walked on.

It was possible that they had been reconciled, she thought. Had Laura ever come back to England? And if so – had she been tempted to look for Ruby? She had to keep on searching for Laura – if only to find some of the answers to her questions.

At the square, where a band was playing rock and roll swing jive, they sat on a bench to listen. Ruby's feet started tapping. She always felt a bit more alive when music was playing. It vibrated inside her, as if it was in her blood.

Mel went to get coffee and returned with two cups and two pieces of Dorset apple cake. 'A continuing battle,' she muttered, taking a bite out of one of them and handing the other to Ruby.

In front of them the rock and roll jivers began to dance, she in a swishy, swirly skirt, him in skin-tight black trousers. 'But there are other starting points,' Mel said.

'Such as?'

She shrugged. 'Finding out where Laura went to school. Putting an ad in the local paper – "Is anyone still in contact with Laura Woods" – that kind of thing.'

'Good idea.' Ruby nodded. She must have had friends here when she was seventeen. Maybe they were still in contact –

or at least knew where those photos had been taken. At least she could extend the radius of her enquiries out a bit further. She took off the cover of her take-out cup. The coffee was strong, frothy and steaming.

'Facebook?' Mel suggested. She was on a roll. 'Friends Reunited?'

'Why not?' Social networking sites were a brilliant idea. Ruby nodded. She would scan the photo on to Facebook. Ask all of her contacts to ask all of their contacts. Didn't they say there were only six steps between any two people in the world?

'But what would I say to her?' Ruby muttered. '"Hey, I'm the baby you abandoned thirty-five years ago. Will you be my friend?"'

Mel laughed. 'Or you could hire a private investigator — they have access to all sorts of public records that the general public can't get to see.' She checked her watch. 'You know, sensitive data and all that.'

'I could do.' She'd thought of that too. But she just had the feeling . . . Laura wasn't in the UK. She was outside of 'public records'. She'd placed herself outside — of all the bureaucracy, all the authorities, all the paperwork. She was a free spirit, wasn't she? *People shouldn't be labelled* — that's what she'd believed when she was twenty. And Ruby sensed that's what she'd still believe now.

Mel got to her feet. 'I've got to get back to work, Ruby,' she said. 'But let me know how you get on.'

'Oh, I will.' Maybe she'd never find her. But she had to at least try.

They hugged and when they drew apart, Mel didn't quite let go. 'And about that Spanish guy from the dinner party . . . '

'*Majoreros*,' said Ruby. 'What about him?'

'Sometimes you have to just close your eyes and jump,' Mel said. 'Otherwise you're not really living at all.'

After Mel had gone back to the shop, Ruby finished her coffee and cake and watched the rock and roll jivers. They were closing their eyes and jumping – really letting go. Mel's eyes had been a bit sad when she'd said that. Was there something she was keeping to herself because she thought Ruby was too fragile right now to be of any help? She'd call her later to find out, she decided.

She thought of her walk with Andrés on the cliff top, the way he had sketched her portrait, a half frown on his face as he focused on getting the drawing right. It had been a good resemblance. But more than that: it had reminded her of something, of someone. The photograph of Laura. In that moment, as Ruby looked at his drawing, she had recognised not only something of herself in it, but something of Laura too.

Was that why she hadn't opened Vivien's letter? Was she forging some silent allegiance with her birth mother, saying not yah boo sucks, but this is where I came from; and this is where I'm going now.

She pulled the photos out of her bag, found the one of Laura holding her when she was a baby. Was that why she had kept looking at this – even before she'd known the truth?

Looking at Laura was like looking at a complete stranger. And yet it was also like looking at someone she had known all her life.

CHAPTER 26

Ruby was playing at the Jazz Café.

Andrés sat at his usual stool at the bar drinking beer. Everything was as before. Tina hustled and bustled behind the bar fetching beer and ice and bottles of wine, chatting to him when she wasn't serving. Couples and singles and groups of friends milled in through the doors and mingled by the bar, sitting down, sometimes getting up to dance. The light dimmed as the evening progressed; the atmosphere was laid-back, the mood was blue.

And yet everything had changed.

Because Tina hadn't asked 'How are you two getting along?' She knew how they were getting along. It was obvious.

They had arrived here together tonight, eyes bright, not touching but nearly touching. Tina had looked at them just once.

Andrés knew that at the end of her set, Ruby would come and sit on the stool next to him at the bar. She would drink beer, laugh, chat a little. She would be tired, but still on a performance high; still buzzing. And when they left, Andrés would take her home.

He had helped her move her things into the cottage in Pride Bay yesterday. Before that he had dropped the work he'd intended to do that week and put forward the work on the cottage, wanting to get it ready for her. His client wouldn't object to the few added extras; Andrés was, after all, increasing the rentable value of the place.

'You really don't have to do all this, Andrés,' she had told him more than once during the past week. 'I don't even know how long I'll be there for.'

He was aware of that. She'd negotiated a rental contract of only three months. It wasn't long, but . . .

'By then I'll know,' she'd said.

And he'd seen the restlessness in her eyes. What would she know? Where she wanted to be? In three months' time her parents' house could be sold. Would she look for something to buy around here – in the landscape of her childhood? Or would she be leaving?

'It does not matter,' he'd said. He understood that she needed to move out of her parents' house and that she had to get on with her life without them. And he wanted her to be able to do that. He wanted to help her. It was a strange and unfamiliar feeling. He barely knew her and yet he felt protective of her. Andrés quite liked that.

He watched her play. She was wearing a red dress, close-fitting and silky, with a slashed neckline and high heels. She had on a black choker and a bracelet of jet that fell from elbow to wrist as her right arm moved up and down over the keys. Her blonde hair was slicked back from her face. She wore the usual red lipstick. She looked amazing.

It wasn't just that though, was it? There was something bright about her, even as she poured her sad soul into the mouthpiece of the saxophone and out in the music whose plaintive beauty wove itself around him until Andrés almost wanted to cry. That something bright just shone from her, like a jewel. He loved her sadness, he loved the shining. Like a star in the sky, he thought. Un-gettable.

When she played, when she took the instrument and bent and swayed to the rhythm of its tune, Ruby travelled some-where, far from the Jazz Café, far from Andrés, far from everything else in the world he could see. Where did she go? Who did she become? God only knew. He understood it though. When he was absorbed in a painting, he often felt that sense of transportation too. Life almost ceased to exist, time stood still, the world might come to an end and he would barely notice.

Last night he had taken her out to dinner to celebrate the move. Their first proper date, he supposed you could call it. It had been a great evening, even though he had been nervous – ridiculously so – and she had seemed distracted. She was in the middle of something, she told him. She had a lot to think about right now. It was something to do with her parents. And she had paused and frowned for a moment in that way she had as though she wanted to tell him about it.

'It's OK,' he had said. 'You do not have to say any more.' He hadn't wanted to pressurise her. It would come in time, he told himself. Ruby would confide in him in time. And that would be the right time.

Andrés took a pull of his beer and held his breath as the final lingering notes filled the café, drifting like dust motes in the space between them. He wasn't quite sure what he felt for her yet but he thought that he kind of got what she was about. He knew they had things in common. And he understood her loss.

In his case, of course, the deaths had been symbolic ones. *Do not darken this door* . . . His father's harsh voice seemed to grate into his ears as it had done so many times before.

There had always been tensions in his home – for as long as he could remember. His father bullying and demanding. Izabella dancing to his tune. His mother scurrying around trying to please everyone. Andrés getting into trouble.

'Why do you have to answer him back?' his mother would say, clicking her tongue in frustration. 'Why can't you be silent, son, and simply leave him be?'

Leave him be. Leave him be. As if Enrique Marin were not after all a mere mortal, a mere man, but some sort of god on high that they all had to worship and adore. While he . . . Andrés shook his head in disgust.

The tensions had grown more tightly strung than ever as he became a teenager, though he hadn't known why. What had changed? His father worked in his studio muttering or yelling, or stomped down to the Old Harbour – bandanna round his head, cheroot hanging from his lips – to scowl at the waves, or to play dominoes in the Bar Acorralado.

Leave him be . . . Mama worked in the house and created her *calados*, her embroidered linen cloths, as she sat outside – sometimes silent, sometimes gossiping with neighbours. Izabella was a dutiful daughter and trotted around after his mother like a puppy. And Andrés continued to paint.

What had changed? The village was slowly becoming richer – there was more planting, more crops. And tourism. Once, the villagers had survived by bartering for fish in exchange for milk and cheese from their goats, cereal from their plots of land, figs and prickly pears – either fresh or sun-dried. But now the tourists had changed all that. And his father was selling paintings. The times of poverty were gone, or so people said. So why was Mama's smile so rare and why was his father's frown so deeply etched on his brow? Why were they both so unhappy?

Andrés had not known. Now, though, he could guess. Perhaps Mama had been aware of what was happening even then and had turned a blind eye to it. *Leave him be . . .* When had it started? For how long had it gone on? These were questions for which Andrés would probably never have an answer.

And then the song was over and Ruby was bowing and smiling and slipping the saxophone strap from her shoulders. The audience were clapping. Andrés got to his feet and clapped too. Tina smiled across at him.

Ruby disappeared backstage.

Andrés fetched another stool and ordered her a beer. That protective sensation again . . . He wasn't sure yet how he felt about it.

Tina put the beer on the counter in front of him. 'She's really good,' she said. 'You can feel her pain.'

'I know.' He could see Ruby making her way over. The woman with whom he went walking in her red fleece and blue jeans and who had sat hugging her knees like a child on Chesil Beach now looked as glamorous and elegant as a film star working the red carpet. She smiled straight at him.

Andrés got to his feet. Whichever way he looked at it, this was important. He wasn't going to fuck it up.

CHAPTER 27

Barcelona, 1973

The streets were busier these days as Sister Julia walked from Santa Ana to the Raval quarter – more people visited the city; people of different nationalities and from different cultures. Tourism had come to Spain. There was much to visit in the city of Barcelona. The cathedral and the Gaudi houses, the parks and the fountains. And so many different voices . . . At first, Sister Julia found this unsettling – perhaps change was always unsettling? – but then she realised. There was less fear on the streets and more of a sense of liberty. This had to be a good thing.

At the clinic there were fewer single mothers and Sister Julia no longer worked such long hours. It was a relief – now, she had more time to read and study the English language; there were many worthy writings in English and she was glad that she could understand them. It was one of her great pleasures. But there were still deaths and there were still adoptions and Sister Julia still kept her book of names – a book which was almost full.

One day, a day of autumn mist and fallen leaves when the city smelt of damp and wood smoke, Sister Julia lingered outside the bookshop in Las Ramblas. It was not just English she wanted to read. Books were once more being published in Catalan. She smiled to herself and offered a prayer of thanks. This was a move towards the recovery of her culture. If only her parents were still alive to see it. Her mother had passed away from this earth only a year after her father – as if she simply found it too hard to cope without him. And since then she had not seen either of her sisters. Matilde and her husband had moved away; Sister Julia only hoped that her sister would find the strength to accept the life that she had been given. As for Paloma . . . As far as Sister Julia was aware, she still lived in Barcelona with Mario Vamos, the man she had married for love. But – much to her regret – she no longer saw her.

It was hard, Sister Julia thought, to even recall the closeness of the family unit they had once had. They had survived when many others had not. But it had never been easy. And hadn't they too been broken – just like all the rest?

She arrived at the clinic to find things much as normal. There were two women in the medical room, both in the early stages of labour, and the doctor was prowling around his consulting room as he often seemed to do these days; never still, always on edge, always ready to brandish his crucifix and demand repentance from the women who still came to them for help. But these days there was an air of fanaticism about him. For how long, she wondered, could this possibly go on?

Sister Julia took the morning prayers as usual and then

helped the nurses with their bedmaking and other duties. A man came to see the doctor about an adoption; she did not see his face, but she heard the confidence in his low, grating voice from inside Dr Lopez's office and she could not help but click her tongue in disapproval.

After Dr Lopez had carried out his morning round, he drew her to one side. 'I am entrusting you with a vital and confidential task, Sister,' he said.

'Very well, doctor.' Sister Julia bowed her head. What could it be?

'There is a payment due from . . . ' noisily, he cleared his throat, 'one of our kind benefactors. You must meet this man and bring the payment back to me immediately.'

A payment?

She must have looked confused, because the doctor waved away her doubts. 'Do not worry, Sister,' he said. 'You will be perfectly safe. It is not far. I will give you the directions.'

But she had not been worrying about her safety. Was she not used to wandering around the city alone? Had she not been doing this for years? No. What had confused her was why she had to go anywhere to collect a payment from a benefactor. Why could the benefactor not bring his payment here to the clinic? It was odd, to say the least.

'I cannot go myself,' Dr Lopez said. 'I have to be careful. I must protect my clinic and my name.' He looked at her. 'You must go, Sister Julia. No one will look twice at you.'

Sister Julia began to grasp his meaning. This was not then simply a payment from a benefactor. There was something more sinister afoot if the doctor was talking about protecting his reputation. She was a nun. No one would suspect her of any clandestine or illegal activity. *Illegal activity* . . . Swiftly, she crossed herself, closed her eyes to find God. *God in heaven, hear my voice. Help me to do what I must do. Amen.*

What should she do? She could refuse to go. But if she went . . . Something told her that if she went she might find out something more, something that she needed to know.

She met the man and the woman under the arches by Calle Fernando. Who knew what kind of dubious transactions took place there? The area was full of shadows; of beggars and thieves.

The man seemed surprised to see her. 'Where is the priest?' he asked.

The priest? He was usually met by a priest? Sister Julia did not know how to answer this and so she was silent.

The man laughed, but without humour. He handed her an envelope. 'Count it,' he said. 'I do not want to be accused of short-changing anyone.'

Sister Julia counted ten thousand pesetas. She had never seen so much money in her life. Whatever was the money for? Was the clinic to be refurbished, perhaps? Would Dr Lopez be taking on more staff? It must take a certain amount of money to run a clinic like the doctor's but she had assumed that it existed on its charitable donations; she knew for a fact that it was assisted by the Church, the reverend mother had told her so.

'I'll be back in six months,' the man said. 'With the next instalment.'

The next instalment? Sister Julia's blood ran cold. 'How many in all?' she was bold enough to ask.

'This is the seventh of ten, Sister,' he said. He bowed his head.

A hundred thousand pesetas then.

Perhaps Sister Julia would not have known for sure what the payment was for if she had not recognised the woman half hiding in the shadows of the arches, her scarf drawn around her face as she stepped forwards to leave.

Sister Julia had seen her at the clinic. She had come there not to give birth, however; she had come there to adopt a child.

So. This man and this woman were adoptive parents. If she tried, she might even be able to remember the name. They were all – were they not? – written down.

A hundred thousand pesetas. So that was how it was. Dear God in heaven. It came to Sister Julia gradually what she had been a part of for so long; what she was a part of still. She had been right to question whether it was simply a matter of helping vulnerable members of society, of giving children more opportunities in life. Of course it was not. How could she have been so blind? So naive? So gullible? It was also a question of money. And the money came from the right sort of families. Right, Sister Julia thought, in more than one sense of that word. This was a corruption that had been going on in front of her eyes for almost three decades.

As she hurried back to the Canales Clinic, the money in her pocket felt as if it was burning through to Sister Julia's very skin. She couldn't wait to be rid of it. Blood money, she thought. Money paid for human life.

The doctor was waiting for her.

She pulled the envelope from her pocket and held it out to him. Took a deep breath. Courage, she thought. 'Will you tell me, doctor,' she said, 'what this money is in payment for?'

'Ah, Sister.' He flicked the envelope from her grasp. 'Perhaps it is best that you do not know.'

Sister Julia met his piercing gaze. She remembered that first day she had been introduced to him in the hospital and how he had intimidated her. She remembered all the questions that she had wanted to ask over the years – and indeed, all the questions that she had asked. 'Perhaps,' she said quietly, 'I already do know.'

He frowned. Scrutinised her up and down in a way he had not done since that first day. 'God moves in mysterious ways, Sister,' he said. 'And ours is not to reason why.' And he took a step closer towards her.

He was so close now that she could feel his breath on her face, smell the scent of him – of surgical spirit and the hint of stale alcohol. He gripped her wrist and in that second she was so scared that she almost stopped breathing. But she did not back down. She would not back down. She stared right back at him. She knew now exactly what he was.

'Perhaps you will not always be able to hide behind God, doctor,' she said, forcing her voice not to shake.

His grip tightened. 'And perhaps you, Sister Julia,' he said, 'should take care.'

She stood her ground and after a moment he seemed to come to his senses. He loosened his hold on her and she pulled her hand away.

He took some money out of the envelope. 'I wish to pay you for the task you have undertaken today, Sister.' His voice now was businesslike and calm.

She stared at him in disbelief. Did he really think that everyone could be bought so easily? Was that what his world was like? 'I want no money,' she said, her voice low. 'I want nothing. And I want no part of it ever again.'

'Very well, Sister.' He opened the door for her to leave. And as she left, a look passed between them. A look so complete in understanding that she felt weak, as if her legs might collapse from under her. But she held her head high and she returned to Santa Ana.

At the convent, Sister Julia hurried to the chapel to pray. And she asked for God's forgiveness – because these things had been done in His name. Names . . . She went to her room, she looked in her book of names and she sighed. There were so many of them. She had done what she could. But now she could do no more. Was she still a person in her own right, as well as a sister at the Convent Santa Ana? Could she make her own decisions? Did she still have a voice?

She went to see the reverend mother and told her she was unable to work at the clinic with Dr Lopez any longer.

'Why is that?' the mother superior asked sharply.

'I cannot,' Sister Julia said. 'I will not.' Her face was wet with tears. But who was she crying for? Was it for the mothers who had lost their babies? The children who would never know who they truly were? Or was she crying for herself and what she had lost?

'But for what reason, my child?' The reverend mother seemed to soften slightly in the face of her passion.

Sister Julia swallowed hard. Should she tell her about the money? What she now knew – for sure – about Dr Lopez and the clinic? Should she tell her of all the things that had been done in God's name? She longed to. It would be such a relief to tell someone, to unburden after all these years. And yet . . . She had tried to tell her before. And each time had been fobbed off with the same story. The reverend mother had always defended him. Why should anything be different now? The truth was that Sister Julia did not know if she could trust her.

'I cannot say.' She bowed her head. 'But it has become impossible for me to continue my work there. I need to take some time for prayer. I need to find again my God.'

The reverend mother regarded her sadly for several moments without saying a word. 'I will speak to the doctor,' she said at last.

Sister Julia could not bear it. If she ever had to return there . . . She straightened her shoulders. 'Reverend Mother, I will not go back,' she repeated.

The mother superior regarded her again and then at last

she reached out her hand and placed it on Sister Julia's head. 'You will not have to, my child,' she said. 'Do not fear.'

'Thank you, Reverend Mother.' And Sister Julia felt the burden ease.

'But you cannot stay here,' she added.

Sister Julia was not surprised. But where could she go? This was the only home she had known for so many years.

The reverend mother seemed deep in thought. 'We will send you to our Canary Island of Fuerteventura,' she said at last. 'To a small convent there which is just starting out. It is quiet. You will be safe. You will have the opportunity to reflect and to pray just as you wish.'

'Very well, Reverend Mother.' It was an appealing thought. To be quiet. To be safe. To have the opportunity to reflect on everything that had happened. Though she knew that if she was safe, then Dr Lopez would be safe as well.

There was one thing that Sister Julia had to do before she left – she must find her sister Paloma and she must say goodbye.

One day in early March, when the breeze was mild and it seemed that winter might be creeping away at last, Sister Julia made her way to the street where her family had lived, and where Mario Vamos too had resided next door. It was not the first time she had been back and yet she stood for several minutes gazing at the house, remembering those family times – some cheerful but many fraught with poverty and hardship. She looked up at the window of the room she had shared with her sisters, and she seemed to hear it once again catching in the wind that funnelled down the narrow street – Paloma's chatter, Paloma's girlish laughter.

Her family no longer owned the house and so Sister Julia knocked on the door of the house next door – the Vamos's. Perhaps even Paloma . . .

But the door was opened by an old woman – Mario's aged aunt, she suspected, whom she remembered from those long-ago childhood days.

'Yes, Sister? Can I help you?' the woman enquired politely, not quite hiding her surprise at seeing a nun on her doorstep.

Sister Julia did not prevaricate. 'Señora, I am looking for Señora Paloma Vamos,' she said. 'It is a matter of some urgency.'

The old woman's expression altered to one of distaste. 'I know her,' she said.

'Then please give me her address.' Sister Julia smiled slightly to soften her words.

'Of course.' She disappeared inside and returned with a piece of paper which she passed to Sister Julia. 'Here.'

'Thank you.'

Sister Julia made her way through the maze of the Raval quarter to the street whose name was written in a spidery scrawl on the paper. Number fifteen. When she arrived there, it was drab and uncared-for. She took a deep breath and knocked on the door.

It was opened by a man of about her own age. She recognised him immediately. But the boyish good looks had slipped from his face – replaced by a hardness that surprised her. He was wearing a cap at a jaunty angle and there was still a certain humour in those eyes. But his mouth was down-turned into a cruel line and his expression was not kind. 'Señor Vamos?' Sister Julia enquired.

'*Si.*' He didn't flinch as he looked at her. 'What can I do for you, Sister?'

Sister Julia held herself erect. Of course he would not recognise her. Why should he after all these years? 'I am come to see my sister Paloma,' she said.

'Oh?'

But behind him she saw Paloma herself materialise from a front room. 'Julia?' She edged past her husband and held out a hand. 'Julia?'

Ignoring Mario Vamos's curious gaze, Sister Julia allowed her hand to be taken as he shrugged and stepped away from the door and Paloma pulled her inside. She smelt the sweet scent of tobacco clinging to his clothes and skin as she moved past him, mingling with the smell of alcohol and sweat. And she noted the way they responded to one another; Mario's curt tone of dismissal as he spoke to his wife.

She and her sister sat facing one another in a small and shabby room at the front of the house. Paloma brought cof-fee and left it on a side table. 'Julia,' she said again. 'It is good to see you.'

'And you too, Paloma.' Sister Julia bowed her head. But in truth, it was a shock. Her sister had changed so much. Her hair was greying and unkempt, her eyes were dull where they had always shone like dark diamonds and the generous curve of her mouth was now tinged with bitterness. 'How are you?' she asked.

As if in reply the front door slammed and Sister Julia saw Mario saunter off down the street, hands in pockets, whistling.

Paloma closed her eyes. 'He will not return tonight,' she said.

Sister Julia did not know what to say. 'You are not happy?' she ventured at last. She remembered what Paloma and their mother had said the last time they visited. 'You and Mario still have no children?'

Paloma shook her head. 'We have no children,' she said. 'And we will not.'

And Sister Julia could see how it was. How Paloma had become bitter and plain as she watched her husband flirt with younger women of the neighbourhood, as they fought a battle which Paloma could never hope to win, as she failed to give him children and lost her husband time after time, more wholly with each year that passed – until he no longer wanted her at all.

'I am leaving our city,' Sister Julia told her as she got up to go. 'I am to live in a convent in Fuerteventura.'

Paloma nodded, seeming unsurprised. 'I wish you luck, Julia,' she said. 'I wish you love.' She smiled. And just for a second she seemed like the old Paloma, the careless, laughing girl.

'And I you, my sister.' They embraced. 'And I you.'

★

Sister Julia left Barcelona in the middle of the Easter festival. The streets were full of people watching the processions and the floats. Peanuts, chocolate and caramelised almonds were being thrown to the children standing by the roadside. By the church, a priest stood holding a missal and a rosary, blessing people as they passed by. There were women wearing mantillas, those delicate traceries of lace, black high heels and black dresses, and men in black suits with slicked back hair. There were upturned faces, people crossing themselves as they murmured a silent prayer. The scents of celebration were in the air for Holy Week – wax, incense, garlic, tobacco smoke . . . And orange blossom, for the blooms were now cloaking the trees in the city. It was a heady cocktail, and one which reminded Sister Julia of how the city had once been when she was a girl. At last Spain's fortunes had changed.

And Sister Julia was to retreat from her world at last.

CHAPTER 28

'Shall we?' Andrés was holding out his hand. Sure and safe.

'Are you joking?' Ruby looked towards the stage. The band – a new band – was playing swing and people had started to dance.

'I never joke about serious things,' he said, 'like dancing.'

'Fair enough.' Ruby slid off the stool. As always when she'd been playing, she felt emotionally drained, a bit of a wasteland. That was OK – she always put a lot in because she wanted to, it was the only way of getting a lot out. But afterwards, she needed to wind down – a few beers or a large glass of red, some food, an easy conversation.

Not dancing.

On the dance floor, the beat picked up. Andrés strode forwards, still holding her hand and looking purposeful. He was wearing faded black jeans, a linen shirt the colour of a pale mushroom and a slightly crumpled linen jacket. His thick dark hair curled against the collar. He had a furrow of concentration on his brow as he found a space on the floor (this was worrying; was he expecting her to move around that much?). He took her in a kind of ballroom hold. She quite liked the proximity of that. So far, so OK.

'Just relax,' he said.

And before she knew it, they were doing some sort of swing jive; him leading, her clinging on by osmosis, telepathy and prayer. At first, she tried to concentrate on the steps, but it was hard to follow the rhythm and they either knocked knees or ended up miles apart. Ruby thought of Mel and what she'd told her. *Jump*.

She'd found out why Mel was unhappy. She'd gone round to their place for supper and Mel had confided in her while they were clearing up. Stuart wanted them to start a family. Time was running out, he said. It meant so much to him to have kids, it was what he'd always wanted.

Ruby touched her arm. 'And you don't?'

Mel looked towards the kitchen doorway. But Stuart was in the sitting room now and he'd put on some music – classical guitar – which was wafting through the house. 'I don't want my life to change, Ruby,' she whispered. 'I don't think I'm . . . ready.'

Ruby took the stack of plates Mel was carrying and put them down on the counter. She hugged her. 'It isn't compulsory to have children,' she murmured into her hair. She couldn't help thinking of Laura and Vivien. And now Mel.

Mel drew away. 'But I'm being selfish?'

'Maybe.' Ruby shrugged. 'But you're entitled, aren't you? It's your life.'

Mel sighed as she bent down to open the dishwasher. 'Our life,' she said.

★

But it was good, wasn't it, Ruby thought now, as she tried not to think too much about the dance steps, to have that with someone? Even if what you wanted didn't always coincide.

So she changed tack. She closed her eyes and jumped. Gave herself up. Went with him wherever he'd decided to take her. Lost herself in the beat. And it worked. This made sense to Ruby. Music had a direct route to the heart.

'Where did you learn to do this?' she shouted mid-spin. She'd always liked to dance, but she'd almost forgotten how. And this was the kind of dancing that was way outside her experience.

He caught her, held her steady. 'I never learnt. Just did.'

Hmm. Ruby relaxed in the cradle of his hold for a moment – cocooned; she liked that – before he spun her out again. She felt the adrenalin bubbling like champagne. Heady stuff. Hang on a minute. Wasn't she supposed to be chilling out?

In the next number, the band slowed it right down. 'That's more like it,' Ruby murmured. They were both breathing heavily.

He held her slightly apart – as if she might break – not pulled close in to his body, which was where she'd rather like to be. She tried not to look at his mouth. His lips were full, the faint shadow of stubble on his jaw; his cheekbones high and defined. There was something primitive about him, something straightforward that drew her. And she could smell the warm resinous scent of him, like amber. The man was seriously sexy. Seriously hot. She must be careful. In her fragile state, she didn't want to get burned.

She closed her eyes for a moment and Laura obligingly stepped into her mind. Laura . . . *Who are you? Where are you? Why did you do it?* Had she thought about Ruby over the years? Had she ever thought about her?

What had it felt like, she wondered, to carry a baby for nine months, to care for that baby for another six months, and then to give that baby away? Why had she done it? Was it for selfish reasons? Or had she wanted to give Ruby what she saw as a better life, one that included all the things that she couldn't give her? Had Laura carried any guilt? Or had she blithely got on with her own life as if she had never been a mother?

Ruby tried to relax in his arms. There were so many questions and she wondered if she'd ever find all the answers. Because so far everything pointed to the fact that she'd been right. The trail had gone dead in 1976 when Laura first went travelling. Laura had apparently been a bit of a loner. And in 1976 she had cut all her ties and simply disappeared. Ruby had found out where Laura went to school – her name was on the old girls list of the local girls' grammar school, now a shiny, rebuilt comprehensive. But no one had answered the ad she'd put in the local paper, nor had Facebook or Friends Reunited yielded any results. Laura must have lost touch with old school friends. It happened – especially after almost forty years.

It seemed then that there was nothing to go on – apart from that Mediterranean beach . . .

Slowly, gradually, Andrés pulled her closer until her face was resting against his linen shirt. Inside every relationship was a deal – whether unspoken or not. And this, she realised, was very different from the contract she had unknowingly made with James. She didn't have to *be* anything. This man accepted her as she was, or even as she might be on some non-specific day in the future. He accepted her grief. He didn't want her to be anything – or anyone – else.

She could feel his heart beating, she could feel the warmth of him. There was something so familiar about him, as if all her life she had been slightly lost, slightly dislocated and now at last she was finding her feet. She felt stronger than she had since the accident. She felt as if she had a purpose.

When the last notes faded and the song was over, he let her go. Ruby moved reluctantly, gave him a small smile. But as they walked back to the bar, he looked at her, touched her hand and something seemed to shift inside her. It was as if the past pain slipped back a little, there was the smallest chink of light and something new and hopeful was emerging in the tunnel of now.

That night, as they walked back to Ruby's new place – small but cosy and exactly what she needed for the moment – she told him how she had discovered she wasn't really her mother's daughter. The darkness seemed to make it possible to talk. The streets were quiet, there were hardly any lights in the windows of the houses they passed; most people were in bed asleep. And only a crescent moon glimmered in the dark sky. The pavement was damp from an evening shower but now the air felt fresh and clean. There was a sense of peace and tranquillity after the music, the dancing. A time for telling. She told him about the shoebox she'd found in the wardrobe and the letter from the doctor. She told him about the family photo album. She told him the story that Frances had told her. And she told him about Laura.

'I can show you a picture,' she said.

They stopped under a lamp-post as they arrived at the cottage and she pulled the photographs out of her bag. 'That's her,' she said. 'And that's me.'

'She's beautiful.' Andrés held the photo up to the light. He frowned. 'Do you know where this was taken?'

'I've got no idea.' She leant against him and peered over his shoulder. 'It looks like a pretty special kind of place though.'

'It looks like Fuerteventura,' Andrés said. He handed it back to her.

'Really?' Well, the light wasn't good. It could be anywhere, couldn't it – with sand and sea and a few black rocks?

'My island is the kind of place people like that come to,' Andrés said. He put his arm around her. It felt good.

'People like that?'

'Surfers, hippies, travellers.' He laughed softly. 'People who drive VW camper vans.'

'I can't get over the fact that she's out there somewhere,' Ruby said. 'That I've got someone somewhere who once had to make such a big decision about me.'

Andrés didn't speak, but he put both his arms around her now and held her tight.

'I've been feeling scared,' she told him. Their faces were only inches apart. 'It's an odd thing. Even my memories don't seem mine any more. I don't know who I am.'

'I know who you are, Ruby,' Andrés said.

She was wrapped in his arms. Really wrapped. Not just like in the dance, but so close that there was no space between them. So close that all she could feel was his warmth. And she wanted more of it. There was something about him that made her nerves jangle; that left her dizzy and wanting to hold on.

She edged out of his embrace and felt for the key that was in her bag. She had let him into her life. There was no going back. She opened the door and turned to face him. Took him by the hand. Led him inside.

CHAPTER 29

Andrés was working in the studio when his mobile rang. He cursed under his breath. But it was his mother so he must answer.

'Mama?'

'Andrés.' Immediately, he heard the held-back emotion in her voice.

'What's wrong?' Something in his belly dipped with foreboding. Was she ill? Was Izabella ill? Was . . . ?

His mother sighed. 'It is your father.'

Andrés tensed. 'What of him?' His voice was flat. He looked down at the painting he was working on. He had prepared it with a background wash of palest blue. On this he planned to paint Chesil Beach in all its glorious shades of toffee, honey, amber. The warmth of the high-bricked sandstone cliffs, the rise of tiny pebbles, the buttercups freckling the grass. And the sea. The end of summer exhibition was coming up and he wanted to put in as many pieces as he could. He had reserved an exhibition space in the Salt House at Pride Bay – a wide open high-roofed barn near the sea – which would be perfect for showing his work. It almost didn't matter to him how much he sold – though sales would obviously be good. What he wanted most, he realised, was recognition.

'He is not well, my son.'

Andrés held his breath. 'What is wrong with him?' He heard his own voice – harsh and grating.

'We are not sure.'

'Well, then . . . ' He released the breath. It would be nothing. His mother worrying about nothing.

Andrés had gained recognition once before in his life – from his father. *The boy can paint . . .* But it had only brought hatred and resentment from the man who was supposed to love him. Because shouldn't you automatically love your own child? *Si, por supuesto*. Of course you should. So. Andrés was looking for a different kind of recognition this time.

'He is losing weight, Andrés. He has none of his old energy. He coughs. How he coughs.'

'He smokes too much.' She'd said it often enough herself.

'He coughs up blood.'

'Has he been to the doctor?' Andrés kept his voice steady now. But his mind was reeling. Coughing up blood was not good. 'He must let the doctor do tests.'

'I keep telling him.' She sounded exhausted.

Andrés sighed. Apart from the rest of it, his father was a stubborn man. 'Call the doctor out to him if you are worried, Mama,' he said. 'Give him no choice. Tell him you will not cook him another dinner until he does the tests.' Be firm with him, woman, he thought. Be strong in the way that you have never been strong before. For God's sake. *Stand up to the man*.

'He has lost his appetite too,' she said.

'You must do it, Mama.' Andrés was unyielding. 'You must make him go.'

'Very well, my son.'

Andrés nodded. 'I will phone you in a few days to find out what they say.'

There was a pause. Well, what else was she expecting? He had cut himself off from his family – he'd had no choice. He knew though what she wanted.

She sobbed. 'Oh, Andrés. I wish that you were here.' He pictured her suddenly, the telephone receiver pressed hard against her ear, her dark hair swept back away from her face. It had been seventeen years and yet he could visualise her as if he had seen her yesterday.

'For him?' he demanded. It hurt to deny her. But was that why she wanted him to come? For a man who hated him? She had always said, hadn't she, that nothing had changed. So what had changed now? His father was ill and Andrés must run home to the island like a puppy with his tail behind his legs? As if Enrique Marin had done nothing?

'For us all,' she whispered.

Andrés sighed. It was no use her wanting a reconciliation between father and son, or for them to pretend there was a thimble of love between them. There was none. The chance for that was long gone. 'I cannot come back,' he said. 'You do not understand.'

'I do understand, my son.'

But she did not. His father had told him never to darken

their door again and only his father could now ask him to come home. And he would never do that. Andrés knew he would never do that.

'It may not be as bad as you think,' he said. What did *he* think? Andrés didn't want to think. Coughing. Blood. Loss of energy and appetite. He guessed he knew what his mother was thinking too. 'Fetch the doctor, Mama,' he repeated. 'And then you will know.' Then they would all know.

After they'd said goodbye, Andrés tried to refocus on his painting. He mixed some colours on his palette and looked at the shots he'd taken of the cliffs in the light he'd wanted to capture; compared them with what was in his mind's eye. Damn his father. Damn him for everything he'd done and everything he did still to mess up Andrés's life. And damn him for making Andrés care.

The colour was right. He filled his brush and began. Broad strokes. Bands of gold.

Ruby was coming down to the studio later and he wanted to have something to show her. Ruby . . . In less than a month, their relationship had swept him away. Friendship and a feeling of wanting to protect her had become . . . What? Sometimes it felt as if there hadn't been a time before Ruby. He wanted her here, but what he didn't know was how long she would stick around.

Happy with the first colour, Andrés deepened it, adding ochre to the initial shade. Ruby was independent. Sometimes she did gigs or rehearsed with the band. Sometimes she disappeared to do research or to interview someone in connection with a story. Sometimes she locked herself in the cottage he'd found for her – to work on a feature – forcing Andrés to go to the studio and paint like he'd never painted before. And sometimes she went somewhere else – inside herself – somewhere he couldn't follow. He knew what – or who – she wanted to find. But he also knew from experience that finding out the truth didn't always make you happy. Sometimes it destroyed the equilibrium, the status quo; that delicate balance of life. Sometimes the truth could hurt.

He bled some of the new colour into the picture. Thought again about his father. It was no coincidence that this landscape reminded him so vividly of the colours back home on the island of his birth; of the lagoon in the bay, of Playa del Castillo, the surfing beach with its umber cliffs and deep, deep sand. How many times had he and Izabella walked that beach, their feet sinking into that sand, spools of water washing their footsteps away? Looking for treasure – *jallos* – just as their forefathers had; netting, driftwood and shells. *Back home* . . . Andrés considered this. Was England now his home? Could it ever be? Andrés was aware that one of the reasons he had wanted to buy Coastguard's Cottage was so that he could say (to his father perhaps), 'Look at me, I have my own life now, I don't need you.' But he never had been able to say that. And now there was this. This news, this bombshell.

The cliffs were not all one colour as they appeared to be at first. Nothing was. An artist had to look deeper – his father had taught him that much at least. Like the desert landscape of the island, these cliffs were, of course, combed through with other shades, darker colours, threads of grey and blue and rust. So. A pale honey to start with. Then build.

But Andrés could not go back to the island and so it could not be his home again. He could not go back as Ruby wanted to go back in order to go forward. He wanted to see them, of course he wanted to see them. His mother and Izabella. But Andrés guessed that it was his father who would never forgive. Just as Andrés would never forget.

CHAPTER 30

Fuerteventura, 2010

Sister Julia sat down to rest for a moment on the bench under the orange tree in the square. She let her breathing steady. It was hot and she was no longer young. The walk from Nuestra Señora del Carmen was just long enough to provide her with some fresh air and exercise, though the main road into the village was lined with date palms which were untended and hung so low that their sharp leaves had threatened to take out her eye. But it was important to go out into the world sometimes. And had it not always been that way for her? Sister Julia relished the peace and tranquillity of the pale stone cloistered convent and the desert landscape all around, but had that sense of serenity ever settled inside her?

Her life was full. She helped with domestic chores in the convent and she prayed to God. She gave what guidance she could to the people in the village. She thought of the sad, dark-eyed woman who had given her that lace tablecloth she still kept in the drawer of her writing desk. Of the stories that even she might not have yet heard. And whenever she thought of the past and looked in her book of names . . . In truth, even after all these years, Sister Julia was still struggling – to find that inner peace.

On one side of the square were the *ferretaria* and the *bazar*; on the other, the Bar Acorralado. A woman passed by. '*Buenos dias*,' she said to Sister Julia.

'God be with you,' she replied.

A newspaper had been discarded on the bench beside her. Sister Julia glanced at it. Even after all this time, she remained curious about the world she had withdrawn from. She picked up the paper. Glanced at the front headline. *Niños Robados*. What was this? *Holy Mother of God*. She crossed herself. And underneath – a picture. A medical room – so like the one at the Canales Clinic that she shuddered as the memory flooded back. A narrow bed with a woman lying in it, an obstetrics trolley carrying the surgical instruments necessary to aid delivery, a nun holding a child – *a nun . . . Glory*. It surged into her mind as if it were yesterday – the women, the babies, the deaths. She could hear their cries. And see their tears. *Dear God in heaven*. She thought that her heart would stop beating.

Sister Julia fumbled for her reading glasses, which were in the purse at her waist. Her hands shook. *Niños Robados*. Spain's Stolen Children. Could this really be what she thought it must be? Yes, it most certainly could. It was a scandal, she read. Arguably the biggest scandal to ever hit her mother country. The scandal of the stolen babies. In terror, she clamped a hand to her mouth. She had no choice but to read on.

There had been an exposé a few years ago, she read. *A few years ago . . . ?* And there she had been, going about her business at the convent, oblivious to what was happening in the outside world. What would she have done if she had known? Sister Julia thought of the book of names. Would she have been brave enough? She had been waiting so long for guidance from God. Now though, she read, there was an organisation fighting for the cause: *ANADIR*.

And something stirred deep within her. That was good. People much younger and stronger than she were fighting. She thought of the Spanish Civil War and the hope in her family's hearts when they had thought the Republicans had won through. They had been rebels – and yet she had been almost too young to realise that. And those rebels had been quashed for many, many years. With methods such as these. Sister Julia let the newspaper rest on her lap for a moment. She gazed across the square at the three-legged dog loping in an ungainly fashion across to the *bazar*. *Dear God . . .* And she had been part of it. A girl whose parents had fought against the values of those same Nationalists had been part of the conspiracy of domination.

She picked up the paper again. Her mind was reeling, but she had to know it all. She read of a young man whose mother had told him the truth on her deathbed: *It is wrong that you do not know you are not of my blood. I bought you from a priest for 150,000 pesetas.* A priest . . . And yet – this was not news to her, was it? Did she not know as much already? Had she not collected money at the Calle Fontana in place of the priest and taken it back to Dr Lopez?

The truth will out. People – her people of Spain – would not be dominated for ever. And those adoptive parents . . . They were not all bad people. They were rich yes, and desperate for a child. And they were weak and open to temptation just as all mankind. But in the end . . . They would not forget. And like this woman on her deathbed they might need to unburden. Just as Sister Julia did herself. She sighed. For now – surely – she must help them find the truth. She could not stand by and allow God alone knew how many people – for they were adults now, not children – not to find out who they were and where they had come from. She could help at least some.

Baby theft . . . she read. *Trafficking*. She had never thought of it that way. Holy Mother of God, even in her darkest moments, she had never thought of it that way.

And she was implicated. Of course, she was implicated. She had comforted the women who had lost their children – but she had never challenged the fact that a baby had been pronounced dead. She had never said to Dr Lopez, *How can he have died? Show him to me. Show me the dead child*. Again, she shuddered. She had not said these things because she had been told it was not her place to question. She – like the unmarried mothers themselves who had been pressurised to give their babies away for adoption – had been weak; intimidated by the doctor, that respectable and God-fearing man, that pillar of society who always knew best.

And yet she had known, hadn't she? Deep in her heart she

338

had known. Else why had she written down the names? Why had she kept the book and why did she keep it still?

Sister Julia could hear the children in the school playground behind the square and music coming from the Bar Acorralado where the men of the village often congregated to drink and play cards and dominos. Life was continuing as if nothing had changed. But for her . . . Everything had changed. It was as if a bolt of lightning had come down from the sky and shown her with frightening clarity what had been done and what there was still left to do.

Sister Julia read on. She read that thousands of Spaniards had come forward, believing that they might be potential victims of the scandal. Women who were sure their babies had been taken from them but who at the time had lacked the confidence to challenge the medical profession, to challenge priests or nuns who were, were they not, men and women of God? Again, she crossed herself. There were those more corrupt who had hidden behind the apparent respectability of priests and nuns. Some of these men and women of God might have been innocent. But others . . . Her eyes filled with tears but she read on. It was too late for tears. She read of women who sometimes had lacked the funds to manage the burial of their own child, who had grasped the straw being given to them; that the State would take care of everything. Who'd had no choice. Who had believed what they were told – because the alternative was impossible to believe.

And she read that as many as three hundred thousand babies might have been stolen in this way. *Three hundred thousand* . . . Sister Julia let this awful statistic sink into her senses. It had then been going on all over Spain. And she had been one of the perpetrators. *Stolen*. It was an emotive word. It stood against everything she had ever believed in. And yet it was true. Dr Lopez had stolen those children to sell on for huge sums of money. And she, Sister Julia, had helped him.

It was still early, but the sun was getting hot and Sister Julia felt that she could barely breathe. She should have brought some water with her. But for now she could not stop reading.

Because of Franco's 1941 adoption law, she read, the only way to prove family relationships was by DNA testing. It would be a lengthy and frustrating business. Babies had been moved around the country too and to other countries; files had been destroyed. Well, Sister Julia knew about that. There were no records. Most of the *Niños Robados* would never know who their true parents were.

She considered this. Thought about her own family, God bless them, who she had lost in different ways, but at least had known.

And that was not all. She put a hand to her head. She felt as if her habit was pressing against her body, her wimple squeezing at her temples. Graves were being exhumed. *Holy Mother* . . . Again, Sister Julia crossed herself. She could feel the rapidity of her own breathing; a fluttering in her heart, an ache in her lungs as if she could not get enough air. Sometimes the graves – supposedly of babies whose mothers had been told they were dead – contained just a limb, sometimes the corpse of an old man or woman, not even a baby at all.

Sister Julia closed her eyes. She put an arm on the side of the bench to steady herself. This was too much. Nuns – like her – had worked in hospitals and clinics all over Spain. And not only on the mainland. There were cases here too in the Canary Islands, in Fuerteventura. It had even happened here because the political arm of the Nationalist party and the Church, working together, had spread like an octopus and manifested supreme power over them all. *Dear God, Holy Father, give me strength.*

But it was true. Nuns – like her – had cared for mothers and told them that their infants were dead. One nun – and Sister Julia could barely believe this story – had apparently been part of a terrible pretence. She put a hand to her mouth and thought for a moment that she would vomit. A pretence of showing mothers a frozen baby as proof that their child had died; a baby who was kept in a freezer for this very purpose. *A frozen baby . . .* Julia shuddered yet again. Her whole body seemed to shudder and shake and for a moment the sun disappeared and her world went black. It was almost too horrific to bear.

But she must be strong. She remembered what her sisters had once said to her many years ago when they visited her at Santa Ana. *You are fortunate*, they had said. *As a nun, you have an important social role to play.* What would Matilde and Paloma say if they were still alive and if they knew of this, Sister Julia wondered? What would they think now of the important social role which she had been asked to perform? Despite the warmth of the sun, the shadows around her were lengthening before her very eyes. And they were shadows stretching back to Spain's Civil War; a legacy that haunted their society to this day. A legacy of pain and betrayal.

Sister Julia pushed her knuckles into her mouth to stop herself from crying aloud. What could she do? Why had she created her book of names if it was to serve no purpose?

She looked up from her reading as another shadow fell over her. It was a man, in his sixties perhaps, with sun-browned, leathery skin and dark eyes. He wore blue overalls and a bandanna around his head and she did not think she had seen him before. He was smoking a thin cheroot. And he was watching her, a curious, almost knowing look on his face.

'*Buenos dias*, Sister,' he growled in a low, guttural tone.

Sister Julia flinched at the sound of his voice and found that she could not speak. She couldn't ignore the man though. So she just nodded. *Please go away*, she thought. It was not charitable, but . . . *Please go away*.

'You are well, Sister?' he asked.

She realised what a picture she must present, how perturbed and emotional she must seem. There were tears in her eyes and she was hot and flushed. She bowed her head and tried to calm herself. 'I am well,' she said at last. Though the words seemed to stick in her throat. Well? After all she had read in this newspaper article? How could she ever again feel well?

The man did not go away as she had hoped. Instead, he sat beside her on the bench. His own breathing was shallow and uneven and she noticed now that he was thin and gaunt. He too, she realised, was far from well.

He leaned forwards, flicked at the paper which was still resting in her lap.

Sister Julia winced.

'You read bad things in the papers, *no*?' He clearly wanted to make conversation.

Sister Julia summoned all her strength. Sent up a silent prayer to God. 'That is so, my son,' she murmured. For she still had a duty to perform. She must not think only of herself. There were many others who had to be helped – and this man could be one of them.

He picked up the paper. Sister Julia froze. She did not think though, that she could bear to discuss it. Not with this man. Not with anyone – at least not at this moment in time.

But he just let out a deep sigh and threw the paper to one side. 'It is life, *si*?' he said.

No, Sister Julia thought. It was death. She got to her feet, a little unsteadily.

The man looked up at her. He cocked his head to one side. 'Can I get you anything, Sister?' His eyes were very dark. Inscrutable.

What she needed was water. But she also needed to return to the convent. Her emotions were in tumult. What she needed even more than water, was to pray. 'Thank you, my son,' she said. 'I am well.'

But he pulled a bottle of water out of the canvas bag slung around his neck. He handed it to her with a shrug.

He had been drinking out of it himself; the bottle was half empty. But Sister Julia did not hesitate. She put it to her lips and as she did so she caught again the intensity of his gaze. Who was he? Why did he seem as if he wanted something from her?

She tried to hand him back the bottle, but he waved it away. 'Keep it, Sister,' he said. 'You may need it on your journey.'

But Sister Julia hurried back to Nuestra Señora del Carmen, heedless of the wind and the sun and her parched throat. She hurried back to the chapel to pray. Only God could help her now. Only God could tell her what to do.

CHAPTER 31

'And how many artists were there in the group to start with?' Ruby asked Steph. She was interviewing her for the local *Echo*. Steph Grainger had founded the art group that Andrés belonged to and she had worked hard to gain recognition for her artists – despite being diagnosed with MS five years ago. The end of summer exhibition coming up was timed to coincide with other Dorset art events and had grown hugely in popularity since the first small exhibition held in the back of a local village hall.

Steph smiled. 'There were three of us. David working in oils, Kathryn in ceramics and me in pastels.'

'And now?'

'Over forty.'

'With a variety of media, I know.' Ruby had already viewed much of the work about to be exhibited in Pride Bay and beyond. And she was impressed. 'And who will be the stars of the show – are you allowed to say? Is there anyone who has real talent – someone we should look out for in the future?'

'There are one or two. A young girl called Patti Tyler who works in earthenware has had some interest. And Andrés Marin's work is very powerful.'

'Really?' Ruby wondered if Steph knew they were a couple. Probably. She would have seen them around and about. In the past month, she and Andrés had spent a lot of time together and they had laid themselves bare – to a degree, she thought. They had shared their history and decided they had enough to build on, that each could trust the other at least. Even so . . . There was still something – she knew – that he wasn't telling her.

Steph nodded with enthusiasm. 'Fabulous watercolours,' she said. 'But of course his father Enrique's a successful artist, isn't he? The talent's obviously been passed on to his son.'

'Mmm.' Ruby realised that she knew almost nothing about Enrique Marin. When it came to his family, Andrés would talk of his mother and his sister. But he rarely spoke of his father. And when he did, his brow creased and his eyes darkened in a way that made Ruby want to change the subject – fast. What had happened, she wondered now – and not for the first time. What had made him not even want to acknowledge Enrique Marin?

'We're grateful for the publicity from the *Echo*,' Steph said. 'The more people we can get here to view the exhibition, the better.'

Ruby got to her feet and they shook hands. 'I'll see if I can generate some interest at a national level as well,' she said. 'Leave it with me.'

When she got back to the cottage she put on a jazz CD and made herself a cup of tea. She picked up Vivien's letter – still propped on the mantelpiece – albeit on a different mantel-piece from before. A new track started. 'Why Shouldn't We Fall in Love?' The music wafted over her. It was one of her favourites. She stared at the writing on the envelope. *Ruby* . . .

She remembered an evening a long time ago when she was a girl, maybe ten years old. It was a few weeks before Christmas. Her father had obtained a lucrative commission – he was to make some dining room furniture for a couple living in Uplyme. He came home excited, a bottle of champagne tucked under his arm.

'I got it,' he told Vivien. His eyes were bright as he thrust the bottle at her, unwound his scarf and pulled off his coat.

'I guessed,' she laughed back at him. Ruby understood that money had been a worry and that this commission would go some way towards easing that worry, what with Christmas coming up too.

He bought fish and chips – Ruby's favourite – and they ate it, accompanied by the chilled champagne. The bubbles got up her nose and made her giggle.

After supper she went upstairs to have a bath and that's when she heard it. Her parents had put on some of their music and it was humming through the house, rich and dark and melodic.

It thrummed through the walls and seemed to vibrate the very bathwater. Ruby heard the saxophone – though it wasn't till later she found out what it was called – climbing up and down the scale of the song; sometimes in little steps as if it was almost out of breath, sometimes long, stretched and fluid like the infinity pool Ruby's friend Jasmine's parents had installed at their posh house on the hill. So mellow.

And something strange happened to Ruby. She closed her eyes and felt it. She wanted to climb that music too. Jazz . . .

After her bath, she'd gone downstairs in her dressing gown for the hot chocolate her mother always made for her. And they were dancing – her parents – her mother's head resting on her father's shoulder, his hand on her waist, the other touching her neck where her dark hair curled into the nape, where the apron she was still wearing looped over and around. Her mother's eyes were closed. *Her mother* . . .

Ruby watched them, mesmerised, then Vivien opened her eyes, spotted her and drew her wordlessly into their special circle. As they moved and swayed, so Ruby moved and swayed. The music was like magic. Black magic. And the saxophone, sinuous and sensual, had wound itself into her heart and soul.

Ruby sighed, ran her fingers over the seal of the envelope. Why? Why had her parents not had the guts to tell her face to face? She propped the letter back on the mantelpiece, turned away.

'Maybe you should give it up,' Mel had said the other day when Ruby had called in to the shop to say hello. She seemed a bit brighter and Ruby wondered if Stuart had taken some of the pressure off. If so, she couldn't help thinking that it was just a matter of time before the subject raised its head again.

'Give what up?' Ruby had perched a deerstalker on her head. She loved coming in here and trying on the stock. But she knew.

'Trying to find Laura,' Mel said.

Easy for her to say. 'I can't.' Just like she couldn't bring herself to open that letter. She needed to find her own genes, to make contact with the girl who had carried her, given birth to her . . . *And given her away*, her heart whispered. Yes, OK. And given her away. And she wanted to find out something about her father too. Who was he? Did he even know of her existence? She knew what Mel was saying. *If it ain't broke* . . . But she needed to find out the reasons, put the pieces all together and create a picture that made sense of her life. Otherwise she'd never find that sense of completion that she was looking for.

Her tea had gone cold. Ruby returned to the tiny kitchen to make some more. She thought of her interview with Steph Grainger. Was Andrés really that good? She liked to think so. Last night, she'd gone down to the studio where he was working on the pieces he was planning to exhibit, and she'd taken a look. She especially loved his Chesil Beach painting, which was to be a massive centrepiece for the exhibition and which featured her favourite golden stacked cliff and the pathway that she'd seen as a promise of her childhood; a memory that she'd never let go of, no matter what else she discovered. A special picture of her own special place. It meant a lot to her that Andrés had painted it – and he'd captured the feel of it so perfectly.

Ruby dropped the teabag in the cup and added boiling water. No one could take away from her those Sunday afternoons at Pride Bay with her parents when she was a girl, walking along the cliff tops with a summer breeze blowing their conversations away, jumping the waves with her father, playing frisbee at low tide. Was it her imagination, or were the days longer and sunnier then? They were certainly more carefree . . .

What subjects did Enrique Marin paint? Ruby realised she didn't know. Was there any similarity in their styles? Andrés's work was mostly landscape – it was easy to see that his passion was for the ginger cliffs, the green fields, the blue ocean with colours so delicious you almost wanted to eat them. But Ruby was curious. She wanted to know everything, she realised, about the man she was involved with. And she was involved. The connection between them was taut as wire, though she had no idea how strong it was, or how fragile. *Why shouldn't we fall in love?* Sometimes she felt as if she couldn't get enough of him. When Andrés was near her, she wanted to kiss him fiercely, to have him inside her, to fuck as if the end of the world was on its way and there were only five minutes left. She hoped it was love; didn't want it to be desperation.

What sort of an artist was her lover's famous father? And what did he look like? Ruby took her tea into the living room, switched on her laptop and went on to Google. She typed in the name. *Enrique Marin*. It was almost too easy these days. Before search engines, research had been a time-consuming activity. But now . . . A few clicks and a whole world would open up for you. Ruby still liked using libraries and interviewing people, especially face to face. Email was useful – but it was no substitute. When you were actually talking to people, things came up that you couldn't have foreseen. And people gave you more – of their lives, their thoughts, their memories. Like Steph Grainger had. It was more personal.

A list of websites appeared. Ruby scrolled down. No doubt her curiosity had influenced her career choice. As a journalist you got the opportunity to find out about things and then tell everyone else. It gave you the chance to expose what was wrong or corrupt. You could do something, you had a voice. And if your story got taken up in the right places, people would read it; people who could do what needed to be done to make things change. Well, that was the ideal. The reality was often more mundane. Articles on health and beauty, travel and interior design – and even the growth of a local art group – might not be world-changing. But at least they could be informative. And if they were the bread and butter of Ruby's existence, there was always the chance that one day a more challenging story might raise its head.

Enrique Marin had his own website and Ruby only hesitated for a moment before clicking on to it. She felt a bit guilty – as if she was going behind Andrés's back. Because he certainly wouldn't like it. But . . . she did a mental shrug. He wouldn't open up about his father, would he? So why shouldn't she find out for herself? He was her lover. Why shouldn't she know more about his life?

It was a professional and expensive website design, she noted. She stared at the picture of the artist when it appeared. She supposed she had been expecting Andrés's features; the high cheekbones perhaps? Or a certain look in the eyes? But Andrés must take after his mother because this man was very different. He was dark-skinned – much darker than Andrés – and his face was squarer, his eyes dense, black and glowering. Angry eyes, thought Ruby. The man had angry eyes. He glared out at her from the screen – clearly a charismatic figure, the red bandanna wound around his head making him look a bit like a Red Indian. She smiled. Not like Andrés at all. But still his father. She touched the image with her fingertip. His father . . .

She clicked on to the biography page. It was brief and succinct and there was no family information other than the fact that Enrique lived with his wife in the village of Ricoroque where he had lived as a child. So success had not taken him to a different place, Ruby noted. He was still living in the same village. Ricoroque, the village where Andrés too had grown up.

She clicked on to Events. There were quite a few – with pictures too. There was the artist working with other artists in a studio in the Centro de Arte, a complex that Enrique Marin had apparently helped set up some years ago to encourage new artists and to give them space in which to work. Which sounded, she thought, like the actions of a nice man, a generous man, a man who wanted to share his good fortune with other up-and-coming artists. Did Andrés know about this initiative? Surely he couldn't disapprove?

There was Enrique hosting a dinner, and Enrique at an exhibition of his work in the capital city of Fuerteventura, Puerto del Rosario. He still sported the red bandanna in this photo, and Ruby could see now that his dark hair was greying at the temples, but he was wearing a smart suit – which went with the bandanna surprisingly well – and holding a glass of champagne, a thin cheroot in his other hand. He looked arty and interesting. He didn't look so angry either, Ruby observed. There were no pictures of his wife or his daughter anywhere. None of Andrés either – but that was hardly a surprise.

There was also a picture of the artist at work – wearing blue overalls this time and looking wild and dishevelled, working in his studio at home, according to the tag on the photo. And finally one of Enrique opening a supermarket. He was quite a local celebrity then.

So what had happened between Andrés and his father? Why did Andrés never visit the island of his birth? And if he cared for Ruby as she thought he did – why wouldn't he tell her?

She clicked on to Work. Just how good was Enrique Marin?

Bloody good, she decided, as she flicked through the images. He clearly specialised in portraits – and there were plenty of them. Some had obviously been done in the studio and others were more casual – as if they'd been painted on the beach or in a café somewhere. Most of the studio portraits were of young women; some just head and shoulders; others were life drawings of female nudes. But the artist had captured a certain sensuality in even the simplest poses. He seemed to have the ability to suggest eroticism in the curve of a hip or the swell of a breast in the subtlest way imaginable. Ruby was fascinated. And there was fire and brimstone too. Enrique Marin liked to paint dramatic subjects. There were volcanoes and fires and even biblical scenes – very different from his other work, but also brilliant in their own way.

The portraits were very sensitively handled. It was a special gift, she supposed, to be able to capture likeness. She had no way of knowing, of course, if Enrique had that talent, but he certainly had the ability to suggest feelings and emotions from facial expressions and movement – through a tilt to the head, a turn of the mouth, a look in the eye. It was as if he found people transparent. As if he could look into someone's eyes and then right through to the other side of them. As if – through his work – he could lay bare their souls. Ruby shivered. She wasn't altogether comfortable with it; there was something probing and almost intrusive about some of these pieces. She thought of the look in his eyes. But it fitted. It fitted with the look of the man. She'd answered her own question – the father was a very different artist from the son. And she was glad.

Ruby was just about to click off the website – she had seen enough, she reckoned, to give her some insight into Andrés's father, and maybe even why they didn't get on – when an image caught her eye. She sat up straighter. She clicked on the image to enlarge it. The face filled the screen; larger than life, it seemed.

It was the portrait of a young woman – probably in her mid-twenties. She had long blonde hair which hung loosely around her shoulders. She was wearing a frilly, peasant-style blouse, but it was just head and shoulders so only the neck-line and shoulders were visible. Long silver earrings hung from her ears like teardrops. Enrique had painted her almost as if she were a flower. A flower child. And she certainly looked like one – small and waiflike, with an elfin face and a wistful mouth. Her eyes were blue – blue and innocent. And her eyes were unbelievably sad.

It was Laura. Ruby stared at it for a long time. But she knew as well as she knew anything that this was a portrait of Laura. Clearly Enrique Marin did have the talent to capture a resemblance. And he had done that with this painting. It was so like the photograph. It was the same girl. Ruby's birth mother. She let the truth sink in. Laura then had lived – at some point in her life after she'd left Ruby with Vivien – in Fuerteventura. It was astonishing. And yet . . .

Ruby remembered what Andrés had said when he looked at the photograph that first night they walked back here together. Hadn't he said it looked like his island? And that Fuerteventura was the sort of place that someone like Laura might go? At the time she'd taken little notice. It was dark and she'd been distracted. Didn't one Mediterranean beach look more or less the same as another? But now . . .

After several minutes of simply staring, Ruby reached for her bag and pulled out the photograph of Laura holding her, the one where she was wearing the love beads and where she was smiling. She held it up next to the portrait by Enrique Marin. It was the same girl. It was Laura.

She got up and found the sketch that Andrés had done of her on Golden Cap – the one that had first alerted her to the likeness between herself and her birth mother. And compared that as well. The same gene pool. You could see it in the shape of the mouth and the eyes.

Why had Laura had her portrait painted by Andrés's father? Ruby guessed that she was short of money. As an up-and-coming artist – as Enrique must have been then – he would have been looking for models; from the evidence on this website he used a lot of them in his work. She doubted he would have paid much. But for a girl like Laura it would have been enough to at least buy food for a day or two.

Ruby couldn't stop staring at the images in front of her. Three faces. But what struck her most of all was that in the photo Ruby had of her birth mother, she looked happy. Whilst in Enrique's portrait she looked so unbearably sad . . .

CHAPTER 32

Fuerteventura, September 2012

Sister Julia left the Convent of Nuestra Señora del Carmen and, instead of walking down the sandy track towards the village, walked instead towards the brown velvet mountains over whose gentle peaks the clouds had gathered. Lately, she had taken to doing this, usually in the afternoon, before going back to the chapel to pray. She was old, but she must take her exercise; she could still walk several kilometres, thanks to God's good grace. And she had begun to walk this way since almost no one else did. This way, she would not come across any of the villagers who might stop and engage her in conversation or want to be blessed or to visit her in the chapel. She knew that this was a selfish act and she was sorry. But for the first time in her life, Sister Julia did not wish to see people; she did not wish to talk. She craved solitude.

In the chapel at the convent and even in her own plain and simple room, Sister Julia could be alone. To be a nun was to be alone with God for much of the time – this was one of the reasons why the sisterhood were encouraged to be silent and not indulge in idle chatter. But Sister Julia was almost ashamed to admit that now she needed a different kind of solitude. She was old. She had turned her face to her God and she had asked Him to show her the way. But as yet there had been no sign and Sister Julia truly did not know what to do.

So she walked into the desert *campo*. She took the trail towards the mountains and as she walked, her steps moved in rhythm with her beating heart. *Show me the way, show me the way* . . . This landscape had always seemed to Sister Julia to be a biblical one. Could the natural world provide her with the answer – or at least a sign – that God would not? Sister Julia did not think this for a moment. The landscape was God's creation, after all. He was everywhere. Indeed, Sister Julia preferred to believe that the communion with nature would enable her to get closer to God without the distraction of the material world. That here in this desert landscape with only the mountains and the ocean for company, she might at last hear God's voice.

When the track divided, Sister Julia hesitated for only a moment before taking the pathway to the coast. Sometimes she saw cars ploughing their way across the *campo* on this route; young people driving to the sea with surfboards tied to the roof, heading for the big waves. Rarely did they seem surprised to see a nun walking across the brown and dusty earth, although once or twice a car would stop and a friendly young person would smile and ask: 'Are you well, Sister?' Meaning, she supposed, *Do you know where you are and what you are doing, or do you need a lift back to civilisation?*

'I am well,' she would say, meaning, *Yes, I do and no, I do not*, and she would continue on her journey.

On this afternoon the wind was high and the road was deserted. Sand blasted on to Sister Julia's white habit, but the material was coarse and she felt almost nothing.

When she arrived at the cliff edge, the waves were wild and crashing violently on to the black rocks below. She watched them for a moment. Sister Julia never walked down to the beach – it would not be a simple matter in these robes and she would probably never make it back up to the top again. She just stood here and admired the elements at their most unfettered and free. Freedom, she had learnt back in Barcelona, had to be fought for. But here on the island it existed naturally. She was sure of that.

So . . . Sister Julia could barely hear herself think as she stood and surveyed the scene. And she let the clamour of sea and wind and the shrieking of the gulls wash over her. It was like meditation or prayer; the aim was to clean your mind, free your mind. Let the path be uncluttered. Let God come in.

The vast sky was streaked with clouds of white and grey; in between, the sun shone from the blue, shimmering on to the inky ocean. The sea bucked and heaved, the waves rolled into shore; rising, rising and curling until they stood, turquoise and luminescent, threaded with golden sand, still and poised for a second before smashing on to the rocks below. Each wave looped forwards, darkening and dipping, and then drew back, hissing from whence it had come. The island was only sixty miles from Africa; behind her the low, smooth hills were soft and velvet, pink and red-gold.

And despite her efforts to cleanse her mind, what Sister Julia had discovered when she read that newspaper all that time ago churned in her head like the turbulent sea, moving forwards, moving back, rolling around like the waves. Even prayer was not the solace it had once been. Even prayer gave her no answers.

'You again, Sister.'

Sister Julia jumped. She knew that voice. She had not heard him approach. She had been lost in her reverie and the ocean was raucous enough to drown anyone's footsteps. Indeed, he must have been compelled to speak loudly in order to be heard above the waves.

She bowed her head in greeting but did not reply. It was the man she had spoken to in the village on the occasion she had read the newspaper and learnt of the breaking scandal of the *Niños Robados*. It was the man who had spoken to her in the square. She recalled how she had felt that day – emotional, devastated at what she had learnt, almost disbelieving at the scale of it. She had been overcome with thirst too. And this man had at least been kind.

'You are still troubled, I see.'

Sister Julia hesitated to look at him. Perhaps she should not speak to him either. It was strange that she should see him again like this when she was in this state of mind. Was it a coincidence? But how could a man like this be any kind of sign from God? It was of course impossible. Sister Julia looked around her at the sky and the cliffs and the ocean, which seemed to stretch into infinity. This situation – even simply standing here with this man – would no doubt be deemed improper by anyone who might be watching.

'There's no one here,' he growled in his low and guttural voice. 'Just you and me and the ocean, Sister.'

Sister Julia tensed. It was as if he had read her mind. Should she be wary? No, indeed. Because God was also here. He was everywhere and He would protect her. Anyhow, the man did not sound threatening. He sounded as if he were simply making an observation. And, of course, he was right.

'Indeed,' she said. 'That is so.'

'Ah, well.' He let out a deep sigh and she was moved to glance at him. He looked much older than when she had seen him last. Thinner, too, and more gaunt. The bones in his face and his collarbone jutted out sharply under the skin, he was unshaven, and his brown skin was leathery and dry. He did not look at all well.

And even as she thought this, he put his hand to his mouth and coughed, low and harsh. 'We all have our troubles,' he muttered.

Once again Sister Julia bowed her head and murmured her agreement. '*Si*. It is true.' What could be wrong in that?

He put his hands in his pockets and pulled out a packet of cheroots and a box of matches.

Sister Julia gave him an assessing glance and he shrugged and put them back in his pocket again.

'I suppose you have no one to talk to at the convent,' he observed.

Sister Julia did not feel that this comment required an

answer. Naturally, what he said was true. At Santa Ana in Barcelona the mother superior had always been available for advice and a listening ear, although in Sister Julia's experience this had been neither sufficient nor satisfactory. But here at Nuestra Señora del Carmen, they lived as in a retreat. Occasionally one of the younger nuns came to her for guidance and she helped as much as she could, but as the oldest member now living at the convent, Sister Julia was regarded as having attained true spiritual wisdom. It would not occur to anyone that she would need guidance for herself.

'Me, I have too many people clustering around me like mosquitoes.' He batted his arms around as if he were swatting them away. 'But can I confide in my family?'

Sister Julia was silent.

'No, I cannot.' His shoulders slumped. 'And so it is for you at the convent, I suspect.' He waved in the general direction of Nuestra Señora del Carmen. 'You have other nuns, *si*, but no confidante, do you now?'

Sister Julia watched him. She blinked. Should she walk away?

'I thought not.' He laughed – a low and rasping laugh.

Sister Julia turned.

'You know what they say? A trouble shared . . . ' he called after her. 'You can tell me, Sister. Who knows? I might be able to help you.' His words were no sooner out of his mouth than Sister Julia felt them being whisked away by the wind. *A trouble shared* . . .

She turned back to face him. 'I cannot do that, my son,'

she said. It would certainly be wrong to tell her troubles to anyone outside the monastic community, let alone a man. And in a situation which—

Before Sister Julia knew what he was about to do, he reached out and grasped her arm.

She flinched. This man was not intimidated then by the cloth of God. It had been a long time since anyone – man or woman – had touched her in this way and Sister Julia felt the strangeness of it seep into her and linger. For a moment she thought of the other life that she might have had if she had been like her sisters at home and not been given to the Church at such a tender age. Would she have been happy? Would a man ever have touched her, have loved her? Or would she – like her sisters Paloma and Matilde – have ended her life suffering perhaps even more?

She looked down at his hand gripping the white cloth of her robes and he withdrew it.

'Would you help me, Sister?' he asked.

Sister Julia met his gaze of entreaty. 'In what way, my son?' She was conscious of the waves, the wind, the sun beating down on them.

'I have sins I want to confess,' he muttered. Once again he coughed.

Sister Julia shuddered inside. She could not help it and yet she did not know why.

'I am ill. My time is drawing near.'

'You must come to the chapel,' she said. She bowed her head.

He muttered an oath. '*Chungo, chungo*. God in heaven. I cannot.'

'Then I cannot speak to you or hear what you have to say to God,' Sister Julia said. 'The chapel is God's house. You must not be afraid to go there.'

'Does not everyone deserve to be heard by God?' he shouted into the wind. His voice had taken on a maniacal note of pure desperation. 'Does not every man deserve forgiveness for his sins?'

Sister Julia's heart went out to him. He was a man at the end of his tether. There was nowhere else for him to go. He was as much in need as any person to whom she had ever given spiritual guidance. 'Be still, my son.' She reached out and placed her palm on the top of his head.

For a moment, he closed his eyes.

When he opened them again he seemed calmer. 'Come with me, Sister.'

And Sister Julia felt compelled to follow him to an overhanging rock where they sat side by side, but not touching, on a ledge that was sheltered from the wind.

Sister Julia bowed her head and she listened.

When he had finished speaking, she was quiet for a moment. She knew now who the man was. What he was and indeed what he had done. 'Is there more, my son?' she said, for now she could indeed see into his heart. She thought of the woman from the village who had come to see her that day, who had given her the delicate tablecloth made of lace. And of the sadness in her dark eyes. Of what remained unsaid. 'Is there more that you wish to tell me?' she asked.

CHAPTER 33

Ruby couldn't wait to tell Andrés. She wouldn't call him though; this was something she wanted to do face to face. Was it such a coincidence – her birth mother sitting for his father, the artist, Enrique Marin? Not really. Because it all made sense. Why Laura had gone to a place like Fuerteventura, the sort of life she would have been leading . . . Ruby could almost feel the pieces of the past slotting together. Her past. And the fact that it was somehow connected with Andrés's past just made her spine tingle.

When she knew he would have finished work and that he'd be down at his studio – time was running out as far as the summer exhibition was concerned and he was there practically every spare hour he had these days – Ruby went down to see him, her laptop in its case slung over one shoulder.

It was a lovely summer's evening and the late sun was glinting on the gently rocking water in the harbour and making the golden cliffs glow. But Ruby didn't linger. She hurried through the back streets to the studios where, sure enough, Andrés was sorting out some framing for one of his pictures. Fortunately no one else was around.

'Hi, Ruby.' She saw him look up as she approached. Good.

She'd been a bit worried about disturbing him but he seemed pleased to see her.

Ruby lifted her face for his kiss; warm and tender. Felt herself folded against his chest. She loved that. Maybe it wasn't too soon for them to think about the future. Why shouldn't they? When something was right, it was right.

'What brings you down here so early?' He released her and turned back to his framing.

'You'll never guess.' Ruby couldn't keep the excitement out of her voice. Ever since she'd seen her image on the screen . . . Well, it was a lead, wasn't it? Almost her first. And the journalist in Ruby couldn't wait to follow it up. Neither could the daughter.

'What?' He laughed. 'You look like you've found your fortune.'

'No.' She grinned back at him. 'But I may have found my birth mother.' She should probably resent Laura for what she'd done – just abandoning her to someone else's care. And yet Ruby couldn't bring herself to. All she could feel for Laura was compassion. Laura had been a young mother. She had given birth to Ruby with no father or family around to help her and then she had lost her own mother just afterwards. How must she have felt? How difficult must it have been? No, she couldn't resent Laura and she couldn't blame her either.

'Really?' He pulled her close again and held the back of her head scooped in his palm, in that way he had. 'Where?'

'I went on to your father's website. And you won't believe

what I found. Look.' She pulled away and opened her laptop, putting it on the trestle table where Andrés was working.

Then she realised that Andrés hadn't responded. 'Andrés?'

His face was dark with anger. Oh, dear. In the excitement of finding the picture of Laura, she'd forgotten how *persona non grata* Enrique Marin was as far as his son was concerned.

'You went on to my father's website?' He stared at her, his green eyes suddenly cold. 'Why would you do that?'

'I wanted to find out more about him, of course.' She should have anticipated this. It was only a website, but she recalled that moment of foreboding she'd had before she'd clicked on it. She'd known he wouldn't like it.

'Why would you want to find out more about him?' He'd stopped working and was still just staring at her, confusion mixing with the anger on his face. 'Why would you be interested?'

'Because he's your father.' For Ruby it was simple. Enrique Marin and his wife had created Andrés. They were his parents, his roots. For God's sake. She had no family to introduce Andrés too. No one. How did he imagine that felt? Didn't he realise how important your family were?

Andrés brought a fist down hard on the trestle table. It shuddered. Automatically, Ruby put a hand out to her laptop. What was the matter with him?

'He is nothing to me,' he said. 'Nothing. Why can't you understand?'

'But—'

'And why should he mean anything to you, Ruby? Why do you care?'

Ruby couldn't answer that. How could she tell him she'd just been curious – when it obviously mattered so much? Andrés hated him. He really hated him and she had hugely underestimated the force of that hatred. 'I'm sorry,' she said. 'I don't care about him – of course I don't. I don't even know him. But he's your father and I was just—'

'Poking around in my affairs.' He finished for her. 'That was what you were doing, yes?'

Ruby was stung. She'd said she was sorry . . . And he was completely missing the point. 'Don't you even want to know what I found on his website?' she asked him in a quiet voice. She really didn't understand what she had done that was so terrible.

'What?' he muttered. 'What did you find?' But he wasn't even looking at her now. He was looking beyond her, out of the open door into the summer evening outside. What was he thinking? She didn't have a clue. She realised with a start how little she really knew about him.

'I found my mother, Andrés,' she whispered. 'Your father painted a portrait of my birth mother.'

'What?' An expression of horror appeared on his face. 'What did you say?'

'Laura must have sat for him,' she said. 'He painted her.'

He stared at her. There was an awful pause which Ruby really didn't understand. Then: 'Show me,' he said.

Hands shaking, she switched on her laptop, found the

folder where she'd copied the image. Double-clicked.

Once again, Laura's image filled the screen. The girl with the long blonde hair and the sad, sad eyes. Laura . . .

Andrés was gazing at the image as if hypnotised. 'This is his work?' he asked. 'He painted this?'

'Yes.'

'I do not believe it,' he muttered. His fists were clenched. He swore softly in his native tongue. 'I cannot believe it.'

'But why not?'

'Because . . . Because . . . ' He turned to Ruby with an air of desperation. 'What makes you so sure it is her?'

Ruby pulled the sketch he'd done of her at Golden Cap out of her bag. 'Can't you see the resemblance?'

'No.' He almost shouted. 'No, I cannot.' He seemed to tear his gaze away from the screen. He paced over to the other side of the unit, to the window that looked out on to the yard. Suddenly he looked like a defeated man and Ruby couldn't bear that.

She followed him and reached out. Put her hand gently on his arm. 'Why does it matter so much, Andrés?' she murmured.

He shrugged off her hand, almost pushed her away. 'It is ridiculous,' he said. 'You're both blonde and blue-eyed. But so are a lot of other people.'

Why was he so cross? Ruby rummaged in her bag once again and pulled out the photo of Laura holding her as a baby. 'Look again.' She pushed it in front of him. She was beginning to get annoyed herself.

He took it, frowned once more. 'It's too blurred.'

'But, Andrés' – she pointed to the background – 'the first time you saw that photo you said you recognised the land-scape.'

'Did I?' He blinked.

'Yes, you did. You said it reminded you of Fuerteventura.' In fact, hadn't he said that he thought it *was* Fuerteventura? 'You said it was the sort of place someone like Laura would have gone to,' she reminded him. 'Hippies and travellers. People who drive VW camper vans. Remember?'

He took a step away from her. And he was avoiding her eyes. In fact his eyes were kind of glazed as if he didn't want to hear any more; as if he didn't want any of this to be true.

But why? Ruby had been so excited and he had just got out a pin and pricked the bubble. 'Don't you think it's possi-ble, Andrés,' she said, trying to sound calm and reasonable, 'that Laura was living there, that she needed money, that she went to sit for your father? She was beautiful, wasn't she? Wouldn't he have wanted to paint her?'

'Yes.' Andrés's voice was bleak. 'Yes, he would have want-ed to paint her. But he didn't. He couldn't. This isn't her, Ruby. You want it to be, but it's not. Can't you see what this means . . . ?' He strode over to the door, flung it open and stomped outside.

Ruby couldn't believe it. And no, she couldn't see what it meant – apart from the fact that she had a lead to Laura's whereabouts at last. She closed down the document and shut the laptop. Slung it back over her shoulder and followed him outside. He was standing in the yard, just staring into the distance. 'So you don't think it's worth following up?' she asked.

He wouldn't even look at her.

She tried again. 'I want to go there, Andrés.'

'To the island.' It wasn't a question. He still wasn't looking at her and she'd swear he was almost crying.

'Yes, to the island.' For some reason, he didn't want her to acknowledge what was happening here; what she'd found. But it was her history, her truth that she was investigating. So she had to be strong. 'Would you come with me?'

Andrés swore softly. But it wasn't a no, Ruby thought.

'Would you introduce me to your father?' she asked.

This time he shook his head. 'Never,' he said.

'I can't speak a word of Spanish,' Ruby said. 'You know I can't. It would be so much harder to do this on my own. And it's so important to me, Andrés.' How could she explain about the feeling she'd had when she'd discovered she wasn't really Vivien and Tom's daughter? It was a sense of not existing, at least not in the way she always had before. A sense of being lost. Of being insubstantial, not really rooted. Whatever she could find out about Laura would help her deal with those feelings and allow her to move on. She might not actually find her – maybe she didn't want to be found. But if there was a chance . . . She had to at least look into it.

'But you will go on your own if you have to.' At last he met her gaze.

She nodded. 'Yes, I will.'

He sighed, a long sigh. 'I cannot go back there, Ruby,' he said. 'I do not want to go back there. And now . . .'

What did he mean – 'and now'? 'What happened?' She braced herself.

'It does not matter what happened,' he said. 'Especially not now.'

She reached out a hand, almost touching him, but not quite. 'If you cared for me . . .' She started to say it. If he loved her, he would tell her. *If he loved her.* But she couldn't quite find the words.

'I care for you.' He took her hand and raised it to his lips. 'But you are asking me an impossible thing.'

'Nothing's impossible.' How could she get through to him?

He shook his head. 'You cannot possibly understand.'

The kiss on her hand – when it came – seemed so final. It felt like goodbye.

What could she do to make him change his mind? She searched his face. Nothing, it seemed. But if he didn't trust her enough to tell her . . . 'I can't let it go, Andrés,' she said.

'No. I understand how it is, Ruby. You just cannot let it go.' He disengaged her hand and she felt that he had disengaged so much more than that. 'But you see – even that hardly matters now.'

CHAPTER 34

How had everything gone so wrong?

Andrés watched Ruby's proud retreating back until she was out of sight. He couldn't believe it. It was too horrible to contemplate. The possibility . . . He swore softly to himself. Everything that could have gone wrong, had gone wrong. Was it possible? Andrés didn't want to believe it, but yes, it was certainly possible. He thought of what Ruby had told him about Laura and how she had left her with Vivien when she was a baby. And that picture she'd shown him. It was more than possible – it seemed overwhelmingly likely.

That old bastard. Would he haunt Andrés's life for ever? Would he fuck it up for ever?

And now he was ill. Was Andrés supposed to be sorry?

A few days ago, he had phoned his mother again as promised.

'How is he?' he'd asked her. 'Has he seen the doctor yet?'

'Yes, he has,' she said.

'How did you persuade him?'

'It was not me,' his mother said. 'It was someone he spoke to on the cliffs beyond Playa del Castillo.'

'Jesus . . . ' It was so typical of the man that he would take notice of some random person he'd met on the cliffs, rather than the wife who had stood by him through all his tempers and tantrums and God knew what else.

'It was a nun,' his mother said.

A nun? Andrés had shaken his head in despair. He knew his father too well to assume he'd had some sort of religious conversion. Never, in a million years. 'What tests did they do?' Andrés asked. For after all, it did not matter who his father had listened to. At least the stubborn old bugger had gone to the doctor at last. And he was glad – for his mother's sake if nothing else.

'What is it called?' She spoke slowly. 'A CT scan? A biopsy?'

'And what was the result?' He found he was holding his breath.

'They do not know yet, Andrés. It will be another day or so, we think.'

'Then I will phone you again in a few days,' he'd told her. Andrés had a right to phone. A right to know. 'Stay strong, Mama.'

But Andrés hadn't phoned – not yet. And now he couldn't bring himself to. But he could not settle to his work either. He had not told Ruby his father was not well. He had resisted. He didn't even want to taint their relationship with a mention of the man. But now . . . Ruby would go there – back to the island – he knew she would. She was almost as stubborn as his father, God damn him. She would go to his parents' house. Andrés realised he was shaking. What would happen when she went to his parents' house? What would she find out when she went there?

He put his stuff away into some sort of order and locked up the studio. It was pointless to try to work when his mind was seething like this.

He strode outside, heading for the harbour and the beach. It was still light and the sky was streaked with the red and yellow of sunset, casting a light on to the old factory premises and cottages that was eerily like the light of the island, the light he loved to paint by. Normally he loved these long summer evenings. But tonight he wasn't in the mood. How could he be?

Andrés thought again of the photographs Ruby had shown him. He thought of the red and white striped lighthouse there in the background of the photo, and he thought of the red and white striped lighthouse of his childhood. Jesus . . . Who would have thought it would come to this?

They used to walk to the lighthouse – he and Izabella – on summer weekends or school holidays when Andrés was twelve or thirteen and his sister eight or nine. He had always looked after her. He enjoyed her company, and he was glad to be away from the atmosphere of home where his father would rant and rail and his mother would race around after him, unable to do anything right. His father never wanted them around anyway; he encouraged them to go out for as long as they wanted to. Yes. And then Andrés had found out why . . .

Before you reached the lagoons at the lighthouse, there was a bay – a perfect horseshoe of a bay surrounded by black rocks where the water was shallow and turquoise, and where the golden sand banked above it so that you could run down there barefoot and paddle in water that was always clear as glass. It was their favourite destination. That day, Andrés carried his rod and fishing bag because he might do some fishing or some sketching, and a blue rucksack containing a bottle of water, his sketchbook, charcoal and some pencils. Izabella held a rose-printed bag containing a book, a loaf of bread, a goat's cheese and some tomatoes. They had their towels slung over their shoulders. They planned to have a picnic among the rock pools, after which Andrés would do some sketches of the red and white wand of the lighthouse pointing to the sky. As the afternoon light changed and the sun was about to set, he would fish.

'Where do you want to go to most in the world, Andrés?' Izabella had asked him, her voice almost disappearing in the wind and in the distant crash of the water on the rocks.

'Oh, I don't know.' He thought of his painting, of Picasso and other artists he admired. 'Paris, maybe, or Seville.' But in truth he didn't want to go anywhere. He had not tired of painting the island; he didn't think he would ever tire of that.

'Hmm.' Izabella wrinkled her nose as she considered this. Andrés knew that she had no time for dry, musty museums or exhibitions. Izabella liked to live and she loved to dance.

She was happiest in the fresh air of the world outside. She needed freedom.

'Where would you go, little one?' he teased her. 'Puerta del Rosario? The Goat Port?' *Puerto Cabras* – as it had once been known. He couldn't see her leaving the island.

She slapped him on the upper arm. 'That shows how much you know! No.' Her voice grew dreamy. 'I shall go to London.'

'Oh you will, will you?' He caught hold of her fingers. 'And what will you do there, my sister?'

She swung their hands back and forth and skipped a couple of steps. 'I shall have fun,' she declared. 'I shall dance and I shall go to parties. I shall live!'

Andrés laughed. He knew that there was a teacher at Izabella's school who had spent some years in England and he guessed that she had been talking to her students, to fire up in Izabella such passion.

They continued to the lighthouse. They had their picnic in the sun, they paddled in the lagoons and he did his sketches – not just of the lighthouse and the sea, but of Izabella as she lay on her stomach fast asleep in the sand, sheltered from the wind by the volcanic rocks of the *corralito*. He drew her as she sat against the lava rocks reading her book. And later as she danced in the bay, slow and rhythmic down by the water's edge, her sarong rippling in the breeze, her long hair cascading around her brown shoulders.

When the wind had died down, when the sun was shimmering gold and silver on the ocean, Andrés and Izabella swam in the shallow turquoise water of the bay. They swam out like fish until Andrés glimpsed the crumbling old jetty by Los Lagos, the village in the distance – squat, white houses with flat roofs jumbled with Moorish styles and sharp flashes of blue, the velvet slopes of the mountains behind, wrinkled in the haze like an old man's skin.

They dipped underwater, holding hands and exploring the sea-life among the rocks and sand – there were always brightly coloured wrasse to be seen, also groupers, snails, crabs and anemones. The sea often had dangerous currents, a strong undertow, but the natives understood the ocean and the waves; they always had.

At last they swam back to the shore, climbed exhausted on to the pale sand and crept back to their *corralito* where they towelled each other dry and laid down in the warmth of the yellow sun.

Later, Andrés fished off the rocks for sea bream and *vieja* – parrot fish – using sardines as bait, and caught a few for their supper. He had barbecued them over a fire of driftwood. The *Majoreros* were accustomed to using the flotsam and jetsam they found in the sea – the *jallos:* gifts from the ocean. The scent of smoking wood and fresh fish and sea had filled their nostrils, filled the air. It was a perfect day.

But unlike Andrés, Izabella had never gone to England. Like her mother before her she had been ground down by expectations and tradition and what was the done thing. Andrés sighed. He had been driven out and yet his sister still lived in Ricoroque. But she had not been blessed with children. Neither of them had achieved any of those old dreams. He wondered if she still went down to the water's edge to dance. He doubted it.

He doubted it very much.

As Andrés reached the harbour, he sat on one of the benches by a pile of crab pots that had been left out to dry and pulled out his mobile. He almost phoned Ruby. He wanted to apologise, he almost wanted to say, *Yes, I will come with you*. But he could not. In the end he could not.

So he phoned his mother in Ricoroque.

'What has happened, Mama?' he asked her gently.

'Now we know for sure.' Her voice broke. 'Now we know for sure, my son.'

'So?'

'He has lung cancer. He has been diagnosed. NSCLC. A carcinoma. He is in stage three.'

'Is that bad?' he asked her. What did it mean exactly?

'Non-small cell lung cancer.' She spoke as if she was reading it out from a reference book. Perhaps she was. 'The most common kind. It is bad,' she said. 'He has a mass, a tumour in the left lung. It is advanced. But not yet spread to other organs – they think.'

But how bad was bad?

'Fucking cheroots,' Andrés muttered. He was angry. Bloody angry. But whether he was more angry about his father or with his father, he couldn't quite say. Enrique Marin was not yet seventy. He was – whatever else – a brilliant artist; a creative man. And he was a bastard of a man who had dealt Andrés a raw deal. Life wasn't fair. And yet . . . He thought of his father's face the last time he'd seen him. *Do not darken this door again* . . . Enrique Marin had always hated Andrés. Andrés had always been a disappointment to him. And now this latest revelation.

'How long does he have?' he asked his mother. The boats bobbed gently on the smooth water in the harbour; the brightly painted fishing craft, the cabin cruisers and inflatables. Every now and again masts clinked with that distinctive metallic sound, even though there was now barely any wind.

'A year. Maybe less.' She sounded calm. Perhaps she had done with the initial hysteria she must have felt when she first heard the news. Perhaps she had been expecting it. Perhaps they all had.

Andrés took a deep breath. *Perhaps not even a year* . . .

'And how did he take it?'

'He said, "What the hell do they know?" and stormed out of the room.'

Andrés almost laughed at this. It was so typical of the old bugger. 'He'll have to accept it though. He'll have to have treatment.'

His mother snorted. 'We will try,' she said. 'All he keeps talking about is how things used to be on the island. The old medicine. He has no time for anything new.'

Andrés knew what she was referring to. He'd heard the stories often enough – about the doctors who cured all diseases with herbal remedies and suchlike. Some of the older *Majoreros* were like his father and had no faith in Western medicine – pills, antibiotics, penicillin. His father had often spoken of the Lamb Doctor – so called because he first arrived on the island from Tenerife with some lambs to sell. He used to move around from village to village, Enrique had told them, staying in people's homes until they were cured, using cupping glasses and candles for prognosis and bleedings; making up medicine with herbs and goats' milk. But for God's sake . . . That was years ago. Medical knowledge had moved on just a bit since then, hadn't it?

'Was he a witch doctor?' Izabella had once asked, eyes round.

'Whatever he was,' Enrique had retorted, 'we need more doctors like him on the island. People used to say – if the Lamb cannot cure you then you are lost.' He thumped his chest. 'But for him your father would not be here now.'

'Why, Papa?' Izabella had run to him and Enrique had put his arm around her shoulders and hugged her.

Enrique Marin had always had time for his daughter, never for his son, Andrés thought now. Never for his son.

'My mother was experiencing a difficult birth,' his father had said. 'They thought she would lose her life – and perhaps the life of her child.'

Izabella had gasped: 'Papa, no!' and Enrique had held her more tightly. 'My father heard that the Lamb was in Lajares curing a case of pneumonia. My father called for him and he came on his white donkey. He saved us both.'

'Mama?' Izabella asked.

'I never saw him,' she said. 'He died the same year I was born. But my parents talked of him too. Everyone did. He was famous on the island. He was a big man, they said. A kind man.'

'And he liked a drink.' Papa roared with laughter.

'Doctors didn't trust him,' said Mama.

Papa had rolled his eyes. 'But the people did.'

'What is the treatment?' Andrés asked his mother now. It wouldn't be herbs and goat's milk, that was for sure.

She sighed. 'Radiotherapy. Maybe chemotherapy. They will not be operating, they say.'

Andrés wondered if this was a bad sign. Probably. But cancer was cancer. The invader.

'He must have a good diet, take lots of rest. But he has so much still to do, he says.' She made a small choked sound of grief.

As if he hadn't done enough, Andrés thought. 'And he must give up smoking.'

The sound changed into a harsh laugh. 'We will see, my son. We will see.'

He supposed it was too late for that; it would make no difference now.

She did not ask him this time if he would come back. This meant what it had always meant, he knew. *Nothing has changed* . . . But how did she feel? How was she coping with the certain knowledge that she would lose her husband?

Andrés said goodbye to her and looked over towards Chesil Beach. He saw a couple walking along the ginger pebbles, hand in hand. Should he have warned his mother about Ruby's visit? Best not, he decided. What will be, will be . . .

But what would be? Andrés repressed a shudder. He got to his feet and in the dimming light made his way back to his house. He wanted to see Ruby. He wanted to be with her, but he knew that he could not. How could he when he did not know? Had he lost her? If not now, then soon perhaps. Depending on what she found out in Ricoroque. He could not now picture his life without Ruby and he could not picture it without his father either. The man had always been such a force. How could such a force ever diminish? Although there had been many times – just like now – when he had desperately wished it would.

CHAPTER 35

There's always a blind spot.

Where was she?

Ruby woke up sweating. She was lying on her back, arms flung out to the sides, legs spread at an awkward angle. Her mother had been lying that way in her nightmare. On the road in a pool of blood. Her mother – Vivien.

Ruby licked her dry lips. She'd gone to sleep thinking about her journey to find her birth mother and had woken with this. With the mother who had brought her up. And the crash. For God's sake. The one thing she couldn't bear to think about and she couldn't get it out of her head.

She sat up, reached out for some water, hiked herself on to her elbow to drink it. It was still almost dark, although the light beginning to filter through the thin curtains of her bedroom in the rented cottage seemed to suggest that it was the early hours of the morning rather than the dead of night. And she was alone.

Andrés. She'd been so excited when she went round to see him. Couldn't wait to show him that image of Laura on the laptop. But she'd ended up at home on her own, booking her flight for one to Fuerteventura via the Internet. She had to go. She knew that Enrique's painting had been of Laura. And so what if Laura wasn't there now? So what if she was there but she didn't want to know her? At least Ruby would have tried.

On the net she'd located a small hotel in the village of Ricoroque and booked a room. No, she wasn't sure how long she would need it for – a week at least. She was leaving the day after tomorrow. She'd get a taxi to Bournemouth Airport. She wouldn't ask Andrés Marin for a thing. She didn't know what had got into him to make him behave that way. But it was better to find out now, she supposed, than later. Andrés. She had really believed that this might be it, that he might be it; the one. But it looked as if she'd got it wrong – again.

Ruby sank back on to the pillows and closed her eyes. She sighed. It had been a while since she'd had that dream. A while since she had wondered . . . At which point had Vivien known she was going to die? Was it when she saw the car veer out to overtake, not knowing the bike was there, not seeing? (Maybe Vivien couldn't see either, maybe Vivien's face was huddled into Ruby's father's back, maybe all she could see was him?)

There's always a blind spot.

Or was it when she felt the bike spinning under them, out of his control? When Vivien was flung away and off the seat of the bike and on to the road? Was it when she heard the squeal of brakes or the cruel discordant sound of metal on metal; harsh, grating? Was it the moment of impact? Ruby shuddered.

Then blackness. Was that when? Was that when she knew she was going to die?

Ruby opened her eyes. She wouldn't sleep any more tonight.

They said it had been instantaneous for both of them. They were dead in seconds. No time then even to think about what might have been.

She curled on to her side and felt for Andrés even though she knew he wasn't there. There was no warm body in the bed beside her. Not even a cosy dent where he had been sleeping – as if he'd simply got up to make tea, perhaps.

No Andrés. No parents. Ruby was alone.

That afternoon, she went back to the house for the last time. Her parents' house; the house of her childhood. The sale had gone through now and Ruby felt only relief. She wiggled the key to open the front door, went into each room one by one to say her final goodbye. The kitchen where her mother had cooked for them all; the bedrooms where they had slept; the living room where Vivien had painted her watercolours. The place seemed so different without their furniture, without them. It was empty, just a vacant shell where once there had been her family, her life; their laughter, their voices, their tears.

She went into the garden her mother had so loved. The grass needed cutting. The white roses and sweet peas were still blooming; their scents heady in the air. Ruby plucked the letter Vivien had written from her bag. It was time. She didn't want to be angry with her parents any longer. This was her chance to find out what her mother had really thought. She slid her thumbnail under the seal.

My darling Ruby,

If you are reading this, something has happened to me before I had the chance to tell you our story. If you are reading this, Frances — who as you know is my closest and most trusted friend — has decided that you should be told everything. Everything.

How can we decide whether or not it is best for someone we love to know everything? I never could. Your father knew what he believed; that what was done was done. Why resurrect the past? Why open wounds that have healed? But I never really agreed with him. I thought you deserved to know the truth. Which is why I asked Frances to do what she has done.

But I hope, my darling Ruby, that I find the courage to tell you myself before she does. I hope that you and I can sit down and talk about it, and that you will find it in your heart to forgive your father and me for what we did. I want to explain things to you. I want to tell you that we did it for you — but we also did it for us. I wanted you so badly, you see.

Please don't blame Laura. She was thinking of you too — I know she was. And if we all did the wrong thing, well, then your father is right and it is done and past and gone.

I want you to know that we love you. I want you to know that I am not sorry. Sorry for deceiving you, of course. But not sorry we did what we did. I would do it again.

And I want you to know, my darling Ruby, that if you want to look for Laura, your true birth mother, then you have my blessing. I understand your reasons and I'm glad.

Always your loving mother,

Vivien.

Tears filled Ruby's eyes until she could barely read the final words. Yes, of course, she forgave her. Yes, of course she understood. *Always your loving mother . . .* And it was true. Vivien had always been her mother in the true sense of the word. She had saved her, nurtured her, loved her. And her father had loved Ruby too. No two people could have done more. Vivien had been generous in her life and she was generous now in these words to her daughter. She had understood that Ruby needed to know the truth and so she had left that shoebox in the wardrobe for her to find. She knew her daughter. She'd known that Ruby wouldn't rest until she found out the whole story. And she'd also understood that Ruby would need to find Laura. To fill in the final gaps.

She walked back into the house. She left the keys on the hall table for the new occupiers. She'd drop another set into the estate agents later.

Ruby opened the front door and she didn't look back. That letter . . . It proved, didn't it, that she was doing the right thing?

CHAPTER 36

Dorset, 20 March 2012

'Ready, love?' Tom stood there in his black leather jacket looking just the part – at over sixty years old. Vivien had to smile. *Easy Rider* . . .

'Ready.' She bent to pull on the laced ankle boots Tom had bought her last Christmas. 'For my biker girl,' he'd said. She wound her hair back in a loose chignon she could tuck under the helmet and shrugged on her own jacket. And she was no spring chicken. More like hell's granny.

Tom was grinning.

'What?'

'You look just as beautiful as the day I first saw you at Charmouth Fair,' he said.

'Get on with you.'

'Truly.'

And you, she thought. *If paradise is half as nice* . . . Had he changed so much? He'd always wanted a bike – right from when he was sixteen. He'd even had one briefly when they were first married. Before money was tight. Before Ruby . . .

Vivien followed him out of the front door. The red speed-machine (as Tom sometimes called it) was waiting, gleaming clean.

He handed her the crash helmet.

And again she found herself thinking. Should she – or shouldn't she? She wanted to talk to her, she really did. She'd wanted to tell her for years. Ruby deserved to know. She ought to know. But there was Tom to consider. *I don't reckon I could do it, love* . . .

Tom swung himself on to the bike and revved the engine. 'Let's be having you,' he said.

Caring for Ruby hadn't altered her life with Tom, Vivien thought, not really. For her part, it had made life richer, and she reckoned that Tom felt the same; he adored that girl. They both did. No two people could have loved Ruby more.

She climbed on behind him and wrapped her arms around his back. Lovely. She leant in close. They were as much in love now as they had ever been. And so much to look forward to. Weren't they always walking, talking, making plans – especially now that Ruby was grown up, happy, independent; everything that Vivien could have wanted for her.

Ruby. She felt the rush as they took off and the bike gathered speed, heading for Pride Bay. Vivien had always loved Ruby as if she was their own. Over the years she'd almost let herself forget she wasn't their own. Only sometimes in the night she would wake in a panic and think: Laura.

Over the years she had often wondered. What if Laura suddenly turned up out of the blue and demanded back her child? How would they cope? How would Ruby cope? But of course she never did. Laura had loved her daughter – what was in that shoebox she left had told Vivien that much, even if she hadn't seen the expression in the poor girl's eyes. But Laura had made a decision that night of the storm – for better or worse – and she had stuck to it. As for Ruby – what was in that shoebox would tell her how much she'd been loved, and that was all anyone really needed to know, wasn't it? How much they'd been loved?

Vivien looked across the road to Colmer's Hill – at the trees perched on the top, always a symbol of West Dorset to her. It hadn't taken her long to fall for Dorset. They'd had to come back here. And Tom was right – it was a beautiful day, the sky a milky blue opal, the hills as fresh and green as springtime.

She had protected her daughter from the truth – all Vivien had ever wanted was to protect her; protect their lives together too. But Ruby had the right to the truth. Vivien tightened her hold. Didn't everyone? Even if it hurt?

Whether she decided to do anything with the knowledge – well, that was up to Ruby. Vivien would tell her the whole story, she decided. Next weekend, when she came to visit. She had to. And then Ruby could decide. Her daughter was strong, resourceful and independent – hadn't she brought her up that way? She'd be able to deal with it. And it was the right thing to do. Tom would see that, he had to.

Tom slowed at the roundabout. 'Isn't life exciting, my lovely?' he yelled back at her.

'Yes!' She could hear the adrenalin in his voice. She

thought of the waltzer and her first sight of the tall boy with the dark hair and the brown eyes flecked with amber, and she held on even tighter as he swung the bike out to overtake a car.

If paradise . . . It was exciting, all right. With Tom, life always was.

CHAPTER 37

Ruby was relieved to arrive at her hotel, have a shower and relax with a cup of coffee before she set out to explore the village.

She walked through the maze of shady backstreets of the old town, past rundown traditional buildings – whitewashed stone with slabs of volcanic lava rock creating pattern and contrast on the walls. The place was quirky rather than pretty – a boat parked in the road where you might expect a car to be, the Vaca restaurant in the harbour – with a statue of a blue cow on its roof. She had to smile. On the other side of the harbour, the grey rocks formed a high cliff, the words: *La Virgen de Buen Viaje* painted in white on the rock, a fisherman's wife set in stone on the cobbles of Calle Muelle de Pescadores, looking out to sea. Wishing the fishermen a good journey perhaps? Or maybe just waiting for her man?

Ruby leant on the wooden rail, looked out at the ocean beyond and thought of Andrés. She'd have to wait a long time for him. She hadn't heard a word from him since she'd left the studio three days ago now. No surprise there. Would he ever forgive her for coming here to the island of his birth? And would she ever forgive him for the way he'd reacted, for letting her come alone? Well, she wouldn't think about that now. She was here – that was all that mattered. She must focus on the search in hand. And she looked up to see a flock of pigeons flying in formation, their wings silver-white against the deep blue of the summer sky. Rundown, perhaps – but there was something special about this place.

'Go for it,' Mel had said when she called her to tell her she was coming out here.

'I'll only be there a week or so,' Ruby told her. But she could hear that sadness again in Mel's voice and she hoped she wasn't deserting her in her hour of need. 'Are you all right?' she asked her.

'I'm fine.' And she could almost see her friend straightening her back, tossing back her auburn hair and applying another coat of lippie. She wasn't about to let Ruby worry about her. Even so – she did.

Ruby pulled the photographs out of her bag. There was nothing here to indicate that this was the same location. The beach in the photos was pale gold, this one was stony and grey; the beach house was built of orange stone, while the houses here were mostly white and blue. Still . . .

The sun was low in the sky and Ruby realised how hungry she was. She hadn't eaten on the plane and had been too churned up this morning for breakfast. Because after all, there was a chance that Laura might live here. There was just a chance that in the next few days Ruby might even meet her. She might talk to her mother, find out the identity of her father. Anything. She felt herself almost regressing into childhood at the thought. She must remember to breathe . . .

At the bottom of the road, looking out over the rocks of the Old Harbour and the inky blue sea, was another sculpture – of a boat, two bronze fishermen pushing it up the beach. And more importantly for Ruby, there was a harbour tapas bar serving beer, fresh prawns and paella. She made her way down there.

Andrés and Laura . . . It seemed incredible that two people so linked to her own life had both lived in this place, she thought to herself. That they might have both once sat here and eaten prawns like she was doing, looked out over the Old Harbour like the fisherman's wife up there on the hill. Watched the sun going down beyond the sea at the horizon, just as she was right now. The sky was filled with pink and red and yellow, the sea was dense as night time. Behind her, the tables emptied and Ruby sat on, watching the sunset, feeling the rhythm of the slinky waves, lost in a dream.

When she finally came to pay the bill, the waiter – just a young boy really, probably the son or nephew of the proprietor, she guessed – took the money and spoke to her in almost perfect English.

Ruby took a chance. 'Do you know where Enrique Marin lives?' she asked. 'The artist?'

'*Si*, but of course.' He sounded surprised that she should have to ask. 'Go up this street, turn right. It is the blue house, Casa Azul. It has a water fountain in the front garden and a carob tree. You will not miss it.'

'Thank you.' Ruby smiled and gave him a generous tip. This seemed a friendly place; there was definitely a good vibe to it. And now she knew where Enrique Marin lived.

She would go there – first thing tomorrow.

The blue house was exactly where the boy had said it would be and Ruby stood there for a few moments, imagining it as the modest traditional building it had once been and which Andrés himself had described to her. Whitewashed stone, blue paintwork, tiny windows, a smallholding out the back. Now, the Casa Azul was rather grand. It was three storeys high – the top storey almost all glass, with outside terraces, blue tiles and what looked like a plunge pool. And in the front garden was the shady carob tree and the fountain the boy had mentioned – a water feature really, very dramatic and made of steel. Definitely the home of an artist – and a successful artist at that.

Ruby took a deep breath, pushed back her shoulders and opened the wrought iron gate – also painted blue. She walked up the path to the front door, knocked and waited.

After a moment, the door opened and a woman of about seventy stood there. Far from looking like the wife of a successful artist, she was small and plain and wore an apron over a simple navy dress. Her dark hair was greying and pinned back from a face that was brown and lined. She wore no jewellery or make-up and her eyes were warm but wary. Ruby scrutinised her carefully, but she could see no look of Andrés about her. But this must – mustn't it – be his mother?

397

'Excuse me,' she said. 'Do you speak English?'

The woman looked even more suspicious at this. '*Si*,' she said. 'A little.' She wiped her hands on her apron and regarded Ruby with a steady gaze. 'What is it you want?'

Ruby guessed that as the wife of a famous artist, this woman would have been catapulted into a very different world – whether she had desired that or not. She would have had to learn to communicate in other languages, dress up for formal occasions, play the role of artist's wife. She didn't look, though, as if she would have relished it.

'I wondered if it would be possible to speak to Enrique Marin?' Ruby said. 'Your husband?'

'I am sorry.' It sounded like a set response. 'My husband, he is ill. He asks not to be disturbed.' She began to shut the door.

How could Ruby make her realise that she wasn't just some hanger-on or art groupie? 'I am looking for my mother,' she said quickly. That should stop her in her tracks.

It did. 'Your mother?' Reyna Marin stared at her.

Ruby nodded. 'I think your husband painted her,' she said. 'Many years ago.'

Inexplicably, Reyna Marin's brow clouded. She looked upset, almost angry. 'I am sorry,' she repeated. 'Those times are gone. He is not well . . . ' The door was closing.

'But—' She knocked again on the door. 'Please . . . ' She hadn't come all the way here to be fobbed off without even seeing the man, without asking him.

And then Ruby heard footsteps from round the side of the

house. Someone stood there – a woman of about her own age.

'I am sorry if my mother was rude,' she said in perfect English. 'But it is true that my father is not well enough for visitors today.'

'Izabella?'

Her expression changed from polite distance to interest. 'How do you know my name?' She came a few steps closer. Ruby could see the resemblance between mother and daughter; the same thick dark hair and full lips. But her hair was long and loose; she wasn't tall like Andrés, but she too was slim.

'I know your brother Andrés.'

'Andrés!' In two steps, Izabella was in front of her, eyes eager and full of hope. 'Is Andrés here with you – on the island?'

'No, he's not.' If only . . . 'He lives near me in England. In West Dorset.' She wouldn't say any more about their relationship though, she decided – that's if there still was one.

'Did he send you here?' Izabella's eyes were wide. Ruby half expected her to call her mother back, to demand that Ruby was admitted. But she didn't. She took Ruby's arm and propelled her back down the path and out of the gate. Was Andrés so unwelcome then? Couldn't his name even be mentioned on the premises? But Ruby allowed herself to be propelled. She was curious about Izabella, she might find out a lot from this sister of his, and anyway – she could always come back here later.

'No, he didn't,' she admitted. 'I wanted him to come with me – but he wouldn't.'

Izabella's face fell and Ruby felt the force of her disappointment. 'Not because he didn't want to see you,' she said quickly. 'But because of everything else that happened, I suppose.'

'I miss him.' Izabella kept hold of her arm and Ruby realised they were walking back towards the sea – not to the Old Harbour near the hotel, but further north.

Why not, she thought. Already she felt drawn to this woman. And Izabella clearly loved her brother very much. 'Of course you do.' She herself had never had a sibling – she could only imagine how comforting it must be. 'And Andrés misses you.'

'Does he really?' Eagerly, Izabella turned to her. 'If only he would come back to us.' She sighed. 'Even for a visit.'

She sounded so sad. But surely his own sister must know the reasons why? 'But you're not unhappy here on the island?' Ruby asked her.

'I am happy enough.' Izabella shrugged. 'But nothing is the same without Andrés. He is my brother. I long to see him again.'

Ruby nodded. He had to come back here one day, didn't he? – if only for his sister's sake? 'What happened, Izabella?' she asked. 'Why has he never come back?' And she realised that this visit was not just about looking for Laura; perhaps it never had been. It was about Andrés too and whatever it was that had made him leave.

They were on the outskirts of the village now. In front of them stretched a beach of pale golden sand, the blue sea beyond. The coastline seemed to go on for ever. Ruby blinked. This was more like it.

'There was an argument,' Izabella said softly. 'Between Andrés and our father.'

'It must have been a massive one,' Ruby said. Families always argued. There had to be more.

'They never got on.' Izabella sighed. 'Andrés, he would always try to protect our mother. Things he said made my father angry. My father is a great painter.' There was pride in her voice now. 'And great painters sometimes have . . . ' She said something in Spanish. Gesticulated with her hands.

'Great egos?' Ruby had been able to see that just from the pictures on his website. He hadn't looked like a man who liked being crossed.

Izabella nodded. 'I think so,' she said. They crossed over the road. Ruby shielded her eyes from the glare of the sun, which was already hot, and looked out along the coastline to a stretch of sand drifting into dunes, crops of black rock at the water's edge and semicircular pods of volcanic lava dotted around the beach, just like in the photographs . . .

'It was a long time ago,' Ruby said. 'Isn't it time they put it behind them and made up?'

Izabella looked at her sadly and shook her head. 'You do not know my father,' she whispered.

No. They were both artists but there the resemblance ended. The father was clearly nothing like the son. Even so,

Ruby couldn't wait to meet him. 'What did Andrés say to him?' she asked. 'Do you know?'

'Not exactly. They wouldn't tell me. But my father has a terrible temper.' She rolled her eyes. 'And Mama said that Andrés had just gone too far this time. My father . . .' She looked beseechingly at Ruby. 'He threw him out of our house. And Andrés was so proud that he never tried to come back.'

'You don't know what it was about?' Ruby asked. Andrés must have really touched a raw nerve with the great Enrique Marin.

'No.' Izabella shook her dark head. 'I only know that after he had gone . . . After he had gone . . .' Her eyes glazed over and she seemed to shake herself as if she realised she had said too much. 'Nothing was ever the same,' she said.

They wandered over the sand and down to the water's edge. Izabella took off her shoes and let the water curl between her toes and Ruby followed suit. The touch of it was soft and refreshing. There were a few people on the beach and in the sea, but it wasn't crowded. And the sand and rocks stretched out as far as the eye could see. 'Shall we walk a little way?' Izabella asked her. 'There's something I'd like to show you.'

'Of course.'

They remained barefoot and stayed by the water's edge as they walked. 'What's wrong with your father?' Ruby asked, though she wasn't sure if Izabella's mother had been making it up as an excuse to keep her out of the house. 'Your mother said he was ill.'

'He has lung cancer.'

'Oh, my God.' Izabella's words were so stark. But as Ruby turned to her, she saw that she was barely holding back the tears. She touched her arm. 'I'm so sorry,' she said. 'I had no idea.' A thought occurred to her. 'Does Andrés know?' she whispered.

'*Si*. He knows.'

'He knows?' Ruby was shocked. 'But . . . ' Why on earth hadn't he told her? It was such a big thing. Wasn't she the woman he was supposed to be in love with? The woman he spent his time with? The woman who – she had thought, not so long ago – he might even have a future with? My God . . . He was clearly a hell of a lot more secretive than she had realised.

And Ruby had had more than enough of secrets. It was bad enough not opening up to her about whatever had happened with his father and his reasons for not seeing his family. But now. His father had lung cancer and he hadn't even bothered to mention it. Did that mean he just didn't care? About his own father? About her?

Izabella led the way up and over some smooth rocks. 'You expected him to tell you?' she said. 'You are in love with my brother?'

Was she? She knew that she'd been falling . . . She looked helplessly at Izabella.

Izabella took her hand. 'Look,' she said.

From the top of the rocks they had a vantage point to the north and to the south. And in front of them was what the rocks had hidden from view before. A perfect horseshoe-shaped bay. A luminescent turquoise lagoon of gently rippling water, surrounded by black volcanic rock; leading down to it from the bank of rocks, a sheet of smooth pale sand. 'It is beautiful – do you not think?'

'It is, yes.' Ruby stared. It was truly stunning.

'And it is a secret.' Izabella put her finger to her lips. 'You have to walk this far to even know it is here.'

Ruby smiled. This was true. On the far side of the bay she could see a strange-looking building built on the beach. Some sort of Moorish beach house, perhaps, with a sculptured roof and chimney. And in the distance . . . She felt like letting out a whoop of excitement. There was a red and white striped lighthouse.

Izabella turned to her. 'But why have you come to our island?' she asked Ruby.

This could be the place. This could really be the place. 'I came here, Izabella,' she said, 'to look for my mother.'

CHAPTER 38

He must get on.

Andrés began to take some of the sitting-room floor-boards up with his crowbar and a hammer, so that he could get to the pipes. He was stripping out some old plumbing for one of his clients. It was the kind of job he could do without, but despite the fact that his business was now very healthy and he wanted to spend more time on his art, he still found it hard to say no to work. It had taken him a long time to get to this position – and it was perhaps the fate of the self-employed; to always worry where the next pay cheque was coming from.

He leant on the crowbar. The dusty old board creaked. Out with the old . . . It was a sobering thought.

Andrés thought of Ruby over there in Fuerteventura. His girl. He had thought that not so long ago. Now . . . He wasn't so sure. If his suspicions proved to be correct then there was no future for them, it was as simple as that. And if he was not correct . . . Well, by not going back to the island with her, by not helping her and supporting her as her man should, then he had already blown his chances, as the English might say.

It was a no-win situation. He put the floorboards to one side and grabbed the pipe wrench from his tool bag. This might be a dirty job but it was just the thing to be doing when you were feeling pissed off with the world. Bloody angry, in fact. Angry that she was there. Angry that she couldn't understand why he hadn't gone back there with her. And angry with him – that lecherous old bastard he called his father. Why should he? Why should he just drop everything and run back to see him – the man who had never had time for him, had barely a word of praise for him; never a moment of love. What did he owe him? What did he owe him really?

Especially after . . .

Andrés switched to the hacksaw, turning the blade so that the teeth faced forwards. He started to saw the pipe; the rasping sound of metal to metal filled the air. Harsh.

And he thought of his father in his studio entertaining all those women – little more than girls, some of them. He'd seen them coming through the house, singly or sometimes in pairs, giggling and whispering together. So impressed by the man. In awe of the great artist. He'd seen his father's face when he looked at them. Lustful old goat. And he'd seen his mother's expression too, although she always went out around the back of the house or turned her face away. How many times had Enrique Marin humiliated his wife? Too many times to be counted.

Andrés had sneaked up to the studio when his father went out to the Bar Acorralado and he'd seen what the old bastard had been doing, how he'd been painting them. People thought that he was a great man, but some used their talents and their greatness to wield power over the more vulnerable. That was Enrique's tool of trade. He had something – a charisma, Andrés supposed you would call it, that made others bend to his will; that enabled him to even know what you were thinking sometimes. But what was he using it for?

Enrique Marin had a huge talent. But he had many strings to his artistic bow.

'Why do you not put a stop to it?' Andrés had asked his mother more than once. 'Show him he cannot go on like this.'

His mother had bent her head. 'He is an artist, son,' she said.

An artist! 'Have you seen what he draws?' he asked her. 'Have you seen what he paints?' Life drawing could be a beautiful thing. But not his. Some of it was so tacky it made Andrés's skin crawl.

His mother turned on him then. 'I do not want to see!' she shot back. 'I do not want to know.'

'But, Mama,' he had pleaded with her. 'It is not right that you hide your head in the sand, you know. It is not right that you allow this to continue.'

She had brushed this away. 'He is a great man,' she said. 'With a great man, you will always have a dark side.'

Andrés didn't believe this for a moment. His father had always had a temper – yes, and he had always been hard to satisfy. But everything had changed when the man became successful. It had turned his head, made him think that he was something he was not; made him use the power he had to control others. To get what he wanted.

But Andrés had to stand by and watch his mother's continued humiliation. Her husband did not take her to exhibitions, launches or parties. Why should he when there was always someone younger or more beautiful to hang on to his arm and on to his every word? Why should he take the woman he was married to, the woman who had borne him his two children? Andrés used to seethe. But what could he do to change things?

Was it just drawing and painting? he used to ask himself. How could it be? And he was determined to catch him out.

One afternoon, Andrés came back to the house when he was supposed to be out till supper time. It was his mother's shopping day and his father was alone in his studio.

But of course, he was not.

Andrés crept back inside Casa Azul and tiptoed up to his father's studio. He could hear their voices and he could tell it was not just painting that was going on. But he must be sure, so he opened the door just a crack and put his eye to the slit. He recognised the girl as Stella, one of his father's models. She was just eighteen and had a boyfriend in the village who Andrés played soccer with sometimes. Enrique Marin played dominoes in the Bar Acorralado with the girl's father; he was one of his best friends.

They were both naked. She was lying on the chaise longue and he was kneeling in front of her, feeding her segments of an orange; dropping them between her moist and open lips.

His father was caressing her breast with his other hand. They were talking and laughing and . . . Andrés shut the door. He did not want to see any more. He could not. And he knew that there had been others – so many others.

That night over dinner, when Izabella had gone round to a friend's house, he told his parents what he had seen.

'I came back to the house this afternoon,' he said. 'I went up to the studio.'

His mother got up from the table and started clearing the plates.

'I saw you and Stella.' He addressed this to his father. 'How can you take advantage of her like that?'

His father shrugged. 'She is desperate to be painted,' he said.

'To be painted!' Andrés laughed. He turned towards his mother but she was opening and shutting cupboards, seemingly not even interested in their conversation. 'I did not see so much painting going on.'

'What do you know of women and their needs?' his father growled. 'You are just a boy.'

Andrés sat up straighter. 'You are taking advantage of her. She thinks you are such a big man. So important. She is young and stupid. And so you are fucking her and fucking up her life.'

His father just sat at the table and watched him. Andrés even thought he saw a smirk hover around his lips. Why should he worry? He had them all under his control.

'Hush, Andrés!' His mother scurried back to the table. She

seemed more shocked that he was saying it than that it had actually happened. 'You do not know what you say.'

'I know exactly what I say.' He looked right back into his father's coal-black eyes. Others might, but Andrés would never look away. 'I saw them. Naked, the two of them. I saw him touching her. It was disgusting.'

'You're a liar, boy,' his father said. He took another swig of his beer.

'I know what I saw.' Andrés looked from one to the other of them. He was doing this to protect his mother, to show his father up for what he really was. So why did he feel that they had both turned against him?

'Take it back,' his father growled.

'No.'

'Take it back!'

'I saw you with her,' Andrés shouted. 'I know what you do. I know what you are. People think you're such a great man. But you're not. You're not. You're a filthy—'

'Enough!' His roar was loud enough to waken the dead. 'Get out of my house.'

'Enrique . . . ' Only now did his mother try to stop him. 'Enrique, no . . . '

'Get out of my house, boy!' he roared. 'Do not darken this door again. And do not dare to come back.'

Andrés continued cutting the pipework into manageable sections with the hacksaw. At one point the blade broke and he had to fit a replacement.

And so he had left.

Those women . . . Those girls . . . If that was what a marriage was, then he wanted none of it.

But now. He had to go back there. He had thought he could avoid it, but how could he? He had to go back. He should be there with Ruby at this time – she needed him. And if Enrique was dying? He would need to help his mother and Izabella through it too. It was his responsibility. Something hurt inside his chest and Andrés breathed deeply, trying to free it, trying to free himself. His blood. His father was his blood.

He owed it to himself. He had a ghost to lay to rest. He had to go home.

And Ruby . . .

He thought of the picture his father had painted of the beautiful young girl with long blonde hair and sad blue eyes. He had to find out if Ruby's mother had been one of those girls.

CHAPTER 39

'Come round to the *casa* again this afternoon,' Izabella had said when they parted. 'I will talk to Mama. She will let you in this time.'

And so Ruby was here again, waiting outside.

Reyna Marin came to the door. 'Come in,' she said. 'You are a friend of my son. Please. You must come in.'

'Thank you.' Ruby followed her into the house, past a spiral staircase which wound from the hall into the upper reaches of the house, and through into the kitchen. It still had the look of a Spanish kitchen about it, Ruby thought, with its colourful tiles and curtains, but it also had all the mod cons.

Reyna Marin ushered Ruby to sit down in a wooden chair at the table. She moved a chopping board and some vegetables she was preparing to one side.

Again, Ruby wondered about their lives. It touched her that despite her husband's success, Reyna Marin – and possibly Enrique too – seemed to prefer the life of simplicity that they had probably always led.

'How is Andrés?' his mother asked hesitantly.

'He's very well.'

Reyna Marin looked as if she might cry. She spoke swiftly and softly in Spanish. Ruby couldn't understand what she said, but she felt the emotion behind her words.

'What I would not give to see him,' she added. She hugged her arms around her chest and slowly rocked her body from side to side. 'What I would not give to hold him in my arms again.' She closed her eyes. 'Andrés. My son . . .'

Ruby got to her feet, put her arm around the woman and tried to offer some comfort. First Izabella and now Reyna. Why wouldn't he come home? And another thought struck her. Here was another woman – like Laura – who had lived for a great deal of her life without her child. Whatever had happened between Enrique and Andrés, she clearly loved her son. Ruby could feel her pain.

Reyna's eyes snapped open. She looked vague, as if she'd suddenly remembered she wasn't alone. 'You want some coffee, *si*?' she asked.

'Yes, please,' said Ruby.

Reyna filled the percolator with water and coffee and put it on the stove. 'And you want to talk to my husband about your mother, you say?'

'I want to trace her.'

Reyna didn't seem to understand. She frowned.

'Look for her.' Ruby sighed. She might as well tell this woman the story. 'She gave me away when I was a baby,' she said.

Reyna spoke again in Spanish, went to the doorway, looked up the stairs. Clearly, she was uncomfortable with the conversation. 'A baby,' she repeated. She shook her head, although whether this was in response to what Ruby had said or whether she was thinking of her own children, Ruby had no idea.

'I saw a portrait of my mother on your husband's website,' she explained.

'A portrait?' Again, her eyes darkened. 'A portrait, you say?' The frown grew deeper.

'I spoke to Andrés . . .'

Reyna was watching her intently. She was on edge, Ruby realised. But why? Was it just because of Andrés – or was there something more?

What could she tell her? 'I am sure he misses you all,' she said weakly.

'And we miss him.' Reyna Marin got up to pour the coffee. 'We miss him from the bottom of our hearts.'

'Reyna?' A man called from upstairs. It could only be Enrique.

'*Si?*' Reyna sighed. 'He is not well,' she said to Ruby. She got to her feet and called back to him, speaking in Spanish.

'I promise not to tire him,' Ruby said when she came back into the kitchen.

'Hey there!' He called out in English this time. His voice was guttural and thick. It must once have been a powerful voice, but Ruby could hear the fragility in it now.

She went out into the hall. He stood at the top of the spiral staircase, and she was shocked to see not the great artist she had expected but a small and wasted man of about seventy.

She barely recognised him from the photos on his website. '*Hola*, Señor,' she said. She could manage about that much Spanish.

'Who are you?' He coughed as soon as he had spoken. But he recovered himself well and stood – more erect – looking down at her. Ruby recognised a glimmer then of what he had been. It was in his stance, in the kind of aura that, despite his illness, still clung to him.

'My name's Ruby Rae. I came here because I wanted to speak with you.' She took a deep breath. 'I believe you painted my mother many years ago.'

'Your mother, eh?' He frowned. Muttered something she couldn't understand. 'What do you want then? What can I be expected to do?' He was shaking his head.

'I'm trying to find her.' Ruby looked up at him.

He sighed heavily. 'What was her name? No, do not tell me, I do not remember names. Come up, come up.' He beckoned her up the stairs.

'I saw a portrait of her on your website,' Ruby said as she climbed the spiral staircase. Her words seemed to echo from the stone walls. 'I just want to talk to her, that's all.'

'Oh, that is all, is it?' She was level with him now and Enrique Marin was looking her up and down, appraising her.

Ruby stood tall. The man was old enough to be her father – older – and yet he was undressing her with his eyes and making absolutely no bones about it. Could you call that artistic licence? Whatever. He simply didn't care.

'She had long blonde hair and blue eyes,' Ruby said. 'I can show you the picture.'

'No need, no need.' Slowly, he walked along the landing, wheezing as he went, beckoning her to follow him. 'Come with me.'

They entered a light, airy and magnificent room with windows on all sides. A studio, Ruby realised immediately. An art studio which was full of canvases, easels, and trestle tables loaded with paints and brushes and other paraphernalia. Automatically, she walked over to the window. From here she could see the ocean, the lagoons, even that lighthouse. 'It's amazing up here,' she breathed. A bird's-eye view.

'Yes, yes.'

He sounded impatient. And why was there no need to show him the picture, she wondered.

'Here she is, *si*?'

Ruby spun around. Enrique Marin was holding a canvas. It showed a woman – Laura – sitting on a flat rock on the beach. She was wearing an indigo sarong and a loose cream blouse. Her legs were bent, she was leaning back slightly on her hands; her hair was blowing in the wind. She was staring out to sea, and she looked as desolate as the scene in which he'd painted her. Laura . . . 'Yes,' she said. 'That's her.' She turned to him. 'How did you know?'

He shrugged. 'You have her look.'

'I do?'

'Noticed it straight off.' His eyes were black and sharp as

flint. 'I loved painting that girl.' He let out a harsh cackle. 'I'd paint you too if I still had the strength.'

Ruby thought of Andrés. What would this man say if he knew that his son had got there first? Andrés hadn't painted her, no, but he had sketched her portrait as they sat on Golden Cap. And even Ruby could see how Enrique Marin had recognised her. There was a resemblance between them; she could see it from this picture more than ever before. Like a stranger, she thought again. Like a stranger you've always known . . .

'You never sold this one?' Ruby asked him. After all, an artist generally sold his work if he could.

He shrugged. 'I made some prints. Call me a sentimental fool, eh?'

Somehow Ruby couldn't quite see him as either. 'Can you tell me anything about her?' Ruby asked him. 'Do you know – is she still around?'

He shrugged. 'I knew nothing about her even then,' he said. 'Apart from her sadness and her bone structure and that she could keep still for hours.' He laughed again, though the laughter turned into a rasping cough that seemed to come from deep within him. 'Why should I know anything more? I did not care. What was important? To talk or to paint, eh?'

Ruby saw what he meant. Even so. There must be something.

'She was a free spirit though, that one.' He chuckled. 'I do not know if she is still here on the island. But I liked her.' He rubbed his hands together. 'Yes, I liked her.'

'And that's all you can tell me?' Ruby asked him. It might be a dead end, but at least she now knew for sure that Laura had lived here – once. Talking to someone who had known her, who had painted her, was helping Ruby get more of a feel for her too.

'*Si*.' He moved with some difficulty towards the other end of the studio. 'I keep all my old sketches and roughs. Some of the originals too. An artist's prerogative, eh?'

'I suppose so.' Ruby smiled.

'And you?'

'Me?'

'What do you do, hmm? Are you as free as your mother?'

'Not really. I'm a journalist. And I play the saxophone. Jazz.'

He stopped what he was doing and stared at her for a long moment. 'Ah. So that is what you do?'

She nodded and he resumed his sorting through the stack of paintings.

'Your mother, eh?' He nodded. 'So do you want to see the rest, hmm?'

Ruby said a quick goodbye to Reyna Marin, who examined her face as if she were looking for the answer to some question, squeezed her hand and said, 'Come again, Ruby, please.'

Then she left the Casa Azul, and pulled out her mobile to call Andrés.

It had been a revelation. She had talked to the father. And now she wanted to talk to the son.

418

'Ruby.'

At least he had answered. 'Hello, Andrés,' she said.

'So you are there?'

Ruby got to the end of the street and turned right according to Enrique's directions. 'Yes, I'm here,' she said.

She heard his exhalation of breath. 'And is it the place?' Though he sounded as if he already knew.

'Yes, it's the place.' She thought of the lighthouse she'd seen in the distance. The bay with the turquoise water and black volcanic rock. 'But I have no idea if she's still here.'

'People come and people go,' Enrique had told her in his gruff voice. 'Some people stay here for ever. This place – it gets you. Here.' And he had thumped his chest.

Had Laura stayed for ever? Enrique hadn't seen her for thirty years, he told Ruby. But in a place like this, that didn't mean a thing. Most of the time he was in his studio, he said. He spent time in Rosario too. He didn't go to the sort of places Laura would go. Not any more.

'And where are you going now?' Andrés asked. He sounded very cool and formal. She wished he was here so that she could grab hold of him and make him tell her what he really felt.

'To the convent,' she said.

'The convent?' He sounded surprised, as well he might.

'It's a strange story.'

Enrique had told her about a nun called Sister Julia who lived at the convent just outside the village. He told her how to get there too. It wasn't far, he said, a few kilometres, that

419

was all. 'I met her,' he said. 'More than once, I met her.'

'Yes?' Ruby was confused. What could that have to do with Laura? She couldn't imagine Laura having any kind of relationship with a nun.

'She is old,' Enrique said. 'But she knows things.' He tapped his nose.

'Things?'

He had shrugged. 'They have records there at Nuestra Señora del Carmen. They know where people can be found. And Sister Julia – she is interested in children; their mothers, their fathers . . .' His voice tailed off into a cough.

'So you think—'

'Just talk to her.' His shoulders slumped and he waved her away. Ruby realised she was being dismissed. 'Talk to her.' For whatever reason, it had seemed important to him.

'Who told you to go and see a nun?' Andrés asked.

Ruby braced herself. 'Your father.'

'Ah.' He sighed. 'You've seen him then.' He sounded resigned.

'He's ill, Andrés.' Ruby took the long straight road out of town as Enrique had directed. It was lined with date palm trees and had a couple of rundown bars where men were sitting outside drinking beer. 'He's very ill.'

'I know.'

'He could be dying.'

'I know that too.'

It was Ruby's turn to sigh. She didn't want to think that this man she cared so much for could be so cold towards his own father. But what was she supposed to think? He knew Enrique Marin was suffering from lung cancer. He knew he might not have long to live. What could he have done that was so bad that Andrés wouldn't at the very least come back and see him one last time before he died? 'But you're still not coming over?' she asked.

There was a long pause. Ruby passed the new supermarket and headed out towards the windmill as directed. The land was brown and arid, the mountains in the distance soft and dimpled.

'Why did he want you to go and see a nun?' Andrés asked.

'I'm not sure.' All that talk about children and parents. It was a bit odd. But it made sense that they might have records at the convent – although Laura was not the kind to allow herself to be recorded in that way. Ruby remembered what she'd apparently said to Vivien about labels and not registering Ruby's birth. A free spirit? A hippy? What was her mother really like? Would she ever have the chance to find out for herself?

'Did you tell him you knew me?' Andrés asked.

'No.' He probably wouldn't have talked to her if she had.

'And my mother. How is my mother?'

'Why don't you come and see?'

Silence.

'And did my father tell you anything else?' Andrés asked.

'Like what?' She wasn't going to make it easy for him.

She heard him sigh.

'He didn't tell me what happened between the two of you,

421

if that's what you mean.' Ruby exhaled. His secret — whatever it might be — was safe.

'I did not mean that,' he said. 'I meant . . . ' He hesitated. 'Never mind what I meant.'

Ruby gave up. The man was infuriating. 'So how's it all going with the exhibition?' she asked instead.

'I'm ready,' he said.

Ruby thought of all those sketches Enrique had shown her — of Laura, on the beach mostly, over a short period of time, he had said. Her sadness and desolation were almost tangible; Enrique had expressed her emotions so vividly in his work. 1978 . . . 1979 . . . After Laura's mother had died. After she had gone back to England. And after she had given her baby to Vivien. Had she regretted her decision then? Had she wished that she had never given Ruby away? So many sketches — it was almost as if he'd been obsessed with her.

'And when the exhibition is over . . . ' Andrés said now.

'Yes?'

'Then it is over,' he said.

Ruby stared gloomily out over the *campo* towards the mountains and the windmill. How had she come to get so involved with such an annoying and inscrutable man? But when he said it was over — was he talking about the summer exhibition? Or was he talking about their relationship? Ruby realised that she didn't have the foggiest idea.

CHAPTER 40

'Why are you here, my child?' the old nun asked Ruby in perfect English.

'I'm looking for my mother.' It was simple as that really.

But the nun gasped – as if she had said something quite shocking.

How could it be shocking to be looking for her mother?

They were seated in a little room off the foyer of the convent – Ruby and the old nun, Sister Julia. She seemed as ancient as the hills. She wore a simple white habit and a heavy crucifix around her neck. Her face was wrinkled as a dried date, but her eyes – although milky and faded – held a startling wisdom. She obviously had a good command of the English language too – perhaps she had studied it when she was a girl?

'Your mother?' Sister Julia seemed overcome. She put a hand to her mouth and her eyes widened, almost in disbelief. 'Oh, my dear,' she said. 'Oh, my dear.' For a few moments she was still and silent, just staring into space. And then she seemed to collect herself and come to.

'Sister?'

'Shall we walk?' She rose to her feet, looking around her,

almost as if she didn't want anyone to hear their conversation.

Which was ridiculous, obviously. But . . .

'It is a lovely day.'

'Yes, of course, Sister. We can walk.' Everyone here seemed to want to walk somewhere with her. And it really did seem rather paranoid. Only, why on earth would this old nun not want to be overheard?

They passed through the cloistered arches of pale crumbling stone. Ruby noticed a small bell tower attached to the chapel on a stone buttress. And outside, she could see some chickens and goats in a pen, and a garden with vegetables and almond trees. The allotment was surrounded by low dry-stone walls made up from what she now knew to be the volcanic black rock of the island.

They walked out through the arched gateway, turning left at the sandy track and heading towards the brown mountains. Sister Julia might be old, but for her age she was quite sprightly.

'Who sent you to me?' she asked as they walked away from the stone buildings of the convent.

'Enrique Marin.' Would she know who he was? Nuns probably wouldn't have much to do with famous artists. 'The artist – from the village.'

'Ah.' But Sister Julia nodded. 'He is the only one to whom I have told the story.'

'The story?' Ruby was confused. Was there a story that concerned Laura? And if so, how did this old nun know it was Laura she was interested in, since she had only just left the house of Enrique Marin? He couldn't possibly have already told her. Nuns didn't use mobiles or even landline telephones – or did they?

'There is something about him.' Sister Julia paused for a moment and looked out towards the mountains. 'Something that compels.'

This was true – Ruby had felt the same. She followed the nun's gaze and saw that dark clouds had gathered there at the peaks, although the rest of the sky was clear blue. All she could see was desert and mountains; in the distance the ribbon of the ocean. 'He is a charismatic man,' she agreed. And so was his son – though in a very different way. She sighed.

'Indeed.' Sister Julia turned to face her. 'It is in the eyes, I believe.' Her own eyes twinkled and Ruby caught a glimpse of the young woman she must have once been. What had made her take vows and enter the sisterhood, she wondered. Had she always lived here on the island? Or had she once had a different sort of life?

But she agreed with her about Enrique Marin's eyes. They bored into you – almost as if they could see into your soul. What had Laura made of him, she wondered. Had she too succumbed to his charm? She doubted that. Artist or not, Enrique Marin would never have had the Mediterranean good looks of Julio – or Ruby's own father, whoever he might be. Another free spirit, she liked to think. Another drifter, like Laura.

'What is your name, my dear child?' Sister Julia asked.

'Ruby. Ruby Rae.'

'Ruby.' Sister Julia nodded as if the name pleased her.

'But that is not my mother's name. Rae, I mean.'

Sister Julia shot her a penetrating look that took Ruby by surprise. 'Naturally not,' she said.

Why naturally not? Ruby frowned.

'Of course you do not know the name of your birth mother,' Sister Julia said. 'How could you? It is not possible. So many things made it not possible.'

'But . . . ' Had she been mistaken to come here? The old nun had seemed sharp enough but maybe she wasn't as with it as Ruby had thought. She was so old. And these nuns lived in retreat from the world. They were bound to lose touch with reality.

They had reached a fork in the path and Sister Julia indicated that they should take the right fork towards the sea. 'We will not go far,' she reassured Ruby. 'These days I cannot go far.'

'But I do know my mother's name,' Ruby said gently. She would walk with her a bit longer and then take her back to the convent. No harm done.

'You do?' Sister Julia turned to face her. 'How can that be, my child?'

'Her name is Laura. Laura Woods.' And Ruby explained how Laura had been living here on the island when she gave birth to Ruby, how she had come back to England after hearing of the death of her mother, and how she had given Ruby to Tom and Vivien Rae to look after because she wanted her to have a different life.

The old nun seemed to understand what she was saying although she remained silent while Ruby was speaking. And Ruby found her presence calming somehow.

'I have a photograph,' she said.

'May I see?'

'Of course.' They had reached the cliff. It was windy but Sister Julia hardly seemed to notice. Down below them the wild sea rolled, heaved and crashed against the black rocks.

Ruby rummaged in her bag and found the photographs she always carried with her. 'I recognised a portrait of my birth mother on Enrique Marin's website,' she told her. 'So I came over here to Fuerteventura to talk to him.'

Sister Julia was looking at the photograph, shielding it with her palm from the wind. There was a slight smile on her face and her expression was serene. Ruby got the impression that she often came here to commune with the wind and the sea and the mountains and God. Or something. There was something primeval and raw about the landscape. You felt the power of Nature – you couldn't help but feel it.

'You must have wanted to find her very much,' Sister Julia said.

'I did. I do.' And Ruby found herself telling her the rest of the story. About the motorbike accident and the death of Vivien and Tom. How she had put the pieces of her birth history together. 'I'm a journalist,' she said, almost apologetically. 'It's my business to investigate stories and write about things. My mother – Vivien, that is – used to say I was born curious.'

'You are a journalist, you say.' Sister Julia was giving her the strangest look.

'Yes.'

'And you investigate stories?'

'I do, yes.' What was this? The nun seemed to understand so much. But it was as if she was thinking of something quite different.

'And you are looking for your mother.' Sister Julia held the photograph to her breast and stared out towards the horizon. 'I see now why Enrique Marin sent you to me,' she said. 'Although I misunderstood at first. I thought that you needed my help, my dear.'

'But I do.'

Sister Julia nodded. 'And I need your help too, my child,' she said. 'I can need no other sign.'

Was she missing something here? How could she help this old nun? Though she'd like to, of course, if she could. 'Do you recognise this woman, Sister?' she asked after a few moments when Sister Julia seemed to have come back to earth again. 'Do you recognise my birth mother?'

'Oh, yes. Shall we walk back now, my child?'

Yes? She recognised her? Ruby felt a jump of hope. 'Does she live nearby?' she asked as they turned around. She must try and be patient, but it was hard.

'She came to Nuestra Señora del Carmen sometimes,' Sister Julia said. 'To pick herbs – for cooking and for medicine.'

Ruby nodded. That fitted with the sort of lifestyle Laura

must have been leading. Simple. Basic. A bit alternative.

Sister Julia smiled to herself. 'She had very little,' she said. 'We were happy to share. And when there were jobs to be done on our allotment, sometimes she and a few of her friends came to help us.'

Ruby felt the excitement beginning to build. 'Recently?' she asked. The trail was getting hotter. She could sense it.

But Sister Julia shook her head. 'Not for some years,' she said. 'But we live some way out, as you know. It may not be easy for her to get here these days.'

Ruby felt the breath tighten in her chest. 'You know where she lives?' she whispered.

Sister Julia reached for her hand. 'I know where she used to live, my child,' she said. 'Laura used to live in a beach house in Los Lagos. Near the bay before you reach the light-house.'

'Oh my God,' said Ruby. Then she remembered who she was with. 'I'm sorry, Sister. But . . . ' Laura lived – or had lived – in that beach house, just beyond where she had been standing with Izabella only this morning.

'I understand.' The old nun nodded. 'You want to see her very much. It is very exciting for you. It may be the end of your journey, perhaps.'

They had reached the white walls of the convent. 'She might not be interested in seeing me again,' Ruby said. Though she didn't want to dwell on that option. 'But I feel I need to at least try.' Especially now that she had seen those drawings of Enrique's, felt that sadness in Laura's eyes.

'There's so much I'd like to know. I think it would help me feel complete somehow.'

'Complete, yes,' Sister Julia repeated. 'It is everyone's right, I think, to discover the circumstances surrounding their birth. It is an integral need. A basic truth. Do you agree?' She grasped Ruby's hand tightly and looked into her eyes.

Her grip was surprisingly strong. 'Yes, yes I do.' Ruby almost felt that she was agreeing to something more. But whatever it was, she was willing. She trusted this woman. She wanted to help.

Sister Julia seemed satisfied. 'When you have gone to Los Lagos,' she said. 'When you have gone as far as you can on your journey – for now – will you return here to the convent to see me?'

'Of course I will.' She would come and tell her what had happened, what she had discovered, whether or not she had found Laura.

'Because there is a story I must tell you,' she said.

'Oh?'

'An important story.' She nodded. 'It is the reason you have been sent here to me, my child.'

CHAPTER 41

After the young woman had left, Sister Julia retreated to her simple whitewashed room on the first floor of Nuestra Señora del Carmen. She sat on the wooden chair, leant on the desk and bent her head into the cradle of her own arms. 'Dear God, dear God,' she murmured. 'She has come.' She had waited so long. She closed her eyes and felt a sense of peace such as she had never known before begin to drift over her. But it was not yet complete. There was still more that she must do.

After a few moments, she raised her head and got to her feet. Sometimes, it was hard even for a woman of the cloth to stay serene. For so many years she had done what she could to help those poor unfortunate women in their times of trouble. She had listened to their stories and she had given them what small comfort she could. She had spoken out to those in authority when she had felt able to do so and she had prayed to God – oh, how she had prayed to God to show her what to do. And then of course she had started writing her book of names . . . It all seemed so long ago now. But, she had made her record of the women, of the adoptive couples, of the children. It had been a risk but she had felt it was all she could do. Wasn't she simply a poor and powerless nun? Wasn't she too at their mercy?

Perhaps. And yet . . . She stood by the arched window and looked out on to their small circular courtyard with the fig tree and the fountain. She had stood by. She had allowed it to happen. She had been complicit in it all.

Sister Julia sighed. It was a heavy burden to bear. When she had first come here to Nuestra Señora del Carmen, she had indeed tried to help the villagers, tried to atone for whatever wrongs she had done. If she could give spiritual guidance and comfort to others, she had thought, if she could spend her days in meditation and prayer, then would not God give her a sign? Would He not show her what she must do? Would He not forgive her and allow her to rest in peace? But for years she had struggled with the knowledge in her heart. And it had seemed sometimes that the struggle would go on until the day that she died.

Reading the story – her story, she reminded herself, the story of the *Niños Robados* – in the newspaper had brought it all back. The pain, the suffering, the tears . . . But it had also brought back the memory of the deception, the corruption. And she had come to the conclusion that she must bear witness.

Outside in the courtyard, Sister Josefina and Sister Maria walked, not talking, but in silent companionship. Sister Julia watched them. Not for her, the calmness of spiritual retreat, the contentment of silence, reflection and prayer. Inside her there had been a battle always raging, a need to unburden, and the uncertainty of not knowing how. Enrique Marin had been right that day on the cliff top. For if there had been anyone she could have told of her part in the story of the stolen children, she would have done so. But it seemed there was no one. And so still she hesitated. She wanted to bring forth her book of names, she wanted the records to be available for those who needed them, those who had been involved. A mother, perhaps, who had never believed her child had died and who now wanted to trace him. A son or daughter who now knew of their adoption and who desperately wanted to seek out their birth mothers. She could help those people. But she did not know how to do it. She was a nun, alone in the world and living in retreat. She spoke to so few people. How could she bring this about? She had needed something sent from God to help her. She had needed a sign. And now this.

Sister Julia moved again to her desk and opened the drawer. She took out the delicate white tablecloth made of lace. The things Enrique Marin had told her that day . . . First, as they sat there on the dark overhanging rock, overheard only by the ocean, he had told her of his life as a struggling artist. The dilemma he had felt about giving everything to his art when he had a wife to care for at home, the resentment at having to tend to the goats and the smallholding when he could have been painting. And then the overwhelming joy when his work began to be recognised, when people paid good money for his paintings, when people stopped him on the street.

'It went to my head, Sister,' he said. 'I make no apology. It went to my head.'

Sister Julia had seen more than enough of life to understand how fame could damage a person. How a person might lose his perspective and abuse his power. Hadn't she witnessed a similar scenario with Dr Lopez in Barcelona? He hadn't been famous, of course, but he had been highly respected and looked up to as a figure of authority who always knew what was best. His head must have been turned. And he had hidden behind the words of God to satisfy his greed and his cruelty. Sister Julia's motivation had never been primarily to see him punished – God would forgive or punish him as He saw fit when the doctor's time came; if it had not come already. It was not Sister Julia's job to judge another. And neither would she judge the man here before her now.

'And what did you do, my son?' she asked him. Though she knew. She knew as soon as he began his story that this was the husband of the woman in the village who had come to see her many years ago. Who had given her this delicate white tablecloth of lace. Sister Julia could still see the look in the woman's dark eyes as she had told her story, could still feel her despair. Sister Julia had often prayed for her. She had been hurt, disillusioned, disappointed. Such was the way of the world.

'I am not proud of all these things,' Enrique Marin had told her, his eyes still fierce as he stared out at the ocean. 'But there is more.'

And Sister Julia remembered what she had always felt about that woman's story – that there was more.

Now, Sister Julia sat down on the chair once again. She was weary. These days, she was so often weary. But at last she had been sent a sign. She clasped her hands together. 'Thank you, God.' This young woman – Ruby – had come from who knew where. A young woman looking for her mother. A journalist. No sign could be clearer. Now, she could tell her story. She could tell her story to Ruby. And Ruby would tell it to the world. Justice would be done. She would give to Ruby the book of names and then at last she would be free.

On the desk was a bottle of water and a glass and Sister Julia poured herself some with a shaky hand. But would there be enough time? Her own time was near. Would the young woman come back as she had promised? Sister Julia sipped the water. She must trust that this would be so.

Enrique Marin had talked of his son and Sister Julia had listened. Fathers, sons . . . Mothers, daughters . . . It seemed that she was destined to be involved in such matters.

'He left home many years ago,' Enrique had said. 'And in his position, I would have done the same.'

Sister Julia bent her head. Enrique Marin had gained self-knowledge. And this was something that many men in an entire lifetime never found.

'I was a bitter, jealous man.' Enrique Marin paused as the wind blew and the tide rolled into shore, the water cascading on to the black rocks, spraying a fountain of spume. 'I blamed him for something over which he had no control.'

And after he had told her the whole story, Sister Julia had let out a long sigh. Her own troubles still hung so heavily in her heart.

But, 'You can tell me, Sister,' Enrique Marin had said. 'I am here. I am no one. Just a man. This is just a deserted cliff top. You can tell me.'

And Sister Julia had looked into his dark flinty eyes and she had told him her story. As the gulls shrieked above them and the waves crashed below, she told him the story of what had happened in Barcelona. Everything that she had seen, everything that she had witnessed, everything that she had done.

'Please God that those names will not be lost,' she said, when she was finished. Perhaps, as she had told the young woman, Ruby, it was the compelling nature of the man – the look in those dark eyes – that had made her tell her story. Perhaps she needed the release for her own peace of mind. Or perhaps she told him simply because she believed that he should know. Perhaps indeed everyone should know.

Sister Julia opened the drawer in the writing desk once again and put aside the tablecloth, lovingly stitched by Reyna Marin. She held for a moment her own mother's worn gold wedding ring and the embroidered sampler she had made as a girl. She picked up the old sepia photograph of herself and her two sisters, Matilde and Paloma. All gone now. Her family was gone and Sister Julia was alone. But hadn't she been alone for such a long time?

And she took out her book of names.

Could she have done anything differently? Perhaps. But she was weak, and like Enrique Marin, she was human. And she was indeed as guilty as he.

But if only she could help the children . . . That was what she had always wanted. For they were the innocent, the helpless. They had done nothing. And it was every child's birthright to know the truth of how they came into this world. Some might not want to know. But for the others . . . Most records had been destroyed. But Sister Julia had worked at the Canales Clinic for a long time. And this book could help so many of them. Sister Julia touched the plain cover. It gave no clue as to what was inside.

Sister Julia thought once more of the young woman – Ruby. She had so much passion. She had loved the parents who had brought her up, but how desperately she still needed to know the truth. The truth. This was important to Sister Julia too. She had done wrong, they had all done wrong. But she could do this one thing. She could tell the truth.

Sister Julia opened the book and read the list of names on the first page. Now there could be some atonement for those sins. And perhaps Sister Julia could find complete peace – at last.

CHAPTER 42

Andrés was unprepared for the feelings of nostalgia that swept over him as the plane began its descent. He caught glimpses of the *campo* as they moved through pockets of cloud. The desert landscape of his childhood seemed unchanged at first. As desolate as ever, it stretched out beneath him in ochre, sand and grey rock tracked with paths and ancient walkways as the plane came in from the north, following the coast line; mountains almost as old as time, their peaks obscured by wisps of cloud. From the east coast, the plane banked out to sea, the fierce blue of the ocean shifting from lacy turquoise at the shoreline to deepest navy, the wing dipping as the plane turned, almost to the south of the island now, so that it could land into the wind.

As they descended, the cloud cleared as if they had emerged from a mist, and now Andrés could see the changes. The stark artificial green of the golf course (using God only knows how much of their precious desalinated water) the chemical blue of the swimming pools, the orange complexes of tourist villas. But it would not be like that in Ricoroque. He sat back and watched the gentle sway of the ocean as the plane prepared to land.

The warmth enveloped him as soon as he emerged from the plane, while inside the terminal it was the smells – Spanish cigarettes, bitter coffee and olive oil; smoked ham and sun cream. It had been a long time but it was beginning to feel like yesterday.

Andrés collected his hire car from the airport car park and set off, heading north. He had pulled out all the stops to get this last-minute flight. And he hadn't told any of them he was coming – not even Ruby. Why not? He supposed he didn't want them to prepare themselves; he wanted to return with as much spontaneity as he had left with. And as for Ruby . . . First, he had to find out the truth. He gripped the steering wheel more forcefully. Only then could he think of Ruby.

He took the bypass around the capital and almost immediately the landscape altered – away from the urbanisation of Rosario. This rural area, these small, scattered villages were much as he remembered. In seventeen years they had hardly changed. Small, squat stone houses and white churches. Smallholdings. Ruins. A bar and a grocery store. Andrés resisted the impulse to stop for a beer. As he drove, he was conscious of the smoothness of the road surface – a contrast to the rugged rocks and eroded mountains which cast deep shadows on the villages below.

Some things were very different, yes. And some were the same.

Andrés opened the window rather than turning on the car's air-con. The warm air seemed pure and fresh – he wanted to breathe it in great lungfuls; it tasted so different from the air in England. He had missed it, he realised; grown used to pollution and not being able to see the stars in a clear night sky.

Andrés thought of the summer exhibition. He'd put everything he had into it, but now it hardly seemed important. Anyway, the work was all done and one of his colleagues, Susie – who did ceramics and rented the studio next to his – had agreed to cover for the periods on the welcome desk which should, according to the rota, be his responsibility. Just before he left Andrés had put the finishing touches to his own section of the exhibition space and placed a red sticker on his central piece – the painting of the cliffs at Chesil Beach. It wasn't for sale. He knew where that was going.

It was late afternoon and already the light was changing. The soft beam of the sun on the pink and brown mountainsides was sharpening into the bitter yellow light he remembered so well – the light he had loved to paint in, to capture; the light that sent shafts of green on to the white houses and the golden sand. It was an other-wordly light that transformed this bleak scenery into an almost lunar landscape; a unique light that made him catch his breath, that Andrés had not seen since he had been gone.

He slowed as Tindaya came into sight. The holy mountain. He had come here once with Izabella, on his scooter; they had ridden down the track between the drystone walls with Montaña Tindaya right in front of them, mushroom-coloured in the pale morning light, streaked with brown and white and rust, channelled by rainwater; the sky clear as a diamond above.

They'd parked the scooter by the brown-stone derelict cottages in the shadow of the mountain itself; walked through the carpet of burgundy cosco and over the bare earth and rubble along the path that led up the slopes of Tindaya and on to the bare rock of the summit. Not an easy path; at times near the top they even had to climb on all fours. But it was worth it. From the top they could see the peaks of other mountains in the distance, the island of Lanzarote, the white sprinkling that was La Oliva and Ricoroque to the left on the coast. They had come to search for the hieroglyphs, the rock engravings. It was a game.

'*Aquí está!*' Izabella had found the first two – on a smooth, upright rock face on the east side of the summit, five or six metres from the peak. 'Here. Come and look!' There were, he had heard, over a hundred such carvings – of feet, podomorphs etched into the *traquita*. Further along the ridge in the next crop of rocks were more – some not so recognisable, but others clear and impressive still. Andrés had heard that they all faced towards Teide – the frequently erupting volcano in Tenerife where the devil was believed to reside. The hieroglyphs were intended to drive away bad spirits. And as he stood there and looked towards Teide, the peak of which was circled by thick cloud – he thought it really could be true.

It was slow going on the way down and they had held hands; Andrés was worried Izabella would go too fast, be careless and lose her footing. But she was as sure-footed as a mountain goat and it was he who stumbled; she who stood firm and stopped him from falling.

But who could stop him from falling now? He and Izabella had lost touch over the years – their lives had gone in such different directions. His parents seemed like strangers. And Ruby . . .

Was the mountain haunted by spirits? Some believed so. He couldn't deny the power of the place. Its magnetic force seemed to draw him in. He had felt it that whole day – as if something or someone dark was hanging over him. An oppression. And it was on the following day that it had happened – that he had seen his father in his studio and challenged him. It was the day before Andrés had left the house for good.

Andrés drove on towards La Oliva. It had always been an important town – the official residence of the colonels in the seventeenth century. Andrés did not go as far as the town, however; he took a left towards Ricoroque alongside the pale green lichen-smeared *malpaís* at Rosa de los Negrines. And he thought of those old history lessons at school, when he had learnt about the history of the island. About the French settlers, who had arrived to an island green with fig, palm and olive trees; to thick woodlands of willow and pine, and freshwater streams. It was, Andrés thought, hard to imagine. And then came the goats (which as everyone knew, ate everything), the lime kilns swallowing vast quantities of wood, the droughts and finally the rabbits and Barbary squirrels. Now, the land was virtually a desert.

On the long straight road to Lajares he put his foot down – he was almost there. Ahead, he could see the hermitage and the windmills – *los molinos*. Were the mills still in operation? Did the ageing miller and his wife still live there, as if time had indeed stood still since Andrés had been gone?

The road to Ricoroque swung to the left and that's when Andrés caught his first glimpse of the lighthouse, the village and the sea. His sea. His village. He could smell it – the dry stone and the earth, the salt-encrusted *casas*. The lava flow continued all the way, alongside the old road bordered by date palms – now effectively a cycling track for tourists, he guessed – and past the track which led to the old convent. This made him think of Ruby. Why had she gone to see a nun?

The straight wide road to town led him all the way in. Andrés took a deep breath. Had he been fooling himself all these years? He had no idea if he would receive any answers to his questions. He had no idea what his reception would be. No matter. He was home.

He parked outside the *casa*. He'd heard from his mother about some of the changes but it was still a surprise. The little house had doubled in size. Was it still his childhood home? Andrés wasn't sure. He surveyed the white-gravelled courtyard and the central metallic sculpture that looked a bit like a giant whisk. It didn't seem so real any more. But at least the carob tree still stood in the far corner of the courtyard.

He paused at the metal gates. Was he being unfair? His father had started from nothing and he had achieved a lot. But at what cost?

Instead of going up to the front door and knocking on it like a stranger, Andrés took a deep breath and walked round the side to the back. He was here now – he had to go through with it. Through the open kitchen window he could see her bustling about preparing food – his mother. He stood and watched, tears in his eyes. He shouldn't have left her for so long – that was all he could think. He shouldn't have gone away and not seen her for so long. What had he been thinking of?

All of a sudden she turned and saw him. She froze.

'My son!'

He heard her cry through the open window and then he pushed open the door and he was in her arms. Cradled like a child.

'Mama.' He buried his face in her hair. She smelt of baking; a fragrance that spun him back to his childhood, to the kitchen where he had spent hours painting while his mother peeled vegetables and shellfish and baked bread; while she cooked dinner and washed dishes, quietly humming. Had she been content with her woman's work? In the early days, perhaps. But later . . . She had been unhappy. He knew she had been unhappy. And what else could he have done to make things change?

'Andrés!' She pushed him away from her with a strength that had always surprised him, coming as it did from such a diminutive woman. 'Is it really you? Can it really be you?'

'It is me,' he assured her. Thank God his father was not around. Andrés was not ready for him – not quite. 'How are you, Mama? Are you well?'

'Me? I am healthy as a pig!' She laughed. For a moment her brow clouded.

'And Papa?' Where was he? Up in his studio, he presumed. If he was well enough to even stand, that was where he would be.

Her expression changed. She looked towards the stairs. What was it she felt? Anxiety? Fear? And then she hugged him again. Drew back to scrutinise his face. 'You are pale.'

He laughed. 'I live in England.'

'You are tired.'

'I'm older.'

'You should have told us you were coming. I would have prepared a special dinner.'

'It does not matter.' He picked her up and swung her from her feet. She was older too. Her face was more lined and weather-beaten and her dark hair was streaked with grey; she had lost weight – now she was light as a feather in his arms. But she had become more worried-looking than he remembered; the years had not been kind to her.

'Andrés!' She hit him on the back playfully, but her laughter was wonderful, like wine.

He put her down. 'And Izabella?' he asked. 'How is my sister?'

'I am well.'

445

The voice came from the open doorway. Izabella, his darling Izabella, stood framed there, a basket of bread and groceries on her arm, a big smile on her face. Small, slender, as beautiful as ever.

'Andrés,' she whispered. 'At last you have come.' She put down the basket she was carrying.

He strode towards her and enveloped her in the biggest hug ever, until she was beating on his chest, laughing and gasping for air. 'Hello, Izabelle,' he said softly. 'You haven't changed a bit.' She had though. He could see now that she too looked tired. Her skin was still smooth but there were fine lines around her eyes and mouth and a faint frown of worry on her brow. But her hair was still long and glossy as a raven's wing, and as she moved away from him to kiss their mother, her body had the same arc and flow of lines and curves that he had drawn and painted so often; though less angular now, more rounded. His mother and his sister. They at least were not strangers.

'Sit down, sit down. I will make coffee.' His mother ushered them towards the table, glanced towards the stairs once again.

Izabella looked too. In heaven's name. What were they both so afraid of? 'Is my father here?' Andrés asked.

'Of course, my son.' His mother ran water into the coffee pot.

'And will you tell him I have come?'

She hesitated. Bowed her head. 'Yes, I will tell him.' Though still she made no move to do so.

Izabella pulled at Andrés's arm so that he would sit down beside her at the table. It was the same table, Andrés realised, that had always been in the kitchen. The one he used to paint on. Simple and wooden; etched with marks, scratches and stains from the family who had used it for a lifetime.

'Tell me everything,' she urged. 'What is happening in England? When did you arrive? Why did you not tell us you were coming?'

'So many questions.' He laughed, looked up, and there was his father standing in the doorway.

Andrés got to his feet. 'Papa.' He looked so much older; it was a shock. His face was like faded tanned leather and what hair he had left was thin and a shocking white. He still wore the paint-spattered shorts, the loose blue shirt, but he was so gaunt. Shorter, too. It was as if he had shrunk. The red bandanna was still fixed loosely around his head; in his mouth was the usual thin cheroot. Despite his illness, he still hadn't stopped smoking then. His expression was thoughtful.

'So . . . ' And his voice as low and guttural as ever.

Andrés stood tall. This was his family. He had a right to be here. He would stand up to the man just as he had before. He had come here to support his mother and his sister. And he had questions to which he needed some answers.

'So you have decided to show your face at last,' Enrique Marin said. 'I wondered how long it would take you.'

'Enrique!' Quietly, his wife admonished him. 'Our son is home at last,' she said. 'We will have coffee together.'

But his father stomped to the fridge and removed a beer.

He shut the door, glanced at Andrés, opened it again and removed another for him. He handed it over.

'Thank you, Papa.'

'Very well.' His mother shrugged and went to fetch glasses. Andrés sat down again but his father remained standing. He swigged his beer from the bottle, wiped his mouth with the back of his hand.

His father coughed violently and spat into a handkerchief. 'Why now?' he demanded. 'Why have you come back here now? Did you think I was on my deathbed, is that it? Nothing like a dying man to bring the vultures gathering round, eh?'

'Enrique . . . ' His mother reached out and patted Andrés's hand.

'Thinking you were too good for us – for this house,' Enrique muttered. 'Thinking you were too good for the island. Going to London. Pah!' His father swore his contempt. He strode out of the kitchen, still muttering, cheroot still in his hand.

They heard his footfall on the stairs, the coughing fit he had when he got to the top.

His father hadn't kissed him or even shaken his hand. His own father who he hadn't seen for seventeen years. He hadn't held him, he hadn't said how glad he was to see him. Why the hell should Andrés bother with him?

But he had a purpose. He got to his feet.

'Andrés . . . '

He turned. 'It's all right, Mama,' he said. Although it

wasn't. The truth was, it hurt as much as it ever had.

'Don't mind him.' His mother leant forward and whispered. 'You know it's just his way.'

She had always whispered to him like that. *It's just his way.* But Andrés knew it was his way. And he knew just like he'd always known – if he was honest with himself. His father had never loved him. His father had never trusted him. Even when he had proved to his father that he too could paint – that he might have inherited a smidgeon of his father's talent – even that only made him angry; as if he was threatened by the boy who could make the sea come alive; as if that boy might take some of his fame, his power, his glory. His father was not glad to see him – why would he be? Yes, it was his way. His way was not to love him.

But Andrés had come here for a reason and he wasn't going to be dictated to by that old goat. He smiled at his sister, gently touched his mother's shoulder. And climbed the stairs after his father.

Enrique didn't seem at all taken aback to see Andrés enter his studio. And he didn't tell him to get out like he always had before. For the first time it struck Andrés that his father's bark might cover something up – some other emotion, perhaps. Was that possible?

'Still painting, are you?' Enrique growled at him.

Surely he couldn't be interested? That too was a first. 'Yes, I am.' Andrés went deeper in, walking over the paint-spattered tiles. Not the way he had crept into his father's studio as a boy, but as if he was entitled to be there. He smelt

449

the plaster of Paris, the dryness of paper and paints, the resinous turpentine and oils.

'What subjects?'

'Mostly seascapes.'

'Nothing new there then.' His father was standing erect in that way he had – as if he were the most important man on God's earth, Andrés thought to himself – but then he took a rasping breath and sat down, almost collapsing into the nearest chair.

'Are you all right, Papa?' Andrés took a step towards him but he waved him away.

'Don't fuss. Don't fuss.' He coughed again, more prolonged this time, and once again spat into his handkerchief. 'Of course I'm not all right. She's told you, hasn't she?'

Andrés nodded. 'She has told me.'

Enrique swore. His face was white. He was angry, Andrés realised. Damn him. Could the man never stop being angry?

Andrés walked past the easels and the dusty sheets, over to the windows, where there were panoramic views of the mountains and the coast. The mountains rested soft and pink against the blue evening sky; the wind had dropped and the sea was slick. From here Andrés could even see the Moorish beach house out towards the lagoons and the red and white striped lighthouse in the distance. The pigeons swooped silently in formation over the orange and white rooftops, outlined against the pink and blue of the sky. Andrés tried to imagine what it would be like working here in this studio. It would be heaven.

He moved back towards his father. 'There is something I need to ask you, Papa,' he said. 'It's important.'

'Oh, yes.' His father nodded as if he already knew what it was. 'I suppose there is. And there's something I need to tell you, my boy. The time has come and as I keep telling your mother, there's no putting it off, not any more. There's something I need to tell you.'

CHAPTER 43

What was she going to find . . . ?

Ruby tried not to think about it, tried not to let her expectations rise too high. She was walking along the beach the same way she'd walked with Izabella, past the semicircular pods of rocks which she had learnt – from the hotel receptionist – were called *corralitos*. Lava rock piles with sandy bases, a natural windbreak and protection from the strong breeze which was even now whipping sand around her ankles and shunting the hair from her face. She liked the feeling though. In the distance, the lighthouse seemed to mock her – seeming closer one minute and then far away as the coastline twisted and turned.

She thought of the nun at the convent – Sister Julia. Why did she want Ruby to go back there? What was this story she had to tell? *Well, you won't know unless you go . . .* She'd have to do it. Apart from letting the old lady down, she was a journalist, wasn't she? Whatever her personal circumstances, whatever her quest, she'd hopefully never lose her nose for a story.

She paused at the top of the rocks, looking down into what Izabella had referred to as the secret bay. The beach was almost deserted and right at the far side of the bay, back by the dunes, she could see the orange beach house, and beyond, the red and white finger of the lighthouse pointing up to the sky. She thought of Laura and the photographs. Now, once more, it looked very far away.

At the water's edge the surf was bubbling over the sand and, on impulse, Ruby ran down and took off her shoes to let her feet sink into the soft grains, the creeping water frothing tantalisingly around her toes. She walked on to where the rocky outcrop bordered the bay, to where the incoming tide was leaving tiny rock pools of sea water where little curlews and terns were scouring for food. The water was so clear that she could see the rocks on the sea bed and the tiny fish swimming above.

She walked over the sand towards the beach house. There was a path lined with the yellow spikes of succulent plants that seemed to wind between the dunes towards the lighthouse. *El faro*. She shielded her eyes to get a better view. Had Andrés walked to the lighthouse – to go fishing, maybe, or beachcombing? This island was in his blood. Whatever had happened between him and his family, it was a part of him. Had he honestly and completely let it go?

She hadn't called Andrés to tell him what had happened with Sister Julia at the convent, what she had discovered about Laura. And he hadn't called her. What was the point of ringing him again? He knew his father was ill and yet he hadn't told her. He knew how important it was for Ruby to come here, and yet he hadn't wanted her to come, let alone

453

offered to come with her. If he couldn't even visit his own father who might not have long to live, if he couldn't come back and support the rest of his family when they needed him, let alone give Ruby some emotional back-up . . . Well, then he wasn't the sort of man Ruby was looking for at all.

Ruby had said as much to Mel who had called her yesterday, eager for news.

'Come on, darling,' she had said. 'Don't give up.'

'On what?'

'On Andrés.'

'It isn't me who's given up,' Ruby reminded her.

'Sounds like you have to me,' Mel said. 'I thought he was special.'

So had Ruby.

'Didn't anyone ever tell you, Ruby?' she said. 'You should never give up on something special. At least not without a fight.'

Which was all very well. But . . . 'How about you?' she asked.

'Funny you should say that.' Mel clearly knew exactly what she was talking about. 'Me and Stuart had a long chat last night. About what we really wanted, you know?'

'I know.'

'And . . . I realised I was scared.'

'Scared?' Ruby couldn't see that. Mel had always been the brave one, even back when they were teenagers and she'd always had the courage to chat to the boys. Or maybe she'd just been better at putting on a brave face? 'What of, Mel?'

454

'Of losing what I've worked so hard for, of my life changing, of not being in charge of things any more.' Mel paused.

'And now?' Ruby asked.

'I talked to Stuart and I realised I didn't have to be scared,' Mel said. 'And that I don't have to lose anything. The shop, being in charge of my own life, I can keep all that.'

'You only have to gain,' Ruby said softly.

'Exactly.'

Our life . . . And Ruby knew that Mel had Stuart and that whatever happened, whatever the two of them decided, she would be fine.

But did she have that with Andrés? She really wasn't sure.

Meanwhile, the breeze was getting stronger. This must be a moving landscape, shifted and formed by the wind. Even the *corralitos* were banked up with drifts of sand that looked more like snow; it seemed that one day a rock pile would exist – the next day it would have disappeared and become part of a dune. And so – things changed and you could never be sure of what you might find.

At last she stopped, the beach house right in front of her. As she had thought when she first saw it, bizarrely, it was built on the sand, near the track that led to *el faro*. And it was an unusual building in other ways too. It was a simple, almost childish design and it was made of cream and orange painted stone, with a Moorish tilt to it in the contours of the windows, the pear-shaped conical chimney, the sloping orange roof. Around it was a low stone wall loosely constructed from stacked black volcanic rocks. Ruby took a few deep breaths. Steadied herself. This was it. This was the place.

There didn't seem to be anyone around as she approached. Should she go straight up and knock on the door? Ruby's heart was thudding in her chest. She thought of Vivien. *I understand why* . . . But Laura hadn't brought Ruby up, nor had she cared for her – apart from in those early weeks. Was Ruby wrong even to be searching for her? Shouldn't she simply just let things be?

But it was irresistible. Ruby had lived here too – if only for a few short weeks. And Laura had lived here for a lot longer. Maybe the place was also in her blood? She pulled out the photos and examined the landscape, working out where each one must have been taken. There was the orange wall of the beach house which Laura had been leaning against when this photograph had been taken; there was the *corralito* – a natural *corralito* with deep curved sides – where she had been sitting, playing the guitar, empty now, save for a shaving of golden sand on the black pitted lava floor. This was the place where the psychedelic VW camper van had been parked; the track from the road was long and rough and it was hard to believe the van had even made it – but it must have done because the evidence was right here in the photo. The red and white stripes of the lighthouse were easily visible now. And there was the sea, clear and enticing. This was, without any doubt, the place.

'Can I help you?'

Ruby spun around. *Laura . . . ?* But no. She saw at once

that the woman – evidently English – who had come out of the little beach house, although around Laura's age, was too tall and too dark to be her.

'Thank you,' she said. 'But I don't know if you can. I'm, er, looking for someone.'

'Oh?' Although the woman seemed curious, she also looked friendly, and so Ruby came closer.

'I'm sorry to disturb you,' she said, for this spot was so quiet, so tranquil. 'But do you live here?' For the first time she noticed the image of a clock engraved into the stone chimney and a smiling face tucked into one corner of the wall. What a strange house. Not as childlike as she had thought before. More quirky and surreal; like a Dali house.

'Yes, I do. I'm Trish.' The woman held out a hand and Ruby took it.

'Ruby,' she said.

'Hello, Ruby.' She eyed her appraisingly. 'Who was it you were looking for?' She glanced around them with a smile and Ruby followed her gaze.

She saw the joke. As far as she could see, they were entirely alone. 'Someone called Laura,' she said. 'Laura Woods. Do you know her?'

'Laura?' The woman called Trish peered more closely at her. She was wearing a faded T-shirt and a simple wrap-around skirt and flip-flops. Her hair was loose and shoulder length and she wore not a scrap of make-up.

Ruby felt ridiculously overdressed in her tailored shorts and red flowery top. She nodded.

'Are you a friend of Laura's?' the woman asked, instead of answering the question.

But of course she had answered the question. So . . . She knew her. Maybe Laura even lived here. 'Sort of,' Ruby said.

'A relative? You look a bit, well, familiar.'

'Um . . . ' Ruby was still holding the photograph. But she wasn't sure she wanted to go through the whole story again. 'Does she live here?' she asked again.

'She did.'

Ruby's heart sank. *She did*. She had gone then. 'When did she leave?' she asked bleakly. 'Do you know where she went?'

'Almost a year ago. And I have no idea where she went, I'm afraid.' Trish was eying the photograph in Ruby's hand. 'May I see?' she asked gently.

What difference did it make, if Laura wasn't even here? With a sigh, Ruby handed it over. 'I'm the baby,' she said.

'And Laura's the mother.' Trish's expression softened. She looked from the photograph back to Ruby and then back again. 'Oh, my dear, I didn't know. But now I can see the resemblance, of course. Come in. Please.' And she led Ruby into the Dali beach house.

The door opened straight into a sitting room. There were bright red tiles on the floor and rugs woven in vibrant patterns, though the colours had faded with time. The furniture was simple – a small wooden table covered with an embroidered cloth, a chest of drawers and a few wicker chairs. Cushions were strewn around the room too – large and colourful – and above them some sheets of fabric – maybe silk – billowed softly in the breeze from the open front door.

'Sit down, please.' Trish waved Ruby into one of the chairs and disappeared to get drinks. She returned with two glasses of fresh orange juice, one of which she passed to Ruby. She sat down on the wicker chair opposite her and regarded her appraisingly. 'I never knew Laura had a daughter,' she said. 'She never told me.' She seemed surprised; as if trying to make sense of it all.

Ruby shrugged. 'Perhaps she was trying to forget.'

Trish frowned.

'I never knew her,' Ruby explained. 'She gave me away when I was a baby.' It sounded stark. But she supposed that it was.

'Oh. I see.' Trish shook her head. 'Or at least, no, I don't see. But—'

'It's OK.' Ruby was trying to put a brave face on it. It was disappointing though. She had come here to find, if not Laura herself, then some answers about her natural parents. She wished Laura had confided in this woman. At least then she might find out who her father was, how Laura had felt about giving her up and maybe even why she'd done it. Did she need to know, she wondered, that it hadn't been easy for Laura, that she had always regretted it, perhaps, that if only she could turn back time . . . ? Rejection, she brooded. It wasn't pleasant. It wasn't easy.

'I'm sorry I can't be of more help,' Trish said, sympathy in her eyes.

Ruby sipped at the orange juice Trish had given her. But perhaps she could? She must after all know Laura better than anyone else Ruby had spoken to so far. So Ruby could at least find out more about her. She looked around the room. 'This is such a cool place,' she said. Trish had left the door open and they were being serenaded by the hiss and rumble of the wind and the ocean. How lovely to fall asleep listening to this. To be soothed into dreams every night; for it to be the first thing you heard every morning when you woke up.

Trish nodded. 'Laura loved it too,' she said. 'She rented it from the German guy who built it – sometime in the seventies, I believe. He had a bit of a crazy dream, you know?' She laughed, but Ruby knew exactly what she meant.

It was just the sort of thing people must have done back then. *Let's go and live on the beach. Get away from it all.* And in a house that was not conventional; which was weird and quirky and symbolic perhaps of how differently its occupants wanted to be regarded from the rest of the world outside. And the late seventies was when Ruby was born – 1978, to be precise.

'Did she live here with Julio when you first knew her?' Ruby thought of Laura's boyfriend, the casual arm slung around her shoulders in the photo. He might not have wanted the responsibility of someone else's baby. But how many boys would at that age? Like Ruby's natural father – maybe he too had simply been one of the drifters who was just passing through.

'She was on her own when I met her. But people here

come and go.' Trish waved towards the beach outside and Ruby remembered what she'd been thinking about moving landscapes, shifting sand. And drifters. Like Laura. Like Trish. People that came and went with the wind, with the tide, as the fancy took them.

'What happened to him?' she asked. 'The German guy who built the place?'

Trish shrugged. 'I think he went off and built some more conventional houses in the village,' she laughed. 'He had a bit of a thing for Laura. But then most men did. She'd get involved with someone, he'd try and pin her down and that was usually the beginning of the end.'

Was her father one of those men? Ruby wondered. Had her natural father also tried to pin Laura down and then lost her – not even knowing that she was already carrying his child?

'Did she pay him rent?' Ruby asked, not really sure where she was going with this.

'I suppose so.' Trish seemed vague. 'Then he just kind of disappeared. Maybe he went back to Germany. I don't know.'

Like Laura had disappeared, Ruby thought. So Laura, she supposed, had assumed ownership of the house. Because it should be looked after, because she needed it and because it was there. *God*. Ruby froze. Exactly like Vivien had assumed ownership of the child Laura had left behind. She supposed it was different when a child was involved. But even so, she could see how easy it would be when the house or the child seemed like the answer to all your prayers. And what about that German builder? What if he had let Laura keep the house because of Ruby? What if Laura had even been part of his crazy dream in the first place? What if . . . ?

'Rather conveniently,' Trish added.

She could say that again. 'How long have you been here?' Ruby asked her. She seemed pretty established and at home.

'Twenty years.' Trish pulled a face. 'I came over here with my boyfriend originally. We were trying to escape.' She leaned confidentially towards Ruby. 'Most people here want to escape from something.'

Ruby could imagine. What had Laura been trying to escape from? Her parents splitting up, perhaps? The loss of her mother? Her baby? She stared out at the ocean. And what happened when you no longer needed an escape route? Or when you got tired of the sun and the waves and the wind? It probably didn't happen – for some people.

'And you met Laura?'

'Pretty much.' Trish nodded. 'I'd just been dumped and I was getting very low on cash. I was walking on the beach one day and I heard someone playing the guitar. The music seemed to weave its way through the wind and the waves. It was magical.' She smiled.

'Laura?'

'Uh-huh.' She sipped her drink. 'We got talking and I told her what had happened. She said I could move into the beach house. "People do," she said, "it's no big deal."' She sat back. 'It was a kind of open house. Anyone was

462

welcome so long as they didn't abuse the hospitality.' She gave Ruby a long look. 'But it was a big deal to me, of course.'

'Of course.' And it gave Ruby a good feeling – like the one she'd got when she'd talked to Sister Julia about Laura. It was nice to know that your birth mother – *even though she'd given you away*, some small voice whispered – had actually been a decent person.

'She helped a lot of people.' Trish became thoughtful. 'She did little things. She let people be. At first she let me share her food and her house, and then later I got another job waitressing in the tapas bar by the Old Harbour and I was able to give her something back – a bit of money for rent.'

'And you never left?'

'I never left.'

Ruby could see why. Even now, sitting here in this wicker chair, listening to the wind and the ocean, she could feel herself relaxing, unwinding and letting go, as if all the stress of the past months since her parents' death were gradually leaking out of her. To be replaced by . . . What? Just a sense of being, she supposed. If that didn't sound too cheesy.

'What was she like?' she asked Trish. She guessed that Laura had experienced that too – the sense of just being. It seemed to go with everything she'd heard about her so far.

'Non-judgemental. Calm. Kind. A bit kooky.' She smiled. 'She used to play and sing in the Beach Bar back in Los Lagos.'

Ruby nodded. She had passed by the place earlier.

'And in a bar in the village. In return for her meals and a bit of cash, that was all. But she created an atmosphere. A warmth.' She smiled at Ruby. 'People liked her. She did some cleaning too, in the holiday rentals.'

Ruby had seen them as well – a couple of complexes built on the beach on the outskirts of the village.

'She lived simply,' Trish said. 'When I got a small inheritance through from my parents . . . ' Her eyes dimmed – as if she too was remembering whatever it was that she had been escaping from – 'I took over the responsibility of this place, and I try to keep the ethos going.'

'Anyone welcome?'

'More or less.' Trish shrugged. 'I tried to give Laura some money but she just wasn't interested. It's not about that, she used to say. I knew what she meant. But we can't all be as strong as Laura.'

Ruby thought of the young girl who had gone to England and given her baby to Vivien and Tom Rae to bring up while she scooted back to Fuerteventura to live with her Spanish boyfriend, making a living from having her portrait painted by Enrique Marin, from playing and singing in bars, from cleaning in holiday rentals. Had she been strong? Was that why she had been able to give Ruby up to what she might have seen as a better life? Because she was strong? Had Ruby been coming at this from an entirely mistaken perspective? She frowned. She'd felt compassion for the girl who had lost her mother, who must have been at her wits' end and who had wanted to be free of her own baby because she simply couldn't cope. And she knew that Vivien had felt that compassion too. But now Ruby realised that it might not be so simple. Laura had different values, a different belief system – perhaps she always had. And she had denied herself her own child because not only might Ruby not have fitted into the lifestyle Laura loved, but also because Laura was strong enough not to need to keep her. It was weird. But it made perfect sense.

'Why did she leave?' she asked Trish.

'I don't know.' Trish spread her hands. 'I got up one day and her bag was gone. Laura too. She'd just . . . moved on.'

'For good, do you think?'

'I don't know why . . . ' Trish hesitated. 'And I probably shouldn't tell you this. But ever since Laura left I've had a really strong feeling.'

'What sort of a feeling?' Ruby asked. What shouldn't she tell her?

'That she might come back one day.'

CHAPTER 44

There was something different in his father's manner, Andrés realised. Yes, he was still a miserable old bastard, probably more so than ever, since he was ill. But . . . Was it the cancer? Had the old man lost his fire? And what could he possibly have to tell him? That he was sorry? That he took back everything he'd ever done to belittle him or make him feel unloved? Some hope.

But his father didn't enlarge on whatever it was he had to say. He just walked over to the opposite window and stared out towards the mountains. God alone knew how they were going to help him.

'What about your subjects?' Andrés asked Enrique, hoping to lead the way into the questions he wanted to ask. 'Are you still painting the same stuff?'

'You can see for yourself.' Enrique flung out an arm to encompass the contents of the light and airy studio.

And yes, Andrés had already spotted some of his father's favourite images on canvases in the studio: biblical scenes of fire and flood, dramatic and dripping colours of flame and blood; the colourful pantomime of the *festa* procession in the village, an ancient forest being razed to the ground, a

466

volcano pouring a river of hot, molten lava on to the brown earth . . .

But more to the point: 'Are you still painting the women?'

'Ah, the women.' Enrique sat forward in his chair, looking pensive. 'They are always too beautiful, don't you think? The women? Too tempting?'

'For Christ's sake.' Andrés strode off to the far end of the studio, ashamed, as he had often been in the past, of his own father. What was the point of being a great and talented artist if you misused your craft in that way? His mother had once said that every great artist must have his dark side, but Andrés couldn't believe that. It was just a cop-out, wasn't it, a way of excusing bad and inappropriate behaviour? Would he never change? He was a man in his seventies with lung cancer but he was still a lecherous old bastard — in his mind at least.

'I confess that I went further than I should have.'

Andrés twisted around. Had he heard right? Was his father admitting that he had done wrong?

Enrique had raised his hand. But now he let it drop, looked rueful. 'You are right. You were right — back then — to try and stop me.'

Andrés was speechless. In that case, what had all these years of exclusion been about? Why the hell hadn't his father got in contact, told him that he would now be welcomed back home?

'And that side of things finished a long time ago, I assure you.' He nodded, though Andrés thought he could see a note of wistfulness in his expression. Well, a man like Enrique Marin could not have changed that much.

'Thank God for that.' Andrés was pleased for his mother, at least. No doubt Enrique found other ways to humiliate her. But the women . . . That had been the worst.

'I didn't do right by your mother.' Enrique got caught in another coughing fit.

He held his side. He was in pain, Andrés realised. He took a step forwards. 'Papa?'

'And I bloody hated you for pointing it out to me,' he growled.

That made sense too. Andrés stopped in his tracks. There was Enrique, the great man. And there was his young son, a mere stripling, a nothing, telling his father what to do. Andrés was surprised now that he'd ever had the nerve. 'What did I know?' he said softly.

'Exactly. What did you know?' Enrique sat back in his chair and pulled the pack of cheroots out of his pocket. He tapped one out and held it between paint- and nicotine-stained fingers. Let out a deep-throated cackle. 'Marriage, eh? They don't warn you, do they? For some people it cannot be for ever. You try, but . . . Eugh!' He took out a sleeve of matches and lit the cheroot, sucking and coughing at the same time.

Andrés wanted to try and stop him but what was the point? He would always go his own way – now, just as he had back then. No one could tell Enrique Marin what to do. And besides, whether he smoked or not, from what his mother had told him, it made little difference now.

'For others, they try to find ways to make that marriage last.' He looked appraisingly at Andrés. 'Do you understand, boy?'

Boy. He would always be that to Enrique Marin. *Boy.* But still, it was perhaps the first time that his father had ever spoken to him like this. If he had done it – even once – when Andrés was growing up, if he had tried to explain, if he had given him just a few minutes of his time now and then, things might have been very different. 'I understand that you put me off marriage for ever,' he said with feeling. What a role model his father had been.

'Hah!' Enrique's shoulders shook. 'I did, did I? Well, I've done something in my life worth boasting about then.'

Andrés shook his head in despair. There was no telling him. He might have admitted that he'd done wrong but he always had an excuse; an answer for everything. Other people managed to make marriages last for ever – or at least they didn't go around seducing girls young enough to be their daughters. On which note . . .

Andrés took a deep breath. 'I want to ask you about one of those women,' he said. He moved closer to the far window. *Now or never.*

Enrique drew hard on the cheroot and held back a cough. 'Funny that,' he said. 'I had someone else here asking about one of the women.'

Ruby. Andrés straightened his shoulders. 'Yes, I know.'

'Ah.' His father let out another harsh laugh. 'I see how it is.'

Did he? Did he see how it was? Or at any rate how it could be? Andrés braced himself for the reply. At least he'd come here. At least he'd tried.

'So you want to know about Laura.' Enrique seemed deep in thought. 'The English girl. The free spirit.'

'I do, yes.'

'Then I'll show you what I showed her – your girlfriend, is it?' Slowly he got to his feet, stubbed the cheroot out in a glass ashtray.

Andrés watched as he went over to where a pile of canvases lay stacked against the wall. He flicked through them, back bent, sighing and muttering. Pulled one away from the rest.

Andrés held his breath. What kind of a picture would it be? But as his father held it out at arm's length to show him, he saw to his relief that it was inoffensive – a portrait of a woman on the beach. It was bloody good, actually. And it was Laura Woods, *si*, most definitely. He nodded. 'Nice,' he said. The artist in him had to give credit where it was due.

'Plenty more where that came from.' And the old man brought out another from the pile, then some drawings from a stack on the desk, then a charcoal sketch from a drawer in the chest by the wall, and finally a set of pastels done in a small spiral-bound notebook.

'Bloody hell.' Andrés looked at him, horrified. His father clearly hadn't been able to get enough of her. Which seemed – didn't it – to answer his question? They must have been lovers. Which meant that his own father could have been responsible for the girl's pregnancy. Which meant . . . Fuck. So where the hell did he go from here?

Looking at all these pictures of her – done, he imagined in the late seventies, Andrés was struck again by the resemblance between her and Ruby. It wasn't obvious – you wouldn't notice it at first glance unless you were looking at bone structure and face shape in the way that an artist might. But it was there. No doubt, it was there. It had always been there. And he'd been stupid really to try and deny it, to try and stop Ruby from coming over here. What had he thought to achieve? The truth would always come out. It was just that he couldn't bear the thought, the possibility that now seemed almost a certainty.

'Did you have sex with her?' he asked.

Enrique snorted. 'What kind of a question is that?' He started putting everything back where it had come from.

Andrés's fists were clenched. 'I need to know.'

'Ah.' He shut the drawer and turned around. 'I see how it is. You are worried. That girl . . . '

'Ruby.'

'Ruby, yes.'

'So, did you?' He'd swear he'd kill him. If he had messed this up for Andrés by his philandering ways, he would kill him.

Enrique gazed at the picture of Laura on the beach and sighed heavily. He picked up the canvas and put it back in the pile. 'I would have if I could have.'

So . . . In a rush, the anger left Andrés's body. He hadn't then. Thank God. 'Truly?' Even now he wondered if the old bastard was lying.

His father shot him a look of disgust. 'Do you think I would not tell you?'

It must be true then. He felt his shoulders relax, his head stop spinning. 'What happened?' he asked. 'What happened between you? Why are there so many paintings?'

'She wouldn't, would she?' He wheezed and coughed. 'That was part of the attraction, was it not? Is this not how these things work?'

Andrés shrugged. His father would know better than he about such things. But thank goodness she had more sense. To think that he had imagined . . . But it had all made a horrible sort of sense. Laura becoming pregnant here on the island with an unwanted child, going over to England, abandoning the baby . . .

'I kept trying.' His father stuck his hands in his pockets. 'Who wouldn't? Every time I painted her I thought, "This time."'

Andrés could believe that.

Even now Enrique couldn't let it go. 'Can you credit it, boy?' He paced over to the easel in the centre of the room. 'She wasn't impressed by the artist and she wasn't impressed by his studio either.' He flung his arms out to embrace the space they were standing in, though Andrés knew of course that he had not had this studio when Laura had been around. When Laura had been around, Andrés must have been a

472

young boy of four or five. The studio had still been on the top floor of the little *casa* – but it had been a very different space in those days. 'Not one tiny bit. None of it meant a thing to her. The parties, the paintings, the exhibitions.' Enrique let his arms fall to his sides. 'The money. The fame. No. She was impressed by none of it. It was a job of work for her, that was all. She sat for me so she could earn enough money to buy food. No more, no less.'

'As it should be, perhaps,' Andrés said drily.

Enrique shot him a sharp look. 'She was a bloody good model though.'

'I can see.'

There was a sound from the open doorway. Andrés looked over. His mother was standing there. 'Enrique . . . ' she began.

His father ignored her. Instead, he came over to Andrés and held both his arms at the elbow. He gripped him hard. 'I said that there was something I needed to tell you, boy.'

Andrés could feel the pressure from his fingers. He looked into his father's eyes. It was an odd sensation. He realised how rarely he had been in this position; how rarely he had looked into his own father's eyes; how rarely Enrique had touched him.

'What?' He met the flinty gaze. 'What do you need to tell me?' Nothing could be as bad as what he had been imagining. Now, if she could forgive him, at least the way was clear for him and Ruby . . .

'You must prepare yourself, boy,' Enrique said. 'Prepare for the truth.'

The truth? What was he talking about? Andrés frowned. He looked across to where his mother was standing. 'Mama?'

She had tears in her eyes.

'Please don't cry.' What was this all about?

'Enrique . . . ' His mother moved towards her husband. Tugged at his arm. 'Don't.'

He brushed her away. 'It is true, Reyna. Why should he not then hear it? He needs to hear it. Do you not realise even now how wrong it would be for him not to hear it?'

Hear what? What were they talking about? Andrés felt his mother's hand slip around his waist. His father was still gripping his arms. Like a bloody vice.

'That question you wanted answering,' his father said. 'About Laura.'

Andrés glanced at his mother but her face was impassive. 'What?' He felt a dip of panic.

'It would not have mattered to you,' his father said.

'What do you mean?' Why would he not just say it?

'It would not have mattered for you and your Ruby.'

'Enrique . . . ' But this time his mother sounded only sad and accepting.

His father let go of Andrés and put an arm around his wife. 'It is time, Reyna,' he said. 'You must accept that. It is time.'

'Time for what?' Andrés was getting fed up with this. 'For Christ's sake—'

'And my time – that too is coming to an end.' Enrique stroked her hair. 'I will not go to my grave not telling him what he needs to know.'

Andrés felt his own breath – shallow in his chest. He waited.

'It is a wonderful thing for you as an artist when you start selling your work.' Enrique sounded almost philosophical now. He left the other two standing by the window and walked slowly to the far side of the studio. 'Your wife is behind you.' He indicated Andrés's mother, who nodded. 'You have a good life, you know?'

Andrés just watched him. He did not think that at this moment he could even speak.

'But what is it all for, hmm, if you have no one to leave it to?' His voice carried across the room with almost as much strength as Andrés remembered from the old days – when he had raised it so often in anger.

'What are you saying?' Andrés tried to control the flutter of foreboding deep in his belly.

'I had contacts.' Enrique put his hands in his pockets. He seemed to have recovered his old swagger now too. 'I had contacts here and on the mainland who put me in touch with the right people.' He shrugged. 'I've never made any pretence about who I am. I might even be called a national institution – by some.' Even now, just as he once had, he was preening himself.

He might have lost some of his old fire, Andrés thought, but he hadn't lost his ego. It was true that he had done a lot for his country, even for Spain, perhaps. But what could this have to do with Andrés? He looked sadly at the figure of his father. He had become almost grotesque. Not even a shadow of his former self. More like a desperate caricature.

'People who mattered knew what I believed.' He struck himself on the chest.

What was he talking about? Had he lost his mind? Andrés looked at his mother but she seemed to be barely listening. Of course his father was one of the old school, Andrés knew that. Politically, at least. He had never been religious – though it might have been useful from time to time when he needed to confess his sins and be forgiven – and despite being an artist he had always been on the side of the Establishment. But . . .

'And so your mother and I . . . ' For the first time, Enrique hesitated and looked back towards his wife. He cleared his throat. 'We – among others – were given the chance to adopt a child.'

'Adopt a child?' Andrés heard the words but they didn't make any sense. 'Adopt a child?' he echoed. He looked once more at his mother. Why didn't she say something?

His mother looked down, wrung her hands. 'Andrés . . . '

'Adopt? You mean . . . ?' But he still couldn't quite formulate what his father did mean.

'You were the child we adopted,' Enrique said quietly.

And then Andrés felt her arms around him; the mother he'd always loved, only ever wanted to protect.

'Me?' He still couldn't think properly. How could that be? The thoughts careered through his head. 'What are you talking about?' Roughly, he moved out of his mother's embrace, grabbed Enrique by the shoulders, hardly able to prevent his hands from squeezing that scrawny neck. 'What the fuck are you talking about?'

'Andrés, please!' His mother was there too, and she was hanging on to Andrés again with that surprising strength of hers.

And the fury left him. Just like that. He let go.

His father coughed and wheezed and spluttered. Andrés stood there, fists clenched.

'I don't blame you, boy,' Enrique said at last. 'I don't blame you at all.'

CHAPTER 45

Ruby listened open-mouthed to the story Sister Julia was telling her. *Niños Robados* . . . She scribbled fast and furiously, not wanting to interrupt the stream of information that was coming from the old nun. And wanting to get it all down. It was dynamite.

'Stolen children,' she breathed. She had heard of the *Niños Robados* – vaguely; she'd mentally collected and filed a lot of stories over the years. But she couldn't recall the details.

'*Si.*' Sister Julia nodded. 'And they were stolen, my child. They really were.' Her eyes were filled with a heavy sadness.

What had it cost her – to tell this story? What had it cost her in bravery and in personal anguish?

Ruby leant back for a moment against the pockmarked wall. The sun was getting hot and they were sitting in the courtyard of the Nuestra del Señora Carmen Convent, on one of the stone benches in the shade of the fig tree heavy with ripening fruit. Despite what Sister Julia had just been telling her, there was an air of tranquillity in the courtyard and now that the old nun had fallen silent, all Ruby could hear was the faint rush of wind and ocean, the scrabbling of the chickens in the dusty earth and the trickle of the fountain.

She scanned her notes. The stolen children might have been covered before but this was different. This was a personal angle – and not from one of the victims. This was straight from the voice of someone directly involved with the scandal. And not just directly involved, but a nun, which surely compromised the whole ethos of Spanish Catholicism at the time. She looked up at Sister Julia, who was watching her patiently. Did she realise the magnitude of what she had been telling her? She certainly seemed to. And Ruby didn't want to upset her, or bring back unhappy memories, but she needed to know everything.

'Was the mother superior involved?' she asked.

But Sister Julia remained serene. No shock or horror reaction from her – she must have seen it all. She considered. 'I do not believe so,' she said at last. 'Not directly, at least. She always professed the utmost respect for the doctor.' And she gave Ruby a gentle look.

Ah. The clue was in the language she had used. *Professed*. So the mother superior might have suspected he was not whiter than white but she would never have rocked the boat. Still, Sister Julia had now done enough boat-rocking to make up for it.

'And for how many years do you think the practice continued?' Ruby asked.

Sister Julia sighed. 'Certainly from the time of the Civil War,' she said. 'And up to the mid seventies, at least, maybe even longer.'

Ruby shook her head almost in disbelief. Though she

could see how it could have gone on for so long — in a dictatorship or where there was poverty, corruption and an unequal distribution of power. After all the emotions of the past few days, after all she had learnt from Trish about Laura, she hadn't thought anything more could touch her. But this . . .

'Do you think others have come forward?' Sister Julia asked. 'Have others told their stories?'

Ruby guessed what she was thinking. If she had been plagued by guilt then so would other people who had been involved. Some would speak out, others would remain silent for ever. 'I have no idea,' she said. She'd have to check on the Internet when she got back to her hotel. But who would admit to such a thing? She felt a tingle in her spine. This story could be a first.

Who would be interested? Ruby leaned back and let her gaze drift past the small bell tower and on to the endlessly blue sky above. Who wouldn't be interested? Automatically, she scanned her internal editor list for possible candidates. The story was risky and it was hot. It was red-hot. There would be accusations.

And it was international. Ruby needed help, she realised. She remembered her conversation with Leah Shandon back in London, one of the editors she wrote for regularly. No contest. She could trust Leah.

Sister Julia rose to her feet. She was so old, so fragile. And yet she had shown incredible strength already. 'I have something I must show you,' she told Ruby. 'Will you wait here?'

'Of course.' As Sister Julia left the courtyard, Ruby listened to the distant sound of the ocean. It was so far away that it wasn't much more than a pulse, a heartbeat. *Andrés, Andrés . . .* it seemed to say. Because everywhere she went, everyone she spoke to, everything she saw, reminded her of him. This was his landscape. And she had already decided that she had lost him. So why had his island already crept into Ruby's very soul?

Was Mel right? Was Andrés worth fighting for? Ruby thought of her parents – of Tom and Vivien and that special something they'd shared. How often had she watched them together and wished she could have that with someone? But perhaps it didn't come so very easily. Perhaps you had to be patient for that sort of love. Perhaps you had to wait and overcome obstacles, like she knew Vivien had waited for Tom, fought for him too when her parents had pressurised her to go to college in Kingston; stayed loyal to him even though they were both so young and he was living in Dorset – a hundred miles away from Vivien. Like Stuart and Mel, it couldn't have all been plain sailing – her mother had longed for a baby, for a start. And when Ruby had appeared on the scene, the pressure must have put strain on their relationship. But in the end it had only made them stronger.

After several minutes, Sister Julia returned. She was holding something close to her chest. It was a big notebook, Ruby saw, plain on the front with navy blue binding.

'No one else has seen this, my child.' Sister Julia sat beside Ruby on the stone bench. 'You are the first.'

Goodness. What could it be? Evidence of what had gone on? Was that possible? Ruby put her hand on Sister Julia's arm. 'Are you sure you want this story to be told?' she asked her. 'I can't say exactly what the consequences might be.' Because Sister Julia had committed a crime, surely? Hundreds of crimes of aiding and abetting abduction of children over a period of over thirty years.

She looked at the old woman sitting beside her – her lined face, her brown eyes milky and faded with age. She had not truly been the one responsible. But would she go unpunished? Or would her age and her vocation give her the pardon that Ruby reckoned she deserved? For a moment Ruby put herself in Sister Julia's place. Would she have spoken out? Would she have risked being thrown out of the convent – or worse – in punishment for what she had witnessed? Would she have been able to stand up to those figures of authority – the doctor, the mother superior – who had claimed that they were doing their God's work? She shook her head. Taken in the context of the times she was living in, probably not. And how could you make any judgement unless you'd been there?

'The consequences will be as God wishes,' Sister Julia replied, bowing her head. 'For those who have done wrong, they will take their punishment on earth – and in heaven if God so decides.' She passed the book to Ruby. 'But he is a merciful God, my child,' she said. 'We may put our trust in Him and in His wisdom.'

Ruby hoped she was right. She took the book from her

and opened it. The pages were covered in faded, almost illegible writing. Spanish writing, she realised. Someone — Sister Julia? — had divided the first page into three columns. Each one had a heading. Each column was full.

Sister Julia pointed to the first heading.

Ruby recognised that word. *Niños*.

'Children,' Sister Julia said. Each one was listed *chico* or *chica*, sometimes with more writing next to it, perhaps a mark of identification. Next to each entry was a date. She pointed to the second heading, under which there were either one or two names for each entry. 'Birth parents,' she said. And to the third. 'The people who took the child away. Who adopted.'

Ruby stared at the page, across at Sister Julia and then back at the page. The chickens in the pen alongside the courtyard continued to scratch at the dry earth and one of the goats flopped down on the ground to rest. And the water from the fountain trickled on. 'You mean . . . ' She flipped over to the next page and the next. The list went on.

'Yes,' said Sister Julia. 'This, my child, is my book of names.'

Book of names. And it certainly was. Ruby continued to turn the pages — almost reverentially now that she knew their true meaning. The impact that this could have . . .

'There was no record.' Sister Julia regarded her calmly. 'Documents were destroyed. Women were told that their babies had died. Incomplete birth certificates and irregular death certificates were written and approved.' Her voice tailed off. 'I worried that no one would ever know the truth.'

'So you made your own record,' Ruby said. She could hardly believe it. How could she be punished when she had done such a brave thing? 'You made your own record because you knew it was wrong.'

'*Si*.' Sister Julia nodded.

'You knew it was wrong to keep this knowledge from the adopted children,' Ruby whispered. She thought again of Vivien and Tom. Vivien too had understood that it was wrong. She hadn't wanted to hurt Tom, but she had made sure she left a record – for Ruby. So that she too could find out the truth.

'Indeed,' said Sister Julia.

'But why now?' Ruby asked her. Sister Julia had remained silent for so long. What had made her speak out at last?

'I read about the extent of the scandal in the newspaper,' she said softly. 'It was not just Dr Lopez's clinic. It was not just Barcelona. It was everywhere in Spain.' She looked around her. 'Even here.'

Here? Ruby followed Sister Julia's gaze. In Fuerteventura? It was hard to imagine – but then a lot of things were hard to imagine and that didn't make them less true.

'I spoke to someone. I realised that I should tell my part of the story.' Sister Julia looked out into the distance, beyond the allotment of herbs and plants, towards the mountains – as if she had forgotten Ruby was there.

'And then?' Ruby prompted.

'And then you came along,' she said.

'Me?'

'You came along, not only an investigative journalist, my child, but more importantly looking for your own birth mother. You were a sign from God. You were the one who could tell my story. I knew then what I had to do.'

Ruby closed the book and handed it back to her. It was a very special document. It might get some people into trouble and it might cause pain. But it could also help bring knowledge and closure – not to mention family reunion and a sense of completion – to an awful lot of people. She'd never been called a sign from God before, but she could see how Sister Julia had come to that conclusion. And if she could help . . . 'Leave it with me, Sister,' she said. 'I need to do some more research. And then perhaps . . . ' She frowned. 'I'll have to go to Barcelona.' Because that was where it had all happened. She needed to see the clinic for herself; needed to talk to other people who might have worked there. And she needed to find out more about Dr Lopez and the legacy he had left so many families.

'It is the children,' Sister Julia said. 'Do you see? I trust that you can deal with this in the right way, the sensitive way, my child. Because you understand. You have been through this kind of experience yourself. I want to help the children. They, of everyone, they are the innocent ones.'

'Of course.' Ruby felt the tears spring to her eyes. She too wanted to help the children. She might not be able to find her own birth mother but she'd try her best, with Sister Julia, to help these children find theirs.

CHAPTER 46

Andrés felt the sun warm on his skin as he sat on the blue-tiled bench in the Old Harbour. It was the place everyone walked through. Would she walk through? He didn't know what he would say to her – but he hoped so.

He had missed this warmth. He had sat here so many times before, painted the brightly coloured little fishing boats that used to be moored here, sketched the fishermen hauling their glittering catches on to the stone jetty. *And all those things he had not known.* It seemed a lifetime away.

He was still assimilating the facts in his head, trying to get to grips – as the English would say. He was an adopted child.

When they had told him, almost from the moment he had heard the words, he had wanted to talk to Ruby. But he held back. He hadn't been around to help her when she'd needed it, had he? Why should he expect her to do the same? Ruby . . . Wasn't it supposed to be Ruby who no longer knew who her natural parents were? Ruby searching for her identity? Not Andrés. He'd always known who he was, never had a moment's doubt. He was the one with the angry father. The great painter with the monstrous ego who had no time for the mere mortals of his family –

especially the boy who was presumed to have inherited some of his own unique artistic talent. The man who had thrown his only son out of his home. The man who didn't love him. Andrés had always wondered why. And now it was becoming clear.

When they had told him – after they had told him – it was Andrés's mother who had broken down. Andrés had simply been numb – what did he feel? What could he feel? His childhood, his family, everything he believed in had been plucked away from him. And this . . . this was what Ruby too had felt. Two adopted people. Was that the bond that had somehow drawn them together? Or was it the years of not even knowing?

His mother had cried and cried and clung on to him. And Andrés had comforted her, assured her that it made no difference, that he still loved her, that he would always love her. And why wouldn't he? She had brought him up, she cared for him. But he wondered. Was this what she'd had to live with since he had been gone? This threat that her husband would reveal all? Andrés stroked her hair and murmured his reassurances. And looked across at Enrique, who wouldn't meet his eye. Why didn't his father say something? Didn't he realise that this was down to him?

'Who were my birth parents?' Andrés asked them at last. The question seemed odd, almost surreal. He was still stunned. And yet he had taken it in – it had almost not even been a surprise. In a way it made sense to him now – that odd feeling of dislocation he had sometimes had; of not fitting in, of being misunderstood. He took a deep breath. 'Tell me what happened. Tell me everything.'

And that was when they had dropped the next bombshell.

Andrés looked out over the glittering sea and the harbour. It had been a day of bombshells, for sure. He was still reeling.

'We do not know who your birth parents were,' his mother had said. 'No one knows – not now.' And she told him about the clinic, the fact that there were no records. And about the payment.

What the fuck . . . ? 'You *paid* for me?' Andrés looked from one to the other of them in disbelief.

'It was all legal and above board,' Enrique insisted.

Legal and above board? Who did he think he was kidding? It made Andrés feel as if he were nothing more than a flashy new car. Only not so flashy, perhaps. Still a disappointment – at least to his father.

Andrés watched the pigeons flying over the harbour. Every time they passed their loft a few stragglers left the main group and weakened the formation.

'But why weren't there any records? What about my birth certificate?' he asked.

Only then did his father tell him the full story. How the adoption had been done on the quiet. How Spain had been in disarray ever since the Civil War – and before. How there were lots of women with unwanted pregnancies or with no man around to care for them, who wanted a good life, a decent life for their child, which they were unable to provide. How Franco's ruling that the adoptive parents' names should be the ones on the birth certificates had been used to hide the truth.

'Did the mothers always want to give up their children?' Andrés had asked him softly.

'No.' Enrique looked him squarely in the eye. 'I have reason to believe that the practice became corrupt. And that they did not always want to give up their children.'

The last of the pigeons returned to the loft. But actually, no. Andrés realised there was one last straggler who was still flying around alone, not knowing where he was going by the look of it. He knew how that pigeon felt.

'And Izabella?' Andrés had asked. Although he already knew the answer. Izabella had belonged in a way he never had. Enrique Marin had at least loved her.

'That is the funny thing. Three years after we had you, she came along. The natural way.' Enrique had shrugged. 'It happens sometimes.'

Finally, the straggler got home and the sky was clear again.

Andrés had brought a towel with him, slung over his shoulder. Now, he got up from the bench – she wouldn't come, why would she come? Besides, she didn't even know he was here. And he walked away from the harbour towards the old jetty where the sea was deep and there was always a strong undertow.

Swimming was good. Swimming hard, fast, against the tide stopped him thinking and Andrés didn't want to think.

Even so, as the water stung his eyes and his muscles throbbed with the effort, it kept coming back to him. He was adopted. He had been given away – or perhaps even taken. He had been stolen by a man who had never even loved him.

Who am I? Andrés swam out into the open sea. He didn't know how long he stayed out there. At one point the waves were so high and the current so strong he thought he'd gone too far, that the sea might whisk him out until he drowned. But of course he hadn't and it didn't and he was such a strong swimmer that he just went on and on, everything his parents had said to him churning around in his head.

'You were all I wanted,' his father had said to him.

They were words he had spent his entire childhood wanting to hear. But . . . 'When did that change?' Andrés asked.

His father could not answer that.

Maybe it was when Andrés started painting. Maybe to Enrique he had seemed like a usurper, an outsider. Maybe it was because Andrés dared to stand up to him. Maybe it was when Enrique realised he could never love Andrés – simply because he wasn't his own.

'Sometimes I wanted to shout at you,' his father had admitted. 'Shout at you, "You are not mine!"'

'And now you have,' Andrés said flatly.

'It is different now.' His father came over to him, put a thin and bony hand on his shoulder. 'I am not shouting it in anger. I am telling you now because it is the right thing to do. I am different now too. I know now all the things I did wrong.' He coughed violently. 'That is what dying does for you, my boy. That is about all it does.'

My boy . . . Andrés wanted to grasp that hand, to hold it, even to take his father in his arms. But he could not. Still, he could not. 'Why did you not tell me before?' he asked instead. He could remember Ruby asking herself the same thing. Why hadn't they told her? Children got adopted all the time. Why had they decided to keep it such a secret?

'Your mother stopped me. I think she always knew though . . .'

That if he came back, Enrique would tell him the truth. Which was why she'd almost encouraged Andrés not to come. All these years.

Nothing has changed . . .

Oh, Mama.

She came to him then, to them both, and Andrés held them close, felt himself being held close by them both – for perhaps the first time. It was a strange feeling. Family . . .

By the time Andrés swam back to the water's edge and dragged himself on to the sand, he was exhausted. There were a few couples and families on the beach nearby, but no one gave him a second glance. Funny, that.

He collapsed into a *corralito* and lay on his back, chest heaving, eyes closed to the sun, feeling its warmth gradually seep into his very core. *How well do you know your own family?* Not very well at all, apparently. He and Ruby shared that at least.

★

Later, he picked Izabella up in the car and they drove to the Centro de Arte. Andrés told her the story as they walked around the place which their father had helped create. He'd had to see it – and despite everything, he couldn't help feeling proud.

Izabella listened in silence. When he'd finished, she flung herself into his arms, oblivious of the people around them and their curious stares.

'It changes nothing, my brother,' she said, when she finally drew away. Her eyes were dark and fierce.

Andrés had to smile. She reminded him of their father sometimes. 'I love you, Izabelle,' he said.

'And I you.' She held his arm as they walked on. 'You will always be my brother – in every way.'

'Of course I will.' It was true that his feelings for his sister hadn't changed. His mother too. But as for his father . . . Was it so simple?

Andrés was impressed by the centre. It had been created to celebrate the rich and exciting artistic talent of the island – sculptors, potters, painters. And it was quite an achievement. In the courtyard and landscaped gardens there were sculptures in wood, bronze, stone and steel around every corner – of shells and stairways, goats and whirlwinds, even one of volcanic lava entitled 'inner bliss'. Andrés had to smile. Inner turmoil was nearer the mark as far as he was concerned. There was a workshop where professional artists ran classes, a studio which could be used by up-and-coming artists lacking their own work premises, and spacious white exhibition galleries where ceramics and paintings hung – every contemporary style, content and colour you could imagine.

'What do you think?' Izabella asked him. 'It is magnificent, is it not?'

It was. Andrés was overwhelmed by the boldness of brushstrokes, by the vivacity of the blues and the greens and the yellows, by the multitude of shades of ochre and brown to be found in just one mountain. He would have given anything when he was younger to be part of something like this.

'He is not a bad man, our father,' Izabella said as they left the centre an hour or so later. 'He has achieved so much.'

Should that make them love him more? Andrés had gone through every emotion now as far as his father was concerned. Adoration, anger, hatred, shame . . . You name it. And now? Truth was, he didn't know what he felt.

Izabella gestured behind them. 'He helped this to become a reality,' she murmured. 'He has helped many people.'

'Perhaps.' Andrés thought of those girls in the studio. And of his mother. But hadn't he also caused harm?

Izabella seemed to know what he was thinking. 'He has made many mistakes in his life,' she said. 'But he is our father.'

'Yes.' Andrés patted her hand. He knew how much she wanted them to be reconciled. And he did not doubt her love – nor her sincerity. But Enrique Marin was not Andrés's father, was he? Could he find a new way of looking at him? Could he find forgiveness in his heart? Silence that voice that would keep whispering: *Remember, he had no time for you.*

'Will you come in?' Izabella asked when they drew up outside the house she shared with her husband Carlos.

'Not now, Izabelle,' Andrés said. There was something he had to do.

'But we will see you tonight?' Izabella's face was eager.

Andrés leant over to kiss her cheek. 'Of course,' he said lightly. Though he was half dreading it. A family dinner with them all. How could they all sit down together and pretend that nothing had changed?

'And what will you do now?' Izabella asked. She put her head on one side and regarded him appraisingly. It was a woman's look. 'Will you try to see her?'

'Her?'

'Ruby.' Izabella squeezed his hand. 'I like her,' she said. 'I like her a lot.'

Andrés smiled at her. 'Yes, I'll try and see her,' he said. If she would agree. 'But first I have to go and see someone else.'

'Someone else?'

'There is someone who might be able to tell you more,' his father had said. 'She worked at the same clinic in Barcelona before they shipped her here to the back of beyond to get her out of the way. I have run into her a few times.'

Andrés frowned. 'Who's that?'

'A nun at the convent,' Andrés said now to his sister.

'She kept some records,' Enrique had said. 'Her name is Sister Julia.'

CHAPTER 47

After a simple lunch of a meat and vegetable stew eaten with chunks of bread, Ruby went for a short stroll with Sister Julia across the desert *campo*. Sister Julia talked. She told Ruby about how she had come to take her vows: about the way her family had survived during the aftermath of Spain's civil war, and about her parents and her sisters. And Ruby listened. 'You must have missed them all very much,' she said.

Sister Julia nodded. 'I did,' she said. 'I still do.'

'I understand.' Ruby thought of the family she had known, her parents, Vivien and Tom, who had been snatched away from her so abruptly. It wasn't easy to be so suddenly alone. And perhaps that was why she had responded as she had to Andrés Marin. Here was a man unlike any man she had met before, a man who she wanted to spend time with, who she connected with on so many different levels, who seemed to understand what she was going through. She sighed. Or so she had thought.

'Of course you do, my child.' Sister Julia patted her hand. 'It is why you have been brought to me.'

Ruby smiled. But it was true – there was a synchronicity to it, just as she had believed there to be a synchronicity with

Andrés, a bond. Two people drawn together, pulled together. That was what it had seemed like. And now it was never going to happen. She'd have to get used to that too. But for now – she simply ached for him.

As they walked back to the convent, Sister Julia talked more of her work at the hospital, gave Ruby more information about the doctor and his methods, opened up more too about her feelings for the mothers and their children. And as she did so Ruby felt her pain and her guilt – and thought of Laura. Would she ever find her? Perhaps not. Perhaps it was more important to find understanding.

'It wasn't your fault,' Ruby told Sister Julia. She knew already how she would write this feature. There was more than one point of view, more than one story to be told.

Sister Julia bowed her head. 'I could have done more, my child,' she said.

Yes, well . . . 'You're only human. We could all do more.'

They returned to the convent and Sister Julia made tea while Ruby scribbled down some more notes.

'Do you think the doctor is still alive?' she asked Sister Julia. He was the one who should have been punished. He had used the others – Sister Julia's innocence, her mother superior's blind belief in his respectability, the mothers' lack of confidence that they could give their baby a good and satisfactory life. Mothers who were like Laura, she thought. Just like Laura. And Dr Lopez had even used the adoptive parents – who were so desprate for a child to love that they would do almost anything and pay almost any price to get it.

'I doubt that he would be,' Sister Julia said. 'Look at me – I am so old and he was several years older than me, although it seemed like so much more at the time.'

Ruby nodded. 'Even so . . .'

'Even so.' Sister Julia sat up straight as she poured the tea. She put the teapot down and looked Ruby straight in the eye. 'I should like to go with you to Barcelona.'

Ruby blinked at her. 'Really?' She hadn't considered that as an option. 'There's no need—'

'But there is.' Sister Julia's gaze was steady. 'You said earlier on that we could all do more, my child. But there is one more thing that I must do. I must return to the old places.'

'The old places?' Though Ruby knew.

'My city of Barcelona. The Convent Santa Ana.' Sister Julia's eyes were glazed now and faraway. Perhaps she was thinking back to that time all those years ago when she first went to Santa Ana as a young girl of seventeen. 'And the Canales Clinic.' She seemed to come to. She picked up her teacup. 'I must go there again, my child. Even I have my ghost to lay to rest. And I must do it before my time on earth is done.'

'Of course.' There was a kind of inevitability about it. Ruby usually liked to work alone and Sister Julia was very old to be jetting about anywhere – let alone back to places that must hold dark memories for her. But she could show Ruby first-hand all the places, tell her again – in situ – exactly how it had been. There was no denying that it would make the story so much more powerful. And it clearly meant a lot to her. It would give her the sense of closure she needed. So how could Ruby say no?

She finished her tea and got to her feet. 'I'll be in touch very soon,' she said.

Sister Julia saw her to the gates of the convent. 'Thank you so much, my child,' she said.

'Goodbye, Sister.' Ruby looked down the red-earth dusty track that led to the village. There was a figure approaching. It was quite a way off but she could see he was tall and male. And there was something else. Something familiar about that long, loping stride. Something about the way he was dressed, the way he . . . She stared. He was getting closer. 'Andrés?' she breathed.

He was waving now, starting to run towards them.

'And who is this, my child?' Sister Julia murmured.

'Andrés,' she said again.

And then before she could even think about it he was there and he was holding her tight. It was a bear hug from heaven. And he was whispering her name into her hair. 'Ruby, Ruby . . .'

Sister Julia cleared her throat.

Andrés put her down.

'What are you doing here?' Ruby grabbed his arm. 'You said—'

'I know what I said.' He put his arm around her shoulders. But he looked at Sister Julia. 'I'm Enrique Marin's son,' he said.

'Ah.' She nodded. 'He sent you to me?'

'Yes.' Andrés squeezed Ruby's shoulders. 'He sent me to you.'

What was going on? Ruby looked from one to the other of them in confusion. 'What for? Why would he send you here?' And then she saw something in Andrés's expression. Something that reminded her of what she too had felt. And she remembered what Sister Julia had said. That she had talked to a man from the village. That the adoption practice had gone on even here in the Canary Islands of Spain.

Andrés cupped the back of her head with his palm in that way he had and looked into her eyes. 'I need to look in Sister Julia's book of names,' he said.

CHAPTER 48

After dinner with his family, Andrés and Ruby took a stroll down to the Old Harbour. Andrés had his arm around her and he wasn't about to let her go. The Old Harbour, he thought. Where it had all begun . . . Who would have thought he'd be back here on a night like this – a warm, late-summer's evening, the scent of prawns and tapas still sweet and spicy in the air, the stars bright in the canopy of night, the crescent moon hanging like a cradle in the sky above the sleek, inky sea. And with this girl . . .

It had been an emotional few days.

When Andrés had arrived at the convent late that afternoon, he almost hadn't been surprised to see Ruby there. Like it was meant to be. Ruby Rae, the island, Sister Julia and the story of his birth. It was pretty much mind-boggling, but after what his father had told him, nothing was going to shock him any more.

'You had better come inside, my son,' the old nun had said. So with her on one side of him, Ruby on the other, they had retreated into the pale stone cloisters of the convent building and Sister Julia had gone to fetch this famous book of names.

Ruby hadn't said much and Andrés was thankful she didn't seem to need to have it spelt out for her. He had been right about her – he had always been right about her. 'Are you sure you want to see?' was all she'd whispered.

He nodded. Yes, he wanted to see. There was a chance his name might not be there; he knew this wasn't a complete record, by any means. But he had been adopted in Barcelona. And he had to know.

Sister Julia brought the book down to them and handed it over to Andrés. 'You are the first, my son,' she said.

And Andrés had taken a deep breath. And opened it . . .

They leaned against the wooden railings and looked down towards the rocks in the harbour.

'I like your parents,' Ruby said.

He laughed. 'Both of them?'

'Both of them.'

He could see why. His mother hadn't been able to do enough tonight. She had scurried around fetching this and carrying that until at last Andrés and Enrique had forcibly dragged her to the table and made her sit down and eat. 'I am just so happy,' she said. 'My son is home and I am so happy.'

My son . . .

As for his father – the old man might be ill but he had lost none of his charm. And as Andrés listened to Enrique letting loose the charisma on the girl Andrés adored . . . Well, the difference was that he didn't mind any more. He even quite liked it.

'And Izabella too,' said Ruby. 'And Carlos.'

Andrés squeezed her hand. Yes, the man his sister had chosen was a good man. It was true that as yet they had no children. But there was still time. Look at her own parents. Izabella's conception had come pretty much out of the blue to a couple who had been forced to adopt their first child because they thought it was impossible for them to have a baby the natural way.

'But how do you feel about your parents now?' Ruby asked. She looked up at him. She of all people would understand the mixed emotions that were running through his head.

And hadn't he been asking himself that same question all day? Andrés looked at the statue of the fisherman's wife standing on the hill of Calle Muelle de Pescadores. Always waiting . . . 'I don't know,' he said. 'Not yet.'

'It will take time to absorb.' Ruby's hand was on his arm. 'You can't take it all in at once, nobody could.'

True enough. But what was also true was that he did still have a family. He had seen his parents' names in the book. Marin. He had seen the entry – *chico*, a boy – and the actual date of his birth. And he had seen a woman's name. Florentina Chavez. He had stared at that name for some minutes. Florentina Chavez. His birth mother. And then he had shut the book and handed it back to Sister Julia. 'Thank you,' he had said. What would he do with the information? He didn't yet know.

But what he did know was the truth. And the fact that he

had more of a family now than he'd had for seventeen years. Because the strange thing was that at the dinner tonight there had indeed been a sense of family between them all. Had it ever been there before? Perhaps. But now . . . His father was not so angry, his mother was not so anxious. It was as if now that the truth was out, they could all relax and be who they really were.

'I know I can't make it up to you,' his father had said as he went up to bed, his face drawn and gaunt. He gripped Andrés's shoulder. 'But in the short time I have left, I am determined to try, my boy.'

So.

Andrés took Ruby's hand and led her down the hill and on to the stony beach. In the distance some Spanish flamenco music played in a bar somewhere. And the waves rolled in, with a hypnotic rhythm all of their own.

On the way back from the convent, Ruby had told Andrés about her search for her mother and what she had found. And she told him the whole story of the *Niños Robados* and what she was planning to do about it. He could sense the excitement in her. Knew that despite her disappointment over Laura, this was something that mattered, something that she could connect with. And now he was part of that story too. He could be one of those voices – if he wanted to be.

'What about the end of summer art exhibition?' Ruby asked him. 'Isn't it the first weekend coming up?' She bent to pick up a piece of green sea glass, glittering amongst the dark stones in the lamplight from the hill, ancient and pitted with the sand it had collected on its journey.

'It is, yes.' He thought of the pictures he'd done, the exhibition space at the Salt House. It all felt like a million miles away, another lifetime. And he thought of the centrepiece – his picture of the cliffs of Chesil Beach. Ruby's childhood path; her dream. He was glad he had decided it was not for sale. Dreams shouldn't be for sale. And the picture would have a home with Ruby – wherever she was.

'You'll miss it.' She turned to him. She was wearing a simple cream linen dress and in the moonlight with her blonde hair she looked almost ethereal.

'It's worth it.' He touched her hand. 'I am so glad that I found you, Ruby,' he said.

'And now?' she asked. 'What will you do now? Will you come to Barcelona? Will you try to find her?'

He took her in his arms and held her like he'd never let her go. God, she smelt good. Of orange blossom and the day's sunshine. He knew who she meant. His birth mother. Florentina Chavez. What was her story? Did he want to know? Did he need to know? How had she felt about giving him up and how did she feel now? Did she ever wonder . . . ?

There was almost too much to think, to say. Andrés closed his eyes and felt it wash over him. The stillness. The quiet. Peace. 'Not yet,' he whispered.

He wasn't ready yet, not ready to take the next step. And he wanted to get to know his own family again first. At least for his father, there wasn't much time. He bent his head close to Ruby's and put his hand around her hand that was still holding the piece of green sea glass. 'What can you see?' he whispered.

She tucked her head in close to him. He felt her hand on the small of his back. And suddenly Andrés didn't feel alone any more.

CHAPTER 49

Sister Julia put her rosary beads to one side. She was not worried about the task that lay ahead of her. She knew exactly what she should do and she had complete confidence that the young woman who had listened so carefully and so kindly to her story would help her – on a practical level. On a spiritual level, of course, she had her God. When she took those first simple vows all those years ago Sister Julia might not have believed in Him; she only experienced the first stirrings of comfort that believing in Him could bring. But her faith today was unshakeable. He had helped her so much over the years and now He had finally given her His sign. The chance for atonement. The opportunity for peace.

It was simple enough to pack for the journey. What did she need in the way of material things? Very little. She had learnt to make do; indeed, to value the simplicity of having little. Having little enabled you to become rich in other ways, ways that Sister Julia was thankful for.

She opened the battered brown suitcase that she had brought here to the island at the time of her banishment, many years ago. She would not take the personal effects she kept in her desk drawer, though it was not easy to leave behind the family mementoes she held dear. Apart from her Bible and psalm book – which she now placed reverentially in the case – the only thing she really needed was this. She picked it up, felt the weight of it in her heart now beginning to lift, beginning to soar. Her book of names.

It had already helped someone – had it not? Not just Andrés, but his father and his mother too could now be at peace. Enrique Marin . . . Sister Julia had always thought she remembered that voice, though in truth that day in the square when she first read of the scandal, she had not quite made the connection.

Ruby had told her that once they arrived in Barcelona they would be handing the evidence – her book – over to an official who would be meeting them at the airport. She had arranged it. She was a clever girl – Sister Julia had the utmost admiration for her. It was vital, Ruby had said, that the book was placed in safe hands as soon as possible so that they would not have to worry about it, so that they would be free to concentrate on their job – which was the telling of the story.

And how Sister Julia longed to feel free.

How would she react when she went back to the Canales Clinic? Sister Julia placed her wash things in the case and the changes of underclothing she would need, and snapped the lid closed. It did not matter, she told herself sternly, how she felt. What mattered was what they were to achieve – for others, for the children who had been mistreated. The *Niños Robados*.

And what would the consequences be? Ruby had warned

her that there would be repercussions – for her, Sister Julia. That she might be facing a criminal sentence, that she might not be free to go, free to return here to the island after it was done.

But that hardly mattered either. She was old. Her time was drawing near. Indeed, she was weary and more than ready to meet her maker once this was done, once her conscience was as clear as it would ever be. She was more than ready to unburden, more than ready to atone for the wrongs she had been part of, to find the peace she so longed for at last.

'Remember, Sister Julia,' Ruby had told her, 'there is no going back.'

And Sister Julia did not want to. Indeed, she did not.

CHAPTER 50

The day that Ruby and Sister Julia were due to leave for
Barcelona dawned grey and still. At midday Ruby and
Andrés had arranged to collect Sister Julia from the convent
so that he could take them to the airport. Ruby wasn't looking forward to that. It felt like no sooner had she found him
– properly found him – than she was leaving. But before
that . . .

'Time for one last walk?' Andrés suggested. And he
seemed to know instinctively where she wanted to go.

They walked hand in hand along the beach, heading for
the rocks that bordered the bay, in a silence that seemed to be
underlined by the heavy, grey clouds above, by the wary
stillness of the day. They'd said so much, Ruby reflected.
Apart from the one thing that mattered the most.

She was eager, though, to drink in the last of the island
landscape that she would see – at least for a while. She
couldn't believe that she'd only been here a week. Already
everything seemed so familiar to her. Sand fine as gold
dust, *corralitos* built with the black volcanic rock which
surely was the island's heartstone, and in the distance those
gentle, mushroom-coloured mountains streaked with rust

and lichen. Andrés's landscape. But was it still his home?

They began to climb up the rocks, Andrés leading the way. He was sure-footed and confident. And she saw it – the way he belonged here.

When he had turned up like that at the convent, the facts of his adoption as he had explained them to her, the expression in his eyes when he saw that entry in Sister Julia's book of names . . . It had been a shock – for both of them. But it all made sense. The pieces slotted together. Enrique had sent Ruby to the convent because he knew about the book of names and because he had realised immediately that the journalist in Ruby could help Sister Julia in her resolution to reveal the truth of the adoptions she had witnessed at the Canales Clinic. And of course Enrique was the only person to whom Sister Julia had told her story, because he had told her his story first. She had known then that he too was involved. That he too had something to pray for forgiveness for. That he had been there and part of it.

As indeed they all were.

They reached the top of the rocks and Ruby looked out once again – over the perfect horseshoe crescent of the bay, in the distance the red and white *faro* and Laura's Dali beach house built by that German boy with a crazy dream where Ruby had met Trish a few days earlier. The clouds were gathering and the bay was deserted.

Just you and me . . . Ruby looked at Andrés. She had come to the island to find her birth mother and had unknowingly uncovered the birth story of the man she had fallen in love with. Because she had, hadn't she? Fallen in love?

Would Andrés try to find his natural parents now that he knew the truth? Would he ever feel that same pull that Ruby had felt? That need to know? Maybe in time. Before he made any decisions, she guessed he would want to make his peace with the family he already had. That he would need to forgive, even though he would never forget what they had done. At least the reconciliation was on the family table. And, like Vivien and Tom, they had only done it because they so much wanted a child of their own to care for. It seemed to Ruby now that they were delighted to have him back in the family fold. Enrique Marin had done wrong by Andrés, there was no doubt about that. He had never bonded with his adopted son and he had unfairly resented him – both for the artistic talent that he knew he couldn't possibly have passed down and for refusing to be controlled by him as the rest of the family were. But Enrique was not well. He was clearly a shadow of the man he once was, and he was sorry. When he had raised his glass at that first family dinner and offered a toast to 'our son' with tears of emotion in those dark eyes, Ruby had almost cried herself. Because she had been right and in the end it was all about love, wasn't it?

Or was it? It was impossible to read Andrés's expression. There was a slight frown on his face. Ruby wanted to reach out; wanted to run her fingertips along those slanting cheekbones, to smooth away that frown, to gently touch his mouth. But she held back. He was looking out to sea, where the wind was picking up and the tide was heaving, the waves rising high before breaking and crashing into the rocks below where they stood. On the other side of the rocks the bay was serene. But it felt as if it were waiting.

Ruby thought about the trip to Barcelona. She had already done some initial research. The Canales Clinic still operated, although it was now run by Dr Lopez's son Rafael. Ruby wondered what he knew of what had gone on before? That, she decided, was where she would start.

Where the investigation would take her, she didn't know. But she would ask some questions and hopefully get a few leads. Most of her information would come from Sister Julia herself. She had already emailed Leah her editor and received a positive reply: *Sounds good. It's a definite for us. Get a feel for how you want to play it and contact me again when you know a bit more.*

She would do that. And then she would write it up. The whole story. It would be a challenge. And she'd have to handle it in a sensitive and compassionate way. The last thing she wanted was to hurt Sister Julia but she would write the truth. She had to. And then— She heard a faint rumble and glanced up at the sky – surely it wasn't going to rain on her final day on the island? She didn't know exactly what would happen then. But Sister Julia's book of names would certainly cause quite a stir.

Andrés turned to her, his green eyes troubled. 'How many do you think you will be able to help?' he asked.

She knew what he was talking about; his mind had been

travelling along the same direction as her own. How many children were looking for answers? How many of the *Niños Robados* would ever be reunited with their birth parents? She shrugged. 'It depends how many of them come forward.' On how many mothers admitted that they had never believed their children had died. And on how many adoptive parents – like Enrique – ever told their children the truth. For some, there would be DNA testing; a long search, in many cases, for a match. But for others there would be Sister Julia's book of names.

The rain came in a deluge as if someone had unbolted a gigantic hatch in the sky.

Ruby gasped and Andrés swore. He pulled her towards him so suddenly that she gasped again. 'It happens like this sometimes on the island,' he muttered into her hair. 'It is very sudden. Very dramatic.'

He could say that again. 'Shall we make a dash for it?' The raindrops were massive. Ruby was soaked to the skin already.

'Where to?' He laughed.

And he was right. There was nowhere to run. What should they do then? Just open their arms and embrace it?

'Come over here.' He pulled her round to the other side of the rocks where there was at least a bit of shelter, and held her into his chest, his back to the worst of the rainstorm.

She was warm there. She could feel his heart beating, the fabric of his linen shirt rough but strangely comforting against the skin of her face as it had been once before. Around them the wind howled like a banshee, the sea whipped over the rocks below and the rain continued to pour from the leaden sky. But Ruby didn't care. She was in his arms, safe and held. She breathed in the scent of him – amber and resin. It was such a good place to be that she felt she could stay there for ever.

After a while, she felt the rain ease and Andrés loosen his hold. She emerged, blinking, and laughed. His shirt was sodden. His dark hair was plastered to his head and to the brown nape of his neck. He was blinking too – blinking raindrops out of his eyes. He looked gorgeous – like a wild man of the storm. Ruby wasn't cold, but still she shivered. He was worth waiting for, she realised. Worth fighting for. She wanted to have the sort of love that she'd seen first-hand while she was growing up. And he was the man she wanted to have it with.

'Come and look,' he said. He beckoned.

'We should get back.' Ruby didn't want to linger. She didn't want to say goodbye. She hated goodbyes. In some ways Andrés was just at the beginning of his journey. But Ruby worried that she might have come to the end of hers. Coming to this place and hearing about Laura's life might be the closest she would ever get to her birth mother, let alone to her father. She might never find out everything she wanted to know. But over the past few days she had come to an important realisation. She was the same Ruby she'd always been. In a way Mel had been right back then when she'd said it. *Ruby Rae is still Ruby Rae.* And would always be. She fingered the gold locket of Vivien's that she still wore around her neck. The parents who had brought her up were the same loving people they had always been too – and they were her parents. She couldn't be angry with them. They had loved her. They had nurtured her. They had shown her what really mattered. Through them she had become who she was now. So in a way it was the end of a journey, wasn't it – even if a new one was beginning?

'In a minute.' He held out his hand and helped her back over the rocks. 'Be careful. It's slippery.'

And it was.

'Look,' he said when they got to the top.

She followed his gaze. It was incredible. The sand hadn't just shifted; the bay had been washed out by the rainwater and the tide. It had been swept clean. No more secrets, she thought. The sun was out again already, bursting through the clouds and making the black rocks glisten. The golden sand looked as if had been sprinkled with diamonds and the clear turquoise water was spangled with light as the sun shone through.

Ruby gripped on to Andrés's arm. Walking across the sand, in the distance, away from them, was a female figure wearing a multicoloured patchwork dress of red, orange and blue. She wasn't a young woman, though she held herself straight and tall. On her back she carried a red, faded rucksack. Ruby stared down at her. She was walking slowly but with a sense of purpose, towards the beach house – or towards the path that led to *el faro*, perhaps? And as she walked, she looked around her at the sea, at the rocks, at the sky. There was something so calm about her. Her fair hair was blowing in the wind. She too looked as if she belonged.

'We'd better go.' Andrés's voice jolted her out of her reverie. 'Or we'll be late picking up Sister Julia.'

'Yes.' But it was hard to look away from her, whoever she was.

Gently, he turned her to face him. 'Will you come back, Ruby?' he asked. His eyes searched hers. He seemed uncertain of what she might say.

'Back here or back to England?' she whispered.

'Back to me,' he said.

It was what she'd been waiting to hear. *Our life* . . . Yellow evening light and sunsets of fire. Was this the place where she would make her future with the man she loved? The place that Laura, her birth mother, had also loved so much? Ruby could continue her work here as well as anywhere – her journalism, her music. And Andrés? That was easy. Andrés would continue with the artistic legacy his adoptive father had created. He had, after all, been born to it. Yes, somehow she knew now where he would be.

She looked again down into the bay, but she wasn't surprised to see that for now the figure had gone.

'Yes, Andrés.' She lifted her face towards him. 'I'll come back. You can count on it.' And she reached up and touched his lips with hers. 'I'll come back – wherever you are.'

ACKNOWLEDGEMENTS

I'd like to thank Teresa Chris my agent for her constant support and faith in my writing. She has been relentless in her encouragement and created some evocative visual pictures which have become integral to this story. And thank you to everyone at Quercus Books including Margot Weale who has been terrific, Kathryn Taussig, and most especially my editor Jo Dickinson, whom I cannot praise highly enough for her structural eye, sensitive editing and for being such a pleasure to work with.

This story has been a long time evolving. At its root was a different story – but one that impacted hugely on the finished product - and for their help in discussing with me the psychology and impact of the characters and events involved I should like to thank Caroline Neilson and Peter Fullerton, both experts in their field. Thanks to Alan Fish whose reading and comments are always much-valued. Thanks to Magda Taylor for helping me get to grips with the saxophone – so to speak – and to Chris Forbes, Grey Innes and Jackie Deveraux for discussions on painting in water colours. Thanks also to Peter English for his musical contributions, Bernie from the Tindaya Arms in Fuerteventura and everyone else I have talked to over there who has given me information on the island's history and culture. And thanks to Mario Pulini for his insight into Barcelona and the Spanish language. Have I forgotten anyone? I hope not. Special big thanks to Grey Innes, my wonderful, favourite idea-stormer, who also listens to everything with a very perceptive ear. And finally, massive thanks to everyone who worked so hard to promote The Villa, especially my daughters Alexa and Ana, who have been amazing.

I should like to add that although I have used actual historical events in this story, any resemblance to any actual person is not intentional; all characters are entirely fictitious. The Canales Clinic does not exist. Neither do the convents mentioned in this story. I have used various sources — both fictional and non-fictional - for the historical information and have tried to be as accurate as I can. Any inaccuracies are my own.

EXTRACT FROM

Back to Mandalay

A new novel by Rosanna Ley
Available in print and ebook spring 2014

E va opened the front door and let herself into the house. She had been feeling pretty low when her grandfather had phoned her last night, and perhaps he had picked up on it because he'd immediately suggested she come home for the weekend. 'You need a rest,' he'd said firmly. 'You sound exhausted.'

She was. But—

'And besides . . .' She heard the determination in his voice. 'I've got something I want to talk to you about, my dear.'

Was that a ruse? Eva didn't know and she didn't care. 'OK, then,' she said. After the day she'd had, she needed something. Home was the best place to come for serious R & R – she could already almost feel the anxiety slipping from her shoulders.

She put down her small suitcase. 'Grandpa!' she called. 'It's me.'

'Hello, my dear.' He appeared in the kitchen doorway – a little more bent than the last time she'd seen him, but still tall and lean, hair snow-white, mouth creasing into a smile, blue eyes twinkling. He opened his arms. 'Sorry to drag you away from Bristol,' he said.

'I wanted to be dragged.' And the way she felt right now, she never wanted to go back there. Bristol meant the auction house and it meant Max. And right now she wasn't sure which was the most unappealing.

She gave her grandfather a hug. Every time she saw him he seemed a bit more lined, a bit more fragile, but she wouldn't think about that now. He smelt of eucalyptus and wood, a fragrance Eva seemed to have lived with all her life. Her grandfather loved wood too; he had worked with it most of his days and he'd passed his passion down to his granddaughter. Eva had left home at eighteen to do a degree in antique furniture restoration with decorative arts; wood and history – it must be in her blood.

They drew apart and her grandfather's brow creased into a frown. 'You do look tired, my dear,' he said. 'And thin.'

'Whereas you look wonderful, darling Grandpa.' Eva smiled, slipped off her coat and hung it on the hook by the door. He meant the world to her. He wasn't so much a grandparent as the life force behind her childhood. 'But what did you want to talk to me about? Is everything OK?'

'Well now . . .' He made his way back into the kitchen and Eva followed. It looked reassuringly the same as ever. The Aga's cosy heat filled the room and there was what looked like one of Mrs Timms's stews on the hob, a rich, meaty fragrance emanating from the pan. A bottle of red wine had been uncorked but not poured and the kitchen table of worn oak was set neatly for two. Grandpa had always been independent and with Mrs Timms to help with cooking and housework, he could manage very well now that he was on his own. To be honest, Eva couldn't see him anywhere else but in his own house, big, rambling and impractical as it was. It was part of him – it always had been.

'I really didn't like the sound of you on the phone,' he said, scrutinising her once again. He shook his head. 'But is it the right time? I had been intending to talk to you, to tell you . . .'

Eva was intrigued. 'Tell me?'

He seemed to come to a decision. 'But I think it can wait a bit longer. Get yourself warm. Have a drink. Relax.' He sat down in the old rocker. 'How's Bristol?'

Eva didn't know whether to laugh or cry. She had dumped her boyfriend and lost her job in one day. How was Bristol? He might well ask.

Two hours later, after a dinner that whizzed her straight back to her childhood and two glasses of warming Bordeaux – Grandpa wasn't so old that he couldn't still appreciate a good wine; he was still a member of the local wine club – Eva had thawed out.

'And what about work?' her grandfather asked her. 'You haven't said much about that, Eva, my dear. Everything still going well?'

'Not really.' No, she hadn't said much about that. Nothing, in fact. The truth was that Eva hadn't loved her job; hadn't even liked it much. But neither had she wanted to leave, at least not quite so suddenly. A job paid the rent – in her case for a small flat not far from the centre of town – and the bills. She'd got to know the people who worked there, the salary was good, she knew what she was doing and it was well within her comfort zone.

OK. When she'd done her degree, she hadn't envisaged working in an auction house in Bristol cataloguing and assessing the value of goods. Because yes, it was a long way from what she'd dreamt of: restoring furniture and textiles to something resembling their former glory, reliving their history, making good; all that seemed a bit like a distant dream these days. But it wasn't the first job she'd had whose thread to the degree she'd done and the work she loved was more than a little tenuous. Before the auction house, she'd worked in a second-hand furniture shop for a man who specialised in house clearances and cold-calling with the express purpose of parting old ladies from family heirlooms with as little money changing hands as possible. That had lasted only six months; Eva could almost feel his smug smile destroying her soul. And before that she'd worked in a museum shop – little more than a glorified sales assistant, which wasn't exactly the kind of museum work she'd wanted to put on her CV. Toss in a year or three working as a seamstress in wedding hire and some secretarial, and that summed up her job experience to date. So what now?

Her grandfather raised his white eyebrows. 'In what way, "not really", my dear?'

Eva sighed. 'In the way that means I'm not working there any more.' It had all been rather strange. It wasn't the first time she'd noticed something odd about the shipment of antiques arriving from a dealer in the Far East. She'd questioned it before and been fobbed off by her boss, Colin Jones. The shipment didn't go through the usual channels – it was whisked into the office rather than the warehouse and then a few days later it would mysteriously disappear. 'It goes to a private buyer,' Colin had said when she asked about it. 'Nothing for you to worry about. The deal's already done.'

When people told her there was nothing to worry about, Eva usually started worrying. She got the bit between her teeth and then waited for an opportunity to find out more. This time, she had managed to get a closer look at the stuff – it was supposed to be teak wood artefacts and she knew all about teak from Grandpa and from her studies. And it was supposed to be antique. But when she sneaked into the office at lunchtime and opened up a few boxes . . .

'What the fuck do you think you're doing?' Colin Jones was standing in the doorway, hands on hips, all jowls and fury.

'I was just curious.' Eva tried to stand her ground. 'I'm interested in teak and—'

'Do you know what curiosity did?' He glared at her. 'It killed the fucking cat.'

And apparently it did more than that because two hours later Eva had her marching orders. 'You can't not give me any notice,' she'd said. She knew her rights.

'I'll pay you.' And he pulled out a wad of notes. 'Three months do you?'

Was she being paid to keep quiet? Eva dithered. She didn't

like that idea. But did she want to stay here if there was something dodgy going on? Or did she want to pay the rent and consider what to do next without Colin Jones breathing down her neck? She shrugged, took the money and left the building. She'd always known Colin was rough – just not quite that rough. But she wasn't going to take this lying down. Just wait till Max heard about it – he'd know what to do.

So she'd scooted round to Max's place where he worked from home as a criminal lawyer – she knew he wasn't in court this afternoon, he'd said something about working on a particularly tricky case. And . . .

'There are plenty more jobs, Eva,' her grandfather said. He was looking very thoughtful. 'Why don't you take some time to think about what you really want to do. What you've been trained for.'

'I know. I will.' He was right – of course he was right. She needed to recapture that dream – the dream that had inspired her to do her degree in the first place, the dream that had more to do with the scent of teak and the history of past lives than sorting and managing auction catalogues. It was no good just curling into a ball and hoping it all went away. It wouldn't. As Grandpa said, it was time for a reappraisal of what she wanted to do with her life. And it was long overdue. At thirty-three years old weren't you supposed to have your life mapped out? Weren't you supposed to at least have some plan? You weren't supposed – were you? – to feel so absolutely lost?

'And I have a suggestion,' he said. He leaned forwards and

adjusted the cushion in his chair. 'I don't want to take advantage of your situation, my dear. But it is, what you might say, fortuitous.'

'Fortuitous?' She'd like to know how losing her job could be fortuitous. And no doubt he was going to tell her. Her grandfather was old and frail – he was ninety-five, for heaven's sake – but his mind was razor sharp; it always had been.

'There's something that needs to be done,' he murmured, still deep in thought. 'And perhaps, now that you have terminated your current employment . . .'

That was one way of putting it, she thought.

'Yes.' He rubbed his hands together in satisfaction. 'The more I think about it, the more I know for sure. You, my dear Eva, are the perfect person to do this for me.' He nodded with conviction. 'It will kill several birds, as they say, with one stone.'

'Oh, Grandpa . . .' Suddenly, Eva wanted to cry. He had such faith in her and what had she done to deserve it? And now he was going to ask her to come back home and look after him. She'd do it – of course she'd do it, if he needed her. She was an only child and her mother lived such a long way away. But . . .

'I'll pay you for your time,' he said. 'And your expenses. And it will give you the perfect opportunity to think about what to do next.'

Eva took his hand. His skin felt paper-thin; it was white and threaded with blue veins and liver spots. 'What is it you want me to do?' she asked him gently.

'I'm old,' he said. 'No one can live for ever. But there's something I should have done long ago. Something . . .'

'Yes, Grandpa?' This didn't sound much like being a carer.

'Get the *chinthe*,' he whispered.

'The *chinthe*?' Perhaps his mind was wandering. But Eva knew what he was referring to. The dark and shiny decorative teak *chinthe* – a sort of mythical lion-like creature, which always stood on her grandfather's bedside table – had been a feature of Eva's childhood, a feature of the stories he used to tell her, about Burma and his life there, working in teak forestry, and then fighting in the war against the Japanese.

Eva had grown up in Dorset, sandwiched between her mother's flat and her grandparents' yellow-bricked, rambling house; between the gentleness of her grandfather's care and the brittle grief of Rosemary, her mother. Her father had died when she was only seven years old and Eva could barely remember him, barely remember how her mother had once been – laughing, carefree and warm. When he died – of a stroke, sudden and cruel – Eva's life had changed out of all recognition; she supposed all their lives had changed. But it was her mother who for years had seemed unable to cope with the grief of losing her husband, unable to move on.

Rosemary Gatsby was a legal secretary and she immediately went from part-time work to full-time in order to make ends meet. The care of Eva fell mainly to her grandparents. Eva often felt now that this had been a relief to Rosemary. That her kind of grieving had made it almost impossible to give her only child the love that Eva needed. Perhaps she was scared, perhaps she associated love with being hurt again. Eva didn't know. She was too young – then – to understand, but she'd had a long, long time to think about it ever since.

Eva's grandmother Helen had been rather delicate, often tired and disliking noise and disruption. But her grandfather . . . He had picked her up from school and taken her on outings down to Chesil Beach and the Dorset sandstone cliffs, or off for muddy walks in the Vale. In the evenings they'd sat here in this kitchen and he'd made them mugs of hot chocolate and told her such stories. Tales of dark wood and darker mysteries. Of a land of scorching heat and drenching monsoons, of green paddy fields and golden temples, of wide lakes and steamy jungles. Those stories had wound their way into Eva's heart until they had become almost a part of her.

Eva got to her feet and went to fetch her grandfather's beloved *chinthe* from the bedroom. It symbolised his time in Burma, she supposed. She picked it up, looked for a moment into its red glass eyes. It was small and delicately carved and looked a bit like a wild lion with a jagged tasselled mane and a fierce snarling face. It had a sturdy body and was made of the rich burnished teak that her grandfather used to work with back in the days before the war; when he lived in the teak camps with elephants, sending the great logs that had been felled tumbling into the Irrawaddy River.

'Here he is, Grandpa.' She put the *chinthe* on the kitchen table in front of him. Her grandfather stared at the little animal for a few moments and then looked back at Eva.

'And that boyfriend of yours?' he asked. 'Are the two of you still . . .' he hesitated, 'involved?'

Eva shook her head. She'd always known Grandpa didn't much like Max. And as usual, he had turned out to be right. Fortunately, they hadn't got round to living together although they had given each other the key to their flat. Fortunately, because Max's tricky afternoon case had turned out to be young and blonde with legs like a giraffe. And it hadn't involved a lot of paperwork either.

'So you're free,' her grandfather said.

'I suppose I am.' Eva tried not to feel desolate. Being free again could be a positive thing. So, she hadn't yet met a man she wanted to spend her life with. Was that so bad? At least now there was nothing and no one stopping her from doing what she wanted to do – recapturing that dream. And if she was honest . . . Max was older, charming, sophisticated. He had been great at taking her out to dinner, buying her gorgeous presents, surprising her with a weekend in Rome or Paris. Which was all very nice and Eva had enjoyed it for almost two years. But . . . She ran her finger across the jagged mane of the *chinthe*; he was a proud animal – she'd always liked him despite his apparent ferocity. It wasn't really love, was it? Part of her had always known that. 'What do you want me to do, Grandpa?' she asked again.

'I can't go to my grave without telling you one last story, Eva,' he said.

'A story?' She didn't like him talking about going to his

grave, but Eva wriggled in the chair and made herself more comfortable.

'It's what you might call a personal quest.' He paused. 'Because there's something I need to know.'

Eva waited, intrigued. And then to her horror his blue eyes filled with tears. 'Grandpa?'

'There's someone I want you to look for,' he said. 'A task I need you to undertake.' He picked up the little *chinthe* and held it gently in his hand. 'There's a promise I made many years ago that now, I need to keep.'

www.quercusbooks.co.uk

Quercus
Join us!

Visit us at our website, or join us on
Twitter and Facebook for:

- Exclusive interviews and films from
  your favourite Quercus authors

- Exclusive extra content

- Pre-publication sneak previews

- Free chapter samplers and
  reading group materials

- Giveaways and competitions

- Subscribe to our free newsletter

www.quercusbooks.co.uk
twitter.com/quercusbooks
facebook.com/quercusbooks